HIGH PRAISE FOR BRIAN KEENE
AND *THE RISING!*

"An apocalyptic epic packed with violence, gore, scares and moral dilemmas. Brian Keene has given zombies their next upgrade."

—*Cemetery Dance*

"Hoping for a good night's sleep? Stay away from *The Rising*. It'll keep you awake, then fill your dreams with lurching, hungry corpses wanting to eat you."

—Richard Laymon, bestselling author

"More power to Brian Keene. He reminds us that horror fiction can deal with fear, not just indulge it."

—Ramsey Campbell, bestselling author

"Brian Keene has raised the living dead to a profound new level. A prodigious talent—*The Rising* takes a bite from beginning to end and you're hooked!"

—Ken Foree, star of *Dawn of the Dead*

"Quite simply, the first great horror novel of the new millennium!"

—*Dark Fluidity*

"Brian Keene is one of the best new writers in the horror genre. Period."

—Edward Lee, author of *Monster* and *City Infernal*

"With Keene at the wheel, horror will never be the same."

—*Hellnotes*

"Stephen King meets Brian Lumley. Keene will keep you turning the pages to the very end."

—*Terror Tales*

"Different, unique and cool—this one doesn't disappoint!"

—*Domain of the Dead*

"Definitely transcends your basic run-of-the-mill horror."

—*The Haunted*

TRAPPED!

"Hey buddy," said a voice from Jim's left, and he smelled the creature the same instant it spoke. *"Having some car trouble?"*

Two leathery arms reached through the open driver's-side window. Cold fingers wrapped around his neck and squeezed. Jim grabbed the bony wrists and his nails burrowed into the decaying flesh. The skin sloughed away and the zombie laughed, squeezing harder.

Another zombie pounced onto the crumpled hood and grabbed through the shattered windshield at Martin. The others busied themselves with prying open the passenger's-side door.

Jim tried to scream, tried to breathe, and found he couldn't. . . .

BRIAN KEENE

RISING
THE

LEISURE BOOKS   NEW YORK CITY

For David. Daddy loves you more than infinity . . .

LEISURE BOOKS ®

January 2004

Published by

Dorchester Publishing Co., Inc.
200 Madison Avenue
New York, NY 10016

ISBN 0-8439-5201-6

Visit us on the web at www.dorchesterpub.com.

ACKNOWLEDGMENTS

Special thanks to Cassandra; Geoff; Mike; Mikey; The Keenes; Gina; Don; Shane; the members of Life of Agony and Power Plant; Tom Piccirilli and Richard Laymon for their help with the first draft; Alan Beatts and John Urbancik for their help with the final draft; and Gary Conner, Sarah Johnson, and Mary Beth Oswald for their technical assistance.

Author's Note: Though many of the locations and highways in this novel are real, I have taken certain fictional liberties with them. So if you live in one of the places we are about to visit, don't look for your house. You won't find it, and probably wouldn't want to know what lives there now . . .

RISING

THE

CHAPTER ONE

The dead scrabbled for an entrance to his grave. His wife was among them, as ravenous for Jim in death as she'd been in life. Their faint, soulless cries drifted down through ten feet of soil and rock.

The kerosene lamp cast flickering shadows on the cinder block walls, and the air in the shelter was stale and earthy. His grip on the Ruger tightened. Above him, Carrie shrieked and clawed at the earth.

She'd been dead for a week.

Jim sighed, breathing in the dank air. He lifted the metal coffeepot from where it sat on the heater and poured himself a cup. The warmth felt good, and he lingered there for a moment, before regretfully turning the heater off. To conserve fuel, he only ran it to heat up his meals. The brief comfort only made the damp chill stronger.

He sipped instant coffee and gagged. Like everything else, it was bitter.

He crossed back to the cot and collapsed upon it.

The noises continued from above.

Jim had built the shelter in the summer of 1999, when Y2K fever was at its highest. Carrie laughed at him, until he'd shown her some of the reports and articles. Even then, she'd been skeptical—until the nightly news' constant barrage had made her a believer. Two months and ten thousand dollars later, the shelter was completed, using most of Carrie's savings and all of his construction knowledge.

It was small; a ten by fifteen-foot bunker that could hold four people comfortably. Despite the size, it was safe, and more important, secure. Jim equipped it with a generator and a vacuum powered toilet that drained into the septic tank behind the house. He'd stocked it with canned and dry foods, toilet paper, medical supplies, matches, guns, and lots of ammunition. Three pallets of bottled water and a fifty five-gallon drum of kerosene stood in the corner. There was a battery-operated boom box and a wide assortment of their eclectic musical tastes. Another shelf held their favorite books. He'd even brought down the old Magnavox 486SX. It wasn't fast, but it was easy on the generator and still gave them contact with the outside world.

They'd started out that New Year's Eve day by keeping a close eye on CNN. When the century passed in Australia and the world failed to end, he knew that all the preparation had been for nothing. Country after country greeted the millennium and the power stayed on.

That evening, they attended a party at Mike and Melissa's. When the ball dropped and the drunken revelers counted down, Carrie pulled him close.

"See, crazy-man? Nothing to worry about."

"I love you, crazy-woman," he had whispered.

"I love you, too."

They were lost in their kiss and barely noticed when Mike turned off the breakers and screamed "Y2K!" as a joke.

As the months went by, the shelter gathered dust. By the end of the next year it lay forgotten. After September 11th raised the fears of biological or nuclear attack, Jim re-stocked it. Even then, it was just an afterthought.

Until the change began. Until the rising started.

In the end, the ghosts of Y2K and September 11th had doomed the world. Tired of the unending stream of "end-time prophecy" and "destruction of Western Civilization as we know it" disasters of the week, the world had ignored the early media reports. It was a new century; one that had no room for those medieval fears and extremist paranoid attitudes. It was time to embrace technology and science, time to further the brotherhood of man. Mankind had perfected cloning, mapped the human genome, and even traveled beyond the moon, when the joint Chinese/U.S. mission had finally set foot on Mars. The world's scientists proclaimed that the cure for cancer was just around the corner. Y2K didn't destroy civilization. Terrorism didn't defeat it. Society had faced both, and conquered them. Civilization was invincible!

Civilization was dead.

A muffled scrabbling came from overhead as something pulled on the periscope. The portcullis wiggled in its turret, swiveling back and forth. The scratching changed to a frustrated grunt, and the view-piece shuddered on its axis. It rose, slamming into the ceiling and dropping back down.

Jim closed his eyes.

"Carrie."

* * *

He'd met her through Mike and Melissa. Like him, she was newly divorced.

"She doesn't want anything serious," Mike had cautioned him. "She just needs to have a little fun again."

Jim knew about that. He knew about happiness and contentment. He'd had a beautiful son, Danny, and a wife, Tammy. They'd been the core of his world.

Until Rick, a co-worker whom Tammy had never mentioned, stole both away.

After the divorce, Jim had his share of fun—drunken one-night stands that blurred together.

He had custody of Danny every other weekend and during those precious times, the beer and bimbos were forgotten. On those weekends, he was Daddy. Those were the only times he was truly happy.

Tammy and Rick married. Rick got a better job in Bloomington, New Jersey. "The chance of a lifetime," Tammy said. That had been it. They left West Virginia, taking the one good thing Jim had left.

The move destroyed him. In an instant, he went from seeing Danny every other weekend to ten weeks in the summer and one week at Christmas, along with the occasional weekend trip to New Jersey. If he'd had the money, if he'd been a little more together, he could have fought it in court. But by that point, Jim had racked up a driving while intoxicated offense. His credit was shot. He'd known that Tammy's lawyer, paid for with *his* money, would eat him alive. He was allowed to call once a week, but the distance along the phone lines only deepened his loss.

Finally, Danny started referring to Rick as his 'other dad' and that had devastated Jim.

There were more women and one night stands. He played at drinking himself to death, knowing he wouldn't because Danny still needed him. He lost his job, his apartment, his driver's license, and his self-respect. The only thing that kept him going were those once a week phone calls and the small voice on the other end that always said, "I miss you, Daddy."

Then he'd met Carrie.

Jim sobbed, bitter tears of rage and loss cutting through the stubble on his haggard face.

For five years they'd been happy and content. The only sadness Jim felt was not being a part of Danny's everyday life. Carrie had helped to dull even that pain.

She saved him.

Eight months ago, Carrie announced over dinner that she was pregnant. Ecstatic, Jim lifted her in his arms, kissing and loving her so much it hurt—an actual, physical hurt deep inside his chest.

Then the world died, taking his new wife and their

unborn baby along with it. Now, joined by their dead neighbors, Carrie was back, digging with rotted fingers to be reunited with her husband.

Mike and Melissa were dead too; ripped apart by a dozen of the creatures. They were among the lucky ones. Their bodies had been so badly damaged that there was no way for them to be reanimated. Shuddering, Jim recalled how the things had swarmed Mike's car, reaching through the shattered windshield and crawling inside. He and Carrie had watched in horror from the living room, ducking into the shelter when the screams stopped and the wet sounds began. The four of them had planned on escaping together. That had been their first attempt to get out of Lewisburg.

* * *

Despite the chill, Jim was sweating. He brushed tears from his eyes and went to the mini-fridge. Still holding the pistol in one hand, he opened the door and paused, letting the draft of cold air wash over him. He marveled again that he'd been down here for three months and had yet to start the generator. The power remained on, as did his cell phone. He thought about the deserted nuclear power stations, still automatically pumping out electricity for a deceased world.

How long until they shut down or blew up? How long would the cell phone and radio and television satellites float up there, waiting for communications from the dead?

* * *

In the first few days, they had talked to people online, learning that the situation was the same everywhere. The dead were coming back to life, not as mindless eating machines like in an old horror movie, but as malicious creatures bent solely on destruction. Various causes were speculated on and debated. Biological or chemical warfare, government testing, alien invasion, the Second Coming of Christ, a meteor from space; all were discussed with equal fervor.

The media soon grew silent, especially after a rogue Army unit executed six reporters during a live broadcast. After that, as civilization collapsed, even the most dedicated journalists gave up, preferring to be with their families rather than bearing final witness to the choas for an audience that could see what was happening just by looking out the window.

Several times, Jim had sent frantic emails to Tammy and Rick, trying to determine if Danny was safe.

He never received a reply.

Each time he called them, he received a message telling him that all circuits were busy. Eventually, even that message stopped.

He'd argued with Carrie, insisting that they make an escape attempt. He was determined to get to his son. Eventually, through gentle reasoning, she got him to see the reality of the situation. Danny was surely dead by now.

Deep inside, he'd wondered if she was right. The father in him refused to give up. He found himself clinging to the conviction that somewhere out there, Danny was still alive. He found himself envisioning different escape attempts, if only to break the monotony of living in the shelter.

Carrie's health began to crumble. Their medical supplies consisted of the bare minimum. She'd long since run out of pre-natal vitamins. Reluctantly, Jim realized it would be impossible to leave. Danny was dead, he knew. In the weeks that followed, as Carrie's condition worsened, there had been times that Jim blamed her.

He still hated himself for that.

One morning, he awoke next to her still form, just as the final, congested breath rattled in her chest. Then she was gone; the pneumonia had finally claimed her. He'd curled up against her cold, lifeless body and cried, bidding farewell to his second wife.

He'd known it was useless to bury her, grimly understanding what needed to be done. But when the madness of grief seized him, he couldn't believe that it would happen to her. Not Carrie. Not the woman who had saved his life. The woman that had *become* his life in these last five years. It was inconceivably blasphemous to think that she would turn into one of *them*.

Alert for the undead, he'd quickly buried her under the pine tree that they had planted together earlier that summer. They'd held hands beneath that tree only months before, talking of how it would watch over the house when they were old.

Now, it stood watch over her.

That night, Carrie raged above him. By morning, she'd been joined by what was left of the Thompsons from next door. Soon, a small army had gathered in the yard. Jim had used the periscope only once since then, giving in to hopelessness when he saw more than thirty corpses milling around on his lawn.

It was then that he started to go mad.

Cut off from the outside world and besieged by the undead, Jim contemplated suicide as the only real escape. He had no way of knowing if there was anyone still alive in Lewisburg, or the country for that matter. For him, the world had become a tomb, outlined by four cinder-block walls.

As weeks went by, the internet went quiet, as did the phone. His cellular was a powerful unit, able to transmit and receive beyond the concrete bunker, but in the past month it had gone silent. In their rush to get to the safety of the shelter, Jim had forgotten the charger. Now he kept it on sleep mode, trying to save the battery and the spares for as long as he could. He was down to his last one.

The television displayed static, except for a channel out of Beckley, which was still showing the emergency broadcast screen. The AM station in Roanoke had stayed on the air until the previous week. Jack Wolf, the station's afternoon talk radio host, kept a lone vigil next to his microphone. Jim had listened in dreadful fascination as Wolf's sanity slowly crumbled from cabin fever. The final broadcast ended with a gunshot. As far as Jim knew, he was the only listener to hear it.

* * *

Jim shivered in the air pouring from the open refrigerator. He pulled out his last can of beer and shut the door. The pop of the tab sounded like a gunshot in the silence. His ears rang, drowning out the cries from above. His pulse throbbed in his temples. He placed the cold can against his head, then brought it to his lips and drained it.

"One for the road." He crunched the can in his fist, tossing it into the corner, where it rattled on the concrete floor.

He returned to the cot and pulled back the pistol slide. The first bullet of the clip slid into the chamber. The clip held thirteen more, but one was all he needed. The pounding in his ears was louder now, and above it, he could hear Carrie. He glanced down at the photos spread out before him on the dirty sheets.

A shot of them at Virginia Beach. That had been the weekend she got pregnant. She smiled at him from the photo and he smiled back. He burst into tears.

The beautiful woman in the photo, the woman who had been so vibrant and energetic and full of life, was now a shambling, rotting husk that ate human flesh.

He put the gun to his head, the barrel cool against his throbbing temple.

Danny stared up at him from the other photo. In it, they were in front of the house: Jim was crouched on one knee with Danny standing beside him. Danny held his soapbox derby trophy, the one that he had received in

New Jersey and had brought along that summer to show his Daddy. Both of them were smiling, and yes, his son *did* look just like him.

Their final phone conversation came back to him now. His finger tightened on the trigger. He hadn't known it would be their last, but each word was burned into his memory.

* * *

Every Saturday, Jim would call Danny and they watched cartoons over the phone together for half an hour. That last time had been one of those mornings. They had discussed the dire peril that the heroes of *Dragonball Z* had found themselves in. They had talked about school and the 'A' that Danny had received on his last test.

"What did you have for breakfast this morning?"

"Fruity Pebbles," Danny had replied. "What did you have?"

"I'm eating Cheerio's."

"Yuck," Danny made a disgusted noise. "That's gross!"

"As gross as kissing a girl?" Jim teased. Like all boys of nine, Danny was repelled and yet strangely mystified by the opposite sex.

"Nothing's that gross," he answered and then grew quiet.

"What are you thinking about, Squirt?" Jim asked.

"Daddy, can I ask you something serious?"

"You can ask me anything you want to, buddy."

"Is it ever okay to hit a girl?"

"No, Danny, that's wrong. You should never, ever hit a girl. Remember what we talked about when you got in that fight with Peter Clifford?"

"But there's this girl at school. Anne Marie Locasio. She won't leave me alone."

"What does she do?"

"She's always picking on me and taking my book bag and chasing me around. The fifth graders laugh at me when she does it."

Jim had smiled at this. The fifth graders, they who ruled the elementary school playground. He'd felt a sudden pang of age when he realized that Danny himself would join those ranks the following year.

"Well, you just have to ignore those guys," he answered. "And if Anne Marie won't leave you alone, just ignore her too. You're a pretty big guy. I'm sure you can get away from her if you want."

"But she won't leave me alone," Danny insisted. "She pulls my hair and..."

"What?"

Danny's voice was a whisper now. He obviously didn't want his mother or stepfather to hear this.

"She tries to kiss me!"

Jim smiled, valiantly struggling to keep from laughing. He then explained to Danny how that meant that she liked him, and what steps Danny should take to protect himself from further torment without hurting Anne Marie or her feelings.

"Know what, Daddy?"

"What, Squirt?"

"I'm glad that I can ask you stuff like this. You're my best friend."

"You're my best friend too," Jim said around the lump in his throat.

In the background, Tammy had hollered something. Jim winced at the sound of her voice.

"Mommy needs to use the phone so I have to get going. Will you call me next week?"

"I promise, cross my heart and hope to die."

"Love you more than Spider Man."

"Love you more than Godzilla," Jim replied, playing the familiar game.

"I love you more than 'finity," Danny answered, winning for the thousandth time.

"I love you more than infinity too, buddy."

Then there was an empty click and a dial tone, and that was the last time he had ever spoken with his son.

* * *

Through his tears, Jim glanced down at the smiling boy in the photograph. He hadn't been there. He hadn't been there when his son had gone to sleep every night, when he constructed epic Star Wars vs. X-Men battles with his action figures, when he played ball in the backyard, or when he learned to ride a bike.

He hadn't been there to save him.

Jim closed his eyes.

Carrie dug at the earth and called to him, hungry.

His finger tightened.

The cell phone rang shrilly.

Jim jumped, dropping the pistol onto the bed. The phone shrieked again. The green digital readout glowed eerily in the soft light of the lantern.

Jim didn't move. He couldn't swallow, couldn't breathe. It felt like someone had hit him in the chest, kicked him in the groin. Consumed with dread, he tried to move his arms and found them frozen.

A third ring, then a fourth. He was insane, of course. That could be the only explanation. The world was dead. Yes, the power was still on and the satellites still kept a silent and mournful watch over its remains, but the world was dead. There was no way someone could be calling him now, here underground, beneath the remains of Lewisburg.

The fifth ring brought a whimper from his throat. Fighting off the emotional malaise that held him, Jim sprang to his feet.

The phone buzzed again, insistent. He reached for it with a trembling hand.

Don't pick it up! It's Carrie or one of the others. Or maybe something worse. Pick up that phone and they'll pour themselves through it and...

It stopped. The silence was deafening.

The display blinked at him. Someone had left a message.

"Oh fuck."

He grasped the phone as if he were holding a live rattlesnake. He brought it to his ear and dialed "0."

"You have one new message," said a mechanical female voice. The canned inflections were the sweetest sound he had ever heard. "To hear the message, press one. To erase your message, press the pound key. If you need assistance, dial zero and an operator will assist you."

He jabbed the button and there was a distant, mechanical whir.

"Saturday, September first, nine p.m.," the recording told him. Jim let out a breath he hadn't realized he'd been holding. Then he heard a new voice.

"Daddy..."

Jim gasped, his pulse jack-hammering. The room was spinning again.

"Daddy, I'm scared. I'm in the attic. I..."

A burst of static interrupted. Then Danny's voice drifted back, sounding very small and afraid.

"I 'membered your phone number but I couldn't make Rick's cell phone work right. Mommy was asleep for a long time but then she woke up and made it work for me. Now she's asleep again. She's been sleeping since... since they got Rick."

Jim closed his eyes, the strength vanishing from his legs. Knees buckling, he collapsed to the floor.

"I'm scared Daddy. I know we shouldn't leave the attic, but Mommy's sick and I don't know how to make her better. I hear things outside the house. Sometimes they just go by and other times I think they're trying to get in. I think Rick is with them."

Danny was crying and Jim wailed along with him.

"Daddy, you promised to call me! I'm scared and I don't know what to do...." More static, and Jim reached out to keep himself from sprawling facedown.

"...and I love you more than Spider Man and more than Pikachu and more than Michael Jordan and more than 'finity, Daddy. I love you more than infinity."

The phone went dead in his hand, the battery using its last spark of life.

Above him, Carrie howled into the night.

* * *

He wasn't sure how long he'd stayed crouched there, with Danny's pleas echoing through his head. Finally, the strength came rushing into his numb limbs and he staggered to his feet.

"I love you, Danny," he said aloud. "I love you more than infinity."

The anguish vanished, replaced by resolve. He grasped the periscope and peered into the darkness. He saw nothing, only a jagged sliver of moonlight. Then a baleful, sunken eyeball glared back at him in hideous magnification. He jumped away from the portcullis, realizing that a zombie was looking back through it. He forced himself to peek again and slowly, the zombie moved away.

Carrie's corpse stood bathed in moonlight, radiant in her putrescence. Her bloated abdomen was horribly distended; the malignant pregnancy still lurking within her, hidden beneath the tatters of the silken robe he'd buried her in. Frayed ribbons fluttered against her gray skin.

He thought about the night that she'd told him she was pregnant. Carrie was lying next to him, the fine sheen of sweat from their lovemaking cooling on their bodies. His head against her stomach, his cheek pressed against her warm, soft curves; the luxuriant feel of skin on skin. Her scent, and the tiny, almost invisible hairs on her belly swaying gently as he breathed. Inside her, their baby grew.

Jim didn't want to think about what was squirming there now.

He rotated the periscope full circle. Life after death had been kind to old Mr. Thompson from next door. His face held a pallor that, although the color of oatmeal, was still brighter than the one that adorned it when he'd been alive. The persistent stiffness of joints that had plagued the elderly neighbor was apparent as he gripped the shovel, except that now, rather than with the throes of arthritis, his fingers swelled with the slow rot of decay. Knuckles poked through leathery skin the texture of parchment, as Mr. Thompson raised the shovel and thrust it into the ground.

The fact that the zombies could use tools didn't surprise Jim. During the siege, he'd watched in horror, listening helplessly to the creature's efforts to dig into the stronghold. Clumsily, but with slow and steady success, the things had managed to remove the sod, revealing the concrete slab beneath the dirt. That slab had been the only thing that had saved him.

Could they get bored, he wondered. *Indeed, could they reason at all?* He didn't know. Obviously, the thing that had once been his wife was drawn to this place. But was it because she remembered it from before, or mere instinct? The fact that they clawed at the ground seemed to indicate that they knew. *That they remembered.* If that theory were true...

Jim shuddered at the implications.

He was nothing more than a sardine, waiting in the silence of a darkened can. Sooner or later, the things above would find the correct can opener and would consume him.

"...more than 'finity, Daddy," Danny's frantic cries echoed in his mind. *"I love you more than infinity."*

He swiveled back to Carrie and noticed that she was smiling, her blackened lips pulled back against stained teeth. The plump end of an earthworm disappeared between them. She raised her head and laughed.

Were there words buried within that ghoulish howl? He couldn't be sure. There had been times over the past few weeks when he could have sworn the things were talking to each other.

Another worm vanished down her decomposing gullet. Horrified, Jim thought of her eating spaghetti on their first date.

Sudden movement caught his eye. The zombies had noticed the periscope turning and now lurched toward it. He glimpsed more of them in the distance, attracted by the commotion. Soon they would be swarming the grounds, searching once again for an entrance into his stronghold. The chance of escaping without a fight had just vanished. They knew now that he was still alive. Although it was unclear what the zombie's reasoning capabilities were, it was obvious they sensed their prey below.

Fifty or more. Not good odds.

He lowered the view-piece.

With his son's pleas for help still haunting him, Jim began to prepare.

"Hang on squirt. Daddy's coming."

CHAPTER TWO

M ount Rushmore was speaking in tongues. That was the first thing Baker noticed. The second thing was the baleful red glare coming from the granite eyes, pulling the chopper towards the rock face.

Struggling with the controls, Baker screamed as George Washington whispered obscenities in a multitude of languages.

The voice continued when he awoke, jerking upright from where he'd slumped at the desk. Saliva had pooled on his blotter, pulling at his skin as he sat up. He listened.

The blasphemies came from down the hall.

From the thing in Observation Room Number Six.

He blinked; still unsure of what was happening. He always experienced a moment of confusion upon waking from a dream. He glanced around, letting the familiar settings settle into reality.

He was in his office, half a mile beneath Havenbrook. Above him, the gates of Hell had been opened wide.

And he had helped to turn the key.

The room bore a strong resemblance to Afghanistan, the cumulative effects of three months without janitorial service. Dingy ceramic mugs, encrusted with the fossilized remains of freeze-dried coffee. Papers, books, and diagrams strewn haphazardly about the room. A trashcan long past the point of overflowing, its contents now spilling onto the floor. In the far corner, a dark stain where the fish tank had spewed onto the carpet.

He shuddered when he looked at it.

Experimenting with the fish tank had been Powell's idea. At that point, they'd lacked a specimen, their research amounting to only speculation without anything to actually study. The three of them, Powell, Harding, and Baker, had closed themselves off from the rest of the complex after the few remaining staff members had fled. They gathered together in Baker's office, venting their frustration and wondering if it was safe to go above even without the all-clear message.

Powell had suggested, jokingly at first, that they try it out on one of Baker's prized tropical fish. Laughter and derision had quickly turned to scientific seriousness when Baker agreed. They netted one of the brightly colored pets, watching with cool detachment as it flopped and gulped in the smothering oxygen. Baker held it in his palm until it stopped quivering. Then they placed it back in the tank, where it floated on top of the briny water— just as a dead fish was supposed to.

Its behavior was surprisingly—and depressingly— normal.

It wasn't until ten minutes later, after the other scientists had retired to the common room for their tenth viewing of old *Jeopardy* reruns on video, that the fish started swimming again.

Baker was only dimly aware of the splashing at first; his attention focused on the game of solitaire laid out before him on the desk. When the splashing became louder, he looked up.

The water had begun to turn red; tiny scarlet clouds swirling amidst the brightly colored pebbles and plastic castle, as the dead fish began to hunt and devour its brethren. At first, Baker could only stare in amazement. Then, gathering his wits, he dashed down the empty corridor and burst into the common room, gasping for breath.

The slaughter was over by the time they crowded into the office. In the few minutes it had taken him to summon the others, the fish had killed every living thing in the tank. Innards and scales floated amidst the carnage.

"My God," Harding gasped.

"God," Baker spat, "had nothing to do with *this*!" He thrust a finger at the tank. "This was mankind, Stephen. This was us!"

Harding stared at him in silence, his mouth working noiselessly, just as the fish had done. Powell sat in the corner, softly crying.

The fish noticed them. It stopped swimming and stared at them with clear contempt.

Baker had been fascinated at the intelligence the fish displayed.

"Look at that. It's studying us, just as we study it."

"What have we done?" sobbed Powell. "Jesus fucking Christ, what have we done?"

Harding snapped. "Get it together, Powell! We need to learn as much as we can from this thing if we expect to undo—"

His reprimand was cut short by another splash. The fish thrashed around, stirring up the muck on the bottom of the tank; obscuring their view. It vanished, hidden by a swirling cloud of blood and feces and slime.

"Somebody get the camcorder," Baker shouted. "We need to be documenting this!"

Before they could, the entire tank stand *moved*. Water spilled over the top, running down the sides in crimson rivulets.

The fish retreated and then burst forward again, slamming itself into the front of the tank. Again and again it charged the glass, heedless of the damage it was doing to itself.

Baker noted the calculating malevolence that filled its dead eyes.

A network of cracks spread throughout the glass,

spider-webbing up the sides. The stand toppled over, crashing to the floor. Glass exploded, showering them all with glittering shards and brackish water.

The fish flopped onto the carpet and began to wriggle towards them. Shoving his books aside, Baker leaped onto the desk while Harding retreated into the hall. Powell collapsed, shrieking and clawing at the carpet while the thing closed the gap between them.

Above Powell's terrified cries, Baker heard the noises the fish was making as it neared the scientist's outstretched legs.

The fish was talking.

He couldn't understand what was said, but the patterns were definitely intelligent speech.

The thing shot towards Powell's groin. He screamed as it brushed his khakis.

Baker leaped to the floor, slamming the computer monitor down on it. Blow after repeated blow, he smashed the creature until there was nothing left but a viscous smear among the shattered glass.

He'd been unaware that he was yelling until he felt Harding's hand on his shoulder. They looked at each other, the full enormity of what they had unleashed upon the world bearing down on them like an airplane.

That night, Powell hacked his wrists open with a butter knife from the cafeteria. They'd found him a few minutes later, when they stopped in to administer a sedative.

Baker looked away from the stain on the rug and closed his eyes. Slowly, he ran a hand through his graying hair and quietly wept.

Down the hall, the thing in Observation Room Six continued ranting.

Baker fumbled in the congested ashtray, finding a partially smoked cigarette. Still weeping, he brought his lighter up to the ragged butt and thumbed it.

Nothing. No flame. Not even a spark. The nearest lighter fluid was a half-mile above him in a world belonging to the dead.

He threw the useless lighter across the room, where it struck a glass frame hanging on the wall. The newspaper that had been so proudly displayed inside fluttered to the floor.

Wearily, Baker walked over and brushed away the broken glass. Shaking the paper in his hands, he began to laugh. The article was dated from earlier in the year.

CONTROVERSY SURROUNDS ACCELERATOR

By Jeff Whitman/Associated Press
A nuclear accelerator designed to replicate the Big Bang has drawn protests from a group of international physicists, politicians, and activists because of fears that it could harm the Earth. One theory even suggests that it could form a black hole, cause 'perturbations of the universe', or even 'rend the fabric of space and time'.

Havenbrook National Laboratories (HNL), one of the American government's foremost research bodies, has spent ten years building its $985 million Relativistic Heavy Ion Collider (RHIC) in Hellertown, Pennsylvania, a rural area near the New Jersey state border. A successful test was held this Friday and the first nuclear collisions are expected to take place within the month.

Last week however, Stephen Harding, Havenbrook's director, set up a committee of physicists to investigate whether the project could go disastrously wrong. Harding was prompted by warnings from other physicists that there was a small but real risk that the machine had the power to create "strangelets"; a new type of matter composed of sub-atomic particles called "strange quarks."

The committee is to examine the possibility that, once formed; strangelets might start a chain reaction that could convert anything they touched into more strange matter. The committee will also consider the less likely alternative that the colliding particles could achieve such a high density that they would form a mini black hole. In space, black holes generate intense gravitational fields that suck in all surrounding matter. The high density formed by the colliding particles could also, in theory, break down the barrier between our dimensions and others.

Inside the collider, atoms of gold are stripped of their outer electrons and pumped into one of two 2.4-mile circular tubes where powerful magnets accelerate them to 99.9% of the speed of light. The ions in the two tubes travel in opposite directions to increase the power of the collisions. When they collide they generate miniscule fireballs of superdense matter. Under these conditions, atomic nuclei evaporate into a plasma of even smaller particles called quarks and gluons. This plasma then emits a shower of other particles as it cools.

Among the particles that appear during this phase are strange quarks. These have been detected in other accelerators but have always been attached to other particles. The RHIC, the most powerful machine yet built, has the ability to create solitary strange quarks for the first time since the universe began.

HNL official Timothy Powell confirmed that there had been discussions concerning the possibilities. William Baker, a professor of nuclear physics who is the leading scientific director for the RHIC, said that the chances of an accident were infinitesimally small, but that Havenbrook had a responsibility to assess them before proceeding. "The big question, of course, is whether our planet would vanish in the blink of an eye or perhaps the possibility of rending the fabric of space and time. It is astonishingly unlikely. We are not seeking to 'rip holes into other dimensions' as you put it. We are seeking to understand more about the universe and our place in it. The risk is so minuscule as to not even be considered."

Baker crumbled the paper in his fists.

Down the corridor, in a sound-proofed room reinforced with twelve inches of steel and concrete, the thing that had once been Timothy Powell shouted in Sumerian. Each syllable echoed through the empty underground complex, drifting up to the dead world above them.

* * *

Baker rubbed his eyes. The tape recorder sat on the table in front of him. He sighed, pressed the record button, and turned on the intercom.

"Powell," he began timidly. "C-can you hear me?"

Powell's corpse lay slumped in the corner of the room. It raised its head, staring at the glass. Baker saw intelligence reflected in that stare. A terrible intelligence—and something else.

"Hello Bill," it rasped, swollen gray-white tongue sliding across peeling lips. *"How's tricks?"*

Baker scribbled on his pad. The creature in Observation Room Six was not Timothy Powell. He knew this. And yet, it had identified him. He said nothing. Beside him, the tape recorder hissed quietly.

"Cat got your tongue, Billy-Boy?"

"How do you feel, Timothy?"

"I'm falling to pieces, to be quite honest with you, Bill. Any chance you could get me something to eat?"

"You're hungry? How about some soup? Blue crabs were in season before—well, before this. The kitchen still has some crab soup left. I froze it—"

"I don't want soup. How about your arm instead? Or a few yards of intestine?"

"You can't eat food?"

"You are food! Now how about coming inside here with me?"

Baker observed in horrified fascination. The zombie shuffled over to the window and sat down, facing him like a prison inmate. Its decaying face pressed against the glass and smiled. No breath fogged the window. Softly, it recited something in a language that Baker didn't recognize. He doubted Powell would have either.

"Who are you?"

"You know who I am. I'm Timothy Powell, Associate Director of Havenbrook Laboratories' RHIC program. I'm your buddy, mi amigo. C'mon, Billy-Boy! Don't tell me you've got post-stress amnesia!"

"Doctor Powell would never refer to me as 'Billy-Boy'," Baker told it matter-of-factly. "You're not Timothy Powell."

The thing plucked a loose piece of skin from its thigh. It appraised it in the fluorescent light, and then plopped the maggot into its mouth. Rotted teeth ground in delight.

Baker turned away.

"Don't believe me? Remember when you and I and

Weston took that week off and flew out to Colorado? We stayed at Doctor Scalise's cabin in Estes Park, and went fishing. Weston caught a big fucking Walleye, and you caught a cold."

Grinning, the corpse placed a swollen hand against the glass. Baker focused on Powell's wedding ring. The gold band had sunk into the sausage-like finger. Then the zombie removed the hand, leaving a greasy smudge on the window.

"Who are you?" he asked it again, fighting to keep the tremor from his voice. "Are you Timothy Powell?"

"Ob," it said with Powell's mouth.

"Is that your name, or is that what you are?"

"Ob," it said again. *"And you are Bill."*

"How do you know my name?"

"The one you call Tim left it behind in here. He left a great many things behind. Delicious things. Were you aware that he frequented prostitutes? His wife obviously wasn't."

"I hardly see how that..."

"He paid them to sodomize him with a dildo."

The corpse chuckled, then coughed, misting the glass with bits of itself.

"Really?" Baker gritted his teeth. "And exactly how did you obtain this knowledge?"

"It is in here with me. All of it is in here for me to pick through. Much of it is useless. All that collective knowledge. Humankind has achieved so little. HE must be very disappointed in his creations."

"Who?"

"Him. The cruel one. The one who...never mind. We shall not speak of it. He shall have his day. I imagined it much while I lingered there."

"And where was that, exactly?"

The thing did not reply. Instead, it began licking the red smear from the glass.

"I hunger," it moaned, and began to grin again.

"Hungry," Baker said to the cold, gray walls. "I didn't think I was this hungry."

He opened the can of baked beans more on instinct than desire, but after the first bite, he proceeded to wolf them down cold. He longed for a hamburger to go along with them, but the huge walk-in freezer was occupied and Baker wasn't about to enter it. Harding lay inside, with a neat, perfunctory hole in his head. He'd suffered a heart attack, one day after Powell's suicide, and the subsequent imprisonment of his reanimated corpse. Baker had used an ice pick on Harding's dead body, wishing for a pistol during the entire grisly process. But the guns were gone, along with the soldiers who had deserted their posts.

The silence in the empty cafeteria was unsettling. He longed for somebody to talk to, other than the thing that called itself Ob.

Walking back down the corridor to his office, his feet echoed on the green tile. He was glad for the noise. The lights flickered, dimmed and then brightened again. The power was going. He wasn't sure if the facility was running on public utilities or its own backup at this point. What would the hallway sound like in the dark?

Down here, alone with that thing...

He collapsed at his desk. The chair groaned in protest. To Baker's surprise, he had actually gained a few pounds during the crisis. Probably from the lack of exercise. His days consisted of the endless tedium of research and more research. His nights, (if they were nights, he couldn't differentiate down here) were spent constantly awaking; escaping the nightmares.

He leaned back, rested his feet on the desk, and turned on the recorder.

"While I am not a biologist or pathologist, I have observed a remarkable transformation in the subject."

He paused as the lights flickered again, then continued.

"The subject is not simply a reanimated dead body. In many ways, it functions like a living being. It seeks nourishment, specifically in the form of human—flesh. I cannot be sure, but it would appear that this is essential to its survival. Observation of the footage provided by the Federal Emergency Management Agency seems to verify this. Of course, it will probably be a long time before FEMA sends another tape."

His nervous chuckle turned into a fit of coughing. Then he continued.

"The subject's musculature appears to adapt to its new state. While decomposition is present, it appears to act not as a detriment, but as a natural process. Hair, skin, even vital organs are irrelevant to the subject's functioning. The flesh that it eats does not pass through the digestive system. It is absorbed through an unknown process; converted into—"

The lights died. Baker sat in the darkness, holding his breath. The squeal of the tape recorder was the only sound. His heart beat once, twice.

The lights came back on, and Baker was surprised to find that he'd been crying.

* * *

"When you feed," Baker asked through the intercom, "why do you not consume the entire body? Why do you leave so much behind?"

"Because so many of our brethren wait to come through," Ob answered, the raspy tone indignant, as if annoyed with the scientist for asking the obvious. *"They would not enjoy it, waiting eons only to inhabit a vessel incapable of movement. A torso with no arms or legs; a mere bag of human-flesh that simply lies there? That would be nothing more than escaping from one prison into another."*

"Tell me more about this place you come from. You called it the void."

"No more," Ob said angrily. "I must summon my brethren. I hunger. Release me and you shall not be harmed."

Baker kept his voice even. "Answer my questions and I'll feed you."

"You play a dangerous game, wise man. Do not think that I am reluctant to damage this shell, in order to be freed. I can obtain another."

"That glass is bulletproof. Those walls are reinforced with steel and concrete. You must realize that I am in charge."

"Your race is no longer in charge of anything. We are free to walk this earth again, as we did long ago."

"Tell me about the void," Baker insisted.

"Very well," the thing sighed, exhaling fetid air from unused, rotting lungs. "But be warned, Professor. Your age has ended. We are your inheritors."

"The void," Baker began.

"THE VOID IS COLD!" Ob roared, suddenly rushing toward the window. It slammed Powell's fist against the glass. Baker skittered backward.

"It is cold because HE is cruel! I dwelled there, trapped for eons with my brothers, the Elilum and Teraphim. HE sent us there! Banished us to the wastes. We watched while you scurried like ants, multiplying and breeding, basking in his frigid love. We waited, for we are patient. We lurked on the threshold, ever observant. And you, wise man, you and your fellow man provided us with the means of our salvation. Just as your bodies provide our temples, you provided our doorway!"

The creature hammered the window again. Baker winced. A small crack spiraled through the glass.

The lights flickered again.

"Do you think that when you die, you go to Heaven?" it laughed. "You don't. You go to what He has set aside for you! Your bodies belong to US! We are your masters. Demons, your kind called us. Djinn. Monsters.

We are the source of your legends—the reason you still fear the dark. We control your flesh. We have been waiting a long time to inhabit you!"

It punched the window again. The crack widened, web-like tendrils spread across its surface. The hand that had once belonged to Dr. Timothy Powell, the hand that had once held a martini glass and swung a golf club and deftly operated the controls of the RHIC, was now a battering ram of rotting meat. Baker recoiled as the fingers split open, revealing jagged pieces of bone that further scratched the inner glass.

Baker fled from the room; Ob's shouts pursuing him down the corridor.

"We are the Siqqusim! We have stood by, waiting to take possession and you are ours. Yidde-oni! Engastrimathos du aba paren tares. We are Ob and Ab and Api and Apu. Our number is greater than the stars! We are more than infinity!"

The glass shattered, and a moment later, the lights died, plunging the facility into darkness.

Baker cowered in the hall, listening in terror as the zombie stumbled after him.

The lights did not return.

CHAPTER THREE

There were two ways out of the shelter. The first was a shaft that led up to the yard. To use it, Jim would have to sling all his gear while climbing the ladder, then unbolt the lock and lift the manhole cover without attracting attention.

He needed to have at least one weapon in hand, so climbing was out. The zombies would swarm on him as soon as they heard the cover begin to open.

That left the cellar.

When he'd built the shelter, he'd gone to a scrap yard in Norfolk and purchased two hatches off a decommissioned Navy troop carrier. When opened from inside the shelter, the first led into a narrow hallway running toward the house. The passageway ended at the second hatch, which was affixed to the walls of the basement.

Twice in the weeks before, when his depression became unbearable, Jim went to this second door, intent on opening it and exposing himself to whatever lay beyond. Both times he'd stopped, listening to the shuffling sounds on the other side. The walls and heavy steel muffled the bumps and gurgles, but they were undeniably there—and undeniably real.

Now, he opened the first hatch, and listened for a footstep, a creak; anything that would betray the presence of the creatures lurking in his house. He heard nothing, but the silence was somehow worse.

Hesitantly, he crept down the passageway, stopping at the second hatch. Placing his ear against the cold steel, he held his breath and waited.

More silence.

He made his way back to the shelter, determined not to spend another hour in his tomb. He replaced his sandals with his black, beaten, steel-toed work boots. They'd served him well during the years he'd worked construction, and he hoped they would continue to do so. He pulled a long-sleeved flannel over his black T-shirt. It would provide comfort against the chill of the night, but was lighter than a jacket and could be tied around his waist during the day.

He unzipped Carrie's blue nylon backpack, catching a faint hint of her perfume; another ghostly reminder of what had been.

Brushing aside the emotions, he began to choose his necessities. A light load would be crucial to speed. Into the pack went a box of shells for the Ruger. He grabbed two more clips for the pistol and filled them with fifteen more bullets each, then placed them aside. He picked up the light, compact Winchester .30-30 lever action rifle that had accompanied him on so many hunting trips, and stuffed several boxes of ammunition for it into the pack as well. Four squeeze bottles of distilled water followed cans of tuna, sardines and instant noodles. Binoculars, a road atlas, the flashlight, boxes of wooden matches, candles, a ceramic coffee mug that Danny had given to him for Father's Day, a small jar of instant coffee, a toothbrush, toothpaste, a bar of soap, spoon and fork, and a can opener all found a home inside as well.

He slung his arms through the straps, testing the weight. Satisfied, he stuffed his pockets with two lighters, his buck knife and the extra clip. The pistol hung in a holster at his side. He picked up the rifle, taking comfort in the familiarity of the smooth wooden stock. Double-checking that it was loaded, Jim took a deep breath.

The room began to spin. Sudden nausea gripped him, as the tension that had been building reached critical mass. His arms and legs tingled and cramps wracked his stomach. Moaning, Jim dropped the rifle and vomited, spattering his boots and the floor.

Eventually, the anxiety spell passed. Shaking, he retrieved the rifle.

"Okay," he said aloud. "Time to go."

He glanced around at the shelter one last time, knowing he would never stare at the four cinder block walls again. His eyes wandered over the photographs of Carrie and Danny, and settled on the cell phone.

He hesitated, then picked it up. After a moment's consideration, he clipped it to his belt. The battery was dead without the charger.

"Just in case," he said to the room, trying to convince himself.

He walked down the narrow passage and placed a steady hand on the door lever. Slowly, he lifted the handle. Each click of the tumbler boomed in the silence. There was a final click, and the hatch creaked open.

Raising the rifle, Jim let the door swing backward, revealing the dark cellar beyond it. The basement was quiet, but once familiar shapes now took on sinister connotations. The tool cabinet became a zombie. The furnace was a crouching beast, ready to leap upon him. His heart pounded ferociously in the darkness.

Carefully, he picked his way around the scattered debris of their past life. He reached the stairway, which led up to the kitchen. He paused again, listening.

Above him, a floorboard creaked softly. Then another. The third creak was punctuated by the distinct squeal of a kitchen chair being scooted across the linoleum.

Jim froze. Finger tightening on the trigger, he fumbled in the darkness for the bottom stair. His foot found purchase and he took a tentative step.

More sounds from the kitchen now, followed by a frustrated growl. He pointed the rifle at the door and took another step. Something brushed lightly against his ear and Jim bit his tongue, stifling a scream. The fly buzzed him again, hovering invisibly.

He shook his head, willing the insect to go away. Now there was a new sound; a droning hum farther up the stairway.

The fly had friends. Lot's of them, judging by the noise. Their buzzing protests filled his ears. A second one landed on his palm, followed by another on his neck.

Then he smelled it; a sickly, butcher shop odor. The reek of roadkill and offal and rotten meat.

He took another step, felt the ceiling brush the top of his head, and realized that he was halfway up. From beyond the door came more plodding steps. The creaking floorboards tracked the zombie's progress.

Steeling himself, Jim prepared to charge up the remaining stairs and burst through the door.

There was a wet squelch as his foot came down in something slippery. The buzzing grew angry, the flies upset at having their dinner disturbed. The stench was stronger now, overpowering. His feet slid out from under him and he toppled forward, his knees colliding with the stair.

The footsteps in the kitchen hurried towards the door.

Grimacing, Jim pulled the lighter from his pocket and looked down.

Intestines. Somebody's intestines lay on the stair in a congealing heap.

The footsteps stopped on the other side of the cellar door.

Gagging, Jim dropped the lighter. The intestines stank worse than anything he had ever smelled. Ignoring the pain in his knees, he stood up.

The doorknob began to turn.

He raised the rifle, aiming blindly in the dark.

The door crashed open, and Jim gaped at the hideous thing standing before him. The viscera on the stairs had belonged to Mr. Thompson. The glistening ends of its intestines hung from their empty cavity, swaying as the zombie raised its arms.

"*Howdy neighbor,*" it rasped. Its voice sounded like somebody gargling glass. "*I see you found the rest of me.*"

The zombie's tongue was a blackened, swollen mass; yet impossibly, the thing *spoke*.

Jim fired, then worked the bolt on the rifle and squeezed off another shot. The crotch of the creature's soiled corduroy pants disintegrated.

"*Oooo,*" it glanced downward. "*Mrs. Thompson isn't going to like that at all.*"

With a speed that belied its ponderous movements, the zombie lashed out, clutching the smoking barrel and snatching it from Jim's grasp.

Stunned at its strength, Jim backed away as the thing examined the gun. It grinned, swung the rifle around, and pointed it at Jim. The leathery skin lining its fingers cracked as it playfully stroked the trigger.

Beyond the kitchen, the screen door banged on its hinges. More zombies paraded into the house. The thing that had once been his neighbor stepped forward. Jim retreated to the bottom of the stairs, yanking the pistol from its holster.

"*I ever tell you about the big war, neighbor? That was a real war, not like Viet Nam or Desert Storm or the 'War on Terrorism'. I was there. Well, not ME, of course. But this body was there. I see the memories.*"

It advanced down the stairs. A plump maggot dropped from the crater that had housed its stomach, and the zombie squashed it underfoot.

"*Of course, you never fought in a war, did you? You don't know the effects that a gut shot has on a human being. You're about to learn.*"

"Mr. Thompson," Jim began, "Please. I just want to

get to my son."

"*Oh, don't worry, you will,*" the thing cackled.
Behind him, more zombies swarmed into the doorframe.
"*You'll still be able to get around. I'm just going to
wound you, make you suffer a bit. Then we'll eat parts
of you. Got to keep our strength up. But we'll leave
enough of you left to walk. There are many of us still
waiting to walk again.*"

"Many of you—?"

"*We are many. Our number is more than the stars.
We are more than infinity.*"

The phrase echoed through Jim's head, grimly
reminding him of Danny.

He fired six shots in rapid succession. The bullets
slammed into the rancid flesh, boring through muscle
and tissue. Laughing, the zombie returned fire.

The blast reverberated through the cellar. The slug
whined by Jim. Above the shots, the other zombies
clamored for him, stampeding toward the cellar. The
thing that had been Mr. Thompson moved aside,
allowing them to slip down the stairway.

Jim fired the Ruger again. Thompson's eyeball
imploded. The hunting rifle dropped from its grasp as it
fell to the floor. Howling, the undead hordes rushed
forward.

Jim backed towards the basement window, aiming
and shooting as he went. There were eight shots left in
the clip. Eight more zombies dropped to the floor. The
others paused, forming a semi-circle around him.

Jim kept the Ruger pointed at them, sweeping it back
and forth. He prayed they wouldn't realize it was empty.

Behind him, half-empty buckets of driveway sealant
sat stacked in front of the window. He stepped up,
balancing his weight on the lids, and quickly considered
his next move. With an empty clip, he couldn't defend
himself. If he turned to climb out the window, they
would swarm him.

"*Concede,*" rasped a zombie that had once been his

paperboy. *"Our brothers await release from the void. Give us your flesh as our sustenance and their vehicle."*

Slowly, Jim inched his hand toward his back pocket.

"What are you?"

"We are what once was and are again. We own your flesh. When your soul has departed, you belong to us. We consume you. We inhabit you!"

His hand closed around the clip.

Glass exploded behind him as two arms crashed through the window. Claw-like fingers clutched his shoulders. He was yanked upward, and jagged spears of glass slashed at his arms and chest. Below him, the zombies cheered.

His attacker flung him through the air. He landed on the wet grass, tasting blood in the back of his throat.

"Hello, Crazy-Man," Carrie teased.

"Oh God," he sobbed, fishing the clip from his pocket and slamming it into the pistol. "Honey, if you can hear me, stay back! I don't want to shoot you!"

Her voice was like leaves blowing in the wind. *"Aren't you glad to see me, Jim? I've been waiting so long and I'm so very hungry. I missed you."*

Jim scuttled backward as she advanced on him. The tatters of her robe billowed in the night breeze.

"Get the fuck back, Carrie!"

"I'm not the only one who missed you, Jim. Somebody else wants to meet you."

Beneath the thin material of the robe, something moved.

Her bony fingers released the drawstring, allowing the robe to slip from her shoulders.

Jim screamed.

Carrie's abdomen was gone, eaten away from the inside. In the hollow cavity, the baby wallowed, clutching the rotting umbilical cord that still attached the two. Smiling, it waved a tiny, desiccated arm. The thing inside the infant tried to speak, but the sounds were unintelligible. Its voice was deep, guttural and old.

"Give your daughter a hug," Carrie squealed.

The fetal zombie leapt to the ground. Wet strands of tissue fell with it. It scampered toward him, the dangling umbilical cord trailing along behind it like a leash.

"We had a girl, darling," the Carrie-thing rasped. *"Aren't you happy? She's sooooo HUNGRY!"*

"Honey," he pleaded. "Don't do this. I've got to get to Danny! He's alive!"

"Not for long," Carrie taunted. *"Someone is waiting to take his place. Someone is waiting to take yours as well."*

The baby padded across the wet grass, panting eagerly as it drew closer.

"Da...Da...Da.."

Its mocking, guttural chant paralyzed him. Each half-formed word sounded like a belch. It tripped over the remains of the umbilical cord. Finally, it ripped the rancid tissue away from its belly and closed the gap between them.

Small, decomposing fingers brushed against the soles of his boot. A tiny hand gripped his ankle.

Shrieking, Jim opened fire. The shots slammed into the baby, sending it sprawling backward. Jim's cries were lost in the barrage.

The infant stopped moving and still he fired.

Enraged, Carrie raced toward him, hatred etched onto her decaying face. Obscenities poured from her; a thousand promised tortures that she would bestow upon him.

Jim continued screaming.

Smoke poured from the barrel, as the gun grew hot in his hands. The tenth shot hit Carrie in the forehead, dropping her to the ground. His finger clenched and unclenched even after the gun clicked empty.

His mouth was still open, but all that escaped was a low, mournful whine.

Jim sprang to his feet as more of the creatures poured from the house. He slid a third clip into the Ruger and opened fire again, mechanically aiming for their heads with each shot.

He ran into the road, feet pounding on the blacktop.

He fled from the house, the neighborhood, his wife, his unborn daughter, and his life; and slipped into the darkness, his tears leaving a trail behind him.

His agonized screams echoed through the empty streets of Lewisburg, West Virginia, and there was no living thing left to hear them.

*   *   *

An hour later, as he staggered along the road, fear and despair gave way to cramps. Exhausted, he tumbled down an embankment, and saw no more.

He awoke in a culvert; cold, wet, and wretched—but not alone. The night was alive with the sounds of the dead. He wiped the rain from his brow and shuddered as a horrible, gibbering laugh echoed over the hills.

After several minutes, it faded, but the silence left in its wake was just as awful.

He lay in the dark. Thunderheads covered the moon. He decided against lighting a match or using the flashlight out here in the open. Instead, he thumbed water from the face of his watch and squinted. Three a.m.

He'd passed out on his stomach, and the muddy water running through the culvert had soaked his jeans and shirt. He fumbled in the dark for the pistol, and found it lying on the bank.

His pack had remained mostly dry. Cautiously, he crawled from the stream and eased it from his aching shoulders. Something rattled inside. He searched the contents, nicking his finger on a jagged piece of broken pottery.

The coffee mug, the one he'd packed as an afterthought, was shattered.

The one Danny had bought him for Father's Day.

The Rising / 41

Jim could hear Danny's voice, full of trust and innocence—and terror.

Groaning, half-nauseous, he got up. His knees popped. He froze, waiting to see if he had attracted the attention of anything hidden in the night.

Cautiously, he began to crawl up to the road. Then he heard it. Distant, but unmistakable.

The growl of a Mopar, distinct and beautiful. Two headlights stabbed the darkness. Tires squealed, and the engine roared as gears were shifted.

"Oh, thank Christ," he sobbed in relief, dragging himself upright. He stepped out into the road, waving his hands above his head. "Hey! Over here!"

The car thundered down the road. The beam from the headlights speared him, bathing him with light.

He took another step.

The car accelerated, hurtling toward him.

"Fuck!"

He leaped out of the way, tumbling back into the culvert. As he jumped, he caught a glimpse of the driver and the passengers.

They were zombies.

Jim rolled to his feet, crouching in the darkness. The car screeched to a halt, the smell of burning rubber filling the air.

He clutched the pistol.

The motor hummed, idling. Then, a car door slammed, followed by another. And another.

"Did you see that?" The voice sounded like sandpaper. *"Sent him flying!"*

"No you didn't," rasped another. *"You didn't even tap him."*

"And you shouldn't have tried," reprimanded a third. *"What use is the body if you've shattered it beyond mobility?"*

"Bah. There's enough for all of our brothers. Let's have some fun with this one."

Jim crept backward, into the treeline. A skull, draped

in tattered flesh, peered over the ravine.

"Hey meat! Where do you think you're going?"

Two more appeared, and slowly, they began to clamber down the hill. Jim raised the pistol, fired, then turned and fled into the woods.

Their catcalls echoed off the trees as he ran. Head down, he barreled his way through the clinging vines, forcing his way through the undergrowth. Branches from a deadfall clutched at him, and for one fearful moment, he thought that perhaps the dead tree had come back to life as well. Then the branch snapped, and he sprang free.

As he made his way deeper into the forest, the sounds of pursuit faded. Pausing for breath, Jim leaned against an oak and listened intently. The forest was quiet. No bird sang, no insect buzzed. There was nothing, not even the wind.

Mind reeling, he tried to figure out what to do next. They could talk, shoot guns, drive fucking cars! Was there anything they *weren't* capable of?

He thought back to the zombie movies he had watched through the years. In the movies, the things weren't smart. They just shambled around—vacant, thoughtless eating machines. In the movies, the zombies didn't shoot back. The only similarity he could find between the movies and real life was that they were slow, and they ate living flesh.

Their lack of speed was an obvious advantage. All he had to do was stay ahead of them. But what they lacked in quick mobility, the made up for in their cunning. They were intelligent. They could plan and calculate.

Outrunning them wouldn't be enough. He had to outthink them.

His goal had been to make it to White Sulphur Springs on foot, and steal a car from the Chevy dealership there. Then, he'd planned on taking Interstate 64 to 81 North. That would take him all the way to Pennsylvania, where he could then head towards New Jersey.

Jim realized the folly in that line of thinking now. The

creatures could drive, and he didn't know what shape the highways were in. They could have traps set all along them, waiting for unwary survivors like himself.

But he *couldn't* do it on foot! He needed to get to Danny and he needed to get there *now*! New Jersey was a twelve-hour drive. Doing it on foot was inconceivable. His son would be long dead by the time he got there. Even the twelve-hour drive offered no assurances that he'd make it in time.

So then what the hell am I doing? He's probably dead already!

Danny's pleas rang in his ears. He thrust his fists against them, shook his head, and trudged forward.

For most of his life, Jim had hunted deer and turkey in the mountains around Lewisburg. White Sulphur Springs was roughly five or six miles away, through a deep hollow and over two mountain ridges. Once there, he'd arm himself better, find a rifle to replace the one he'd lost to Mr. Thompson, and move on. Barring any trouble, he'd make it to White Sulphur Springs by dawn.

He needed to come up with a plan between now and then.

He walked on, the shadows between the trees swallowing him.

From high above, a whippoorwill sang its lonely song.

Jim's grandmother had always said that if you heard a whippoorwill at night, it meant someone close to you was going to die.

The bird sang again, and Jim froze. It was perched directly in front of him.

And it was alive.

It chirped at him, and spread its wings.

"Nice to see I'm not the only one," he whispered. "I wish I had your wings."

The bird took flight, vanishing into the darkness.

He pressed on.

CHAPTER FOUR

The old man sat on the park bench feeding the pigeons.

Their bloated corpses buzzed around him. Frankie watched from the safety of the restroom as the dead birds devoured him. A pigeon swooped down, one of its eyeballs dangling from the socket, and claimed the old man's left eye in return. Strips of flesh were sheared away by snapping, razored beaks.

The old man did not scream.

He sat in stony silence, seemingly unaware of what was happening. He absentmindedly brushed at the side of his head. The mangled ruins of his right ear stained his white collar.

"Damn skeeters," she heard him mutter. A pigeon darted for the plump offering of his tongue. When the beak clamped and tore off a small morsel of meat, blood flowed into his mouth.

"Fly! Be free!" he flapped his arms as he sat on the bench. The pigeons around him fluttered and circled. No sooner had he slumped back than the birds descended again.

"Fucking nutcase," Frankie muttered, grinding her teeth.

The old man continued to move under the barrage of beaks. He squirmed and laughed, as if he were being tickled.

She started shaking again, though whether from revulsion or withdrawal or fear she could not tell. The jones called to her. The scabs dotting her slender arms itched, and three blunt, cracked fingernails dug at them without hesitation. She needed a fix. She needed some skag. She needed.

That need landed her at here at the Baltimore Zoo. Out of the frying pan and into the fire.

T-Bone and Horn Dawg and the others *had* to have seen her climb the fence. The question was, would they follow? Would they leave her be, so she could rest in peace?

Rest?

Yes, rest. Rest from the running all over town.

Rest forever. In peace.

Frankie thought she could damn well die here, in a men's bathroom with dead, hungry animals walking around outside, and a gang of pissed-off dope dealers who wanted the bag of dope she now carried. The street value on that particular bag of dope had skyrocketed, because there would be no further bags of dope like it.

Unfortunately, she was down to the last of it. Somehow, she didn't think T-Bone and the rest would be happy to hear that.

The old man was silent now. Cautiously, Frankie peered out the door. His black suit was a pink, quivering mass of exposed muscle and nerve endings. His chest continued to rise and fall. Stubbornly, the life his parents gave him continued with tenacity. It would not quit without a fight.

Death was stronger.

Patient.

She watched him die and wondered *how long before he rose again?*

Her arms howled. Her gut clenched, and she felt the pang of emptiness there. She dug into her pocket in search of something to take it away. The last of it.

She cooked up the batch, blotter and spoon,

disposable lighter, and she began to lick her cracked lips. Soon, none of these thoughts would matter. Not the old man, the pigeons, T-Bone and the others; not even the baby. What mattered was the greedy, puckered mouth track marks that dotted her arms, like the insistent mouths of newborns, hungrily demanding a nipple.

She tied off. The needle found a good vein. She shot.

Her blood sang sweet harmonies that lulled, pulled her along. A few seconds after, the familiar euphoria hit. The warmth settled in her belly. She felt like she was wrapped in cotton. Her face flushed and pupils constricted, Frankie drifted out of the restroom and above the zoo, floating beyond the ruins of Baltimore and the living world.

* * *

Frankie lay in the hospital. The bright lights were harsh on her eyes. Faces stared impassively; covered in shrouds. Her blood glistened on the doctor's glove.

She was in pain. She was turned inside out and the doctor and nurses didn't understand, or seem to care. They were talking about the morning's news report (a dead man coming back to life?), and she could see it in their eyes, see the thought reflected.

"Just another junkie whore delivering her unwanted baby into the world."

Fuck them. What did she care? They should be impressed! Most heroin users developed spontaneous abortions. She'd been strong enough to carry full-term.

The sooner she was done, the sooner she could take her baby and leave—

(get a fix)

—something tore and as she howled in agony, the doctor said he would have to cut.

"Don't push."

"Fuck you!" she screamed.

Frankie pushed, pushed with everything she had,

pushed till her spine felt like it would snap.

Something broke. She felt it, even through the pain.
Something small broke, but it changed everything.

"Push!" the doctor urged.

"Make up your fucking mind!" Frankie screamed,
but she continued to try.

The agony built to a crescendo, and then the
pressure vanished, all at once, and Frankie was crying.

She was the only one.

She heard a nurse mutter: "I'm not surprised."

"I'm going to call it as 5:17 p.m.," the doctor replied.

"My baby," Frankie pleaded through dry and
crusted lips. "What's wrong with my baby?"

The nurse walked away with her baby—

"MY BABY!"

The nurse turned and stared. She said nothing, but
Frankie knew. She knew.

Dead.

Stillborn.

Then the needle pricked her arm. Finally, the blessed
needle...

The nurse vanished out the door, along with her
baby.

Frankie closed her eyes, just for a moment. They
jarred open when, out in the hallway, her dead baby
cried and the nurses screamed.

* * *

The screaming continued when Frankie awoke. She'd
nodded. Usually she was out for three to four hours, and
she was unsure as to the time. It was dark now, and she
shivered against the cold bathroom stall.

The scream had come from outside. It took her a
moment to get her bearings. The listlessness still clung to
her limbs.

Tingling from a combination of heroin and fear, she
crept to the door and peaked outside.

The old man was moving again—

—and Marquon had found him.

More terrible shrieks poured forth from the gangster's gaping mouth as the old man reached into his belly and pulled forth a prize, ropy and wet. He thrashed, legs and arms flailing wildly as the zombie dug deeper. Marquon's Tec-9 lay discarded, forgotten in the grass. Something inside him popped, and ran through the clawed fingers like Play-Doh.

Marquon grew silent.

Frankie slid down the wall, panic eradicating the remains of the high. If Marquon had made it in, that meant the others were here too.

They were inside the zoo with all the other beasts.

As if on cue, she heard distant gunfire, followed by a shout. Marquon's cell phone began to ring.

She didn't believe what happened next. She was sure it was the dregs of the smack.

The old man picked up the cell phone, stared at it, and then spoke.

"Send more..."

It turned off the phone with one gore-streaked hand, and then resumed eating.

On hands and knees, Frankie crawled into the nearest stall. She reached into the stained porcelain, splashing water on her grubby face. Then she stood, trying to think.

She heard voices now, much closer. Voices she recognized.

"Damn, G! Check that shit out."

Horn Dawg.

"Mother-fucking Marquon. I told that nigga to watch his ass. Now look at him."

T-Bone.

"Hey, look at this. Dessert! I'll be right with you gentlemen."

The zombie.

Their reply was a volley of gunshots, followed by more ringing. At first, Frankie thought it was in her ears, but dimly she realized it was another cell phone.

"Yo," T-Bone snapped, cutting the chime off abruptly. "Whassup?"

Silence, and then "You stupid mother fuckers! Wha'chu mean he let it out of its fucking cage? Shit, did he think the bitch was gonna hide in there wit it?"

Frankie resumed watch at the door, in time to see T-Bone viciously jamming the phone into his pocket. The zombie lay in a bullet-ridden pile at his feet.

"Who that is?" inquired Horn Dawg.

"Fucking C. He said Willie let the damn lion out of its cage. Thought that ho' might be hiding inside. Stupid mother fucker shot the lock off."

"Yo, maybe we should forget about all this," Horn Dawg replied, his face turning ashen. "A fucking lion on the loose? Naaa yo. I don't think so."

"Man, fuck that lion," T-Bone spat. "And fuck you too. We ain't leaving until we find her. And put a bullet in Marquon's head. We don't need him getting' back up and trying to eat a brother."

Horn Dawg complied with a single shot. He looked at T-Bone.

"Did C say whether that lion was alive or dead?"

"What the fuck you think, nigga? They been stuck in those cages for how long now. You think it was still alive? And I'll tell you something else. Fucking C is on fucking crack. He say the lion be talking to him and shit!'"

The sudden growl from the bushes beyond the fountain was deep and rumbling, a symphony of perfect bestial rage. Then the foliage parted and it padded into the moonlight, the king of the jungle.

The king was dead. Long live the king.

The lion *grinned*.

It broke into a run and the two gangsters fled for sanctuary.

Frankie's sanctuary.

She dashed into a stall, slamming the door shut and pulling her feet up just as the outside door crashed open.

"Shoot the fucker," Horn Dawg screamed. "Nail that sumbitch!"

Instead, T-Bone shoved the door closed and braced his shoulder against it.

"I can't shoot it, nigga! My clip's empty. That's why I had you shoot Marquon! Now drag that trash can over here and put it in front of the door!"

"Man, ain't no damn trash can gonna stop no dead lion," Horn Dawg said as he slid the trash can into place. "I jus' hope he's too big to fit through the door. Otherwise, we're fucked."

"That bitch—that *ho* is fucked if I catch her stinkin' junkie ass. Gettin' me into this shit—"

A scratch at the door silenced them. Frankie stood on the bowl in the locked stall, her breath locked tight in her chest. If the thing got in here, it would not stop with T-Bone and Horn Dawg. If she moved, and alerted them to her presence, the lion would be a blessing. Of that she was certain, and the certainty expelled through her pores in thick sweat as she realized that she was going to die.

Oh, God, *why* did she have to run out of junk? Why like this? She could not die like this—why couldn't she die happy? Why couldn't she die high?

The toilet was cold under her feet.

The lion spoke, each word punctuated by a growl, as vocal cords that had never formed words before began to do so now.

The words were in no language Frankie had ever heard—nor anybody on the planet had probably ever heard. It was like something inside the lion was trying to speak—as if it were borrowing the animal's vocal chords for its own purpose. But a lion's tongue wasn't designed for speech.

Was it?

"Motherfucker," T-Bone whispered as the lion scratched at the door again, this time more insistent.

"Damn yo, we need to get the fuck *out* of here, like, with a fuckin' quickness."

"Well," T-Bone shouted, "start lookin' for a fucking way!"

The scratching was furious now, as were the growls of rage, and the terrible, mangled words between them. The garbage can vibrated and shook as the lion's paws batted the other side of the door. Frankie heard them run past her stall, and try to climb up to the window on the other side. It was set high in the wall, so T-Bone was standing on Horn-Dawg's shoulders to reach it. She heard the smash of glass as his pistol butt crashed into the pane.

Frankie willed every cell in her body to silence, to stillness. If she betrayed her presence here, she was dead.

At least T-Bone was out of bullets. She might have a chance. A slim one, but it beat squatting on top of the toilet as a dead lion forced its way into the bathroom, or getting caught by T-Bone and Horn Dawg.

She held her breath because if she gave her position away right now by drawing air, that would be the last breath she ever took. She had to wait until the lion got in.

T-Bone cleared the glass out of his way, and started to pull himself up as the bathroom door crashed open. Horn-Dawg screamed. T-Bone scrambled to the window ledge.

"Pull me up, nigga! Pull me up!" Horn Dawg yelled. Frankie heard him trying to climb the slick tiled wall. His shoes scraped uselessly against it. Then Frankie heard a thud. T-Bone pulled himself through the window.

"You fucking piece o'—" Horn Dawg never finished before the lion's jaws snapped his spine.

Frankie closed her eyes, tried to ignore the sounds of the lion eating, tried to ignore the smacking, ripping sounds. There was another sound too. Smaller, hidden beneath the symphony of carnage. A constant, incessant buzzing. It took her a moment and then she realized it was the flies living beneath the dead lion's skin.

The stench was horrible, a cloying miasma of wet fur and decaying flesh that made the urinals in the far corner pleasant by comparison.

Leaping from her crouch, she shoved the stall door open as her feet hit the ground. All sound had stopped, save for her harsh, ragged breathing, amplified by the tile. The lion turned its tattered mane slowly toward her, roaring on mute. T-Bone screamed something from his vantage point at the window, but this too was silenced.

The lion turned, faced her. Bits of Horn-Dawg dangled from its blackened gums. Hunger flashed within its sunken eyes. Dead muscles, free of rigor mortis, coiled like steel cable as it prepared to leap.

Frankie grasped at the door handle, kicking out desperately at the trash can that the lion had knocked aside. She pushed hard, but the door didn't budge. Whimpering, she slammed against it with her shoulder. Still, the door didn't move.

The sounds were rushing back now, growing louder. The lion roared, a dry, desiccated rasp that lost none of its ferocity. The carrion stench filled the room.

"You dumb bitch," T-Bone cackled from the window. "Can't chu' read the sign? That's it for your ass!"

Frankie glanced above her head.

PULL the grimy sign screamed at her.

Frankie yanked the handle.

The lion sprang.

Then she was out the door and into night. The air was foul and unmoving. It was the sweetest air she ever breathed. Filling her lungs deep, she ran.

Behind her, the bathrooms shuddered on their foundation as the door swung shut and the lion slammed against it. More clawing sounds from inside. The lion roared, trapped.

Frankie walked backward, her senses hyperaware. The sound of the lion's rage, the dry papery rustle of leaves in the bushes; each sound electrified her spine with dread. She felt like a field mouse knowing an owl was watching from a tree branch, or a snake from its subterranean pit.

She felt the ground beneath her left foot change: from the bathroom's concrete path to the asphalt-paved walkway leading through the zoo. In the distance, T-Bone shouted into his cell phone for reinforcements.

Two monkeys, long dead, reached for her through the bars of a cage to her left, and that was all the incentive she needed to keep running. Better to be dead than the living dead.

A stagnant breeze ruffled her greasy hair, carrying with it another distant sound. The sound of a baby crying.

She came to a low, flat building on her left. She pulled a door open, and stepped inside. Something wet crunched under her foot.

She did not want to look down, but did anyway. Whatever it used to be was now red and wet and unidentifiable. Maggots, pale and blind and bloated, wriggled throughout it, carving highways in the unknown flesh. Whimpering, Frankie skittered out of the mess. Her feet left gory tracks on the tiled floor.

The maggots continued about their business, unperturbed. *Were they alive or dead,* she wondered. *Did it matter?*

Above her, concealed in the shadows and spider webs, something rasped—like sandpaper on a board.

She backed up quickly and collided with a glass wall display. Biting through her lip, Frankie turned. The terrarium was dark. Inside it, something crawled lazily toward her. An skeletal iguana head, cadaverous and menacing, bumped against the thick glass, leaving bits of itself stuck to the barrier.

Above her, the sound came again, a dryness to it that she couldn't place. Before she could determine its location, a shadow crossed the doorway.

"Well lookit here," said C. "Got you now, Frankie!"

Frankie froze. Her tired, bloodshot eyes locked onto the knife C clutched in his right hand. Behind her, the iguana slammed against the glass, its insatiable hunger refusing to be thwarted by the barrier.

"Yo," C said into his cell phone. "I got the bitch. She in the snake house."

"Listen C," Frankie pleaded. "We can work this out. I can take care of you. T-Bone doesn't have to know."

"Bitch please," he spit. "Like I'd stick my dick up *you*? Shee-it! Sides, I ain't gonna waste you just yet. T-Bone will want to have some fun wit you first."

He leaped, and Frankie dodged. Dropping the cell phone, C snatched a handful of her hair and yanked—hard. Frankie screamed in fright and pain. The cell phone slid across the tiles, in time with the slithering sound from overhead, drawing closer.

C slammed Frankie to the floor. Her head cracked on the tile. Her ears rang, and her vision swam away from focus. Warm, salty blood ran down the back of her throat.

Laughing, C straddled her. His weight crushed her chest. He sliced open her shirt. His blade drew a bead of scarlet between her breasts.

"Yeah, now we talking," he gloated. "Maybe I will break me off a little somethin' before the crew get here." His grin was lascivious, and his gold tooth glinted in the near dark, as he slid the blade just below her nipple. "You hear what I'm sayin'?"

Frankie held her breath, too afraid to move.

C pushed the knife a little harder, drawing more blood. "Answer me, bitch. You hearin' me?"

"Please, C, don't—"

Something long and white dropped from the ceiling and coiled around him.

C's eyes bulged in terror as decomposed flesh wrapped around him. The anaconda had once been the talk of the Mid-Atlantic region, and even in death, it was still magnificent. Frankie didn't stop to ponder its morbid beauty however. She was too busy scurrying backward and bleeding to marvel at the snake's power and speed.

Her mind did take in its swollen length, and the bones that protruded through the parchment-like hide. It squeezed its prey, glaring at her with one malevolent eye. The other socket was empty save for the maggots wriggling within.

Again, Frankie screamed.

C did not. His dark skin turned purple as the undead serpent twisted around him, hiding his legs and his waist and his chest beneath one hundred and fifty pounds of decaying flesh.

Frankie slid to her feet and stumbled into a side office. Trembling, she slammed the door shut behind her. She pressed the tattered remains of her shirt around her wound, stopping the flow of blood, and examined the cut. She was relieved to find that it wasn't deep. Her nipple was still intact.

She glanced around the room, searching for a weapon. Oak bookshelves displayed dusty tomes of forgotten zoological lore, never to be used again. A matching desk was in the room's center. Occupying it was a blotter, an in-and-out basket overflowing with paperwork, a tape player, and a coffee mug from which several pens jutted.

She crossed the room and began to rifle through the drawers. A family, framed in glass, smiled back at her, watching her actions with eternally frozen stares. An all-American family: husband, wife, and two kids—a boy and a girl. The girl was the youngest, probably around four or five. Adorable.

Was she still alive?

Again, she thought she heard the cry of a baby.

She flung her hands to her ears, clenching her eyes shut. "Stop it stop it *STOP IT!*"

The ghost noise continued.

She considered the pens on the desk. Did she have the courage to just jam one into her eye, forcing it back until it puncture the membrane and sank into her brain?

She opened the bottom drawer, and a revolver stared

back at her. An old one. She scrabbled through the drawer, searching for bullets and finding only the moldy remains of several packages of Twinkies. She opened the cylinder, and laughed out loud when she saw that it was full. Six bullets gleamed at her from their snug confines.

She slammed the cylinder back into place, and began to believe.

Then she heard the baby again; louder, more insistent.

She went to the window and peered outside. A hedge blocked her view from the main concourse, but the backside of the Reptile House looked deserted.

Gritting her teeth, Frankie forced the window upward and crawled outside into the night air.

Crouching, she crept toward the bushes.

Something rustled on the other side. Frankie raised the pistol.

She burst from the foliage and almost tripped over the baby stroller. It was lying on its side, half on the curb, half in the grass. Strapped safely in the belts was an infant. It raised its tiny head, looked at her, and wailed.

The frilly pink blouse it wore was dirty and stained, both from the elements and from its own juices. The scalp, once covered with a fine layer of downy hair, had peeled back in places, exposing the dull gleam of bone. It struggled uselessly in the restraints, reaching for her. Its lilting cry continued and in that keening sob was hunger and a need to be comforted.

Frankie's face crumbled. She shuffled toward it, tears streaking through the grime and blood that spattered her pale cheeks. She reached for the stroller, setting it upright, and the infant cooed at her, grubby outstretched fists pumping the air. She offered her finger and the cold, skeletal fingers curled around it happily.

Slowly the infant's eyes rose to Frankie's. Its hollow-eyed stare was extinguished as the infant suddenly lunged forward, its ravenous blackened maw widening in an attempt to latch on to her hand.

Frankie screamed, snatching her finger back from the zombie.

"What the fuck was that, yo?"

Frankie dived behind the hedge just as T-Bone and two other thugs rounded the corner, attracted by the baby's cries.

"Latron, go on around front," T-Bone ordered one of the men, who trotted off around the corner of the Reptile House.

"Damn, holmes," sputtered the other. "That's a baby!"

"No shit, nigga," spat T-Bone. He had to shout over the infant's shrieks. "I look stupid to you, Terrell? Blast it while I go check out that window."

Terrell leveled the shotgun he was carrying at the stroller and jacked the pump. His eyes were wide.

"I ain't never shot no babies, T-Bone."

"It ain't no baby no more! Now shoot the fucking thing and let's go get that ho!"

As if to prove his point, the infant's squeals turned to curses.

Terrell blasted it in half. Still it continued to curse. Ejecting a shell, he fired again, obliterating its head.

Yelling, Frankie erupted from the shrubbery. She emptied four bullets into the would-be gunman before he could even pull the trigger.

She snarled, and fired at T-Bone. The gangster flung himself to the pavement, raised Marquon's recovered pistol, and squeezed off a burst of his own. The shots went low, spraying Frankie with fragments of asphalt and dirt, but missing her.

From inside the Reptile House came a horrified shout, as Latron discovered the same fate that had befallen C. Startled, T-Bone was distracted by the man's screams. Seizing the moment, Frankie fired. A crimson flower bloomed in the middle of T-Bone's forehead. He grunted once, his chest rising, then lay still.

Frankie emptied the last bullet into Terrell's head,

making sure he wouldn't get up again either.

In the aftermath, the zoo had grown quiet.

She glanced over at the remains of the baby, then turned away.

Escaping through the city streets was hopeless. On any night, the streets of Baltimore teemed with people. Now they would be crawling with the walking dead.

She wondered just how many had been attracted by the gun battle, shuffling toward the zoo even now.

The streets and alleys were out, as was the beltway. She considered hiding on a nearby tenement rooftop, but that was no good either. She shuddered, remembering the old man and the pigeons.

Her skin began to itch. Already, her body was demanding another fix.

A nearby manhole cover caught her eye. She ran to it.

Something chittered from the shadows. A monkey perhaps. Alive or dead she did not know nor did she want to find out. She clawed at the iron cover, straining. It didn't budge. Her yellowed nails bent, then snapped, and still she pulled.

Footsteps rang out behind her.

Still struggling, Frankie turned and screamed.

Three of them approached her, still dressed in the garments of their former existence. A businessman, red tie now sinking into the bloated, mottled throat. A nurse, whose formerly white uniform was now a tie-dye of various bodily fluids. A maintenance worker, the zoo logo still prominently displayed on his left breast. He carried some type of electric prod, and thrust it outward. It crackled in the darkness.

Laughing, they advanced on her.

Frankie shrieked, yanking frantically at the stubborn cover. Something in her back tore. Still she pulled. The abscesses in her arms burst, spurting with pus-yellow blood.

The cover rose with a screech, and she slid it to the side.

The zombies drew closer. They did not speak, and Frankie found their silence even more disturbing than the others. She thought of the baby. That evil zombie baby that had seemed so harmless...

Arms weak, collapsed veins turning to water, she still found the strength to raise her arm and extend her middle finger. Then she dropped down into the hole and was swallowed by the darkness.

She was on the run again, and while she could outrun the zombies, she couldn't escape herself—or the craving that was building in her veins.

CHAPTER FIVE

Martin stared at Jesus on the cross and thought about resurrection.

Lazarus had lain dead in his tomb for four days before Jesus came along. Martin opened his Scofield Reference Bible and turned to the Book of John. In Chapter 11, Verse 39, Martha told Jesus "by this time he stinketh; for he hath been dead four days."

That was pretty specific.

So was the account of Jesus bringing Lazarus back from the dead. "Lazarus come forth!" and the dead man did just that, still bound in graveclothes. Jesus then commanded the crowd to turn Lazarus loose, after which John dropped the narrative and moved on to the conversion of the Jews and the Pharisee conspiracy.

Nowhere in the Bible did it say Lazarus went around eating people.

The Bible that Martin had known, taught, and loved for the last forty years was full of examples of the dead coming back to life. But not like this.

"He that believes in me shall have eternal life," Martin spoke aloud. His voice sounded very small in the empty church.

He wondered if the things he had glimpsed in the street were still believers. At one time, many of them had been members of his congregation.

Martin had seen a lot in his sixty years. He'd survived a copperhead bite when he was seven and pneumonia when he was ten. He served as a Navy chaplain during Viet Nam, and made it back home alive, only to have Desert Storm claim a son of his own in return. That had been their only child. He'd outlived his wife, Chesya, gone five years now to breast cancer.

His faith had gotten him through it all.

He needed that faith now, clinging to it as a drowning man would grasp a lifeboat.

But he also found himself questioning it. Not for the first time—the Lord had given him all kinds of tests over the years, though never anything so fundamental as this. But, as Martin was fond of telling his flock, the good Lord didn't waste his time testing those who didn't have much to offer.

He moved across the church to the boarded-over stained glass window and peered through a knothole in the plywood.

Though not quite dawn, the darkness was already receding. Becky Gingerich, the church organist, had lost her soiled dress overnight. Now she squatted among the shrubs, clad only in a filthy pair of once-white cotton panties. Her sagging breasts swayed freely. She gnawed on a forearm as if it were a chicken leg, then cast it aside, staring off into the distance and moaning softly. Something had attracted her attention.

A man appeared, cautiously limping down the street. His jeans and flannel shirt were dirty and torn. He clutched a pistol, but the weapon dangled limply by his side. He did not seem to notice the corpse moving in the shadows. Wearily, he collapsed to his knees on the sidewalk.

The hedges rustled and Becky darted forward. Half conscious, the man seemed unaware of the danger.

"Hey!" Martin shouted, beating his fist against the plywood. "Look out!"

Mouthing a quick prayer, he dashed into the narthex

and struggled to move the heavy wooden pew propped against the door. Sliding it aside, he grabbed the shotgun from the coat rack, undid the four recently installed deadbolts, and ran outside.

Hearing the commotion, the stranger turned as the zombie lurched toward him. He raised the pistol and fired. The bullet tore through her shoulder. Running across the yard, Martin ducked as the second shot missed its mark completely.

The man squeezed the trigger again, and missed. He fired a fourth time, but the clip was empty. Confused, he looked at the pistol, then stared up at Becky.

He closed his eyes, and Martin heard him whisper "I'm sorry, Danny."

Martin slammed the shotgun into the creature's back. The former organist toppled face first to the sidewalk; yellowed teeth breaking on the pavement.

Martin jacked a shell into the chamber, and placed the barrel against the base of the zombie's skull.

Becky screamed in rage.

"Go with God, Rebecca."

Brain matter and skull fragments sprayed across the sidewalk like a Rorschach pattern.

The sun peeked over the rooftops. The roar of the shotgun echoed through the quiet streets, greeting the dawn.

"I'm afraid that's going to attract attention. We'd best get inside!"

The elderly black man held his hand out to Jim who took it. Despite his age, the man's grip was firm. He wore crumpled khakis and black shoes. Something white peeked out from beneath the neckline of his yellow sweater.

A preacher's collar.

"Thank you, Father," Jim said.

"Pastor, actually," the old man corrected him, smiling. "Reverend Thomas Martin. And no need to thank me. Give your thanks to the Lord after we're safe."

"Jim Thurmond, and yeah, let's get off the street."

A hungry cry, followed by another, was all the incentive they needed.

"Is this your church, Reverend?"

The old man smiled. "It's God's church. I just work here."

* * *

Martin fixed him a makeshift bed using blankets and a pew. Jim resisted, insisting that he only needed to rest for a moment, and promptly fell into a deep but troubled sleep. Martin sipped instant coffee and stood watch, listening to the occasional shriek of the things outside.

Shortly before noon, a wandering zombie discovered Becky's corpse and began to feed on her remains. Martin watched in revulsion as, like ants, more of the creatures were attracted to the feast. Occasionally, they would glance around at the surrounding houses and the church. Martin wondered if they would be moved to investigate, but they seemed satisfied with the free lunch.

An hour later, when the knot of fetid things scattered, nothing remained of Becky except bones and a few red bits, smeared across the sidewalk and grass.

Jim awoke at sundown, alarmed at first and unable to remember where he was. He sat up, looking around the church. *This wasn't the shelter!* Then he saw the preacher, smiling in the candlelight, and he remembered—

—and in remembering, he thought of Danny.

"Here you go," Martin handed him a steaming cup of coffee. "It's not very good, but it'll wake you up."

"Thanks," Jim nodded. He sipped it and took in the surroundings. "Pretty secure. You do all these fortifications yourself?"

The preacher laughed softly.

"Yes, by the grace of God. I managed to get the place squared away before it got bad. I had some help. John, our janitor. He's the one who got the windows boarded over."

"Where is he now?"

Martin's face darkened. He didn't speak for a moment, and Jim wondered if he had heard him.

"I don't know," he said finally. "Dead I suppose. Or undead more likely. He left two weeks ago, insisted on getting his pickup truck. Planned on driving us out of here. He was convinced this was a localized problem, thought the government might have this section of the state cordoned off. John figured we should make for Beckley or Lewisburg, or maybe Richmond. I never saw him again."

"It's like this everywhere, as far as I can tell," Jim told him. "I—I came from Lewisburg."

"On foot too, it would seem," Martin commented in wonderment. "How did you manage that?"

"I almost didn't," Jim admitted. "I was on auto-pilot I guess."

"These are times when men are forced to do what they must," the Preacher sighed. "I had hoped it was different elsewhere. I prayed for a ham radio set, or even a decent pair of those AM/FM headphones I see the kids wearing, just so I could know what was happening. I've had no contact with folks, and the power has pretty much been out, except for a few streetlights here and there. I heard a plane go overhead a few days ago, but that's been it."

"The power was still on in Lewisburg. I had radio, TV, and the net. They're worthless though. There's nothing— no one. As for this being a localized event, it's been over a month. I think they'd have had troops in here by now, if that was the case."

The Preacher thought about this, then excused himself and disappeared into a side room. Jim began to lace up his boots.

Returning, Martin offered him Oreo cookies, bread, animal crackers, and warm grape juice for dinner. "Got the cookies and crackers from the Sunday School room.

The bread and juice were for communion."

They ate in silence.

After a few minutes, Martin caught Jim staring at him.

"Why?" Jim asked.

"Why what?"

"Why did God let this happen? I thought the end of the world was supposed to be when Russia invaded Israel and you couldn't buy anything without having a 666 on your credit card."

"That's one interpretation," Martin nodded. "But you're talking about end-time prophecy and you've got to remember, there are many, many different ideas about what it all means."

"I thought that when the Rapture happened, the dead would return to life? Isn't that what's happening?"

"Well, the actual word 'Rapture' never occurs in the Old or New Testament. But yes, the Bible does speak of the dead returning to life, after a fashion, to live with the Lord upon his return."

"No offense Reverend, but if He's returned, He's made a hell of a mess of things."

"That's just it, Jim. He hasn't returned—not yet. What's happening isn't of God. It's Satan who was given mastery over the Earth. Yet even in this, we must stand firm and trust in the will of the Lord."

"Do you believe that, Martin? Do you really believe this is God's will?"

Martin paused, choosing his words carefully.

"If you're asking me if I believe in God, Jim, yes. Yes I do. But more importantly, I believe that there is a reason for everything, good and bad. Despite what you may have heard, bad things are not caused by God. When there's a tornado, that isn't God's will. But it's his love and power that gives us the strength to carry on in the tornado's wake, And it's that same love that will get us through now. I believe we have been spared for a reason."

"I have a reason, alright," Jim nodded, standing. "My son is alive, and I've got to make it to New Jersey and save him. Thanks for the meal and the shelter, Reverend, and more importantly, thanks for saving my ass today. I'd like to pay you, if you'll let me. I don't have much, but I've got some extra sardines and Tylenol in my pack—"

"Your son is alive?" Martin repeated. "How can you be sure? New Jersey is a long way off."

"He called me last night on my cell phone."

The old man looked at him as if he were crazy.

"I know it sounds crazy but it happened! He's alive and hiding out in my ex-wife's attic. I'm got to get to him."

Slowly, Martin rose from the pew.

"Then I'll help you."

"Thanks Martin. Really, thanks. But I can't ask you to do that. I need to move quickly, and I don't want—"

"Nonsense," the preacher interrupted. "You asked me about God's will and the meaning in all of this. Well, it's His will that you received that call, and it's His will that kept you alive to receive it. And it's also His will that I help you."

"I can't ask you to do that."

"*You're* not asking me. God is." Martin stamped his foot, then more quietly, said "I feel this in my heart."

Jim stared at him, unflinching. Then, slowly, a grin spread across his tired face.

"Alright," he reached out a hand. "If it's God's will and everything, I guess I can't stand in the way of that."

They shook hands, and sat back down.

"So what's your plan?" Martin asked.

"We need a vehicle. I don't reckon the church has one that we could use?"

"No," Martin shook his head. "That's why John left. To get his truck. But there's plenty in the streets and driveways."

"I don't suppose a man of the cloth knows how to hot wire one?"

"No, but there's a dealership just off the interstate. We could get one there, keys and everything. It's right off Sixty-Four."

"Works for me," Jim said, mulling it over. "When can we make a move? I can't waste any more time."

"We'll leave tonight," Martin said. "Those things don't really sleep, but the darkness will give us more cover. That's how I've avoided discovery so far. I stay quiet, watch for them during the day, and sleep at night. With the boards over the windows, they can't spot the candlelight, and I've been careful not to give them a reason to be curious."

"Well, let's hope that luck holds."

"I told you, Jim. It's not luck—it's God. All you have to do is ask Him."

Jim began reloading his clip.

"In that case Pastor Martin, I'm going to ask for a tank."

* * *

"They can drive?" Martin sputtered, astonished.

Jim pored over the atlas spread out on the pulpit in front of him. "The ones I saw last night sure could. They can shoot, use tools. Everything you and I can do. They're just a little slower at it. That's our only advantage."

"I saw one a week or so ago," Martin told him, while waterproofing his boots. "Mike Roden's boy, Ben. Mike was the manager over at the bank. Anyway, Ben was carrying a skateboard at his side. Not riding it, but carrying it, as if he was planning on riding it if he could find a suitable spot. I just figured it was some kind of rudimentary instinct—a trace memory of before."

"It's more than just memory, I can tell you that," Jim said, then paused. He thought back to the basement, and to what Mr. Thompson and Carrie had said. A part of them, the physical part, were people he had known and loved. But there was something else too. Something inside of them that was—old. Ancient.

And very, very evil.

"I was there," Mr. Thompson's corpse had said, when talking about the war. *"Well, not ME, of course. But this body was there. I see the memories."*

"I don't think these zombies are the people we knew."

"Well of course they are, Jim. That one I shot this morning was Becky Gingerich. She'd been our organist for almost seven years."

Frustrated, Jim struggled for the words to express what he was thinking. He was a construction worker, damn it. Not a scientist!

"The bodies are the same on the outside, yes, but I think what's making them come back is something else. A force of some kind."

The zombie's taunts came back to him. *"We are what once was and are again. We own your flesh. When your soul has departed, you belong to us. We consume you. We inhabit you!"*

Jim told Martin of his escape from the shelter. He paused when he came to Carrie and the baby, then finished, swallowing hard. "It's like they possess our bodies, but not until after we're dead. Like they have to wait for our souls to leave or something."

The old man nodded patiently. "Demons."

"Maybe," Jim agreed, "but I've never taken that stuff seriously."

"The dead walk the Earth, Jim. What could be more serious than that?"

"I know, I know!" Jim slammed his hand down on the pulpit. "But if they're demons, then shouldn't we be able to throw holy water on them, or exorcise them or something? There's so much we don't know! Why can you fill them full of holes and they keep coming, but hit them in what's left of their brain and they drop? They eat us, but is it for nourishment, or just because they're sadistic bastards? Their bodies keep rotting, the meat just slides right off the bone, and yet they keep going!"

He stopped, shocked by his outburst. He hadn't realized he was crying till he felt the wetness on his cheek.

"I'm sorry, Reverend," he apologized. "I'm just worried about Danny."

"I don't have the answers, Jim. I wish I did. One thing I can tell you is that God does have the answers, and with his strength, we will win the day. We *will* save your son!"

Jim nodded in acceptance, and turned back to the atlas. Inside, he wished he could believe it.

* * *

An hour later, they were ready, and sat discussing the plan one last time.

"I still think we should avoid any population centers," Martin said. "The more people that lived in a town, the more zombies there probably are in that area. Let's stick to the back roads."

"I agree," Jim conceded, "and if it was just you and me, I'd say we head higher up into the mountains. But the longer we take, the less chance Danny has. Other than the Appalachians, the whole East Coast is pretty much one big population center. At least on the Interstate, we can avoid going through the center of any town, large or small. If these things are on the move, and driving in numbers, we'll have a better chance outrunning them on an Interstate I'm familiar with, rather than some winding back road."

"So," he continued, "we hit the Chevy dealership, get us a vehicle, and see what kind of attention we've attracted. If we don't have company, we do a quick stop at the Super Mart next door, stock up in the sporting goods section, and then we're on the road. Sound good?"

"Not really," Martin grinned, "but I've got nothing better."

Jim smiled back. "Let's go."

They walked to the door, moved the pew aside, undid

the bolts and peered out into the night.

The street was empty.

Stealthily, they made their way across the street and slipped into the shadows. Martin led the way, and Jim was surprised at the older man's stamina and speed. They crept between houses, careful to stay out of the moonlight and the few, scattered areas where the automatic streetlights still worked. Martin led him through backyards, a small urban woodland, around a baseball diamond, and through a culvert.

Occasionally they spotted or heard the undead, but were careful to stay hidden until the danger had passed.

Finally, upon exiting a cornfield, they reached the car lot. The dealership shared the highway exit with a strip mall and several fast food restaurants. Ghostly sodium lights bathed the parking lots in a yellow glow.

"Looks deserted," Martin whispered. "Do you think it's safe?"

"I don't think anything's safe anymore, Reverend," Jim said grimly, "but we've got no choice."

Crouching between the rows of new vehicles, they crept across the lot. A few of the cars showed signs of vandalism—a smashed windshield, several slashed tires; but most still looked brand new. Banners and stickers in the windshields promised *0% FINANCING* and warned *TWO-DAYS ONLY!!*, begging them to *TAKE ME HOME TODAY*.

A black Suburban caught Jim's eye.

"How about this one?"

"I reckon that should do us just fine," Martin agreed. "But how do you plan to get us going?"

"Follow me and I'll show you," Jim told him. "My friend Mike used to sell cars. They usually keep the keys in one location." Jim stood quietly for a full minute, memorizing the Vin number on the sticker by repeating it over and over to himself. Then they walked toward the showroom.

Something hissed behind them. Something else

joined in. Then several more.

"What the hell?"

They turned, and with a howl, something small and black and furry launched itself at them. They stumbled backward, pressing against the garage doors, and the blast from Martin's shotgun cut the leaping cat in half.

Three more undead felines crept forward. Their fur was matted with dried blood and gore. One's entrails dragged uselessly along behind it.

They feline zombies leaned back on their haunches, preparing to jump.

Martin stared in disbelief.

"They're cats!"

"They're zombies, Martin! Shoot the fuckers!"

They opened fire, dropping two where they crouched. Spitting with rage, the third ran beneath a car and darted out the other side. Martin fired after it, but Jim held up a hand and stopped him.

"Forget about it! If the shooting didn't let the whole town know we're here, then that furball will. We'd better find those keys quick!"

"Even the animals," Martin hyperventilated. "Oh Jim, I had no idea."

"I forgot to tell you about that. I'm sorry about my language too."

"No need to apologize. It was the heat of battle." The old man reloaded the shotgun. "Besides," he gave Jim a wink, "I've been known to say worse upon occasion."

How you boys doing this evening?

Both men whirled around as the glass doors swung open. A zombie stepped into the lot. It grinned at them, revealing blackened gums and a grayish tongue. Fly larvae wriggled in its nose. The formerly white shirt and gray dress slacks that it wore were stained with the corpse's juices. A tie hung askew around its neck.

"Shit." Jim raised the gun.

Now son, the zombie rasped. *There's no need for that. Tell me, what do I need to do to put you in a new* car today?"

"No thanks," Martin's voice quavered. "We're just looking."

Jim fired, the shot sinking into the creature's chest. It took another step toward them.

"Well then, maybe the question is, what do I need to do to put my friends in the two of you!"

It ducked a second before Jim's follow-up shot. Weaving to the left, it lunged forward and it made a grab for Martin's thigh. The black man shrank away.

"Mmmm, dark meat!"

Jim's third shot found a home in the zombie's temple, and an exit on the other side. It collapsed to the pavement, thudding against the bumper of the truck in front of them.

"Let's move!"

They scanned the showroom and cautiously entered the building. Jim quickly found what he was looking for; a lock box mounted on the wall, directly across from the sales manager's desk.

"Here goes nothing."

He fired a shot at the lock, and they both ducked as the bullet ricocheted off the metal lock box and into a filing cabinet.

"Damn! That thing's strong. I thought we'd be able to shoot the lock off."

"Maybe he has a key," Martin offered, pointing outside at the re-killed corpse.

"Maybe," Jim agreed. "Go look. It should be a small, round key. I'll check the shop."

Jim disappeared into the back, and Martin said nothing, staring after him.

He walked back outside and eyed the zombie warily. It lay in the same position it had fallen in.

"The Lord is my shepherd," Martin recited, creeping closer. Then he was above it. The stench was overpowering. Something wriggled beneath the skin of its forearm, tunneling beneath the waxy flesh.

Taking a deep breath, Martin bent down and reached for the creature.

The lights went off, plunging the lot into darkness.

Martin cried out, scrambling backward. He heard Jim holler in surprise as well. Something crashed inside the dealership. The building was dark too, as were the strip mall and the restaurants.

"Jim?" He ran back inside. "Jim! You okay?"

"I'm fine." Jim stumbled back into the showroom. "Looks like the rest of the power finally went out. Wonder if it's just this grid or a wider area?"

"I don't know, but if that cat and all the shooting didn't get them stirred up, this certainly will. We need to go. I didn't get a key."

"That's okay," Jim said, hefting a crowbar. "I found one."

He went to work on the lock box. Breaking into it with the crowbar was harder than he'd thought it would be, and it was ten minutes before he cracked it.

"Shit!"

"What's wrong now?"

"We need the Vin number! After everything that happened, I forgot it! Run back out and get it for me, but be careful." He grabbed a tablet and a pen off the salesperson's desk and tossed them to him.

Breathing another silent prayer, Martin walked across the lot to the Suburban. The sticker was hard to read now that the lights were off, and it took a moment for his eyes to adjust. Finally deciphering it, he jotted the number down and trotted back toward the showroom.

Halfway across the lot, he smelled it. Like the zombie they'd just killed, but stronger.

Much stronger.

Martin ran back into the building.

Eye's wide, he exploded into the showroom.

"KLKBG22J4L668923!"

Jim rifled through the keys, searching for a matching number.

"What's the last four numbers?"

"8923! But—"

"Wait a minute."

"There's something else, Jim!"

"Just a second—-got it!" The grin on his face died when he glanced up at the preacher.

"What is it?"

"Sniff the air for a moment." Martin told him. "Do you smell it?"

Jim breathed deep and then gagged.

"Jesus, what is that?"

"They're coming!"

They charged across the lot, reaching the vehicle as the first few zombies loped through the rows of cars. More of the dead stepped out of the cornfield, or shambled across the adjacent parking lots. Dozens poured out of the doors of the Safe Mart next door.

Spying them, the zombies lifted up a horrifying cry, and began to half-run, half lurch toward them.

"Time to go!" Jim shouted and pressed the button on the remote dangling from the keychain.

The door didn't open. He pressed harder and still nothing happened.

"Shit!"

"What's wrong?" Martin demanded, watching in horror as the zombies drew closer.

"It's one of those remote locking systems, and the batteries in this thing aren't working!"

A zombie in overalls and suspenders had almost reached them. It stopped less than fifteen feet away and raised the pitchfork it was carrying, shaking it at them.

"Give it up, humans. Our brothers await release! Surrender now, and we promise we'll make it quick."

Jim's answer was a shot to its head. Gurgling, the creature fell, and the others rushed forward.

Martin raised the shotgun and blasted the passenger window. Knocking glass out of the way with the stock, he clambered through the opening. His joints groaned and creaked in protest.

Jim picked his targets carefully, waiting till they were close, aiming for the head, and then firing.

"Hurry!"

Martin dropped into the seat, felt something pop in his back, and fumbled with the lock as a white-hot pain raced down his spine. Gritting his teeth, he gripped the latch and opened the door.

Dozens of the creatures swarmed the car lot, and reinforcements were closing the distance quickly. Jim dropped two more in their tracks and then jumped inside, throwing his backpack onto the seat between them. He thrust the key into the ignition and turned. The engine purred to life. Jim slammed it into drive, and they lurched forward in their seats.

The SUV roared in protest, refusing to budge.

A pair of mottled arms reached through the shattered window, clutching at Martin.

"The emergency break!" he gasped, and shoved the barrel against the zombie's chin. He squeezed the trigger as they sped forward, the roar of the shotgun momentarily deafening them both.

Another zombie jumped in front of them and ran straight toward the vehicle. Jim stomped the gas, running it down. Cursing, it bounced off the bumper and lay writhing in their wake. They impact jolted them, and Martin screamed as another bolt of pain tore through his back. Through watering eyes, he watched as the undead flashed by them. Jim guided the Suburban up the ramp and onto the highway.

"Well now," Jim chuckled, pointing ahead. "Look who it is!"

The cat that had escaped them earlier stood frozen in their headlights. A second later, it crunched softly under the tires. Jim glance back in the rearview mirror and saw it splattered across the road.

Martin groaned in pain.

"What's wrong?" Jim asked, concerned. "You okay?"

"I'll be fine," he gasped, opening his eyes. "Hurt my back when I climbed through the window, is all. I'm not as young as I used to be."

Leaning forward, Jim turned on the wiper fluid. It sprayed across the windshield, washing the blood away.

"There's painkillers in my backpack. Help yourself."

"Bless you," Martin sighed, and undid the hasp. He reached inside and shuffled through the contents, looking for the bottle. His fingers closed around a photograph, and he took it out, appraising it.

"Is this your son?" he asked.

Jim glanced over. Martin held the photo from the shelter, the one of them with the Soap Box Derby trophy.

"Yep," he said quietly. "That's my son. That's Danny."

They drove into the night.

CHAPTER SIX

B aker camped in the janitor's office of a Rest Stop along the Pennsylvania Turnpike. Smashing open the vending machines, he ate a dinner of chips and candy and washed it down with warm soda. He'd used the butt of his rifle to break the glass on the machines, and for a brief moment, wondered if anybody would call the authorities. Then he chuckled at the absurdity of the thought.

He wished his only crimes against humanity were mere vandalism and petty theft, but two days of panicked observation had confirmed otherwise.

This was his fault.

The escape from Havenbrook had been harrowing. Fleeing down dark tunnels and hallways, the sounds of Ob's furious pursuit echoed closely behind him at all times. Finally, he'd made it out, but only after an exhausting climb up an elevator shaft.

What he escaped into was far worse.

There was no hole in the sky, no gaping wound from which another dimension could be glimpsed. Baker surmised that the experiment had probably weakened the walls between this world and the place Ob and his brethren came from, blurring the invisible boundaries. Whatever the portal was, it wasn't obvious.

The facility grounds were deserted, and he had no trouble temporarily outfitting himself from the guard shack. He then ransacked the first house he came to and managed to find a hunting rifle and a pistol, along with a supply of food.

He easily avoided the few zombies remaining in Hellertown, simply by sticking to the woods. But it was in those woods, halfway to Allentown, that the real pursuit started.

Baker had forgotten about the fish.

Walking like a zombie himself, the full enormity of what he had helped unleash upon the planet starting to sink in, Baker didn't hear the squirrels until they were almost upon him. He was grateful for the annual hunting trips he'd taken with his colleagues. He managed to drop four of the creatures in quick succession. But while he was reloading, the rabbits emerged from the brush, and the chase began.

Branches and thorns tearing at him, he'd run through the woods, chased by a pack of undead bunny rabbits. Thinking about it in retrospect, Baker could almost laugh, but he was afraid if that he started laughing now, he'd never stop. Something inside of him felt like it was ready to break.

He'd managed to kill or elude his smaller pursuers, as well as an undead turkey buzzard and four human zombies.

That first night, he'd come across a baseball diamond overlooking Allentown. He'd taken shelter inside a portable toilet and was awakened by screams. He'd watched in horror as a group of zombies mounted on off-road bikes hunted down a young couple who were still very much alive. Baker had considered helping them for a moment, but paralyzed with fear and hopelessly outnumbered, he could only watch from his hiding place as the creatures shot them, aiming to wound, and then feasted upon their flesh.

They're hunting us, he'd realized.

Baker had noted with horrified detachment that while they consumed organs and skin, the zombies left enough intact for the victims to remain mobile.

Soon they were. Inhabited by something else, the humanoid shells rose, joining their brethren. Then they moved on.

Baker spent the rest of that night shuddering in the darkness, unable to sleep.

The next day had been a long, slow, and terrifying trek, until he'd stumbled onto the Turnpike. The highway had been surprisingly vacant; the zombies having moved on to better hunting grounds. He cautiously passed around a few abandoned cars and some orange construction cones, but that was all.

Now that he was settled and relatively safe for the moment here in the rest stop, the fear slid away, replaced by shock and an overwhelming guilt.

He couldn't stop thinking about his responsibility for all of this. He was surely damned, and this was hell.

Swooning, Baker clenched his eyes shut and gripped the corners of the janitor's sink. He wailed, forgetting for a moment that silence was the key to staying alive. The tears were too much to keep bottled up inside—too great to be controlled. A scream of anguish burned in his throat. The tears kept coming, and he crouched there for a long time.

He did not hear the door open behind him.

Baker's back was to it, his shoulders heaving as he cried. He opened his eyes for a moment, peering down into the sink. The room was spinning, and Baker began to shiver, despite the sweat on his brow.

A shadow fell across him.

Baker's legs buckled, and his head struck the rim of the sink as he crumpled to the floor.

Moaning unintelligibly, the figure in the doorway shuffled toward him.

* * *

Baker stirred, then froze; his eyes shut.
Something moved in the darkness.

"Nnnuuhh."

Oh God! One of them got in here while I was passed out!

He kept his eyes closed; thinking. Judging from the sounds, the zombie was right on top of him. His pistol was inside his pack, which meant it might as well have been on the moon. He was helpless.

The creature warbled to itself in a strange, lilting pattern; as if its tongue had been removed.

"Nnnuuuhh. Nooonah."

Baker realized it was singing.

The thing brushed up against him, draping something cold and wet across his forehead. Water ran into the corners of his eyes and down his cheeks.

"Wata. Nowh ooo beh awwllyht. Ayk uhp."

A firm hand patted his cheek softly. Baker willed himself to remain still, fighting the urge to scream.

The flesh against his face didn't feel dead. It was warm and smooth. The creature didn't reek of decay either. Rather, it stank of unwashed armpits and sweat—much like Baker himself.

"Ayk uhp fo Wohrm."

Heart pounding, Baker opened his eyes.

A round, grimy face drooled over him, smiling happily when it saw he was awake.

The boy leaned back on his haunches and spoke.

"Ooo ayyk! Yaaayy!"

Baker removed the wet rag from his forehead, studying his benefactor. His age was indeterminate, somewhere between fourteen and nineteen, Baker guessed. Judging by his facial features and deformities, the boy suffered from some form of retardation. Baker couldn't determine what type.

"Thank you," Baker nodded, smiling gently.

"Ellkohm!"

Welcome, perhaps?

Baker turned away to lay the rag on the sink, asking "My name is Professor Baker. What's yours?"

The boy made no reply. Baker looked back over his shoulder. The boy peered up at him curiously.

"Ellkohm!" he cheered again.

"What's your name, my friend?" Baker asked. The boy stared at his lips, brow knitted in concentration. He shook his head in frustration, and continued staring, waiting for Baker to repeat himself.

He's reading my lips! He's deaf!

Baker knelt before him on the floor, forming his words carefully.

"My name is Baker," he pointed to his chest. "What is your name?"

Understanding flickered in the boy's eyes and he clapped.

"Wohrm!" he chirped, poking a thumb at himself.

"Worm?" Baker queried. The boy nodded gleefully, and then pointed at Baker.

"Baykhar?"

"Yes, Baker." He placed his hand on the boy's shoulder and squeezed. "It is very nice to meet you, Worm."

"Nyyyz to eeet oo!" Worm agreed.

Baker laughed, his tears and guilt forgotten for a moment.

* * *

Baker shared his vending machine spoils with his new companion. Conversation was nonexistent, save for Worm's delighted grunts as he devoured the candy bars. He whistled and hooted in enjoyment, and Baker grinned.

How had he survived, alone and without guidance? Baker had no way of knowing.

He tapped Worm on the shoulder. The boy looked at him expectantly.

"Where are your parents?"

Worm's glance fell to his lap, a shadow passing

beneath his soulful brown eyes.

"Mmm—myss," he stammered. "Myss eeght Mawmee."

"I don't understand," Baker told him, moving his lips carefully.

Worm reared backward, holding his hands before him like claws. His lips wrinkled back into a sneer, and he squinted his eyes and began to squeak.

"Myss," he said again, crawling around the room on all fours. Then he looked at Baker for understanding.

"Mice?"

Worm nodded excitedly, then stopped, sadness washing over him again.

"Myss eeght Mawmee."

"Mice eight—?"

Worm made hungry sounds and gnashed his teeth.

Suddenly, Baker understood.

Ate," he whispered, turning away. "Mice ate his mother. And I bet they weren't alive when they did it."

Baker's guilt came flooding back, and he grew quiet.

After finishing his dinner, Worm produced a small, brightly colored rubber ball from his pocket, and began to bounce it on the floor, catching it in his palm each time. Baker watched until, finally exhausted, the scientist fell into a deep and troubled sleep.

The nightmares followed him.

* * *

The thunderstorms arrived just before dawn, and the two of them awoke to a world that was as dark as when they had fallen asleep. Worm stared at the lightning in fascination, unable to hear the thunder that boomed across the valley with it.

Baker stepped into the parking lot and was drenched within seconds. Fat, cold raindrops splatted against the blacktop like bugs against a windshield.

Resigned to staying put until the storm passed, Baker

took the opportunity to explore the Rest Area. Worm followed eagerly along behind him.

They raided a vending machine that dispensed bottled water, along with the rest of the snack machines. Baker paused at a newspaper box; frozen headlines from a not so distant but bygone era staring back at him. The President of Palestine warned that his country's economic problems could destabilize the entire Middle East, while the Israeli army was blocking aide shipments into the state because of terrorism concerns from the newly reactive Hezbollah. Phenyalamime, a popular food additive, had been found to cause cancer. The popular boardwalk at Ocean City, Maryland had washed away due to beach erosion and global warming effects. The President was assuring Americans that the Pentagon had not authorized human cloning, despite what sources were claiming.

And then there was the RHIC, and Baker saw his name in print, along with Harding's and Powell's.

He moved on.

The restrooms yielded nothing useful, save for some extra rolls of toilet paper. The lobby sported dozens of tourist attraction fliers and not much else. A full-color road map hung on one wall, and Baker stopped to study it. Worm bounced his rubber ball behind him, singing softly.

Baker refused to believe that it was all over. Surely, somebody out there was still alive, and working on regaining control; reversing the catastrophe. It was folly to consider mankind extinct.

So where could he find them?

From where he stood, he was close to many East Coast hubs. Philadelphia, Pittsburgh, Baltimore, New York City, and the nation's capitol were all within five or six hours driving distance. But these major metropolitan areas had such high population areas, that they would be virtual death traps.

Baker ran a dirty finger down the map, frowning. It

seemed best to continue south into Pennsylvania, possibly crossing over into Maryland or Virginia. He traced the blue highway line. Harrisburg, while small, had a large urban population and would present the same problems. York and Hanover might be feasible. Although they had dense populations, both were surrounded by miles of rural communities and uninhabited farmlands and forests. The local governments in these areas could have kept up a fight, possibly barricading themselves against the enemy.

Farther south, just beyond Hanover, his finger stopped on Gettysburg. More than just a Civil War memorial, Gettysburg was near Camp David, and was rumored to be the location of something called "the underground Pentagon." Baker had earned himself friends in both congress and the military over the years, and his own security clearance was quite substantial. He knew things—things the public didn't know.

Things like the fact that in the case of a war or a crippling terrorist attack, several of the country's leaders would be shuttled to a location in Gettysburg, where they'd be safeguarded while they did what was necessary to get the country operational again.

If there was any semblance of order left, the closest place to find it would be Gettysburg. They could take the turnpike southward, skirting only the outskirts of Harrisburg, then on to York, where they could lose themselves in the countryside and travel through the less populated back roads to Gettysburg.

He nodded to himself, convinced it was a good plan.

Of course, they could be killed at any time along the way.

He considered transportation. Under normal conditions, Gettysburg was an approximate three-hour drive from where he stood. What the drive—and the roads—would be like now was anybody's guess.

Should they even drive, he wondered, or would a moving vehicle just attract more attention? He thought about the young couple that he'd seen hunted by the zombies. The creatures could operate vehicles and use firearms. Their dexterity was slower, but they were still cunning—and lethal. Wouldn't a speeding vehicle, or even a slow-moving one, provide a much more apparent target for them than if he and Worm were to just stick to the fields and woods, and go on foot?

He sighed in exasperation. Walking was just as deadly; perhaps more so. That left them vulnerable not only to the human zombies, but to the rest of the living dead bestiary. Distance was also a factor. On foot, a three-hour drive became a one hundred and twenty-mile hike. Baker was by no means in bad shape. He'd taken advantage of Havenbrook's extensive physical fitness center every other day. Nevertheless, at fifty-five, he was no longer a young man, and two hours on an exercise bike three days a week were no comparison to a grueling journey on foot, especially one where danger was so prevalent.

Adding to his frustration was Worm. He couldn't just abandon him. The boy seemed to have survived on his own quite well so far, but now that Baker had discovered him (or was it the other way around, he wondered), he felt responsible for his new ward. Perhaps, Baker realized, he was making amends; trying to get back in God's good graces for the mess he'd helped to cause down here.

Driving it would have to be. That decided, he turned his mind to the task of finding transportation. There had been a few cars and trucks scattered among the rest area's parking lot, so that seemed a logical first choice.

He got Worm's attention, and placed a hand on his shoulder.

"Stay here," Baker commanded. "I have to go out."

"Shugh Baykhar!" the boy smiled, giving him an okay sign with his fingers.

Verifying the pistol had a fully loaded clip; he stepped out into the rain. Doubt gnawed at him. What was he doing? He was a scientist, not a car-jacker. He hadn't the faintest idea how to hot wire a car, or even how to break into one without smashing the window or setting off one of those annoying car alarms that would alert every zombie in the tri-state area as to their location.

The first three vehicles; a Saturn, Dodge truck, and a Honda, were locked. The fourth, a rusting "K" car, was unlocked, but missing it's keys. Baker rummaged half-heartedly through the glove compartment and under the seats before giving up and moving on.

The fifth car, a gray, compact Hyundai, was not only locked, but occupied.

The keys lay on the ground, just beyond the driver's side door, still clutched in a severed hand. The rest of the body was missing; eaten or walking around Baker couldn't be sure, and all that remained was a dried reddish-brown spot on the blacktop.

The child in the backseat had probably been five or six years old. It glared at Baker through the window, baring its teeth in undisguised savagery and loathing. The child had been oriental; Chinese, Baker was sure.

After a moment of fright, he paused, realizing that the zombie was trapped inside. He studied the situation, weighing the evidence. Obviously, he surmised after careful observance, the parent and this child had been set upon by the creatures. The parent had made certain the child was safely in the car first, but there was no time for themselves. Somehow, either through the parent's doing or the child's mistake, the child-safety locks had been engaged. After the death of the child (starvation, previous wound, shock—Baker ran off a litany of possible causes), the entity that took over its body was unable to work the safety locks *because the child itself had no former memory of how to work them*. It lacked the physical strength of an adult host, so attempting to smash through the window, as Baker had seen Ob do at Havenbrook, was fruitless.

How long had it sat there, trapped in this cage of

Detroit steel and Japanese engineering?

It looked *very* hungry. Ravenous in fact.

Baker tapped the glass with his finger, and the creature snarled; its rage muffled by the glass and the rain.

Stooping, he snatched the keys from the dead hand.

The zombie tensed.

Baker placed the key in the lock and turned. The zombie sprang over the console and into the front seat.

With a speed that surprised even himself, Baker whipped the driver's side door open and aimed the pistol. Eyeing it, the zombie froze. A bulbous, gray tongue licked the split and cracked lips.

It spoke to him in Chinese. When Baker didn't respond, it switched to the form of Sumerian that Baker had heard Ob use as well.

"You don't speak English," he observed in calm detachment, "because your host didn't know English."

The thing spat, its mottled fingers clutching at the seat tightly.

"But you know what this is, don't you?" Baker gave the pistol a slight shake. "That's sad. The child learned about guns before he learned to speak the language of his adopted home country."

The creature launched itself at him, but Baker was quicker. Thunder crashed overhead, and was answered by his pistol. The inside of the dead child's head splattered across the dashboard.

Baker made sure it was destroyed, then grabbed the corpse by its skinny ankles and dropped it unceremoniously onto the pavement.

His stomach fluttered.

They aren't human, he reminded himself. *This is the only way to survive.*

"I'm sorry." he whispered to the grisly pile of flesh and bone.

Then he fished the key from the door, slid behind the wheel, said a Hail Mary (something he hadn't done since college), and turned the ignition.

The engine turning over was the sweetest sound Baker had ever known, and he cheered.

He checked the gauges, and was delighted to find that the car had a full tank of gas. Everything else looked okay as well.

He ran back to the shelter and burst through the door, rainwater pooling on the rug in the lobby. He found Worm, dejectedly bouncing the ball against a stall in the women's bathroom.

"We're leaving," Baker mouthed, trying to convey his excitement. "Let's get your things!" He had to make several attempts before his meaning was clear, at which point Worm cringed, backing farther into the restroom.

"Don't you want to leave?" Baker asked "Don't you want to find other people?"

Shaking his head back and forth, Worm whimpered and dropped his eyes.

"Eeeet uss," he protested. "Peepol trhi to eet Wurhm!"

The boy refused to look up. Baker cupped his chin and forced him to meet his stare. Tears streamed from the frightened boy's eyes.

"Worm!" Baker insisted. "Nobody is going to eat you. I promise. I'm going to take care of you now."

"Nooo myss? Noo dahd peepol?"

"No, Worm," Baker assured him gently, cradling the boy to his chest. Worm trembled, and then clung to him. Though he knew Worm couldn't see his lips, he continued talking in soothing tones.

"I'm not going to let anything harm you." Baker promised, and in doing so, realized he had taken his first step on the path to self-atonement. "I'm going to make up for it."

They gathered their belongings and with a last, perfunctory check of the building, they walked outside to the car.

The rain had stopped.

CHAPTER SEVEN

Raindrops fell like tears from a black tar god—or drops of rancid milk from a dead mother's breast. The industrial residue that Baltimore's recently defunct factories had spewed into the sky for decades was now falling back down to be claimed by the earth.

Emerging from the sewer, Frankie baptized herself in the slick rain, luxuriating in the oily film that it left behind. She imagined the pollutants burning away her old self, revealing the new.

She'd just come from hell.

"Troll." she whispered.

She shivered, remembering her escape from the zoo and what happened after.

* * *

The first zombie tumbled down the manhole shaft after her, hitting the tunnel floor and rupturing like a sack of rotten vegetables; its innards spilling out around it. The shattered limbs wriggled like worms, then lay still. Covered in gore, Frankie fired blindly up the shaft, deterring the rest.

The tunnel was pitch black. She had a flash of memory; from the distant past before the smack and turning tricks to get more smack became her life. A murderer in Las Vegas had once eluded the authorities' dragnet by using a sewer drain to escape. The man was underground for five hours and, according to maps, he'd trudged at least four miles. She wondered how dark it was in the drain, what he'd encountered and what he was thinking. Was the hardened felon frightened? When he finally saw light at the tunnel's end, was he relieved?

What if there was no light at the end of her tunnel?

She slogged forward, fingers trailing along the invisible wall to her right, feeling the slimy dampness.

Abandon hope, all ye who enter here. Another snippet of the past; from Mr. Yowaski's class, right before she'd started screwing him in exchange for a passing grade in English. She wondered who or what might be lurking down here; crackheads, deranged survivors, zombies. What was hiding in the dark, watching her even now? Weren't there alligators in the sewer? Maybe in Florida, but she didn't think Baltimore suffered from that particular urban blight. But there *were* rats; of that she was sure. She had no idea how many shots she had left, and couldn't tell in the darkness. How could she possibly fend off a swarm of hungry rats?

She yawned, shivering as the first chills of withdrawal set in. Large goosebumps broke out on her skin. Cold Turkey, they called it, because you looked like a fucking plucked bird when it hit.

She paused. Was there something there, in the dark? A soft padding sound faded and stopped.

She stood still, holding her breath. The sound was not repeated.

She shuffled forward, flinching when her fingers came in contact with something round and metallic. After a moment's experimentation, she realized that it was a doorknob.

Unlocked.

Taking a deep breath, she turned it. The door grated open. Particles of dust flaked down into her hair and eyes.

The space beyond the door was even darker than the

tunnel. Carefully, she stepped through the opening and pulled the door shut behind her. There was no draft of air. No sound. She could *sense* walls but she could not see them. A maintenance or storage room of some kind, she guessed. She was safe for now.

Or was she?

What if there was a zombie in here with her, lurking in the darkness, waiting to lunge out and eat her? She sniffed the air. It was stale and damp, but there was no telltale smell of the putrefaction that signaled one of the undead. There was no rasp of flesh or exposed bone, no whisper of something moving.

Crouching on all fours, she crawled forward. Her hands traced the alien outlines of unfamiliar objects. Then she collided with a wall. She put her back to it and began to twitch.

The hot flashes followed, and though she couldn't see her ears, she knew they were scarlet. Her breathing grew short and jerky. Her eyeballs were getting hot too, and felt like they were going to melt right out of their sockets. She knew they were bloodshot, even in the darkness.

She was going to die here, underground. In a fucking storage room. In the dark. With no heroin. She should have let the lion eat her, or let T-Bone and the others scrag her ass. That would have been quicker, at least.

She knew she had at least one bullet left.

She thought about the baby.

(It wasn't my baby)

The hot flashes passed, and the chills returned; intense and biting. She knew that the drowsiness would follow soon. She usually slept for eleven or twelve hours when it happened. What fresh horrors of the withdrawal came after that, Frankie didn't know. She'd never made it that far. There was always another dick to be sucked by then; to be milked for ten or twenty bucks that could be converted to junk with ease.

She yawned, deep and long.

Sleep. That sounded good.

Frankie had no intention of waking up again.

She put the barrel of the gun against her head, and then thought better of it. What if she missed? She'd heard about that. Attempted suicides where the bullet traveled around the brain like a car on a racetrack, horribly maiming the victim but not bringing the desired effect.

She yawned again, and stifled it by placing the gun in her mouth. She tasted oil and cordite, and found she preferred them to the man-sweat of the cocks that had been there before it.

She steeled herself and then, before she lost her nerve, squeezed the trigger.

There was an empty click.

She screamed in frustration and flung the pistol into the darkness. There was a metallic clang as something fell over. Frankie sobbed, and the tears did not stop.

She was still crying when she passed out.

* * *

When she awoke she wasn't aware of it at first. Lying in darkness, she opened her crusted eyes and saw more of the same.

The cramps seized her almost immediately, and she barely had time to turn her head before the vomiting began. Her stomach was empty, and turned itself inside out, savagely heaving what little fluid she had left. Warm bile spattered her shirt and clung to her hair. She was sweating profusely, and her ragged clothes quickly became drenched.

There was a brief respite, and then another cramp stabbed her abdomen. Her bowels erupted, and everything below her waist grew warm and wet. The smell made her gag, causing another round of dry-heaves.

She groaned, biting through her lip as a third wave of cramps set in. Blood trickled down the back of her throat, and was thrown up a second later.

She cried out, struggling to sit up. Sweat ran into her eyes, stinging them. Her muscles began to twitch, legs convulsing as she 'kicked the habit.' Each jerk sent a bolt of pain through her bones, rocketing up her spine where it exploded into the center of her brain.

She was still moaning, eyes clenched tightly shut, when the doorknob turned.

Frankie gasped, fear overriding the lack of opiate her body was protesting.

The door inched open, revealing a flickering torch.

"You're not one of them." The voice was deep and quiet, and spoke matter-of-factly.

Trembling, Frankie squinted, trying to see beyond the light. The pain grew worse and she fought back a scream as another spell of watery diarrhea hit.

"I've seen this before," the voice whispered. "I guess we'll have to wait, won't we?"

The door closed softly and then Frankie was alone with the fire and the voice.

"Wh—what are you?" she whimpered.

"I am a Troll."

She laughed; a fragile, wilting sound that was interrupted by a hacking cough.

"Don't suppose you happen to have any methadone on you?" she asked weakly.

Then she traded the light of the torch for the darkness behind her eyelids, and she knew no more.

* * *

Grinding her teeth. Hard. Hard enough to feel them wiggle, to feel the blood well up between decaying tooth and receding gum line.

Sweat oozes from her dirt-clogged pores like pus from a zit. It stinks. The reek makes her vomit and then the smell of that makes her vomit again. She lays in her own shit, feels it covering her quivering buttocks and running down her spindly legs, coating her lower back too, like a warm blanket.

She finds comfort in this.

Comfort in shit. Comfort in Hell.

The baby is here with her, somewhere. She hasn't seen it yet, but she can hear it. T-Bone and C and Marquon and Willie and the others are here too, whispering promises of pain and death. She welcomes these promises; holds her arms out expectantly, but death never comes and that makes her cry. The doctors and the nurses whisper in the ether. A john undoes his zipper, and the sound makes her violently shudder.

In between the madness (for she knows that's what this is) the Troll is there. He cleans her face with a cool, wet rag, and whispers assurances, and makes her drink hot chicken broth from a rusty coffee can. She curses the Troll because she didn't ask for chicken broth; she asked for skag. The chicken broth just churns in her stomach and is rejected but he continues giving it to her anyway. She can see bits of debris in his unkempt beard, and perhaps even some pieces of the chicken broth she threw up. For a moment she feels sorry and she sees the concern in his kind, grey eyes; and then it hits again— THE NEED—and she hates him all over again and wants to die. She begs him to kill her, but he doesn't listen.

There are minutes and hours and days of hot flashes and cold flashes and she can't breath (she doesn't want to anyway but it still bothers her that she can't) and cramps—twitches-convulsions-nausea-tremors—and her nose and throat feel like mucous factories and Frankie screams.

And screams.

And screams.

And screams...

And through it all the Troll is there by her side, shushing her and promising that everything will be alright, that it's almost over and maybe he's right—

—because the baby's cries aren't so loud anymore.

She can't hear them anymore.

Something inside her dies, and finally, Frankie sleeps.

* * *

Frankie opened her eyes. Her bones and muscles ached, her head throbbed, and her nose was running, but she'd never felt better.

The Troll sat in the center of the room, reading by candlelight. When she stirred, he looked up in surprise, smiled, and closed the book. Frankie glimpsed the front cover—*The Birth of Tragedy* by Friedrich Nietzsche.

Frankie licked her lips and tried to speak. Her tongue felt like sandpaper.

"Thought I was going to die. I wanted to."

"I was just reading about that," the Troll replied. "Nietzsche quotes Silenus; 'What is best of all is beyond your reach forever; not to be born, not to be, to be nothing. But the second best for you—is quickly to die.'"

Frankie said nothing. The room was surprisingly warm, almost homey.

"How long?"

"Were you out? A little over seventy-two hours by my estimation. Can't be sure because my watch stopped working weeks ago. You're not out of the woods, of course, but you're past the bad portion. Heroin withdrawal usually lasts about ten to fourteen days, but the first three are the real killers."

"How did you—?"

"I used to work at a clinic. I was a counselor. Are you thirsty?"

She nodded, and he brought her a canteen.

"Here, try to sit up," he urged, and placing a hand under her back, he helped her sit forward. Her spine popped, and it felt good.

She took a drink of water. Cold and clean and

revitalizing, it imbued her with life as it traveled down her raw throat.

"That's enough," he cautioned, stopping her from gulping. "You've thrown up quite enough. You need to start keeping something in you."

"Thanks," she gasped. "I guess I owe you my life."

He laughed, then patted her leg.

"You owe me nothing. You only owe yourself."

"My name's Frankie," she offered, extending her hand, noticing as she did that the trembling had subsided.

"People called me Troll," he said warmly, clasping her hand. "Welcome to my home."

"You live here?" she asked, not surprised, but feeling a little guilty that she'd trespassed. In Frankie's world, people lived where they could; in alleyways, under railroad trestles, cardboard boxes, anywhere there was space.

"Not this particular room, no. But down here, yes. Been here for a while. Long before things went bad up top."

"You got hooked yourself, didn't you?"

He laughed, a short, brittle, humorless sound. "Not hardly. What makes you think that?"

"I'm sorry. You just seem like a smart guy. Reading philosophy and shit. And you knew about smack. I figured you got lost in your work."

"No," he said, and grew silent. He stared at the flickering candle flame, and it was several minutes before he spoke again.

"My daughter started snorting heroin. Fifteen years I worked with this, and I was the be-all end-all of drug counseling, wasn't I? Accommodations on the wall, testimonials on file from former junkies that I'd helped. But when it came to my own daughter, I was blind. I never saw it coming."

Frankie said nothing, listening.

"I don't know why she started. Maybe the divorce,

maybe it was trouble with a boy. I thought we were close. Thought she told me everything. But I guess fourteen-year-old girls aren't really Daddy's best friend, are they?"

He paused, fingers trailing through his scraggly beard.

"She was at a party. Snorted it. The junk had been mixed with some kind of household chemical. I never found out what, but I'm sure you know how it is."

Frankie nodded. She'd seen friends go out the same way. It was brutal.

"She died on the way to the hospital. My ex-wife blamed me. And I couldn't disagree with her. So I came down here."

"I'm sorry," Frankie said.

"Don't be. It's not so bad. You'd be surprised at the types of people you find underground. Stockbrokers and lawyers and medical school dropouts and Liberal Arts majors. People live anywhere they can, and there are worse places to bunk down for the night, believe me. And surprisingly, not all of them are running from something."

"They are now."

"Yes," he agreed. "I suppose they are. But it's not just up there. They're down here too. Not a lot of humans yet, but the rats are pretty bad."

Frankie shuddered, remembering the zoo.

"It's going to get worse down here too," he continued. "I was actually on my way out when our paths crossed." He motioned to his backpack and gear. "Figured I'd follow the tunnels out to the harbor, and then take a boat somewhere."

"Where would you go?"

He shrugged. "Anywhere but here, I guess. To be honest, I don't know. I need to determine if this is a localized event, or worldwide. An island would be a logical choice, but even those have animals and birds, so the safety and security would be relative. I considered just drifting, far from land. But I don't know if even that would be safe. There're things like sharks to consider. I imagine a school of zombie sharks or an undead killer whale could make quick work of a boat."

"It's hopeless," she sighed. "Sooner or later, they're going to get us all, and we'll be walking around like one of them. You should have let me die; should have caved my head in so I wouldn't get back up."

Troll shook his head. "You saved yourself, Frankie. All I did was watch over you. The feat and the triumph are yours and yours alone. Somewhere inside you, you found the strength to fight—to survive. Your will is a strong one, and that is what you will need out there."

Frankie considered this. Her stomach grumbled and she grinned, embarrassed.

"I imagine you could use something to eat. But first, why don't you clean up." He moved over to some metal shelves in the corner, and rummaged through them. "I don't know how these will fit you," he said, holding up a city worker's maintenance uniform, "but they've got to be better than what you're wearing now. Probably smell nicer too."

Frankie laughed, and gratefully accepted the clothes. He gave her a clean rag and a wash basin with water. Then, like a magician performing a particularly fine trick, he produced a bar of soap and a small bottle of shampoo.

Frankie disrobed and began to scrub while he turned his back and prepared dinner. The soapy water ran over her bruises and sores, over fresh track marks and ghosts of fixes past.

Never again. She'd vowed this before, of course, but something inside her meant it this time. Never again.

Troll turned to her, holding a paper plate piled high with granola bars, beef jerky, and apples that had only started to go brown in spots. She heard his intake of breath from across the room, as she stood naked in the flickering candlelight.

She licked her lips. "You took care of me. Would you like me to take care of you?"

"No," he said, his voice thick with emotion. "I'm honored, but there's no need for that. I imagine you've repaid plenty of favors in the past that way, but not now. This is the new you, remember?"

She smiled, more pleased than she could find the words to express.

"You're something else, Mr. Troll." She shrugged into the uniform, and found it fit like a new skin.

They ate, and as she chewed, Frankie thought to herself that everything tasted different now.

* * *

"So far," Troll told her, lighting the torch while she reloaded the pistol, "fire has kept the rats away when I came across them. But there are other things down here too, and I don't know how it will work on them. So let me lead."

She nodded, biting her lip.

"Ready?"

She nodded again, unable to speak.

He opened the door into darkness.

They started down the tunnel. Passing a manhole shaft, Frankie saw signs of occupancy in the tiny ledges. Sleeping bags and shelves hung over the rungs of the ladders rising up to the street. There was no sign of the people who dwelled in them.

They walked on in silence, with only the sloshing of their shoes and the sound of their breath as company. The tunnel seemed endless, barreling into the distance beyond the reach of the torch. Troll walked with unerring assurance through innumerable twists and turns.

They came to a section where the floor was covered with muddy water. It stank like the walking corpses in the world above, and a layer of scummy film floated atop it. To avoid stepping in the muck, they walked with their legs spread apart, feet gripping the sides of the tunnel and heads lowered.

Cockroaches scuttled blindly through the mud, living on rotted leaves and detritus from the streets and buildings. Albino fish spawned in the water by the dozens. Frankie wondered if they were some type of deformed goldfish, flushed down here long ago. Some of them had grown too big to fit completely in the water. Unable to swim properly, they flopped through the scum, gulping noiselessly in the suffocating oxygen.

But that was it. No human or rats, zombified or otherwise.

Troll led on tirelessly through the vast network of catacombs. Eventually, they arrived at a crossroads of sorts. Several tunnels of varying height and angles merged together into an open area.

"This way," Troll whispered, the first sound he'd made in over an hour. "Then it's just another mile or so to the harbor."

He continued forward, and Frankie followed close behind. This new tunnel was almost perfectly straight. The ceiling rose and sank like the underbelly of a roller coaster, but the floor was dry, and her cramping legs were grateful.

Eventually, she felt a cool draft on her face.

That was when the first sound came from behind them.

They both turned. Troll held the torch high, just as a second splash echoed down the corridor.

"Quickly," Troll urged, grabbing her arm. They started walking, briskly; not yet running.

More sounds, closer now. A clicking. The sound of nails or claws.

Lots of them.

Then the smell. That all-too-familiar reek of the undead.

Troll pushed Frankie ahead of him. Then he stopped and turned, thrusting the torch forward.

Dozens of beady red eyes reflected back at him from

the darkness.

The rats charged, spilling towards them like a brown wave coming down the tunnel. They made no sound, save the clicking of their claws as they scurried forward.

"Go!" He shoved her forward and she almost fell. Catching herself, Frankie ran, not sparing a glance behind. Her footsteps pounded against the tunnel. Troll's breathing was harsh behind her. The sounds of pursuit grew stronger. The rats began to squeal, and the sound was like fingernails on a chalkboard. Frankie fumbled for her gun.

"That's no good!" Troll shouted. "By the time you pick off one, ten more will be on you! Just run!"

She obeyed him, flying ahead. She'd gone several yards before she realized he wasn't behind her.

Troll stood in the center of the tunnel, legs spread wide, blocking it with his girth. He held the torch before him like a flaming sword, sweeping it back and forth. The army of undead vermin cowered, the menace in their eyes almost palpable.

"Troll!"

"Go," he screamed at her, not looking back. "I'll meet you outside!"

Frankie stood rooted, and took a step toward him.

"God damn it, girl," he hollered. The rats paced back and forth, testing the limits of the fire. "Survive, Frankie! You've got a second chance. Don't blow it."

Something small and brown and furry dropped squeaking from the ceiling, and Troll swung at it with the brand. It erupted into flame, and the rest scampered back. He thrust it at them, growling.

Reluctantly, Frankie ran...

* * *

...and that was how she found herself standing here; in a wide, swampy area close to the Fells Point Marina, enduring her baptism of acid rain. The Sylvan Learning Center skyscraper and the Inner Harbor Marriott towered over her, their windows dark and brooding.

She waited for a long time.

Troll never emerged from the sewer.

Eventually, Frankie limped on, her tears swallowed up by the rain.

CHAPTER EIGHT

Interstate 64 skirted only a few sparse towns as it wound through the mountains of West Virginia and into Virginia, and Martin breathed a prayer of thanks for that. The lack of populated areas improved their chances to avoid encounters with the undead.

Jim drove toward the rising sun, while Martin experimented with the radio, scanning both the AM and FM frequencies. All the stations were playing twenty-four hours of non-stop silence.

Thick fog covered the highway, but Jim kept the speed at a steady sixty-five, ignoring Martin's pleas to slow down. Other than the morning mist, the road was clear. Both of them had been surprised by the lack of vehicles. They'd seen only half a dozen abandoned cars, and most of those had been at the last exit.

Still, to make the old man happy, Jim agreed to wear his seatbelt.

"How's your back?"

"Getting better," Martin grunted. "I reckon those pain killers you grabbed at the gas station did the trick."

They passed the exits for Clifton Forge, Hot Springs, and Crow; each town sitting far off the highway and shrouded by the mountains. The trees masking Crow glowed orange, and wisps of black smoke were beginning to drift through the forest and onto the road.

"Should we stop?" Martin asked.

Jim passed the exit and didn't slow.

"No. There's nothing we can do there."

"But if the town's on fire and there are people still alive—"

"Then they're probably better off. Besides, if there *are* people still left there, maybe they're the ones who started it. Maybe it was the only way to save themselves."

Martin considered this quietly.

"You know," he said a few minutes later, "we haven't seen any other survivors since we left White Sulphur Springs."

"Yeah, but we haven't seen any zombies either."

"This is true. Still, you would think we'd have seen more. Where do you suppose everybody's gone?"

"If you mean the zombies," Jim answered, "I don't know. You've got to remember, the towns in this part of the state are small and spread out. Most folks live on farms or homes with no close neighbors, or in a hunting cabin down in some hollow. I reckon if they're dying and coming back, we probably *wouldn't* see that many around here. The most I've seen at once was back in Lewisburg, and that's only because we lived in a housing development."

"But wouldn't the zombies be on the move by now?" Martin asked. "They eat folks, same as we eat a hamburger. If they had no food, surely they'd start migrating to where there was more."

"Yeah, and I think they probably are," Jim agreed. "But you've got to remember that there's hundreds of miles of mountains covering West Virginia. Most of the state is forested. If they are making their way through that type of terrain, it cuts down on our chances of running across any, even the animal zombies. I'll tell you one thing though. I'm still confused over the whole 'food' thing."

"What do you mean?"

"Well, there's no doubt that they're eating us. We've

both seen it. But have you noticed something? They don't eat the whole body. It's not like the movies where they rip a victim apart, gnawing every last scrap of meat off the bone."

Martin shuddered.

"Sorry about that, Reverend, but do you see my point? They are eating us for food. But for the most part, they seem to be making extra sure that their victims can remain mobile; that they can become one of them. Most of the zombies we've seen have kept their limbs, especially their legs. And all of them still have their head."

"I saw one without a lower jaw."

"But I'm betting its brains were still intact, right?" The preacher nodded and Jim continued. "The brain seems to be the key. Like we were talking about yesterday at the church; it's almost as if something else is settling in the brain after death, and reanimating the body. Like a parasite or something. You said it was demons, and maybe that's so. I don't know. Whatever it is, I'm willing to bet there's a lot of zombies out there that lacked mobility at first."

"Why?"

"Because when this first started, most people died as a result of something other than being a zombie dinner. People who'd been in accidents or fires or what have you. Severed spine. Broken neck. Legs cut off by a riding mower. Things like that. Later, as more and more of the living were being killed by the original wave of zombies, deaths in that manner decreased. As more people die as a result of the zombies, we're seeing more corpses that have the capability for moving around."

"So you think we'll see more and more of them as time goes on?"

"Oh yeah. I imagine if we were farther north, where there's more people, we'd be seeing it already."

"But what about survivors, Jim? Doesn't it seem odd to you that we haven't seen another living person?"

"I don't know," Jim admitted. "Maybe we're all there is in these parts. But I know Danny's alive, and that's all that matters to me."

"We can't be all that's left," Martin said. "I truly believe with all of my heart that there are others, Jim. Folks like us. We just have to find them."

Moments later, the headlights pinpointed a lone deer, standing along the median strip. When it saw them, it bounded across the lanes and disappeared into the treeline.

"I think that one was alive," Martin said. "It didn't move like one of them."

"I guess we should wish him luck then," Jim agreed. "He's gonna have a lot more to worry about than just hunters come this fall."

Eventually, the sun burned off the haze. They crossed the border, a green sign informing them that they were *LEAVING WILD, WONDERFUL WEST VIRGINIA* and asking them to *COME AGAIN*.

"Well, we're in Virginia already," Martin said. "So far, so good."

"We can hope, anyway. We're doing good with the gas. We've only used about a quarter tank. But I don't reckon that our luck will hold. The closer we get to New Jersey, the more congested things will become. To be honest, Martin, I'm not sure how we'll get around that without a fight."

"Perhaps God will clear a path for us."

Jim gripped the wheel.

When he spoke again, Martin had to strain to hear him.

"Why?"

"Why what, Jim?"

"Why did God let this happen? Why did he do this?"

Martin paused, choosing his words carefully. It was a question he'd been asked a thousand times before, a question that he himself had asked on more than one occasion. Deaths in the family, sickness, divorce, unemployment, bankruptcy; all of these had led his flock to inquire the same thing.

"You asked me that before and I told you that I didn't know," he answered, the words catching in his throat. "I still don't. I wish I did, Jim. I truly do. But I do know that God didn't do this. The Bible tells us very clearly that Satan is the master of this Earth. He has been since the fall—him and his minions."

"Even if that's so, why does God allow it to happen? The Devil may rule the planet, but are you telling me God couldn't lift a finger and stop all of this?"

"Believe me, I know. It would seem that way. But it doesn't work like that, Jim."

"He works in mysterious ways and all that?"

Martin smiled grimly. "Something like that."

"Well, that's bullshit, Martin. He can leave my son out of it! He's got a son of his own, and he let him get murdered! He doesn't need to kill mine too!"

The preacher didn't reply. Instead, he sat staring out the window and watching the trees rush by them.

"I'm sorry, Martin" Jim exhaled. "I didn't mean to offend you. I really didn't. It's just..." He trailed off.

Martin placed a hand on his shoulder.

"It's alright Jim. I understand. I just wish I had an answer for you, something that would give you comfort. But I do know this and I believe it with all of my heart. Our meeting wasn't coincidence. It was planned by God. And I think Danny is alive, Jim, and I think we're going to find him! I feel this in my heart."

"I hope so," Jim said. "God, I hope so."

Turning, Martin fished around in the backseat and produced a bottle of water for each of them, and a bag of potato chips. They ate hungrily.

"Have you given any thought of what we'll do once we rescue Danny?"

"I have, actually. There's a couple of things we could do."

"Let's hear the choices," Martin said, and never

finished. Instead, he gripped the dashboard. "Look out!"

They squealed around a curve, and the twisted carcass of a brightly colored Volkswagen Beetle was spread across the road. The car lay on its collapsed roof, and the tires, one flattened and another off the rim, pointed up in the air like the legs of some dead animal. The passenger side was smashed in, and shards of shattered glass dotted the blacktop like crystalline snow.

Four motorcycles (*not Harley's*, Jim noticed, *but those damn rice burners*) stood propped up on their kickstands in the middle of the highway—one directly in front of them.

Jim's foot reflexively slammed the brake, and as the SUV skidded toward the motorcycle, he saw two things, as if in slow motion. Two zombies were crouched in the grass of the median strip, feasting on the innards of a teenage girl, and two more were pulling the driver, a young male, out of the driver's side by his hair. Even as the zombies turned in surprise, one of them sliced the boy's throat before jumping clear of the onrushing vehicle.

Martin's prayer and Jim's shout were both cut off as the Suburban crashed into the bike. Metal shrieked and glass shattered. The air bags exploded from the dashboard, pummeling them both.

Jim felt the front tires go flat, and he fought for control. Anti-lock breaks didn't help against a punctured tire. The Suburban careened right, then crashed through the guardrail, slamming against the thick trunk of a gnarled oak tree.

"Mother-fucker," the zombie with the knife snarled. *"They trashed my fucking bike!"* He hauled the teen out of the Volkswagen's wreckage, and dropped the body. The carcass slumped to the ground. Then he advanced on the Suburban.

His companion ripped open the young man's shirt, and bit down on a hairy nipple, shaking his head until it ripped free.

"Hey," it rasped. *"You better eat some now. The soul's departing and I feel the impatience on the other side."*

"Let our brothers have that vessel now. There's more meat over there."

Jim shoved the airbag out of his way and fumbled with the ignition. The dashboard looked like a Christmas tree with all the blinking lights. The engine light, the oil light, the battery light; nothing was working. Frantic, he looked back at the highway to see where the zombies were.

All four stalked towards the truck.

"Shit!"

"Huzzat?" Martin stirred next to him. Blood trickled from his nose, and there were dark circles under his eyes.

"Martin, we've got to go!" Jim hissed. "Can you make a run for it?"

"I tol' you we shzould wear our sheatbeltz," the old man slurred. Then he closed his eyes and slipped from consciousness.

Jim reached down for his pistol, only to find it gone.

"Fuck!"

Unfastening his seatbelt, he felt around beneath the seat for the missing gun. The skid and the impact had tossed around the contents in the backseat. He found a pack of instant coffee, a roadmap, and a rifle shell, but no gun.

"Hey buddy," said a voice from his left, and he smelled the creature the same instant it spoke. *"Having some car trouble?"*

Two leathery arms reached through the open driver's side window. Cold fingers wrapped around his neck and squeezed. Jim grabbed the bony wrists and his nails burrowed into the decaying flesh. The skin sloughed away and the zombie laughed, squeezing harder.

Another zombie pounced onto the crumpled hood and grabbed through the shattered windshield at Martin. The others busied themselves with prying open the passenger-side door.

Jim tried to scream, tried to breathe, and found he couldn't. His throat burned, and his pounding head felt like it was going to explode. The pain was so intense that he didn't hear the gunshot until after his attacker's brains sprayed across his face, blinding him.

The dead arms immediately loosened as the zombie fell to the ground. A second shot ripped through the creature on the hood and burrowed into the seat, inches away from Jim's chest. Shouting, he ducked down.

Forgetting about Martin, the other zombies turned to face the forest. Six more shots rang out in quick succession. Then there was silence.

"Hey in there!" a voice called out. "You alive?"

Martin was stirring again, and he looked at Jim in confusion.

"What's going on?" he whispered.

The voice shouted again. "Ya'll come on out with your hands up where we can see 'em!"

"I don't know," Jim admitted. "but it doesn't sound any better than the zombies."

"Maybe you done killed them, Tom." hollered another voice.

"Shut up, Luke!" the first voice snapped. "I wasn't about to ask them zombies if they'd share."

"Hello out there," Martin called, his voice wavering. "We don't want any trouble."

"And you won't get none as long as you do what yer told! Now c'mon out and keep your hands high."

They did as they were instructed, crawling from the wreckage with their arms above their heads. A burly, bearded man in camouflage stepped out from the foliage, clutching a shotgun. A moment later, another man, this one skinny and balding, also rustled forward. He pointed a hunting rifle on them.

The big man sized them up, then spat brown tobacco juice in the dirt. The other grinned and Jim noticed a thin ribbon of drool leaking down the side of his chin.

"Thanks for saving us," Jim began. "Is there some way I can repay you?"

"You can repay us by shutting your pie-hole," the first man snapped, then spoke to his companion. "Whaddya' think, Luke?"

"The nigger ain't nuthin but skin and bones. He looks a little gnarly. But t'other one looks mighty fine."

Martin shuffled nervously, and visions of Ned Beatty getting raped in *Deliverance* swam through Jim's mind.

"Now look—"

"You can have the nigger," Tom said, ignoring Jim. "Might as well do them here. I reckon we can field dress them, take them back to the hollow, then come back for their gear."

Luke's growling stomach indicated his agreement.

My God, Jim thought, *they're cannibals!*

"Alright, you boys turn around and get on your knees."

Jim considered lunging for the Suburban and finding one of the guns, and immediately decided against it. He'd be dead before he could even reach it.

"Look," he stammered. "we've got food—enough for both of you. We'll gladly give it up if you'll let us go. I've got to rescue my boy."

Tom answered by jacking the shotgun's pump.

"Didn't you hear me? My son lives in New Jersey and we've got to save him!"

"Mister, I don't care if your Grandma lives in Bumfuck, Egypt. We got no time to waste. We got families to feed and you boys were in the wrong place at the wrong time. That's all. If it's any consolation, I can promise you that you won't end up like them things we just killed. I can shoot you in the face or the back of the head. If you don't want to see it comin', I suggest you turn around and get on your fucking knees—now! Makes no difference to me."

He pointed the shotgun at Jim's head, but Jim stood his ground.

"You're no better than the zombies, you son of a bitch!"

"That may be. But we sure as hell ain't gonna starve to death while we wait for the government to come in and fix things. They've been planning for a bio-attack like this for years, but I don't think they knew China had something like this chemical that would make dead folks get up and run around."

Martin began to pray.

"Our Father, who art in Heaven, hallowed be thy name."

"Tom, heads up!"

Luke jabbed a finger over Jim's shoulder.

Thy kingdom come, thy will be done on Earth as it is in Heaven.

"Those prayers cannot help you now. He has departed from His throne and your kind belongs to us!"

Jim turned, dropped, and rolled, dragging Martin with him. The young couple from the wreckage, who minutes ago been spread out along the highway, were now stalking towards them. Their cruel smiles dripped with malice.

"Get ready," Jim mouthed at Martin. The old man nodded in agreement.

"I got 'em," Luke called. Sighting through his rifle, he clacked the bolt and squeezed the trigger.

Nothing happened.

The zombies jeered at him and advanced, their steps never faltering.

"You dumb fuck," Tom spat, raising the shotgun. "You forgot to reload."

He squeezed the trigger and the shotgun jerked against his shoulder. The young male zombie's ear and cheek vanished, revealing teeth and gristle. A permanent sneer now frozen on its face, it continued toward them as the roar of the shotgun echoed across the hills.

"Shit!" Tom jacked the pump again.

"Yam gohgna klll eww." The zombie's tongue rolled

out of its ruined mouth.

"He says he's going to kill you," the girl informed them.

"Go!" Jim hissed. Pushing Martin, they scurried past the cannibalistic rednecks and half-limped, half-dashed towards the forest.

"Luke, would you shoot them cocksuckers already?" Tom shouted in exasperation. The boom of his shotgun followed, and the first zombie dropped to the ground, the top of its head now obliterated.

The sharp crack of Luke's rifle rang out behind them as Jim and Martin pushed through the brush. Thorns tore at their skin and branches whipped their faces but they didn't slow. They heard Tom berating Luke.

"You dumb shit! You couldn't hit the broadside of a barn if it was painted orange!"

Two more shots followed. They slid down the embankment of a dry creek bed, hobbled across the stones, and then panted up the other side.

"GET BACK HERE YOU FUCKS!"

Their pursuers plunged into the forest, snapping branches and curses indicating their location.

At the top of the next hill, Martin collapsed, gasping for breath and clutching his side with one hand and his back with the other.

"Come one, Martin!"

"You go ahead," he winced. "I can't make it."

Jim glanced down the hill. He could hear them but could not see them yet. "Martin, let me carry you."

"No, Jim. I'm too old to be running through these woods playing hide and seek from the good ol' boys. I'll draw them off until you can get away."

"Bullshit!"

"No, it's not bullshit! Think about Danny, Jim!"

"I'm not leaving you here."

"God will protect me."

"Well he's done a bang-up job of it so far, Martin!" Jim stomped away, eyes searching the ground. He picked up a tree limb; heavy, solid and about three inches thick, and swung it like a bat.

"These redneck sons-of-bitches are holding us up and jeopardizing my son's life. Every moment we spend out here leaves us open to attack by a zombie squirrel or bird or what-have-you!"

He stalked away.

"What are you going to do?" Martin called softly.

"Call them," Jim told him. "I'll be close by."

Martin closed his eyes and fought to get his breathing under control. His chest ached, his limbs were cold, and his back was in agony. He opened his eyes and looked around, hoping for some reassurance from Jim, but Jim was gone. He was alone now. Alone in the forest.

Then he heard footsteps rustling toward him through the leaves.

"Oh Lord," he wailed. "Help me Jesus. I can't take no more of this!"

The footsteps rushed toward him, and both hunters emerged from the thicket of brambles.

"Howdy nigger," Luke grinned. "Looks like your friend got away. That's a shame. I suspect gnawing on you would be like gnawing on a chicken wing."

Tom shot his companion a stern look, then carefully approached Martin till he was within ten feet of the preacher.

"Where's your friend, old man?"

"He—he ran off and left me."

The big man glanced around warily, then raised the shotgun.

"Oh well. I reckon you'll have to do."

He set the shotgun in the crook of his shoulder and arm, and wrapped his finger around the trigger.

Jim lunged out from behind the tree and swung his makeshift club. The branch connected with Luke's mouth. The hunter let out a muffled scream, then dropped his rifle and fell to his knees, cupping his ruined lips and teeth with his hands.

Snarling, Jim brought the limb down on his head. Luke's scalp split open, and he went limp.

"Drop it you fucker!" Jim warned Tom.

The shotgun bucked in Tom's hands. Jim felt a moment of pain, as if dozens of bees had just stung his shoulder, and then he grew cold. His legs betrayed him, and he collapsed, squirming amidst the dead leaves.

Tom ejected the spent shell, and jacked another one in place.

Squinting, he drew a bead on Jim. "I'll come back to you in a second, Blackie."

There was a second blast, and a crimson flower bloomed on Tom's chest. Still clutching the shotgun, he looked down in surprise. He turned in a semi-circle, and Martin could see a gaping exit wound, about the size of a coffee cup, in his back.

"Well fuck me..." he gasped, and toppled over.

Martin stared in astonishment as a man stepped out of the brush, followed by a young boy. Like everyone else they had encountered, the newcomers carried rifles.

"It's alright. We ain't gonna hurt you." He stuck out his hand and helped Martin to his feet.

"Thank you," Martin stammered. "But my friend—"

"We'd best take a look," the man said.

Jim rolled around on the ground, balling his fists against his head.

"Fuck fuck fuck fuck fuck FUCK," he repeated through tightly gritted teeth. "It hurts! It hurts bad!"

They crouched next to him. Blood was seeping from his shoulder.

The man pulled out a large hunting knife, and Martin grabbed his wrist.

"It's alright," the man reassured him. "I just want to cut this shirt off him."

He sliced the fabric away, talking as he did.

"I'm Lloyd Clendenan. This here's my boy, Jason. Say hi, Jason."

"Howdy," the boy said shyly. "Pleased to meet you."

"I'm Reverend Thomas Martin, from White Sulphur Springs. This man is Jim Thurmond, a construction worker from Lewisburg."

Jim moaned, his eyes clenched shut.

"Been fixin' to do something about Tom and Luke. Planned on doing it today in fact. Didn't figure we'd end up saving two folks in the process."

"We're very much obliged," Martin thanked him. "They wanted to..." He swallowed, unable to finish the sentence.

"Yeah, I know. They started with Ernie Whitt last week, and moved on to some other folks. That's why I intended to put them in the ground, before they could set their sights on me and my boy."

He appraised Jim's wound and nodded to himself.

"Your friend here will be alright. Looks like it just went through the meat, is all. Hell, I got worse than this in Viet Nam. Need to get this bleeding stopped though." He turned to the boy. "Jason, give me your belt."

The boy stood over them, removing his belt. Jim opened his eyes and stared up at him.

"Danny?"

"Shhh. Lay still Jim. Danny's okay."

Jim shut his eyes again.

"Why'd he call me Danny, Pop?" the boy asked.

Lloyd looked at Martin.

"Danny is his son's name," Martin explained to them. "He's about your age. We were on our way to New Jersey to rescue him when we ran into some trouble."

"New Jersey?" Lloyd whistled. "Pastor, what makes you think he's alive *to* rescue?"

Martin didn't answer. He was starting to wonder that himself.

Faith, it seemed, was beginning to be in short supply.

CHAPTER NINE

"I don't like this." Skip said.

"You don't have to like it," Miccelli sneered. "All we've got to do is keep our mouths shut and do what we're told."

A trio of zombies emerged from an alleyway and rushed at them. Skip raised his Baretta, but the other soldier beat him to it.

"Mine!" Miccelli shouted and unloaded his M16 on the creatures. All three dropped to the street.

"Fuck that, man," Skip continued. "I can't live like this anymore, man. It's just not right!"

A German Shepherd, its fur matted with gore and its back legs missing, dragged itself down the sidewalk toward them. It was followed by a girl of no more than nine or ten. Her intestines trailed along behind her, and the remains of several other organs had dried and shriveled on her dress.

"Mine!" Skip called. Carefully, he picked them off, putting a single 9mm round through each of their heads.

The sounds of battle echoed through the streets around them.

"What ain't right? Shooting zombies? Man, you're fucked up."

"Not shooting zombies, you douche-bag," Skip snapped. "I'm talking about *that*." He cocked his thumb back to the tractor-trailers following slowly along in formation behind the HumVees, Bradleys, and the tank.

"That's what Colonel Schow wants, so that's what—"

An explosion cut him off, as Warner used his M203 grenade launcher to blow out the hardware store's display window.

"Shopping spree!" he called out to them, and then ducked into the building, weapon at the ready. Blumenthal followed him. Skip heard them laughing inside as they ransacked the displays.

There was a lull in the combat on their street, and Skip checked his rounds in both the M16 and the pistol.

"You better watch saying shit like that," Miccelli hissed in his ear. "Remember what happened to Hopkins and Gurand?"

Skip nodded. Hopkins and Gurand had questioned the Colonel's orders one too many times. Captain McFarland caught them trying to desert, and they'd been dealt with swiftly; without the benefit of a hearing or a military tribunal. Colonel Schow ordered both men crucified, after which the entire unit had been forced to watch as a flock of undead birds tore them to pieces.

They'd gotten off lucky, as far as Skip was concerned. What happened to Falker had been much worse.

Private First Class Falker had fallen in love with one of the whores at the encampment. She didn't reciprocate, and when she became Schow's personal property, he made a failed attempt to assassinate the Colonel.

When he was caught, Colonel Schow ordered a hole drilled into the wall of a small utility shed. Falker was stripped naked and nailed crucifixion style to the side of the building, so that his penis protruded through the hole, while the rest of him hung from the outside wall. Then, they rounded up some zombies and imprisoned them inside the shed.

It took about two minutes for the creatures to discover the dangling morsel, and Falker shrieked and writhed as it was consumed. The zombies then tried in vain to reach more of him through the hole, but only succeeded in tearing away some dangling flaps of skin from his mutilated groin.

Falker hung there until he bled to death, and then Staff Sergeant Miller put a bullet in his head, before he could reanimate.

Satisfied that he wouldn't run out of ammunition, Skip surveyed the perimeter. The sounds of battle were dying down now; replaced by the crackling of fires and the moans of the injured and dying. The staccato beat of the 50 caliber punctuated these as Lawson picked off a few straggling zombies from his perch on the HumVee.

Sergeant Ford and Privates' First Class Kramer and Anderson strolled towards them, leading two handcuffed women at gunpoint. They made a wide berth around a mangled corpse lying in the middle of the road. Its lower section had been crushed by the treads on one of the Bradleys, and one arm was badly maimed. Refusing to surrender, it still clawed at them with its one remaining arm.

Terrified, the women sobbed, hunching against each other. An extended burst from Kramer's M16 destroyed what was left of the wriggling corpse.

"Nice," Miccelli leered at the captives. "Where'd you find them, Sergeant Ford?"

"Hiding in the bathroom of a little coffee shop four blocks down. We've already got first dibs on them, so don't even think about it!"

"What's the status?" Anderson asked them.

"Warner and Blumenthal are in there," Miccelli pointed to the hardware store, "and Wilson and Robertson both bought it. They went down an alley and the zombies ambushed them. They tore Wilson to shreds, man. Didn't even leave enough for him to get back up and walk around like they usually do. Robertson was still alive when they opened his stomach up, and he swallowed his Baretta. We couldn't get to him. There were too many."

Ford kicked the sidewalk curb and shook his head. "Roman's dead too. He and Thompson were running point and they walked into an ambush. It amazes me how these fucking things can calculate."

"Is Thompson okay, Sergeant?" Miccelli asked.

The big man shook his head.

"He'll lose a leg, at the very least. When we left, he was begging the doc to shoot him. I'm guessing if he don't, Thompson will do it himself, first chance he gets."

Kramer spotted a lone crow, watching them from a telephone pole. Moving in one fluid moment, he shot it. Black feathers floated to the ground.

"That one was alive, I think." Anderson mused.

"Not anymore, it's not."

"You're awfully quiet, Skip." Ford observed.

Skip stirred, carefully meeting the Sergeant's eyes. They were all looking at him, and Miccelli scowled a silent warning.

"Sorry, Sarge," he lied. "I was just thinking about poor Thompson. We went through boot camp together."

In truth, he'd been watching the two captive women. They were obviously mother and daughter, and although recent events had taken a toll on them, they were both still very attractive. This first night in the meat wagon would be hard on them. It would be even worse when they got back to Gettysburg.

Deep inside, Skip felt his rage growing. He imagined himself gunning down his fellow Guardsmen, and escaping with the women. But that was no good. They'd be dead within minutes, and even if they did manage to escape, they'd be caught and would suffer a fate like Hopkins, Gurand, and Falker.

Even if they managed to elude capture, what would they do? Reluctantly, he resigned himself to the same conclusion he always came to. There was safety in numbers, and those numbers were right here in his unit. He was trapped.

"Get them on the truck," Ford ordered Kramer.

"Make sure they get washed down good. Partridge has the hose hooked up to the town's water tank. Don't know how much pressure it's got, but make sure you don't bruise them any worse than they are now."

Kramer led the cringing women toward the rigs.

Miccelli pointed down the street.

"Here comes Capriano. Looks like he's hurt!"

The wounded man limped towards them, dragging his right leg. As he drew closer, Skip noticed that his right foot was turned completely around, his toes pointing back the way he had come. He made no sound as he approached them.

"Don't move, Capriano!" Anderson ran towards him. "We'll get you some—"

The injured guardsman raised his M16 and squeezed the trigger. The rounds punched through Anderson's chest and out the other side. Ford, Miccelli, and Skip instinctively ducked and returned fire. Capriano shook violently under the bombardment. Then he toppled backward and, after a final wild burst, spraying stray shots into the air, he lay still.

"He damn sure didn't look dead!" Miccelli cried.

"If he wasn't before, he is now." Ford said through gritted teeth. His burst had caught the shooter in the mouth, virtually erasing everything from the jaw and up.

Skip rushed to Anderson's side, shouting hoarsely for a medic, but immediately saw that it was too late. The man's chest was a wet ruin, and his glazed eyes stared sightlessly.

Ford joined him. Calmly, the Sergeant pulled out his pistol and shot the dead man in the head.

"Let's round em up," he ordered. "Warner! Blumenthal! Let's go!"

Gravel crunched under his feet as he walked away.

Miccelli unbuckled Anderson's belt and began gathering up his gear. "Yo, Skip. You want his boots?"

"No, you can have them."

"How about these extra clips? You can have those if

you want them."

He pulled a switchblade from Anderson's pants pocket and whistled in appreciation. "Nice."

Skip turned away.

He didn't want Miccelli to see him crying, or to notice the anger that burned in his red-rimmed eyes.

* * *

They had once been a Pennsylvania National Guard Infantry unit, stationed out of Harrisburg. They'd been proud—heroes.

Skip didn't know what they were now, but they sure as shit weren't heroes.

When the collapse hit and the dead started coming back to life, they'd been sent to Gettysburg. Like the other Guard units deployed to various towns and cities across the state, they were supposed to safeguard the citizens; keep them secure and stop the creatures from spreading until the government could figure out how to fix the situation.

They'd failed, and it wasn't long before they figured out that the government wouldn't be fixing the problem, because the government no longer existed. That had been confirmed by the news footage (most of the networks were still broadcasting at that point) of the dead President making a meal of the Secretary of State during an interrupted press briefing. The President darted out from somewhere off camera, spewing obscenities and grappling with the victim. The camera zoomed in on the grisly scene as his teeth clamped down on the man's arm, biting through the sleeve of his tailored suit and into the flesh beneath. One Secret Service agent drew his weapon on the undead Commander-In-Chief, and a second agent immediately shot the first. Pandemonium ensued, as more agents exchanged gunfire and reporters scrambled.

The Vice-President, it was reported, suffered a fatal heart attack following the press conference. There was no confirmation on whether steps had been taken to ensure that he didn't rise again.

Hours later, someone in power (speculation varied as to whom; some said it was the Secretary of Defense, while others said it was a renegade General) had ordered the House and Senate buildings bombed from the air, ostensibly because it had been overrun by zombies. That had sparked isolated skirmishes between the various armed forces units in and around Washington, and after the loss of the Pentagon a day later, the inter-branch fighting spread like wildfire.

Skip had heard horror stories, like the Captain of the U.S.S. Austin, a troop carrier with over four-hundred sailors and two-hundred marines assigned to it, who had ordered the execution of the entire 24th Marine Amphibious Unit—who were onboard his ship in the North Atlantic at the time. He'd accused the marines of mutiny, and the squids and jarheads fought each other from bow to stern. Skip had heard that the sailors made the surviving marines walk the plank.

It was happening in other countries too. He was amazed that nukes hadn't been launched yet. He'd heard rumors of limited nuclear exchanges between Iran and Iraq and India and Pakistan, but nothing that could be confirmed.

After weeks of fighting, the decimated armed forces began to band together into larger warring groups. From the command post in Gettysburg, Colonel Schow was in sporadic contact with General Richard Dunbar on the West Coast. The general had launched a campaign for control of Northern California, eliminating both zombies and enemies at the same time. He'd even managed to unite several citizen militias in the state, and was using the alliance to push farther into other states. Schow's plan for Pennsylvania was similar, and the two exchanged information on a regular basis.

Skip had overheard them talking via radio, and after Schow informed the General of their recent progress and victories, the disembodied voice (sounding hauntingly like Marlon Brando in *Apocalypse Now*) had repeated "The Dick is pleased" over and over like an insane mantra.

Probably because he *was* insane, Skip knew. Just like Schow.

They were all insane. You had to be, if you wanted to survive this.

Gettysburg was secure. The town had been swept clean of the undead, and those that died from sickness, injuries, or natural causes were disposed of immediately, the bodies incinerated.

After the initial sweep and purge operation, they'd tried placing barbed wire around much of the town, and planted mines in the surrounding Civil War battlefields. The defensive measures had proved to be hopelessly ineffectual against the living dead. Hordes of zombies simply poured over the barbed wire, slicing themselves to shreds with unflinching disregard. Worse were those who had their legs blown off by a mine, only to then pull themselves by their arms across the fields in search of prey.

Finally, guards had been posted all around the perimeter to insure that it remained secure. The mines and barbed wire remained in place as a semi-effective early warning system—and to keep marauding gangs of bikers and survivalists at bay.

Roving bikers and renegades weren't the only problem. Refugees streamed into the town early on, attracted by the false rumor that the government had established an underground Pentagon there during the Cold War. Skip had always found that amusingly ironic. Stupid civilians—as if the government would ever allow the location of something like that to be known to the general populace. Still, they came, looking for shelter and order, and found Schow's men instead.

They still were attempting to come up with an effective defense against the avian zombies and other types that could make it through the secure zone. Undead snakes, rodents, and other small animals also presented a problem, and still managed to slip through. As a result, most of the civilian population stayed indoors at all times.

Not that they had a choice, Skip thought to himself.

By orders of Colonel Schow, any civilian, be they man, woman or child, caught carrying a weapon was to be shot on sight. No exceptions had been made and after a few examples, thoughts of dissent were now virtually non-existent.

It wasn't like the civilians had any great reason to venture outside anyway, Skip knew. Downtown Gettysburg had become an armed military encampment. Smoke from burning trash barrels choked the sky and the air was thick with the stench of the latrines and the bodies burned in the pit on the town outskirts. Garbage rotted in the gutters, despite the work detail's efforts to pick it up. The streets were filled at all times with armed Guardsmen. There were no utilities; things like running water and electricity belonged to the past now, but generators had been set up for the officer's quarters, and for some of the enlisted men.

When the townspeople were allowed outside, it wasn't exactly a cause for celebration. Able-bodied men were used for slave labor, although nobody called it that out loud. Instead, it was referred to as a work detail, and it was strictly enforced. The soldiers were, for the most part, happy with the arrangement, as it meant somebody other than them got to do the grunt work like digging latrines and disposing of bodies.

Those civilians who resisted were used in more onerous tasks, the most popular of which was bait detail. When a patrol ventured into the surrounding fields and villages, they would take a dozen or so civilians with them. One at a time, the unfortunates would be put 'on point', and forced to walk ahead of the group. Any zombie lying in wait would inevitably attack the lead individual, giving the soldiers plenty of advance warning. Individuals sent on bait detail were considered expendable.

Women were used for 'morale'. For most, this involved sexual enslavement in the Meat Wagon, although a few of the elderly or the absolutely unappealing were allowed to work in the mess hall and at other menial tasks.

Those women who repeatedly resisted the use of their bodies were also sent to bait detail.

What disgusted Skip most of all was the compliance of the civilian populace. Their spirits broken, the vast majority simply accepted this lifestyle. Some of them even seemed to prefer it. A few of the men had proven themselves and were "drafted" into the unit and allowed to carry a weapon. Especially appalling to Skip, were the women who *enjoyed* being a sexual conscripts: post-apocalyptic whores who didn't seem to mind sucking ten dicks a night, as long as it kept them relatively safe and alive.

He clenched his fists.

Why didn't they rise up? When the unit was away like this, they easily outnumbered the soldiers left behind. Why did they just blindly accept it, like sheep? Maybe the alternative didn't seem all that appealing to them. Or perhaps they were scared.

Like him. Scared of staying alive but even more terrified of dying.

These days, death offered no escape from the futility of their lives.

When he was in high school, Skip had dated a Goth chick that had been obsessed with death. So much, in fact, that she'd tried to commit suicide several times. He'd been upset by this, blaming himself, her parents, the school and a number of other things; until he realized that killing herself was part of the fantasy—part of her obsession. She hungered for what came after.

Riding in the Bradley, listening to the tracks rumbling

beneath his feet, Skip found himself wondering if she was still alive, and if she was still hungry for what came after.

* * *

Second Lieutenant Torres pointed on the highway map at a town labeled Glen Rock. "We are here. Captain Gonzalez wants you to take some men and recon this town here." He indicated a small town marked Shrewsbury, nestled on the Pennsylvania-Maryland border. "The Captain says that Colonel Schow wants to abandon the Gettysburg encampment in favor of a more secure location. Determine if Shrewsbury fits our requirements."

Staff Sergeant Miller nodded. "I can do that."

"Staff Sergeant Michaels, you will take another squad here." Torres pointed to York. "Again, this is only a recon mission. Do not engage any hostile forces unless you are attacked. Just observe and report back. Meanwhile, I am to take the rest of the unit and the prisoners and report back to Gettysburg."

"I'll take PFC Anderson," Miller said.

Michaels cleared his throat. "Anderson was killed during this morning's raid."

"Shit," muttered Miller. He ran a hand through his greasy hair; his military buzz-cut long since abandoned. "Alright, then I want Kramer."

"Fair enough," Torres nodded. "Staff Sergeant Michaels, you can take Sergeant Ford."

"Good deal. I want Warner, Blumenthal and Lawson too."

"No, screw that!" Miller protested. "That leaves me with Skip, Partridge and Miccelli, and I don't trust that shifty little fucker Skip! I think he'd rather shoot us all in the back than shoot a zombie. You notice that he *never* fucks the whores? I think he's a faggot."

"Too bad! You got Kramer, so you're stuck with them! I'm not taking all the fresh meat!"

"Enough," the Lieutenant barked. "You've got your orders! Carry them out. Miller, if you have reason to believe Private Skip does not have this unit's best interests at heart, and you can prove it, then we'll deal with that. Otherwise, that is all."

Staff Sergeant Miller snapped off a salute, lit a cigarette and stormed away.

"Prissy little fucker. Who does he think he is? I was patrolling Atlanta after the terrorist attacks while that fucker was still in high school."

After successfully raiding Glen Rock, they'd camped at the nearby National Guard Ammo Dump as planned. The secure site was removed from the town and the highway, accessible only by driving down a two-mile gravel road that led into the woods.

The ammo was stored above ground in engineered bunkers that looked like hills of dirt, all identical in size and lined up in neat rows. Each bunker had a door built into its side and each door had a sign indicating what type of ammunition was stored inside. A security fence surrounded the entire complex.

The tractor-trailers were parked between the mounds. The doors of one hung open, and a line of soldiers were wrapped around it all the way to the cab.

He dropped the butt to the pavement, ground it out with his boot heel, and considered the line.

"I need to get laid before we go."

He approached the HumVee that the three Privates were assigned to and banged on the hatch. A moment later, it opened and an acne-scarred Private, barely out of high school by the look of him, peered out.

"Get me Skip, Partridge and Miccelli."

"Miccelli and Partridge are in the meat wagon, Sergeant," he pointed at the tractor-trailer. "but Skip's in here sleeping."

The Staff Sergeant poked his head inside.

"Skip, fall out and bring your gear," he bawled, and stalked toward the rigs.

Skip scrambled out, blinking the sleep from his eyes, and trailed after him.

"Find PFC Kramer and then both of you report to my vehicle and wait for me," Miller ordered him. "We've been assigned recon, fifteen miles southeast of here. I'm going to find Partridge and Miccelli, grab a quick piece of tail, and then we'll take off."

He elbowed his way through the line of waiting men, and climbed up inside the trailer.

Skip leaned against the HumVee and checked his weapons.

Five of them on this mission. Miller, Kramer, Miccelli, Partridge and himself.

Five of them away from the rest of the unit.

Safety in numbers, he thought, and grinned.

Here or there; either way, he was a dead man walking. The knowledge gave him a cold sense of comfort.

He slapped at a mosquito, wondered if it was alive or the living dead, and decided that there wasn't much difference anyway.

He waited a while, then stalked away to find Kramer.

CHAPTER TEN

J im stopped the car, stretched, and ran a hand
through his hair. It came away greasy, just like his
skin. He tried to remember his last shower and
couldn't. The wound in his shoulder throbbed. The
center of the bandage was black with dried blood, and the
edges crusted with dried pus. Steeling himself, he opened
the door, got out of the car, and started down the street.

The illusion was almost perfect—as long as he didn't
look too closely. The sun hung high in the sky, bathing the
neighborhood in warmth and brightness. The houses
were lined up in two neat rows along the street, each one
identical except for the color of their shutters or the
curtains hanging in the window. Cars and SUV's
occupied the driveways and curbs, and childrens' bikes
and scooters lay discarded in the front yards.

A solitary ceramic lawn gnome watched him pass.

The street was alive.

A dog sat panting on the sidewalk. Jim thought that
perhaps it would wag its tail if it could, but the tail had
been torn out by the roots, leaving only a maggot-infested
hole. A swollen cat stretched in a nearby windowsill,
watching the dog with its one remaining eye. The feline's
hiss sounded like a steam engine.

The wind playfully chased a discarded popsicle
wrapper across the street. Jim heard a child's laughter as
it tumbled by. The wrapper caught on a row of shrubs
and the laughter faded.

It had rained the night before, and earthworms wriggled blindly in the puddles. Jim stepped on one and the mushed remains continued to writhe after he moved on.

Elm and oak trees lined the street, forming a barrier between the curb and the sidewalk. Birds huddled in their branches, whispering to each other; marking his advance. Most of their feathers had molted away.

The trees reached toward him with outstretched grasping limbs, but Jim was careful to stay in the middle of the street where they could not reach him.

The street was alive. Dogs. Cats. Worms. Birds. Trees.

All dead. And all alive.

He stopped in front of the house.

They'd added some new aluminum siding since the last time he'd been here. Nice investment. His child support money had probably paid for it.

The grass was green and freshly cut. The clippings had been raked into neat little piles. On the front porch, a handful of discarded plastic army men stood guard. Roses bloomed along the side of the house. Their thorns dripped blood.

Jim checked his Walther P38 and approached the front door. His feet felt leaden, as if the grass clippings were quicksand sucking at his boots. His could feel his pulse in his temples.

Down the street, the dead dog howled, long and mournful.

Jim knocked on the door and Rick answered it.

His ex-wife's new husband was a grisly sight. His bathrobe hung open, stained with dried bodily juices. Most of the thick, perfect hair that Jim had hated so much was gone, and the few clumps that remained were wildly askew. His skin was mottled and grey. A worm tunneled through the cheesy flesh of his cheek and another burrowed through his forearm. One of his ears was missing, and brownish-yellow ichor ran from the corners of his eyes.

"Jim, you're not welcome here."

Its foul breath clung to him. Jim shuddered in revulsion as a rotted tooth fell out, landing on the carpet.

"I'm here for Danny."

"Jim, you know you don't have visitation during the school year. This is a violation of the court order."

Jim pushed him out of the way. The skin was cold and moist, and his fingers sank beneath the surface of the thing's chest. He pulled them away, dripping, and called for his son.

"Danny! Danny, Daddy's here! I've come to take you home!"

"Danny isn't here right now Mrs. Torrance," Rick cackled. It cocked its head. *"You know, I always wanted to do that."*

Jim ran toward the stairs but the zombie stepped in front of him. Bony fingers coiled around his wrist, pulling his arm towards the gaping hole that had been its mouth. Jim yanked his arm away and the creature's teeth snapped together.

"Where's my son, goddamn it?"

"He's upstairs, taking a break. We've been playing football in the backyard, just like any other father and son."

"I'm his father you son of a bitch!"

The zombie laughed. The pale end of a worm dangled out of its nose and it sniffed it back up.

"Some father you are," it crowed. *"You weren't here to save him. He belongs to us now! He's our son!"*

"Like hell he is!" Jim raised the P38 and fired, the bullet passing neatly through Rick's skull. The zombie collapsed to the floor and Jim kicked it in the head. His boot sank into the soft flesh, and he laughed at the bits of brain matter on his steel toes.

He was still laughing after he emptied the clip into the corpse.

"You know, I've always wanted to do *that*."

He ran up the stairs two at a time.

"Danny, it's okay now! Daddy's here—"

Tammy lunged out of the bathroom at the top of the stairway. Squealing in wicked delight, she shoved him backward. Jim tumbled backward, collapsing in a heap at the bottom of the stairs.

Hissing furiously, she lumbered down the stairs after him.

"KillyoukillyouKILLYOU! Gonna eat your guts and your useless cock and tear out your eyes and eat them too because you were never a man and you were never a husband and you were NEVER A FATHER!"

Jim had dropped the empty pistol in the fall. There was a fresh gash on his forehead and blood filled his eyes. Groaning, he wiped it away.

"You were never a father. You were never anything. But now you'll finally get to be something, Jim. You can be one of us! Forever!"

"You promised me forever once before, bitch. No thanks."

Shrieking, she sprang at him. Her putrid, bloated body crushed him to the floor. Jim turned his head away. The stench of her proximity made him gag. Her jaws clamped down on his arm and she yanked her head back, taking a chunk of flesh with it. Hungrily, she began to chew.

Blood spurted from the hole in his arm. Grabbing a fistful of her oily hair, he slammed the zombie's head into the wall. The meat fell from her mouth, and he had a crazy urge to stick it back on his arm.

"You fucking bitch! Give me my son!"

He rolled them both over. Straddling her chest, he pounded her head into the floor repeatedly. After a half-dozen blows, something cracked. Tammy screamed and still he kept at it. Finally, she lay still.

The screaming continued long after her head was a pulpy smear, and Jim realized it was coming from him.

For a second, he thought of Carrie. Then he wiped his

gory hands on his shirt, and crawled up the stairs. Reaching the top, he limped towards Danny's bedroom door. Despite the commotion, the door remained closed.

"Danny, it's Daddy! Come on out, son. Everything's going to be alright now."

The door creaked open, and his son stepped out into the light.

"Hello Daddy," the zombie tittered. *"I thought you'd never get here."*

Jim screamed.

* * *

"It's okay Jim. It's okay now."

Martin stood over him, shaking him gently.

Still in the throes of the nightmare, Jim shrank away from the preacher. Immediately the pain in his shoulder flared. Wincing, he looked at the gauze taped around it; white and clean with only a small red stain in the center.

"Delmas bandaged it. He fixed you up real good. He was a medic in Viet Nam."

"Who?"

"Delmas Clendenan. He and his boy saved our skins. This is their cabin we're in." Martin chuckled. "Boy, you've been out of it. Thrashing around and sweating in your sleep. Delmas said it was shock, fatigue and blood loss, but you're okay now. The bullet passed clean through your shoulder, and there's no infection or anything. He sewed you up nice, praise God. I imagine it'll be a little sore for a time though."

Jim sucked his tongue, working up saliva to coat his parched throat.

"How long?" he stammered.

"Have we been here? Day and a half."

Instantly, Jim swept back the covers and was on his feet.

"Two days? Martin, we've got to go! We should have been in New Jersey by now!"

He stumbled as the room spun out of control. Quickly, the old man caught him and gently but insistently forced him to lay back down.

"I know, Jim," he assured him. "but you're not going to be any help to Danny if you can't walk."

"Don't need to walk. I can drive."

"I believe you probably can. But we're going to have to walk to find ourselves another car, and you're in no shape to do that. You can't even lift your arm yet!"

Jim struggled to sit up again.

Martin pushed him back down. "Rest. Get your strength. We'll leave first thing in the morning."

"Martin, we—"

"I mean it," the preacher warned him. "So help me God, Jim, if you don't lay back down, I will knock you out! I aim to help you save your boy, and I truly believe that God is going to help us do just that—but we won't even make it a mile with the shape you're currently in. Now rest! We'll leave in the morning."

Jim nodded weakly, and lay his head back on the pillow.

Moments later, there was a knock at the door, and a man entered the room. A young boy trailed shyly along behind him.

"You're awake," the man observed. "That's good, but you ought to be resting."

He was a big man; not flabby, but by no means skinny either. A thick reddish-brown beard, sprinkled with strands of gray, covered his ruddy face. He wore muddy work boots, a flannel shirt, and a pair of denim overalls.

"Delmas Clendenan." He thrust his hand out and Jim shook it, wincing slightly as tendrils of pain spiraled through his shoulder. "This here's my boy, Jason."

"Howdy," Jim smiled.

"Hello, sir."

The boy was older than Danny, maybe eleven or twelve, and leaner.

"Thanks for helping us, Mr. Clendenan," Jim said. "Is

there any way we can repay you?"

The woodsman snorted. "Naw, there's no need for that. We're happy to have some company, truth be told. Things have—well, it's been a bit quiet around here since my wife passed on." A shadow seemed to fall across his face, and the boy dropped his eyes to the floor.

"Was it...?" Martin began.

Delmas nodded, then placed a hand on Jason's shoulder.

"Why don't you check on the stew for me?"

After the boy had left the room, he continued.

"Happened about four weeks ago. She was birthing a calf out in the barn, and it was stillborn. The mother died along with it. My wife, bless her heart, was just as soft as a daisy, and she sat there in that stable and cried. Cried so much, she didn't notice when they started moving around again."

He grew quiet and looked out the window towards the barn.

"I'm sorry." Martin said.

Delmas sniffed, but said nothing.

"I lost my wife too," Jim told him. "Second wife, actually, but I loved her more than anything. She was pregnant with our first child. But I've got a son about your boy's age, from my first marriage. He's alive, and we need to get to him."

"Mister Thurmond, I know that you've been through a lot, but how do you know that your boy is still alive?"

"He called me on my cell phone, just four nights ago. He was hiding out in my ex-wife's attic."

"On your cell phone?"

"The battery still had some life in it. He got through before it was spent."

Delmas shuffled his feet. "I don't mean no disrespect, but are you sure he called you on your cell phone?"

"I didn't imagine it, if that's what you're thinking! Most of the utilities were still working back home. Haven't they been on here?"

"Off and on, sure. But they're spotty. Luckily we've got a wood burning stove in the kitchen. Power went out about a week ago and hasn't been back since."

"But the power was on until recently. You've seen other survivors?"

"Well sure, but that don't mean—"

"It means that my son is alive, Mr. Clendenan, and I aim to keep him that way."

Delmas held up his hands. "Whoa there! I didn't mean any disrespect. Reverend Martin here said your son was up in Jersey. Hell, that's hundreds of miles away. You just need to think about it, is all. Consider the possibilities."

"Believe me, I have. But let me ask you one thing, Mr. Clendenan."

"Call me Delmas."

"Okay, Delmas. If it was Jason out there, wouldn't you do the same thing for him?"

"You bet I would."

"Then help me," Jim said. "Please."

Delmas looked at them both, and shrugged his shoulders.

"I reckon you boys will need a full stomach before you leave. We ain't got much, but we'll be glad to share. I'm fixing to go out and bag something for dinner. You want to come along, Reverend?"

"You mean in the woods?" Martin stammered. "But isn't that dangerous?"

"Sure it is, but I'm careful. We got no choice, really. The grocery store is a long ways off, and I don't reckon they're open for business anyway. Hunting's still pretty good in these hills. I'm sure we can round us up a squirrel or a rabbit or maybe even a wild turkey that ain't been turned into one of them things."

"Well, okay I guess." Martin cast a sidelong glance at Jim, but his companion seemed lost in his own thoughts. "I haven't been hunting in, oh, well I guess it's been about ten years. Ever since the arthritis started acting up. This

Join the Leisure Horror Book Club and
GET 2 FREE BOOKS NOW—
An $11.98 value!

— Yes! I want to subscribe to — the Leisure Horror Book Club.

Please send me my **2 FREE BOOKS**. I have enclosed $2.00 for shipping/handling. Each month I'll receive the two newest Leisure Horror selections to preview for 10 days. If I decide to keep them, I will pay the Special Members Only discounted price of just $4.25 each, a total of $8.50, plus 2.00 shipping/handling. This is a **SAVINGS OF AT LEAST $3.48** off the bookstore price. There is no minimum number of books I must buy and I may cancel the program at any time. In any case, the **2 FREE BOOKS** are mine to keep.

Not available in Canada.

NAME: _____

ADDRESS: _____

CITY: _____ STATE: _____

COUNTRY: _____ ZIP: _____

TELEPHONE: _____

E-MAIL: _____

SIGNATURE: _____

might be fun!"

Laughing, Delmas slapped him on the back and sauntered out of the room.

Martin turned to Jim.

"Try to rest, okay Jim? I'll be back as soon as I can."

Jim made no reply and Martin assumed he hadn't heard him. But then Jim stirred and looked at him.

"Be careful Martin."

The old man nodded and followed after Delmas.

Jim closed his eyes and tried to fall back asleep, but he was haunted by images from his nightmare. Images of Danny.

"Hang in there, squirt," he whispered to the darkness. "Daddy's coming. I promise."

* * *

Delmas unlocked the cedar gun cabinet and removed two rifles. He hefted a 30.06 in one hand, and passed a Remington 4.10 to Martin.

The preacher eyed the gun skeptically.

"Kind of small, isn't it? What if we run into something bigger than a groundhog? Will this do the trick?"

"I've got some punkinballs you can use," Delmas grunted. "Jason's brought down a four-point buck using that there rifle and punkinballs. As for anything else we might run across—just make sure you aim for the head." He winked, and began loading his rifle.

"Yes, I'd established that much." Martin said, and accepted a box of ammunition from Jason. The weight of the rifle felt good in his hands. The gun was a bolt action, and he loaded three shells into it.

"Ready?" Delmas asked.

"Ready as I'll ever be!" Martin declared, trying to sound confident. The feeling wasn't mirrored in his eyes though, and the big man grinned.

"I'm telling you, Reverend, there ain't nothing to

worry about. We're just going down yonder in the hollow. Jason and I hunt it a couple times a week. We've got no choice. We ate the last of the chickens, and the cows—well, I told you about the cows already. Garden's done for the year, and I don't have enough canned goods to spare. You boys want to eat, it's gonna have to be wild game."

Martin kneaded the rifle stock, letting his aching fingers slide over the smooth faux-walnut finish.

"I'm sorry, Delmas. We're grateful. We really are. I'm just a little nervous is all." He smiled, patted the gun, and motioned to the door. "After you."

The mountain man chuckled and pointed at Jason.

"No leaving till I get back, you hear? I want you to stay here and help Mr. Thurmond if he needs anything."

"Yessir. You want me to fix some potatoes?"

"Sure," Delmas answered, going out the door. "Start peeling them awhile."

They stepped out onto the porch.

Delmas turned and pressed his bearded face against the screen door.

"Hey Jason?"

The young boy turned expectantly.

"Yeah Pop?"

"I love you son. Behave."

"You too, Pop."

* * *

Hearing the exchange between father and son, Jim swallowed hard. Rising, he looked out the window and watched them walk across the field, their forms growing smaller until they finally, vanished into the hollow.

He crawled back beneath the covers, gently kneading his throbbing shoulder. He was unable to shake the weird sense of foreboding that had fallen over him. He hoped that Martin said a little prayer.

Then his thoughts turned back to Danny, and the

foreboding grew worse.

He slipped back into a troubled sleep.

* * *

The hollow was quiet; brooding. Spanning a little over a square mile, it was created by four sloping hills leading down to its center. A serpentine creek wound through its length, exiting into a cornfield on the other side of the Clendenan homestead.

The silence was pervasive; and to Martin, unsettling. No squirrels danced playfully in the branches. No birds sang from the boughs. There was no sound, save the occasional squirt as Delmas spat a wad of brown tobacco juice from his mouth, and the trickling of the creek.

The greenery was alive, of course. Gentle ferns covered the banks of the stream. Twisting thorns, vines and tree limbs blocked their passage at every step. Moss clung to the gray stones thrusting up from the forest floor. The rocks reminded Martin of tombstones.

Delmas parted the leafy canopy in front of them and made his way down the hill. The branches rustled back into place, and after a moment's hesitation, Martin followed.

The ground sloped steadily downward. There were still no signs of other life, and Martin had the uncanny impression that the hollow was holding its breath.

"I love this place," Delmas whispered. "Ain't no salesmen or bill collectors to deal with. Just the air and the smell of the woods—the wet leaves. And when that wind whistles through the branches? God, that's the best."

"You've lived here a long time?"

"Yeah, since the war. I got out in sixty-nine, just before the dope smokers got over there and fucked everything up. Came home, married Bernice, and we built this place. Had two girls; Elizabeth and Nicole. They both moved away a long time ago. Nicole's in

Richmond, married to a veterinarian. Beth moved up to Pennsylvania."

He kicked at a root jutting from the ground.

"I don't know if they're alive or not. I suspect not. We never heard from either of them once this all started. Anyway, after the girls made us grandparents, Bernice surprised me with the news that she was pregnant again. Let me tell you, Reverend, I was scared by that. I'd just turned fifty, and didn't have no business raising another child. But secretly, I'd always wanted a boy. Figured I was never meant to have one. So when Jason come out, I was happier than a pig in shit. I love my girls, but do you know what I mean?"

Martin nodded.

"He's a fine boy, your son."

"Yes sir, that he is. And he's all I got now. That's why I feel for your friend. That's a hard thing. Damn hard! I can imagine what he must be going through."

"I think any father could." Martin agreed.

"Tell me something, Reverend. Between you and me, do you *really* think there's a chance his boy's alive?"

Before Martin could answer, the limbs above them rustled. Suddenly, shattering the stillness, a huge black crow took flight.

"My God," Martin clutched his chest. "I thought I was going to have a heart attack there for a second!"

Delmas laughed. "I told you there's some critters still alive in here! Only folks that hunt it are Jason and me, and Old John Joe over yonder." He pointed in the direction of the cornfield.

"He's a neighbor of yours, I take it?"

"Crazy old coot is what he is, though I don't reckon it's his fault. Same thing happened to Bernice happened to his wife too. Except John Joe didn't put her in the ground like Jason and I."

"He didn't? Please don't tell me he tried to—eat her..."

"John Joe? Hell no! He wasn't crazy like them

cannibals you run across. He just couldn't accept the fact that she wasn't his wife no more."

"So what did he do with her?"

"Well, he put her in the chicken house. Put chains and shackles around her legs, and fixed it up just like a little cell. And he fed her."

"He *fed* her?"

"Yep. Chicken. Beef. Fish he caught in the Greenbrier. Cooked it up and set it in there, using a long pole with a hook on it so he wouldn't have to get within grabbing reach of her. She wouldn't touch it. Then he tried some vegetables from the garden. She didn't want anything to do with those either. So he quit cooking and fed her the meat raw. She ate that, but John Joe knew it wasn't normal for a body to be eating raw meat. Finally, he asked me to come have a look. I don't think he really grasped just what was going on with the world. John Joe wasn't one to watch the news."

"I went over and had myself a look. It was horrible. She'd eaten through one ankle to get free of the shackles, and she was gnawing on the other when I saw her. She got agitated, and started cursing." He blushed. "Well, I never heard words like that coming from a lady's mouth; not even the gook hookers during the war. Terrible things. And she wasn't just speaking English either. She'd start ranting in English and then slip into some gibberish I've never heard before. Couldn't make heads or tails of it, but I'm here to tell you, it sounded ugly. There was something evil in those words."

Martin fingered his rifle.

"So what became of her?"

"Well, I told John Joe what he needed to do, but he didn't do it. I guess she nibbled off enough of her body to get loose, because a week later, John Joe come walking across the field, just as dead as she was. Had bite marks all over him and his throat was torn out. Jason put him down with one shot."

They marched down the hill to the creek. Delmas

stopped short and pointed at the mud. A line of hoof prints crossed the stream and headed up the hill.

"Those are fresh," he whispered. "Hell, they've just been through here!"

Martin glanced around but there was no sign of the deer.

"Alright, here's the plan," Delmas told him. "I'm gonna go up on that ridge yonder, and try to flush them down this way. You put yourself over against that tree," he indicated a massive, gnarled oak, "and whichever one of us gets the first shot, the other one has to clean it."

"Fair enough," Martin agreed. He was grateful he didn't have to climb the hill. The pain from his arthritis was spider webbing its way through his legs and back.

"Let me put a dip in first."

Delmas stuffed a pinch of Kodiak between his lip and gum, and snapped the lid back on the can. Returning it to his jacket pocket, he rubbed his hands together briskly, then picked up the rifle.

"Can's just about empty. I suppose I'll have to quit soon. Don't reckon I'm gonna get anymore anytime soon."

He began to creep away, when suddenly, on the other side of the stream, a twig snapped.

Martin jumped, backing up a few steps. Another twig snapped, followed by the rustle of leaves.

Delmas spotted it immediately and froze—holding his breath. His mouth filled with tobacco juice, and he swallowed, rather than spitting and announcing his presence.

Beneath the outstretched limbs, a shape emerged. Four legs, a mid-section, then a head. And what a glorious head it was! Even enveloped in the branches, Delmas could spot the rough outline of a rack—possibly a twelve-point or more.

Fuck me, he thought to himself. His finger twitched.

The deer bent its head, as if to sniff the ground, and Delmas raised the rifle.

Two things happened at once.

Martin caught a whiff of rotting flesh, and with a blur and a whip of branches, the buck vanished into the forest. They glimpsed a fragmentary telltale flash of white as it ran.

"White-tail!"

Thumbing the safety off, Delmas sprinted after it.

"Wait!" Martin called. "I think it's a zombie!"

The roar of the big man's rifle drowned him out.

Martin ran after him. Out of breath, he tried to shout another warning, but only managed to wheeze. The deer was still standing. Carefully, Delmas raised the 30.06 to his shoulder and sighted again.

The deer snorted and turned towards him. He still couldn't see its features because of the foliage, but he was sure it was staring directly at him.

He squeezed the trigger. The rifle bucked between his armpit and shoulder. It was a good pain.

The bullet passed straight through the animal's heart, and the deer dropped in the shadows beneath the trees.

The shot's echo rolled across the hollow. Delmas grinned in anticipation. The buck would provide venison for months if they cured it right.

Leaning against a tree, Martin gasped, trying to speak.

With a whoop, Delmas dashed toward his kill. His nose crinkled in disgust as the smell hit him.

"Oh shit."

The deer had been dead before he shot it.

The zombie sprang to its feet and lowered its antlers. The foliage parted and three more deer, two bucks and a doe, stepped forward menacingly. The one that Delmas had shot made a noise, and Martin swore it sounded like laughter.

They planned this, he thought to himself. *Dear God, they set us up!*

* * *

Jim awoke to the distant sound of gunshots. Yawning and dazed, he took a moment to study the room more closely. It was sparse: only the bed, nightstand and a dresser to keep him company. A painting of Jesus hung on one wall, and a picture of Jason holding a stringer of trout and beaming proudly hung on the other. A framed picture of a pretty but tired-looking woman sat atop the dresser. Jim guessed it was Clendenon's wife.

A pitcher of water and a bottle of aspirin sat on the nightstand. Jim downed four pills and explored his wound, probing the bandage with his fingers. From the kitchen, he heard the sounds of pots clanging together. Stretching, he got out of bed and dressed, then went to the window.

The scene outside was idyllic; tranquil. A faded red barn leaned precariously to its left, surrounded by a chicken-house, corncrib, and several wooden utility sheds. A John Deere tractor that had seen better days sat forlornly, weeds growing up to the top of its oversized tires. A large garden plot, now barren and empty, lay to the right. Near the garden, under a large willow, was a lone makeshift tombstone. It read simply:

BERNICE REGINA CLENDENAN
BELOVED WIFE AND MOTHER
REST IN PEACE

The property reminded Jim of where he'd grown up; the Shennandoah Mountains in Pocahontas County. He hadn't thought of his parents in a long time, and he suddenly felt ashamed. He hadn't been back to his childhood home in years; not since they died and the bank had taken the farm to settle their outstanding debts. It had always bothered Jim that Danny would never know his grandparents.

But Jim was also thankful that they hadn't been around to see what had become of the world. He'd lost too many people already; Carrie, the baby, friends like Mike and Melissa. He wouldn't have wanted to go through the anguish of losing his parents all over again.

The door opened and Jason peeked his head inside. Jim wondered why he'd thought the boy was older than Danny. He could clearly see now that they were the same age. In fact, the kid bore an uncanny resemblance to his son. Why hadn't he noticed that before?

"Didn't mean to disturb you Mr. Thurmond, but I figured you might be getting hungry."

"You didn't disturb me." Jim smiled warmly. "Please, call me Jim. You're Jason, right?"

"Yes sir, I mean Jim."

"Are Martin and your father back yet?"

The boy shook his head. "No, but I reckon it shouldn't be too much longer. I heard some shooting a few minutes ago."

"Yeah, that's what woke me. Wonder what they managed to bag?"

"Oh, there's all kinds of critters in the hollow! Why, I've killed me rabbits, pheasants, groundhogs, squirrels, deer, even a turkey or two. I missed a bear last year though."

"Well, that's pretty good shooting for a little guy like yourself," Jim exclaimed. "Your Dad must be proud."

"I'm no little guy," the boy said, puffing out his chest. "I'll be twelve in December."

"Twelve?" Jim studied him and could see it now. Jason looked nothing like Danny. *What the hell was wrong with him? Was he losing his mind?*

Jason had asked him something while he pondered this, and now the boy was staring at him in puzzlement.

"I'm sorry," Jim apologized. "I'm still a bit woozy. What did you say?"

"I said there's tomato soup if you want some. It'll hold you over till they get back. Then we'll have some meat and potatoes."

"I think a bowl of tomato soup would be just fine."

He followed the boy through the living room and into the kitchen. Bernice's presence could still be felt throughout the house, but it was strongest here; everything from the embroidered potholders to the matching toaster cover bore her distinct feminine touch.

"You miss your mother, I guess." Jim regretted saying it the moment the words left his mouth, but it was too late.

"Yeah," Jason replied, his voice grown sullen. He retrieved a bowl from the cupboard and ladled soup from a black iron pot bubbling softly on the wood-burning stove.

"When Mamma died, Pop said we had to burn her. That's just like cremation, so I figured it wouldn't be so bad. But Pop wasn't sure burning would be enough. Before he did it, he told me to go inside. Instead, I snuck around the house and hid behind the corncrib, and I saw what Pop did. He had this big machete that he uses to cut weeds down around the pond. He—he cut Mamma's head off with it. Then he burned her."

Jim wasn't sure how to respond, so he said nothing. Jason handed him the bowl and he sat down at the table, waiting patiently to see if the boy would continue.

"I was mad at Pop after that, but I guess I understand why he did it. He was crying, so I know it hurt him as bad as it did me."

"I'm sure that was a very hard thing for your Pop to do," Jim agreed. "But he did it because he loves you and wants to keep you safe, I suspect."

"Yeah, I reckon so," Jason sniffed.

"I have a son too," Jim said around mouthfuls of soup. "His name is Danny. He's a little younger than you are, but I think you guys would get along. He lives in New Jersey with his mother and step-father, and Reverend Martin and I are on our way to get him."

"Does he know you're coming?"

Jim considered this.

"Yeah, I think he does. He knows I wouldn't let anything happen to him. Wouldn't you feel the same about your Pop?"

Jason shrugged. "I guess so. But New Jersey is a long ways away."

Jim's stomach growled, the hot soup reawakening his appetite.

"It's tough for a father when you can't be there every day," he told Jason. "I wanted to be there for my son, but I couldn't. I wasn't allowed. My ex-wife got an expensive lawyer and I couldn't afford one. I wish I could have been there every time he fell off his bike and skinned his knee, or tucked him in when he had a bad dream. But it didn't turn out that way. The important thing is that Danny knows I *wanted* to be there. And pretty soon, we'll be together again."

Jim finished off the soup and thanked Jason, and their conversation turned to other things. Jim asked him about life on the farm. Jason wanted to know more about what he and Martin had seen on their journey, and Jim told him, editing out the grislier details. Jim learned that the boy had no concept of the outside world, other than what he'd seen on television.

"What's the farthest you've ever been?"

"To my big sister's house in Richmond. Mamma and Pop were going to take me to Busch Gardens next summer, but I don't guess there'd be much to see there now."

He grinned. Surprised, Jim laughed along with him.

"You're a pretty tough kid, you know that Jason?"

"That's what Pop tells me."

That was when the screaming started outside.

CHAPTER ELEVEN

Coasting along the turnpike, Baker considered their options.

There was a shopping mall just off the next exit, a few miles down the turnpike. They could probably find supplies there: food, clothing, weapons—but after further consideration, he finally decided against it. The shopping mall was located on the edge of a suburban area, and was bound to be heavily populated. The farther they could get away from towns, the better off they would be.

Still, the wilds presented a problem as well. While remote areas had less humans, there were more undead animals to worry about.

In the passenger seat, Worm cooed happily to himself, engrossed in a children's book that he'd found lying in the backseat. Baker gave him a sidelong glance and smiled, then turned his attention back to the road.

It would be easier without Worm, of course. Baker hated himself for thinking that, but the analytical portion of his brain kept reminding him of it. Besides, what if something happened to Baker? What would become of his young charge then? Cold, rational thought dictated that it would be an act of kindness to kill him while he slept. Better than leaving him alone to face the terrors of this new world.

He could never do that, though. He felt responsible for Worm. Who was he kidding? He wasn't an assassin—

some ruthless, emotionless killer.

Sure you are, said the voice in his head. *You killed the world, Baker. You're a murderer. The greatest mass-murderer in history!*

He mentally shrugged the voice away, and focused on their current dilemma. Towns were out. The wilderness was out. What did that leave? An island perhaps? There were islands scattered along the Susquehanna River, but they presented the same problem as the mountains or forests, only on a smaller scale. A rural farmhouse, removed from the rest of civilization? No, that didn't provide any more security than the wilderness. A small plane or a helicopter might be nice, like in that zombie movie he'd seen years ago on video. But even if he knew how to pilot one (which he didn't), where would they go after they went up? In the movie, the survivors had gone to a shopping mall.

Which brought him back to square one.

A billboard caught his attention.

INDIAN ECHO CAVERNS—EXIT 27—TEN MILES

He arched his eyebrows. A cave! He'd taken his visiting niece and nephew to the attraction several years before. He mulled over the possibilities; a deep, underground location, hidden from prowling eyes. Only one entrance and exit, so it was easily guarded. Perhaps most importantly, it was completely devoid of life; a tourist trap without the bats and other cave-dwelling creatures.

It could work. At least for now. At this point, anything was better than driving down the wide-open Pennsylvania Turnpike in a bright red Hyundai.

He tapped Worm on the shoulder, gaining his attention away from the adventures of Self the Kitty.

"Do you suffer from claustrophobia?"

The young man blinked, uncomprehending.

"Are you afraid of caverns or being underground?" Baker tried again, but still his companion didn't understand. He tried a different tact.

"Are you afraid of the dark?"

"Dawk?" This got a reaction. Worm considered the question and then touched Baker's arm. "Goht Bayker. No dawk."

"As long as you're with me, you won't mind the dark," Baker translated, and was touched. He felt a balloon of emotions welling up inside his chest, and remembered the promise that he'd made.

"Kihtee fuhnee," Worm told him, returning his attention to the book.

His mind made up on their destination, Baker edged the speedometer to forty-five. He still wanted to be cautious, in case they came upon a wrecked vehicle, but at the same time, he was anxious to get there.

He wondered how long their supplies would last them, but decided that it would be enough for the interim. Once they'd safely established shelter in the caverns, Baker could make a trip to replenish their stores. He also considered the possibility that the caverns weren't totally deserted. What if an employee or a tourist had turned into one of the undead and was holed up there? Even worse, what if somebody else, another survivor or a group of them, had already had the same idea and laid sole claim to it?

There were too many variables. They would just have to deal with the consequences when they arrived there.

The exit for the shopping mall flashed by, and Baker studied the landscape. Far below the exit ramp, scattered zombies could be seen shambling around the parking lot and fields. Incredibly, as he passed by them, two of the creatures turned their heads and pointed at the speeding Hyundai. Then, they flung open the doors of a nearby pickup truck, and hauled themselves into the cab.

He saw the truck's reverse lights in his rear-view mirror, and then the mall passed from sight. He stomped on the gas pedal and shot a reassuring glance at Worm, but the boy was oblivious to their pursuit. Nervously,

Baker appraised the situation. He had a head start; one that was broadening as the speedometer inched past seventy-five. It would take the zombies in the truck at least a couple minutes to maneuver out of the mall, up the ramp, and onto the Turnpike. If he could reach the next exit, the one for the caverns, before they regained sight of the car, they might be alright.

He decided against parking the car in close proximity to the caverns. It would announce their location on the off-chance that the zombies took the exit and drove around in search of them.

"Buherdz," Worm said suddenly, bouncing in his seat.

"What?"

"Buherdz!" He shouted now, clearly agitated, and pointed upward.

The sky was black with clouds of undead birds. Crows and finches. Sparrows and robins. Cardinals and turkey buzzards. Thousands of them blotted out the sun, swooping downward in one massive flock.

Soaring towards the car.

Gripping the wheel, Baker pressed the accelerator to the floor. The Hyundai protested, then the automatic transmission caught up with his urging and the car shot forward. As it did so, he heard a horn honking behind them, loud and persistent.

The truck was coming up behind them, and the birds swept in for the kill.

* * *

Watching the airborne zombies out of the windshield of the cab, Private Warner was glad he was driving the truck. The HumVee sat five interior passengers, with a sling seat for the gunner topside. In Warner's case, he would have occupied that seat. But while he loved handling the .50 caliber machine gun, and even the occasional Mach 19 grenade launcher or TOW missile launcher, a series of botched missions had taught the unit that when mobile, it was best to keep all hands and legs inside the vehicle at all times.

This was one of those times. Had he been manning the machine gun, he'd be easy prey for the swarming flock. The enormous round wouldn't do much good against so many small targets, and at six feet long and one hundred and fifty pounds, he couldn't exactly carry it around with him.

Instead, he was driving a civilian box truck that had been commandeered weeks ago. Once used to ferry bread deliveries all over the state, it now served as a mobile detention unit, transporting prisoners back to Gettysburg. It was currently empty, but Warner had no doubt that would change before this reconnaissance mission was over.

Warner carried no illusions about what they were doing, nor did he care. He was on the winning team, and if cracking some civilian in the head with a rifle butt to keep them in line was what he had to do to stay on the winning team, then he was all for it. Besides, he figured, they'd been protecting these soft mother fuckers for so many years, it was about time civilians showed some respect and busted their ass for them. Forced labor and prostitution? Maybe—but at least they were alive. They should be grateful.

Warner had never had any illusions about his position. The way he saw it, he got paid to protect people from themselves; and cracking heads, whether they were a rioting protestor or a looter after a flood or tornado, was one of the benefits. He didn't care about the citizens he was sworn to protect. Most of them didn't deserve protection anyway. They wanted their houses and businesses kept safe, but they were the first ones squawking on the news when the media showed a Guardsmen taking out a few of the very same fucks they wanted protection from.

Although he had never said it aloud, Warner secretly liked things the way they were now. He got laid on a nightly basis, and who cared if some of them fought back at first? Pussy was pussy, whether it was willing or unwilling. You just had to break the bitch down was all. He ate well, slept well, and got to utilize his skills. He was still alive, and more importantly, his life had purpose.

"Warner," Sergeant Ford's voice crackled over the radio. "You see that shit overhead?"

He keyed the mike, eyes still trained on the birds.

"That's affirmative. Something tells me they ain't flying south for the winter."

"Staff Sergeant Michaels says to stop. He wants to wait them out. If it looks like they're going to attack and they breach your truck, make for us. We'll cram you in until it's over."

"Roger that," Warner replied, as visions of beaks smashing their way through the truck's windshield ran through his mind.

* * *

"Warner's clear," Ford informed Michaels, warily eyeing the circling birds. He'd never seen so many at once. Their attention seemed, so far, to be focused on something beyond the curve in the road.

In the back, Lawson and Blumenthal readied their weapons and fidgeted nervously.

"This entire mission has been a cluster-fuck," Michaels grumbled. "First York, now this. Schow's going to be pissed."

Their reconnaissance of York had found the town to be hostile; filled not just with the living dead, but with warring factions of skinheads and street gangs too. A large portion of the downtown district had been destroyed by fire, and most of the surrounding areas were inhospitable as well. Certainly not worth wasting manpower on. The bottom line was that York was unsuitable for a new base.

He turned back to the birds, in time to see most of the

group drop downward. One flank separated from the main body, wheeling back toward their location.

"Shit," Ford barked. "They've spotted us! Get on the horn and tell Warner to move his ass!"

Blumenthal turned to Lawson and whispered conspiratorially "No bunch of birds is going to peck their way through *this* tin can."

"Maybe," he shrugged non-committaly, "but I'm glad we got the flame-thrower, just in case."

* * *

Baker swerved left, then spun the wheel to the right, searching for an escape, but the creatures were everywhere. The birds zoomed down upon the car. Bodies smashed against the windshield like living dead torpedoes, heedless of the damage being done to themselves.

Whimpering, Worm clawed at his seatbelt and closed his eyes.

The windshield began to crack under the barrage, and the cracks quickly spread. The sheer force of numbers rocked the car back and forth along the road. Each splattering body sounded like a rock as they pinged off the roof and hood. Baker turned on the wipers and blew the horn, but it did nothing to dislodge them.

Suddenly, the car slammed forward as something hit them from behind. The truck! In his panic, he'd forgotten about it. Terrified, he glanced into the rearview mirror.

The pickup truck was right behind them, close enough that he could see the leering grins of its two undead passengers. The truck sped forward and the car lurched again as their grille crashed against the Hyundai's rear bumper.

Metal shrieked as something drew its talons across the roof. Baker spun the wheel again but the car wasn't responding. The birds' bodies littered the road, and the tires slid uselessly over them. More carcasses collected in the wheel wells, choking the tires and sending the car careening toward the guardrail. Just then, the truck rammed them a third time and the car began to spin. Now the birds pounded it from all sides, and the rear window began to crack as well. A crow forced its head through the shattered windshield and cawed at them.

The car shuddered to a halt and the cacophony of the assault grew to thundering proportions. Eyes tightly clenched, Worm placed his quivering hands over his face. Baker reached for the gun, knowing how futile the weapon it would be against this enemy. There was only one way out of this.

There was a loud bang as something heavy landed on the hood. Baker peered through the feathery mass of wings and saw the eagle; once a proud symbol of freedom and democracy. Now symbolizing corruption and death. Spreading its massive wings, it darted towards the shattered windshield.

Baker put the gun to Worm's head and prayed that he'd have time to finish them both before the creatures reached them.

* * *

Warner watched a squadron of birds break off from the rest of the formation and wing directly towards the truck and the HumVee.

"Oh hell!"

"Warner," Ford shouted over the radio, "get your ass moving! Now now now now NOW!"

Flinging the door open, he dashed toward the HumVee. Blumenthal emerged from the top-hatch, clutching an M-16 and urging him on.

Something sharp whizzed by his head, and he felt a sudden pain. He placed his hand to his ear, and his palm came away red. Another bird snapped at his ankles, and a third clawed at his hair.

Shrieking, he clenched the bird in his fists and squeezed. It fought back, snapping at his hands and fingers with its razored beak, drawing more blood.

Warner stumbled, falling to his knees in the middle of the road. His back felt heavy, as the weight of more birds forced him to the ground. He rolled and thrashed, crushing them beneath him.

The HumVee backed towards him, and Blumenthal fired off a burst from his M-16. He managed to actually hit a few of the small moving targets, but the rest scattered, flitting out of range.

Warner pulled himself up, screaming as something pecked it's way into the back of his neck.

Inside the HumVee, Michaels' attention had been focused on operating the vehicle and not running over Warner. Ford was the first to notice the red Hyundai that careened around the bend in the road, spinning uncontrollably before it slid to a stop. A rusty pickup truck skidded to a halt behind it, and two human zombies got out of it.

"Christ," he muttered, then turned to Michaels. "We've got company!"

Still firing, Blumenthal jumped out of the moving vehicle and ran towards the injured soldier. Warner was covered in feathery bodies. The birds chattered excitedly, picking at his exposed flesh, as he writhed in agony. Blumenthal took a few more strides toward him and then retreated as more of the creatures bombarded him. Screaming, he dropped the M-16 and flung his arms protectively over his eyes.

Lawson clambered into the sling chair atop the HumVee and aimed the flame-thrower. A liquid orange burst roared through the air, setting dozens of birds aflame. He swung the weapon in a wide arc, and the rest of the airborne hordes retreated.

"What about Warner?" Blumenthal shrieked

Their fallen comrade was a mass of quivering meat, red and raw. His uniform had been ripped to pieces as had most of his skin. Zombie birds landed on him, tore away strips of flesh, and then took flight, making room for their brothers.

Without a word, Lawson turned the weapon on Warner and his attackers, turning both into an inferno. As the fire engulfed everything behind them, Blumenthal climbed inside the HumVee.

"Eyes front," Ford shouted to Lawson. "More of them!"

Lawson swung the flame-thrower around, gasping in astonishment when he spotted the huge eagle on the hood of the car. He sent a fiery spray arcing toward them.

"Slide the fuck over!"

Blumenthal popped his head through the opening in the roof and opened fire with the .50 cal, laughing as the enormous rounds tore through the two human zombies and their truck, scattering heads, limbs and torsos along the blacktop.

The few remaining birds lurched toward the sky.

"We've got movement in the car," Ford cautioned them. "Non-zombie. Hand me that bullhorn."

"I'm surprised it didn't catch fire too, way you were spraying everything."

"Shut up, Blumenthal," Lawson growled. "It worked, didn't it?"

The driver's side door of the Hyundai swung open, and both men trained their weapons on it. A man, bleeding and singed but still very much alive, raised his hands toward them.

"Don't shoot!" Baker cried. "We're human!"

He ducked back inside, hugged Worm, and convinced the quaking boy to open his eyes.

"We're safe, Worm," he mouthed. "Safe. Army men!" He pointed towards the HumVee and the box truck.

"Passenger, please exit the vehicle with your hands in the air! Driver, remain inside!"

"My companion is deaf," Baker called. "He can't hear you—"

"DO IT NOW!" Ford roared.

Using hand signals, Baker urged Worm to get out. After some coaxing, the terrified boy reluctantly complied.

"Driver, now it's your turn. Keep those hands up!"

Baker did as he was told, trying to ignore the fragile bodies and wings crunching softly beneath his feet. The stench of burning flesh hung heavily in the air. The zombies from the truck lay scattered over a wide area.

Two soldiers—Baker could see that they were Army National Guard—dismounted and walked slowly towards them, weapons at the ready.

"Thank you," Baker clamored. "Thank you gentlemen so much! I really thought we were—

Blumenthal slammed the butt of his M-16 into Baker's abdomen, cutting him off. Clenching his stomach and gasping for air, Baker fell to the ground and curled into a ball.

"Bayhker!"

Worm squealed in fright and tried to run. Lawson flung him to the ground and placed a booted heel on his head.

Baker wheezed, unable to speak. He clawed at the road with his hands, fighting for breath.

"Put them in the truck," Michaels ordered. "Lawson, you take over driving."

Kneeling, Blumenthal snapped a pair of handcuffs around Baker's wrists. Then he plucked the RHIC identification badge from his coat. He scrutinized the picture on the card, then grabbed Baker's chin and stared at his face.

"Same guy?" Lawson asked. "What's the ID say?"

"Havenbrook. Wasn't that where that Top Secret government lab was? You know, the one that was on the news just before everything went to shit?"

"Yeah," Lawson shrugged, putting cuffs on Worm as well. "So what? The President of Palestine and that transvestite supermodel were on the news too, but I don't see them here."

"Hey Sarge," Blumenthal called. "I think we've got something here that might make this trip worth it after all!"

Lawson dragged Worm to his feet, watching the sky closely for any returning birds.

Blumenthal handed the badge to Michaels. "Wasn't this the place where they were doing those experiments?"

"Maybe. I thought it was a weapons lab or something like that."

"Well," Blumenthal cleared his throat, "I was thinking maybe Colonel Schow would like to interrogate this guy, on account that he obviously worked there. At the very least, there's probably all kinds of weapons laying around, but also—"

He faltered, unsure if he should proceed.

"Go on, Private."

"Well, if I remember correctly, most of it is underground. I'm thinking that would make a perfect place for us to move to."

Michaels looked from Blumenthal to the cowering Baker and then back to the Private again.

"Blumenthal, if you're right, you may have just earned yourself a promotion."

The soldier grinned. Forcing Baker to his feet, they loaded the captives into the back of the truck, then rolled the door down, padlocking it.

It was pitch black inside the truck. Worm sobbed uncontrollably as the engine roared to life. Baker slid toward the sound of his voice and the frightened boy cowered against him. Baker wished he could murmur words of assurance, but Worm wouldn't be able to see his lips moving in the dark.

The intense pain in his stomach and chest had drowned out much of the soldier's conversation, but he gathered they wanted information on Havenbrook. That meant they would keep him alive.

In the darkness, Baker wondered how he and Worm

would remain that way after he'd given them what they wanted.

CHAPTER TWELVE

Jason grabbed a rifle from the gun cabinet and dashed out the door before Jim could stop him.

"Jason, wait! We don't know what's out there!"

Unheeding, the boy jumped off the porch and ran across the front yard. Weaponless, Jim ran after him.

Martin limped across the field, carrying Delmas with him. The elderly preacher looked pale and haggard, and his mouth hung open. His unseeing eyes stared past them. His pants were torn and blood streamed down his leg. His feet shuffled along automatically. From his belt loop, a length of baling twine had been tied around the trigger guards of the rifles. He dragged the guns along behind them, the stocks and barrels digging furrows in the dirt.

Delmas was in worse shape. Chunks of flesh were missing from his arms, legs, and face, and his body was covered in bite marks. He was coated in blood, and his eyes were shut.

"Pop!"

Jim caught them both as Martin stumbled, and gently eased them to the ground. Martin blinked, gazing up at him, and licked his lips.

"What happened? Are you alright?"

"Ambushed," the elderly minister coughed. "They were waiting for us in the hollow. They set a *trap*!"

"How many?" Jim demanded.

"More than—more than I could count. First it was just deer, but then there were squirrels, birds, and a couple of humans. Working together. We managed to destroy a bunch of them. I don't know how many are left."

"Are you okay?"

"A dead groundhog bit me on the leg, but I'm alright. Thought I was going to have a heart attack getting us back here. Just let me rest a minute."

Jim checked him over. His skin was hot and flushed, and he had an ugly gash on his leg. The cut had started to clot already though. Otherwise, he seemed okay.

Jason cradled Delmas' head in his arms. His father wasn't moving.

"Let me see him," Jim said gently, and Jason looked up at him, tears streaming down his face.

"Please don't let him die."

At the sound of his son's voice, Delmas opened his eyes.

"Jason..."

"I'm here, Pop. You're gonna be alright. I'm gonna take care of you."

"Delmas," Jim asked, "can you walk?"

"My leg's busted."

"Then I'm going to have to carry you. Jason, can you help Reverend Martin? Maybe carry the guns?"

The boy stood up, wiping his nose with his sleeve.

Delmas wrapped his arms around Jim's neck and bit his lip in anticipation.

"Ready?"

He whimpered in the affirmative. Jim lifted him off the ground and the wounded man screamed in anguish as his leg banged against Jim's thigh. The gunshot wound in Jim's shoulder flared to life in response.

Struggling with the effort, Jim got him into the house and laid Delmas in the same bed that he had occupied only hours before. Martin stumbled in behind them, followed by Jason. Wide-eyed, the boy put the rifles on the floor and slammed the door shut.

"There's more coming!"

Jim ran to the window. Three shadowy figures stepped out of the twilight; two humans and a doe. The zombies lurched toward the house.

Getting his second wind, Martin grabbed shells from the gun cabinet and began reloading the rifles.

"See to your father," Jim told Jason. "We'll handle this."

"How many are there?" Martin asked.

"Three that I can see. Maybe more that I can't. I don't know. You ready?"

"No, but let's do it anyway."

Jim flung the door open and leaped onto the porch, firing as he went. The shots were wild, but they deterred the zombies long enough for him to take position, eject his shells, aim, and fire again. He drew a bead on the doe and quickly squeezed the trigger. The gun jumped in his hands and the bullet tore into her neck. The next shot dropped her.

Martin targeted the closest human, an obese hillbilly who had swollen to hideous proportions in death. His first shot shattered the creature's kneecap. He readjusted and the second plowed into the prodigious stomach. The stench spilling from the monster's intestines clouded the porch. He aimed higher and the next two shots separated the zombie's head from its body. It dangled on a few thin scraps of sinew and flesh, before falling off the shoulders and rolling across the ground. The body dropped beside it.

Martin approached the head. The eyes followed him and the lips moved, forming words but now lacking the lungs and vocal chords to express them.

He knelt down next to it and the teeth snapped at him soundlessly. Rising, he thrust the barrel into its mouth. The eyes grew wide. He fired.

The third zombie turned to run. Leading it for a moment with the barrel, Jim drew a bead on it, fired, and watched its brains exit through the back of its skull.

Breathing hard, the two men smiled at each other grimly. The echoes of the last shot rebounded off the hills. Finally Martin spoke.

"Clendenon's in bad shape." It wasn't a question.

"Yeah, I'm afraid so."

"Jim," he paused before continuing. "You realize we can't leave them like this."

"I know."

He stared into the setting sun. New Jersey—and Danny—had never seemed farther away at that moment.

* * *

They used two bottles of peroxide and several boxes of cotton balls on the bites. Martin gave him a liberal dose of aspirin and a bottle of Jim Beam to kill the pain while they bandaged his wounds. Delmas had lost a lot of blood, and his skin was chalk-white. His leg was swollen to almost twice its normal size, and Jim had to cut the pants leg off around it. They elevated it with pillows, and when Jim touched his thigh, the flesh was hot and tight.

Mercifully, Delmas finally passed out, moaning himself to sleep.

"We've got to do something about that leg," Jim said, "but I don't know how."

"We could try to set it," Martin said. He looked at Jason. "Did your Pop ever teach you how to do anything like that?"

"No. Mamma taught me how to make a poultice, but we don't have the stuff to do it."

"Are there any neighbors who would be able to help?"

"No. Tom and Luke and old John Joe were the last."

Jim paced the floor while Martin cared for his own wounds and washed up in the sink.

"Try to get some sleep," the minister coaxed Jason.

"Can't, sir. I'm not sleepy."

"Well then, why don't you go sit with your father a

spell. Mr. Thurmond and I will try to figure out what to do next."

After the door closed behind him, Martin sighed, loosening his collar.

"So what do we do?" Jim stopped pacing.

"I don't know. I've been thinking about that. Best case scenario; we fight off any infection and the man is a cripple for the rest of his life. How long do you think they'll last if he can't walk?"

Jim didn't reply.

"We could take them with us," Martin suggested. "Find a van or something. Sooner or later we'll have to run into a doctor or at least somebody with medical knowledge."

"He's in no shape to travel, Martin. A few hours ago, you weren't even sure that I was."

"You certainly act like you're feeling better."

"I am better, but driving him is out. We can't move him with that busted leg."

"So we wait."

"And Danny—" He choked, unable to finish.

"I'm sorry, Jim."

Martin sank into the sofa and propped his feet up. Jim began to pace again.

"Maybe this is how it's supposed to be, Jim. I could stay here with them while you went on."

Jim considered this.

"No, Martin, I can't leave you here. You came with me, offered your friendship and support. It wouldn't be right."

"It may not be right, but that doesn't mean it's not God's plan. Maybe the Lord needs me here."

"Let me think about it. We're not going to be able to do anything until it's light outside anyway."

In the darkness, a whippoorwill sang its lonely song to the accompaniment of chirping crickets. Martin went to the window.

"My Mama used to say that when you heard a

whippoorwill at sunset, it meant that somebody close to you was going to die."

"My folks used to say the same thing," Jim responded. "If it's true, they must be singing an awful lot these days."

* * *

Jason woke in the middle of the night, slumped in the chair next to his father's bed. He stretched his legs, yawned, and went to his father's side. Delmas lay utterly still, and Jason felt a momentary twinge of panic. He placed his ear next to the sleeping man's mouth, and sighed with relief when he heard him breathing quietly.

Jason's bladder let him know with a sense of urgency that he needed to pee. He tiptoed to the door and peeked out into the living room. Pastor Martin lay on the couch, mumbling and thrashing fitfully in his sleep. Jim sat facing the window, silhouetted in moonlight. He was staring at something in his hands.

"Mr. Thurmond," Jason whispered, but Jim didn't turn or acknowledge him.

Jason crept behind him. In Jim's hands was a wallet-sized photograph of a little boy.

"Jim," Jason whispered again, and this time he heard him. Bleary-eyed, Jim turned to face him.

"Hey Jason," he murmured wearily. "Couldn't sleep?"

"I had to pee. What about you?"

"Can't sleep."

"Is that Danny?"

"Yep, that's him," Jim sighed, turning back to the picture before putting it back into his wallet. "How's your Pop?"

"He's sleeping. I guess that's good."

"It certainly can't hurt," Jim agreed. Jason was hopping back and forth from foot to foot now. "Go ahead and pee. I'll watch your Pop while you're gone."

"Thanks."

Rising to his feet, Jim tiptoed into the bedroom.

Delmas' worsening condition shocked him. He hadn't expected the injured man to be up and dancing a jig, but the deterioration was happening much quicker than he had thought it would.

His skin had taken a ghostly pallor and dark circles surrounded his sunken eyes. Despite their efforts, Jim could smell the infection rotting Delmas from the inside out. The stench reminded Jim of hot dogs in a microwave, and he gagged. Delmas' leg was swollen and the flesh glistened in the candlelight. Purplish-black splotches dotted his thigh and calf, and the veins bulged through the skin.

From the bathroom, Jim heard the sound of the toilet flushing and with a last, pitiful look at Delmas, he turned to leave.

"Kill me."

He wheeled around. Clendenan was awake and staring at him.

"Kill me," he wheezed again. "Don't let me—"

Jim went to his side, trying to calm him down.

"That'll be enough of that talk. You don't want to scare your son."

Kill me!" Delmas insisted. With a sudden burst of strength, he grabbed Jim's shirt, clenching it tightly.

"Hey," Jim protested, "what are you doing?"

"Listen to me, Thurmond! I don't want to be like one of those things out there! I don't want Jason to see me like that. You've got to put me in the ground yourself."

"Don't be silly," Jim soothed. "You're going to be okay, Delmas. We're going to find you a doctor—"

"Bullshit! Ain't no doctors around here! We both know I ain't gonna make it, Jim. I can smell myself rotting. I'm burning up with fever."

He broke off into a violent fit of coughing. Jim tried to lean him forward but Delmas waved him away and brought it under control. Jim noticed in dreadful fascination that rusty colored fluid was leaking from the corner of his mouth.

"Kill me."

"I can't, Delmas. I'm sorry, but I can't."

"Then I will."

They both turned. Jason stood in the doorway, and Jim could tell by the expression on his face that the boy had heard the exchange. Martin stood blinking behind him, one hand on his shoulder. There were sleep seeds in the old man's eyes.

"You can't be serious," Jim said. "You're just a boy."

"Yes sir, and he's my Pop. I reckon I should be the one."

Delmas stared at his son gravely.

"You know what you're saying, boy? Are you sure about this?"

Jason nodded, struggling to contain the torrent of emotions that threatened to break loose. He was afraid if he started crying now, he'd never stop.

"For Christ's sake, Delmas, give it a few days," Jim urged. "Maybe we can stop the infection!"

The big man silenced him with a wave of his hand.

"I'm dying," he said simply, "and if we give it a few days, what happens if I pass on in my sleep? Then I'm a danger to all of you. No, it's better this way. This way we're sure."

Scowling, Jim moved away from the bed and knocked his head against the wall in frustration.

"Jason," Delmas rasped, and held his hand outstretched. The boy floated to his side. A tear ran down his cheek as he took his Pop's hand in his own.

"You've got a job to do, Jason," he wheezed. "You understand why I had to do what I did with your mother. Now I need you to do it for me. It won't hurt me, I promise. It happens so quick—" A sob caught in his throat.

"I can do it, Pop. I'm not afraid."

"I don't want you to look at me when you're done,"

Delmas commanded him. "After you pull the trigger, just close your eyes and walk away. I don't want you to be haunted by it. Just leave the room. I'm sure Pastor Martin and Mr. Thurmond here will bury me."

Martin nodded slowly, his gaze fixed on the floor. Jim struck the wall with his fist.

"Go and get the twelve gauge."

As Jason left the room, he called them over to his side.

"You still heading on to find your boy?"

"Yes."

"Take Jason with you?"

"Sure," Jim vowed, meeting Delmas' pleading eyes. "We'd be honored. I promise you, from one father to another, that I'll watch over your son and not let any harm come to him."

"Thank you." He coughed again, spraying the sheets with blood and grimacing in pain as his leg rolled off the stack of pillows.

"I've got it," Jason said quietly, and shuffled toward the bed.

"Delmas," Martin queried, "I must ask you—do you know Jesus as your personal savior? Have you accepted him into your heart?"

"Yes, about twenty years ago when we went to a revival and the preacher gave an invitation. I haven't always done right, but I've tried to live the way he'd want me to."

Martin nodded.

They formed a circle; Delmas lying in the bed, Jason on one side, and Martin and Jim on the other.

"Let us pray," Martin requested, and placed his hands on top of Delmas and Jason's heads. He began to pray, and his voice was soft, yet strong and firm at the same time. There was no hint of old age or weariness or doubt in it. "Heavenly Father, we ask that you watch over Delmas and Jason, and that you be with them in this hour of need; that you give them strength and comfort and the will to do what must be done. We ask that you guide Jason's hand, and that he not be troubled, and that you accept this man, your humble servant, who knows your power and glory, into the place you have prepared for him by your side, that he may bask in the wonder of Heaven. We ask Lord, that you comfort both father and son with the knowledge that they will see each other again, because of your gift, that they shall not perish, but have eternal life.

"Lord, we know that these bodies you have blessed us with and this flesh that you have breathed life into are just that—bodies. We know that our soul is eternal and we ask that you welcome Delmas Clendenon's soul now. We ask these things in the name of the Father, and of the Son, and of the Holy Spirit, as we pray: Our Father, who art in Heaven, hallowed be They name..."

"Thy kingdom come...Thy will be done..." the others repeated the Lord's Prayer along with him.

"...and deliver us from evil..."

And please let my son be alive, Jim thought.

"Amen," Martin finished.

"Amen," Jim echoed softly. He raised his head and all of them were crying.

"Goodbye, Mr. Clendenan." Martin shook his hand. "May the peace of our Lord and Savior Jesus Christ be with you."

"Thank you Reverend."

Jim was next.

"I promise," he whispered firmly, "I'll watch over him like he was my own."

Biting his lip in pain and sorrow and preparation, Delmas nodded. He squeezed Jim's hand tightly, then sobbed "Thank you."

They filed out of the room and Jim shut the door behind them, leaving father and son alone to confront the inevitable task at hand.

"Should we let him go through with this?" Jim asked. "Is this right?"

"I don't know if it's right," Martin admitted, "but it's something that both have decided and we must respect that. The boy is old enough to know what it is he is doing, and the ramifications that come with it. In a strange way, there is almost a familial dignity in this."

"I didn't have you picked for a supporter of assisted suicide, Martin."

"And you would be right, but this is a new world we live in, and the rules have changed. Jason is but a young man. Let him learn those rules now, while he is a young man, that he may do what is necessary when we cannot."

"Necessary," Jim mused, "that's pretty harsh."

"Is it? I suppose it might be at that. But isn't it harsh that that man is suffering, dying a slow death? Isn't it harsh that the corpses of our friends and neighbors are being corrupted by some evil force after their souls have fled? Isn't it harsh that your son is in danger, and you are beset with perils on your way to rescue him? Wake up, Jim! It's a harsh world! This is the path the Lord has put before us. It is not one I would choose to willingly walk, but God has given me no choice and I will follow. You must let Jason and Delmas do the same."

They lapsed into silence. Martin knelt before the couch and began to pray again.

Jim began to pace the floor again.

They waited.

* * *

"I want you to know that I'm proud of you son," Delmas wheezed. "and that I love you."

The tears were streaming down Jason's face now, and sniffing, he wiped his eyes.

"I love you too, Pop."

"Put the barrel right here," Delmas indicated, tapping the space on his forehead right between his eyes. "And then just let go and don't think about it."

With trembling hands, Jason started to lift the shotgun. Then his shoulder sagged and it pointed to the floor.

"Pop," he sobbed in protest, "I can't do it!"

"Yes, you can," Delmas said softly. "You're a good son, Jason. The best a man could ever ask for. I know that you can do this. You have to, just like I had to with your Mamma. It's not easy, but it's got to be done. Promise that you won't let me come back! Don't let me turn into one of those things."

Unable to speak, Jason nodded.

With fading strength, Delmas squeezed his hand. His face was wet with tears.

"Don't ever forget me," he croaked, "and if you have a boy of your own some day, I hope you'll teach him all the things I taught you."

He glanced around the room one last time and then looked out the window at the barn.

"The sun will be up soon, and I'm tired. My leg hurts something awful. It will be good to see your Mamma again."

He reached down along the side of the bed and lifted the barrel of the shotgun to his head, placing it firmly between his eyes. It was cool against his feverish skin, and he found comfort in this.

"I love you Jason."

Jason pulled the gun away and leaned forward, kissing the indentation the barrel had made.

"I love you too, Pop."

He put the shotgun back in place and wrapped his finger around the trigger. His tears were gone now.

Delmas closed his eyes.

* * *

The roar of the gunshot ripped through the house, silencing the songs of the whippoorwill and the crickets. Martin jumped, then continued to pray, more fervently now. Jim stopped pacing and walked toward the door.

"No," Martin stopped him. "Let's give him a moment."

Jim nodded and then a second blast tore through the night.

They ran for the room and Jim knew what they would find before the door was even opened.

Martin gasped. "Oh my Lord! Jim, don't go in there!"

The room stank of cordite and wisps of smoke still floated in the air. Delmas' body lay slumped in the bed, the top of his head running down the wallpaper behind him. Jason was sprawled on the floor, fingers still clutching the shotgun tightly. A pool of blood spread out behind him.

Jim crossed the room and knelt by the body, removing the weapon from Jason's lifeless grasp.

"No no no no no!" He repeated the word over and over, like a mantra. Then he turned it into one long and mournful wail. Martin was reminded of fiction, when writers expressed that sound with *Noooooooooooo*. He'd never heard a human utter it before now.

"Jim, maybe we should—"

Jim turned his face to the ceiling and screamed.

"Dannyyyyyyyyyyyyyyyyyyyyyyyyy!"

Outside, the whippoorwill began to sing again.

CHAPTER THIRTEEN

"Slow down!" Frankie shouted. Her arm dangled out the car window. "You wrap us around the guardrail and we're going to have a hard time finding an ambulance!"

"If this were Texas," Eddie drawled, "we'd have wide open spaces to drive through." He revved the car and the speedometer crept past ninety as he snaked around the twisted wrecks littering the highway,

"If this were Texas," Frankie replied, "then I'd already be in hell."

"You don't like Texas?"

"Never been there and I don't plan to go now. Isn't it all cowboys and cattle?"

"Awww, shit no, honey. We've got cities that'd make Baltimore seem tiny by comparison. We've got nightlife like you wouldn't believe! Best country music outside of Nashville. Well, at least before all this."

"Country music? Gag."

"What's wrong with country music?"

"It's nothing but redneck noise." She turned back to the road and shouted "Watch out!"

A tanker truck lay on its side in the middle of the highway, blocking all three lanes. Cursing, Eddie swerved into the breakdown lane and the Nissan bumped and lurched over the grass-covered embankment. The wheels spun, threatening to drop them down into a culvert. Then they found traction and Eddie struggled to weave around the truck and back onto the highway.

"That was close," he muttered. He tipped his cowboy hat backward, wiping his brow with a meaty palm. "Sorry about that."

"That's alright," Frankie said sweetly. "NOW SLOW THE FUCK DOWN!"

"Punch buggy red!" John of Many Colors shouted from the backseat as they passed a wrecked Volkswagen. He playfully tagged Frankie's shoulder.

"I don't know why we had to bring that fuckstick along," Eddie sulked. "Anybody with a lick of sense can tell he ain't right in the head."

"We brought him along because he's alive," Frankie explained again, her patience with the burly Texan wearing thin. "And if he's alive, he deserves a chance to stay that way. The only way we're going to make it is if we start banding together."

"Well, just don't you go forgetting your promise," Eddie warned her. "I help the two of you get out of the city, and I get to sleep with you tonight."

"A promise is a promise." She turned away.

His sweaty hand left the steering wheel and began to paw at her breast. Frankie's nipple stiffened; not in arousal, but in revulsion. Professional detachment took over. Here was skill; the one thing she was good at. While Eddie grinned, mistakenly believing she was turned on by his crude attentions, Frankie was working. She did what she'd always done with her Johns; left her body and let her mind go someplace else. Before the rising started, that place had been a daydream of the oblivion that her next fix would bring.

Now, she thought about her baby.

What kind of mother would she have been, she wondered, had she never gotten hooked on junk and finished college and ended up married? Would she have been a good one?

She liked to think so.

"Lookie there," Eddie pointed through the windshield. "Possum burger."

A fat possum, its hind end crushed by a previous vehicle, crawled with excruciating slowness across the highway. Frankie idly wondered if it had died before it had been run over or after it had been run over.

Eddie headed directly for it, and there was a sickening thump as the tires passed over its front half. The car bumped and then continued on.

"Ten points!" Eddie yelled happily, and went back to roughly kneading her thigh.

"Gray," John of Many Colors played along. "That possum was gray!"

Eddie laughed. "It's red now!"

John of Many Colors whipped around in his seat, staring out the back window to confirm Eddie's declaration.

"Gray and black."

Frankie closed her eyes. A headache was forming in her temples and the air inside the car, even with the windows down, was hot and oppressively humid. John of Many Colors stank of feet and unwashed armpits, and Eddie reeked of cheap after-shave (he'd pulled a bottle from the glove compartment and splashed it on immediately after picking them up).

She wondered if despair and futility had a smell, and if so, did the car reek of those as well?

* * *

After Troll's sacrifice and her escape from the sewers, the first living human Frankie encountered was James. In his previous life, he'd been a photographer for the Baltimore Sun, and he still carried his camera slung around his neck.

Frankie had found herself pursued by several zombies, and it had been James who gunned them down, picking them off one by one from the rooftop of a crumbling tenement building .

She expected him to want sex as payment for saving

her life, and was pleasantly surprised when he made no overtures in that direction. Instead, he proposed that they escape the city together, since there was safety in numbers. She'd readily agreed and they skirted their way around the harbor.

Arriving at the National Aquarium, they encountered John of Many Colors, and Frankie had been overjoyed. The homeless man was somebody she recognized from before the dead started rising. He'd long been a source of hilarity among all of Baltimore's street people. Think your life couldn't get any worse, sucking ten dicks a night for enough money to score, only to sleep in an abandoned warehouse and do it all over again the next day? It could be worse. You could be John of Many Colors.

Rumor had it that once upon a time, he'd been an actor; summer stock mostly, and had enjoyed more than his fair share of cocaine. When the addiction delivered its inevitable blizzard, he had been starring in a production of *Joseph and the Amazing Technicolor Dreamcoat*. He ended up on the street; broke, snowblind, and with only the coat as the last remaining vestige of his previous life.

John of Many Colors spent his days panhandling for money in front of Baltimore's World Trade Center, and shouting out to passersby what seemed to be the complete inventory of every color Crayola included in their crayon box.

Finding him alive, a recognizable link to the old world, filled Frankie with hope.

Frankie and James made an effort to convince him to come with them, but if the unstable vagrant understood, he gave no indication. Still, when they finally began walking away, he'd trotted after them like a faithful pet dog.

They came across a pawnshop that had somehow miraculously avoided being looted, and spent an hour arming themselves. Several blocks later, they came across a grocery store and completed outfitting themselves. The produce, meat, dairy and frozen goods aisles reeked of rot and putrefaction, but the canned and dry goods were still safe. They loaded up their backpacks, avoiding any cans without a label or dented or rusty.

Then, they slowly made their way out of the city, cautiously ducking and running across the industrial outskirts, until they'd reached Interstate 83.

That was where they'd lost James.

Insisting on finding them a car, he convinced Frankie that they should search a nearby parking garage. They'd entered the dark, six-story building, and a zombie hiding behind a pylon on Level Two attacked him with an axe and tore his still beating heart from his chest before he'd even managed to switch the safety off his pistol.

Frankie shot the zombie, and after closing James' eyes with her fingertips, put a bullet in his head as well. She added his weapons to her own, and transferred as much of his share of the food as she could carry to her backpack. Then she'd spent ten minutes tracking down John of Many Colors, finally finding him cowering in the back of a dark blue pickup truck ("Blue," he'd kept repeating. "This truck is blue.") before continuing on.

The zombie in the parking garage had apparently had friends. Attracted by the shots, hordes of undead humans, dogs, rats and others spilled from the surrounding factories and abandoned lots. More rushed out from the strip of trees beneath the overpass. Frankie shot as many as she could, and John of Many Colors contented himself to screaming out the various colors of their rotting garments as they fell around them, when a black Nissan sports car screeched up beside them.

"Ya'll need a lift?" a man called from the partially open window.

Frankie squeezed off another shot, dropping an elderly zombie whose false teeth looked garish and sinister in her twisted mouth, then gave the car a backward glance.

The driver was a big man: thick chested, heavily muscled arms with a tattoo on his left bicep that said *Feo*

Amante. He wore a black cowboy hat and mirrored sunglasses, below which a thick mustache drooped like a hairy caterpillar.

"Yeah, we could use some help," she'd calmly replied, and took aim at another creature.

"Cost you a blow job now," the driver casually informed her, "and you've got to let me fuck you later on." He was a southerner by the sound of his accent.

"No deal," she bartered, and emptied her clip at a row of advancing zombies. John of Many Colors was clawing at the Nissan's back door, whimpering with fright.

"Suit yourself, brown sugar." The cowboy rolled up the window, and the car began to slowly pull away.

"Wait!" Frankie shouted, hating herself for it.

The car stopped and the window came back down.

"Yes?"

"How about a blow job and that's it?"

"No deal."

Frankie's clip was empty and the zombies were forming a semi-circle.

"Alright, I'll fuck you later." She started towards the car.

"Promise?" he asked.

She yanked the door handle but it was locked.

"Yes!" she hollered in frustration. She could smell them behind her now, hear their rasping curses and profane assurances of what they would to do to her. "I promise! Now open the fucking door!"

There was the telltale snick of the locks disengaging and then she and John of Many Colors jumped inside the car. Frankie slammed the door shut, locking it.

The cowboy floored it and the car squealed away just as the zombies began to pound on her window.

And that was how they'd met Eddie.

* * *

As they drew farther away from the city and into the Maryland suburbs, the number of wrecked vehicles decreased. Eddie contented himself by driving with one hand on the wheel and shooting out the window at the occasional zombie with the other.

They passed by a strip mall, and a deceased biker on a massive touring bike roared up the entrance ramp after them. Eddie let it pull alongside and then swerved into the lane. There was a horrible screech of metal as the car lurched sideways. Then both the zombie and the bike lay scattered across the lanes.

Eddie's laughter grated on her nerves.

"Asshole," Frankie muttered beneath her breath.

"What's that, bitch?" He gave her nipple a hard pinch and Frankie dug her ragged nails into her side to keep from giving him the satisfaction of hearing her scream.

"You shouldn't be doing shit like that," she told him. "We could have wrecked."

"You're getting awfully mouthy, brown sugar. I'm starting to think you're mighty ungrateful."

Frankie backpedaled quickly. The last thing she needed was for the Texan to put them out along the side of the road with so many of the undead lurking about.

"I'm sorry," she said sweetly and massaged the crotch of his dirty jeans. She fingered the growing bulge playfully, then licked her index finger and traced the tattoo on his arm.

"What's that mean—'Feo Amante'?"

"It means 'ugly lover'. My ex-wife gave me that nickname."

Frankie felt the laughter bubbling over but it was too late to stop it. She leaned back in her seat, giggling uncontrollably and holding her stomach.

Eddie's face grew red, then scarlet, and then purple as thunderclouds of anger flashed in his eyes. He slammed the brakes hard and the car slid to a screeching halt. Frankie flung out a hand to keep from hitting the dashboard and John of Many Colors collided with the back of Eddie's seat.

With a sudden movement, Eddie grabbed her by the throat and shoved the pistol under her nose.

"Bitch, I've had enough of your mouth. I'm gonna put it to good use right now. Start sucking."

"Fuck off and die, you needle-dick mother fucker."

Eddie went pale with rage. His mouth became a cruel, thin line.

"What did you say?"

"You heard me, needle-dick. Go fuck a zombie because that's the only way you're gonna get any pussy. You ain't touching me."

"You just signed your death warrant, you cunt!"

In the backseat, John of Many Colors began to whine.

"Red. Too much red in the car. Red."

Eddie pulled the trigger.

"You're empty, asshole," Frankie told him as his eyes grew wide. "I counted your shots."

She brought her hand, the hand clutching the pistol, up from under the seat and blew his brains through the back of his cowboy hat.

John of Many Colors giggled.

"You liked that, huh?"

"Red," he told her. "Red and pink and gray."

"You know, you could have helped me a little more."

She glanced out the windows quickly, making sure there were no zombies in their immediate vicinity. She didn't see any but she knew they'd be coming within minutes. There was no disguising the gunshot. Quickly, she reached around Eddie's still twitching corpse and opened the door. Grunting, she shoved him out onto the road. Using napkins from the glove compartment, she wiped the blood and skull fragments from the upholstery, and slid behind the wheel. She dropped the car into drive and they sped away, as the first of the undead scavengers loped onto the highway toward them.

She checked the rearview mirror in time to see them swarming around Eddie's remains.

"Too bad he wasn't alive for that, huh John?"

"Too bad," John of Many Colors agreed. Then he pointed excitedly at a green Volkswagen laying on its side and punched her playfully in the shoulder.

"Green punch buggy!"

Frankie laughed, then realized she was shaking.

I just killed a man, she thought. *Good. It's a good start.*

They flashed by a sign that said PENNSYLVANIA 32 MILES.

"It's a good start," she repeated aloud.

* * *

"What a pissant little town," Miccelli grumbled. "Ain't nothing here except that water tower, some houses, and a gas station. And it's all built on a fucking hill!"

"That's why the Colonel wants us to scout it, genius," Kramer sneered. "Easy to clear, easier to guard and control. Say hello to your new home."

"Let's not get ahead of ourselves," Miller warned them. "Tell Partridge to stop."

Skip radioed the command back to Partridge, who was driving the white cargo van behind them. They slowed to a stop at the top of the hill. The town lay spread out in the valley below them, and Skip noticed that Miccelli was right. If you were driving by on the nearby highway, you'd never even notice the town. There were two roads; the one they were on and another that ran north to south. Both intersected in the town square. There was a small cluster of homes, a gas station and convenience store, a church with a cemetery behind it, and a water tower. The outskirts were mostly cornfields. Far off to the north, beyond the corn, the interstate wound its way through the countryside.

"I don't like it," Miller grunted. "There's nothing moving down there. No zombies. No survivors. Nothing."

"So what do we do?" asked Kramer.

"We go in," Miller replied. "Skip, I want you on the fifty cal."

Skip jumped in his seat.

"And let a zombie with a sniper rifle pick me off?" he argued. "No thanks! What about those fucking zombie birds?"

Miller's hand slid down to his sidearm.

"You disobeying orders, Private?"

Everyone inside the HumVee froze, watching the exchange. Miccelli was sneering at him in clear anticipation. Kramer casually lit a cigarette and shook his head.

"No Sergeant," Skip said quietly. "Just pointing out the risks."

"The only risk you need to keep in mind is that I'm ten seconds away from putting a bullet in your ass! Are we clear?"

Skip didn't answer.

"ARE WE CLEAR?"

"Yes Sergeant."

He heard Miccelli snicker as he crawled through the turret. "Should have shot the fucker."

Skip slid behind the weapon and glanced nervously at the empty sky. Time was running out for him, he knew. If the undead didn't kill him, the men from the unit were sure to. He'd read about this type of collective psychosis before. Squads in Viet Nam who burned villages to the ground and collected ears. The seven soldiers at Fort Bragg who killed their wives within a week of returning from Afghanistan. There was something about constant battle that made men crazy—evil.

The HumVee rolled forward and Partridge followed along behind them. Skip's eyes scanned back and forth, watching for movement.

They passed the church and its quaint graveyard and Skip wondered about what was buried there. The recently dead were capable of reanimation, but what about those who had been dead and buried? What if they'd decayed to the point where they couldn't free themselves? Were they still sentient—lying uselessly beneath the soil and lacking the musculature to dig their way out?

He shuddered at the thought, watching the houses carefully for any sign of a threat. Some of them were boarded up but most looked surprisingly normal, as if the inhabitants had just stepped out for a moment. Scattered cars were still parked neatly along the curb and in driveways. Lawns were still green, although overgrown.

Where were all the people? he wondered. Even if they were dead, their reanimated corpses should be lurking about. Had the zombies moved on to better hunting grounds?

He was musing over this when he heard a car's engine turning over. The car raced down the driveway of a house they had just passed, and slammed into the passenger side of the cargo van with a loud crash. Skip swiveled around in time to see Partridge fighting with the steering wheel as both vehicles slid into a parked car.

The doors of the surrounding houses opened and the living dead swarmed towards them.

"Ambush!" Skip screamed.

Zombies were crowding into the street, and more were appearing on the rooftops, armed with rifles and pistols, and even a crossbow, Skip noted.

"Shit!"

Firing, he swung in a circle, spraying the creatures on the rooftops first. Even the thunderous roar of the fifty caliber wasn't enough to drown out Partridge's hideous shrieks as he was dragged from the van and into the street.

"Go!" Miller screamed, and the HumVee lurched forward.

Skip laid down another burst and then jumped free of the rolling vehicle, landing in the street. He crouched there, glancing about frantically. He'd dropped most of the zombies on the rooftops, and the ones in the street were busy eating Partridge and avoiding the HumVee as the massive juggernaut backed towards them, crushing them beneath its weight.

Skip saw his chance and took it. With only a momentary consideration of the M-16 he'd left on the HumVee, he ducked between the houses and ran, fleeing both the zombies and his fellow soldiers.

Partridge's final screams and a fresh volley of gunfire echoed in his ears.

* * *

As they crossed the border into Pennsylvania, John of Many Colors suddenly seemed to experience a moment of lucidity, as if awakening from a dream. One moment he was cataloging the colors of the billboards they passed, and the next, he was staring fixedly at Frankie.

"What is your name?" he asked her, almost timidly.

"Frankie," she smiled, "and yours is John, right?"

"It was at one time. I suppose it still is. It is very nice to meet you Frankie."

"Likewise."

"Names are important, I guess. Although I don't think they matter as much now."

"Sure they do. Why would you say that?"

"Because we're all going to die soon anyway."

"I'm not," Frankie replied. "I'm going to live."

"It's foolish to think that way," John scolded her gently. "Look around us. The only things living in this world are now dead. Soon, we'll be like them."

"There's got to be others like us. All we've got to do is find them. I've been through hell to make it this far and I don't intend to give up now."

He sat quietly, pondering this, and when Frankie turned towards him again she saw the familiar haze seeping back into his eyes.

"Black," he told her. "The color of death is black."

* * *

Skip found an aluminum baseball bat in a child's abandoned clubhouse. Gripping it with both hands, he wielded it before him like a sword.

A mummified canine, its feral corpse dry and desiccated, lunged toward him from the shadowy confines of a doghouse. It sprang for his throat before the chain around its neck jerked it back violently. Skip noticed in abhorrent fascination that the dog's collar had sunk several inches into the flesh.

He could hear the sounds of pursuit behind him now, even as the sounds of battle took on a fevered pitch. The heavy staccato of M-16 fire was interspersed with the short, sharp reports of single action rifles. The zombies were shooting back at them.

A hoarse shout behind him indicated that he'd been spotted. He jumped over a fence and cut through another backyard. A child's swing swayed lonely in the slight breeze. A plastic wading pool sat off to the side. The water inside it was black and full of algae.

He dashed by it and a child-zombie that had been lying at the bottom of the pool erupted from the brackish water, clawing at him and dripping slime. Ragged, filthy nails sliced through his shirt and into the skin of his back. Skip spun on his heels and swung the bat. It connected with a wet thud and the creature's head collapsed in on itself, reminding Skip of the rotten jack-o-lanterns he used to smash apart after Halloween. The foulness escaping from the thing's ruined head was overpowering, and he staggered backward, wiping the bat in the grass.

Another zombie emerged from the house, carrying a rifle. The screen door slammed behind it as it lurched toward him and clumsily raised the weapon. Skip grinned, shot it the finger, then turned and fled. Determined, the zombie chased after him in single-minded pursuit.

He came to a wide-open soybean field and paused. Hands on his knees, gasping for breath, he hastily considered his options. The water tower was close, and a rung ladder snaked up its side. He could easily fend off his pursuers from atop the tower, as they would have to climb up single file to reach him. But that left him vulnerable to attacks from the birds and other creatures that could easily reach the top. Also, there was no escape if the living dead simply surrounded the bottom of the structure and decided to wait him out.

The Interstate glinted in the distance, a black and silver ribbon cutting through Maryland and Pennsylvania's rolling hills and farmland. If he could make it to the highway, maybe he could find a car. At the very least, he'd be away from the town and the majority of the living dead. But the highway also offered no protection from above.

He glanced nervously into the sky and his fears were realized as he spotted a black cloud far away on the horizon. His terror grew as the cloud changed direction in mid-air and moved swiftly towards the town.

On the ground, an army of the living dead moved steadily towards him.

Out of choices and out of time, Skip turned and fled across the field toward the highway.

The dead followed him.

* * *

"I see him," Miccelli hollered over the bursts from the fifty caliber. "Little fucker's heading across that field!"

Miller and Kramer turned to where he was pointing. Sure enough, a green clad, fast-moving figure was crossing the open field next to the water tower. An army of slower moving figures followed in his wake.

"He's heading for the highway," Miller observed. "But we can get to him before those zombies do."

"I think we should just let those ugly fucks tear him to

pieces, the way he let them do it to Partridge."

"No, Kramer. Schow is going to want to make an example of him. That boy is definitely going back with us, even if I have to shoot him in both legs and keep him alive until we get there."

"Hey Sergeant," Miccelli called from the roof. "There's a flock of bird zombies coming in!"

"Then get your ass back in here!" He nodded to Kramer. "Floor it and get to that fucking Skip before those zombies do. Cut across the field."

"Roger that," Kramer replied and gunned the motor. "I can't believe he deserted like that."

"I can," Miller commented. "He knew he was fucking up, questioning orders and shit. Ain't no room for somebody like that. And we almost paid the price for his cowardice."

Miccelli slid back into his seat and checked his weapon. He wiped the grime from his forehead and face, and took a long swig of water from his canteen.

"Fucking things were waiting in ambush! I still can't believe that."

Miller didn't respond. His attention was focused on the fleeing man on the horizon, and the figures trailing along behind him.

"That's your ass, Skip," he muttered under his breath. His knuckles turned white as he gripped the console and fantasized about the tortures Colonel Schow would have in store for the Private upon their return. And if Skip got a little injured between here and Gettysburg, who would care?

* * *

Frankie was opening a bag of chips with her teeth when a haggard-looking man in a tattered military uniform ran into the road, frantically waving his arms. His hair was askew and his face was streaked with dirt and blood, but she could tell that he was alive and not one of the living dead. He clutched a bat in one hand, waving it above his head as well.

Frankie braked, made sure the doors were locked, and rolled the window down halfway. She pointed the pistol at him and waited.

"Jesus Christ, lady, don't shoot!" Skip gasped.

"Drop the bat, and keep your hands up where I can see them."

Gasping, he did as he was told. The bat clattered to the pavement and Skip shifted nervously from one foot to the other.

"Green," observed John of Many Colors. "That man is green. And red too."

"Look," he said slowly, fighting to keep his voice calm, "there's a shitload of zombies chasing me. We need to get away from here, and we need to do it now!"

Frankie glanced across the field. A throng of the living dead, both human and animal and in various stages of decomposition, swarmed towards them. Closer, and cutting between the hordes and the highway, was some kind of military vehicle. As it bore down on them, the man grew agitated.

"Lady, if we don't go now, they'll fucking kill us! They're crazy!"

Frankie didn't know if he was talking about the zombies or whoever was inside the onrushing vehicle, but one glance at the darkening sky made up her mind. It was filled with undead birds, all soaring directly towards them.

"Get in," she barked, cocking her head to the passenger side. "Don't try anything either, or I'll kill you."

Visibly relieved, the soldier ran around to the side of the car and jumped in.

"Thanks!"

"What are you? Army?"

"National Guard," he gasped. "Can we go please?"

The HumVee crashed through the guardrail and

slammed to a stop in front of them. A man popped out of the top like a jack-in-the-box, and leveled the biggest machine gun Frankie had ever seen directly at them.

"Out of the car, now!"

"Shit!" Skip turned to Frankie. "Do you have another gun?"

Before she could reply, two Guardsmen were running towards the car, weapons pointed at them. Bewildered, and still not knowing who was who, but only that any of these men were preferable to the zombies closing in on them, Frankie stared in silence.

"Drop it, bitch!"

Miccelli yanked the driver's side door open with one hand and shoved his M-16 at her head.

"Into the HumVee, now! Move it!"

"Hi Skip," Kramer taunted, pulling him from the car. "Where'd you think you were going, you chicken-shit little fuck?"

He slammed the butt of his weapon into Skip's back, knocking him to the ground. Then he began to club him, savagely bringing the stock down again and again on his back and shoulders.

"Fuck you, Kramer," Skip spat blood at him and rolled over. He saw the butt of the M-16 descending and then he knew no more.

Miccelli bound Frankie's wrists and she screamed as the first bird swooped down and nipped at her hair while he was doing it.

John of Many Colors crawled from the car and hopped up and down, hooting in fright.

"What about him?" Miccelli asked, tossing a thumb at the vagrant while he shoved Frankie into the HumVee.

Kramer leveled the weapon at him. "No room at the inn."

He opened fire. John of Many Colors danced in the road, his body jerking as the bullets slammed into him. No sound escaped his lips, except for a low sigh as he collapsed to the ground. Blood pooled on the pavement beneath him.

Kramer knocked a bird away, took aim at a human zombie that was clambering over the guardrail. Then he and Miccelli threw the unconscious Skip into the HumVee and closed the hatch behind him.

"Nice-looking black cooze," Miller said, leering at Frankie as they sped away. "I've got first dibs."

Frankie closed her eyes and shuddered. She was in trouble, of that she was certain. But she was still alive.

We're all going to die soon. John of Many Colors had said.

"I'm not. I'm going to live."

* * *

John of Many Colors lay twitching on the hot pavement. The birds began to peck at him, but he couldn't feel it. They flew away with strips of his flesh hanging from their beaks. Then the other zombies encircled him, pawing at him hungrily.

"I was wrong," he told them. He held his bloodstained hands up to them, and they proceeded to gnaw on his fingers.

"The color of death isn't black. It's red."

He saw a zombie sever his index finger, biting through both flesh and bone, and then his sight faded.

"It's red. Everything is red. The whole world is dead."

Later, after his soul had departed and another entity had taken possession of his body, he learned that he was right.

CHAPTER FOURTEEN

Dear Danny,

I don't know why I'm writing this, because even when I find you, I probably won't let you read it. Maybe I will when you're older, and you can understand it better. I guess I'm writing it just to make me feel better. I keep thinking about you all the time, and remembering stuff.

I miss you son. I miss you so bad. It's like somebody took something out of my chest and left a big hole. I can feel the hole in there. It hurts. I'm used to feeling that way. I felt it every time I took you back to your home (well, where you lived with your Mom and Rick—I never thought of it as your home), and I felt it when you were gone. I used to go into your room after the summer was over and I'd sit on the bed and look at your toys and books and videos and I knew they would sit there, unused, until you came back again. Some nights, I would try to go to sleep and I would start to think about you, and suddenly, I couldn't breathe. Carrie called them panic attacks, but they were much more than that. I missed you all the time, and I felt so empty.

It's worse now. There are times I feel like one of those zombies out there. A lot of bad things have happened, Danny. Carrie is gone and your baby sister is gone. You remember our friends Mike and Melissa? Gone. Our home is gone, and I don't guess we'll ever be able to go back. I wish I had thought to grab some of your favorite toys before I escaped, but I didn't. When I find you, the first thing we'll do is raid a toy store. And this time, you can have whatever you want. We don't have to worry about whether or not I can afford it. Then we'll find a comic book store, and you can get whatever you want there too (except Preacher and Hellblazer—you're still not old enough to read those). We'll go to someplace safe, someplace without monsters.

I'm on my way, Danny, and I need you to hang in there. I need you to be strong and I need you to be brave just a little while longer. Daddy is coming and I know that you know that. I know you're sitting in that attic right now, waiting for me.

Danny, I'm sorry that I couldn't always be there for

you. I wanted to be, but I couldn't. I never bad-mouthed your mother to you, and I'm not about to start now, but I hope that you understand why I wasn't there, and that you'll still love me. It might be hard for you now, but I know that one day, when you're older, you'll understand. I know that your mom and Rick may have told you things, but you're a smart boy, and I know you'll figure things out for yourself. You'll understand why I couldn't be there.

But Danny, I swear to you, I will never leave again. No more courts and no more lawyers. I am your father and I love you, and when I find you, I will never leave your side again.

I'll be there soon, I promise. It used to be a full day's drive from West Virginia to New Jersey, but it's taking me a little longer. We've run into trouble and some bad things happened. I told you about Carrie and the baby, and that almost destroyed me. If I didn't have you, Danny, I think it would have. I would have given up there. But I didn't, because I DO have you, and I will not fail you again. I've made a new friend, a preacher named Reverend Martin. I think you'll like him. He's a nice man. He says he can't wait to meet you. But there are some bad things happening, and it's slowed us down. We made two other friends, a man named Delmas and his son, Jason.

But they won't be coming with us now.

We're getting ready to leave here soon. Martin is sleeping and after I finish this, I'm going to grab a little sleep too. Or at least I'll try. I don't want to sleep, not even for an hour, because that's one extra hour I'll have to be away from you. But I'm tired, Danny, and I can't help it. I'm very tired.

But after I wake up, that's it. No more. Nothing else will delay us or slow us down. I'm coming, Danny. Daddy's coming and you've got to hang in there. You've got to stay strong. I'll be there soon, I promise. And when I get there, I'm going to wrap my arms around you and hug you so tight. And I'll never let you go.

I love you son. I love you more than infinity.

Daddy

CHAPTER FIFTEEN

Before moving on, they buried Delmas and Jason next to Bernice. Martin said a prayer over their graves, and Jim fashioned two makeshift tombstones using scavenged wood from the barn and a can of paint.

Leaving the Clendenan household and the solemn graves behind, they hiked through the woods, retracing their steps back to the Interstate. Along the way, they encountered several zombies, but had little trouble with them.

Both the preacher and the construction worker were becoming expert marksmen.

"Practice makes perfect," Martin joked.

Jim said nothing. Since Jason's suicide, Martin had noticed a change in his companion's behavior. He was silent, taciturn. Driven.

They were forced to walk from Interstate 64 to the spot where it merged with Interstate 81 before they finally found transportation. That added another full day to their progress and Jim grew even more withdrawn.

When they finally found a vehicle that still had the keys (an old, gray-primer Buick), they drove in darkness. Jim elected to not turn on the headlights, saying they would act as a beacon to anything lurking in the night. Reluctantly, Martin agreed with him. Luckily, the lanes on the Interstate were wide and mostly clear of debris, and they encountered no traffic.

Jim refused to stop and rest for the night, and Martin dozed in the seat next to him after receiving Jim's assurances that he would wake the Reverend up when he grew tired.

The air inside the car was stifling, and Jim rolled the window down, letting the cool breeze blow through his hair. The night was quiet. No tractor-trailers or cars passing in the southbound lane. No truck stops or restaurants lit up off the highway. No insects or horns or radios or airplanes.

It was a dead silence.

Martin stirred next to him.

"Go on back to sleep," Jim said softly. "You need your rest."

"No, I'm okay." He stretched, stifling a yawn. "Why don't you let me drive for a while? Get some rest yourself?"

"I'm alright, Martin. To be honest, I'd prefer to drive right now. Keeps my mind off things."

"Jim, I know that things look bleak. But you've got to trust in the Lord."

Jim snorted. "Martin, you're my friend and I respect you, but after everything we've seen, I'm not even sure that I believe in God anymore."

Martin didn't blink. "That's okay. You don't have to believe in God, Jim. Just know that He believes in you."

Jim shook his head and the old man pressed on, chuckling softly as he did.

"We've made it this far, right? I don't know about you, but I'd say we beat the odds. We should be dead by now, Jim, but we're not. Seems to me like He's been helping us along our way."

"Seems to *me* like He's throwing up roadblocks."

"No, that isn't His doing. 'God helps those who help themselves', remember? He's been helping us out of those scrapes."

"Like He helped Delmas and Jason? Like He helped my wife and our baby? If this is God's way of helping us,

Martin, then no offense, but He can fuck off!"

Martin was silent for a moment.

"You know," he said, "I used to hear young people joke about Hell, without any concept of what they were saying. 'I don't care if I go to Hell. All the cool people are there. It'll be a big party.' And when I heard them say that, part of me wanted to laugh and part of me wanted to cry. Jesus described Hell as an eternal fire, filled with the gnashing of teeth. It's a very real place, and it's anything but a party."

"And?"

"My point is, when it comes to the Lord, you can't make off-the-cuff comments like that, Jim. God is a god of love, but he's also the God of vengeance from the Old Testament."

"Sounds like he's got a split personality then."

Martin gave up, knowing that further discussion would be useless. There was too much bitterness in his companion's heart. It was hard to speak of faith to those who had none.

Martin closed his eyes, pretending to sleep again, and silently prayed for Jim's faith—and for his own as well.

* * *

Exhaustion finally forced Jim to let Martin drive. Just before dawn, the Buick's gas gauge dipped to empty and Martin woke him.

"We'll need to find another car soon."

"I can siphon, if we need to," Jim said. "I used to do it in high school."

They pulled off near Verona, spying an abandoned dairy farm just off the Interstate. They took the exit and then backtracked down a dusty, one-lane dirt road.

They heard the cries before they reached the end of the lane; a horrible, braying cacophony. It was coming from the barn.

"Cows?" Martin asked, dumfounded.

"I think so," Jim nodded, "but they don't sound alive."

A John Deere tractor, a huge combine, a mini-van with handicapped tags, and an old, rusting farm truck sat nearby.

"We should be able to get enough gas from those."

Exiting the Buick, they checked their surroundings for any signs of the living dead. Satisfied that it was clear, they listened to the wailing. Siren-like, it called to them, and they walked towards the barn.

The smell hit them before they opened the door, and Martin gagged. Guns at the ready, Jim gave the door a shove and let it swing open. The hinges creaked loudly as it opened.

The cows stood lined up in their stalls in neat rows. The cause of death was clearly apparent—for some, lacking a farmer to milk them, their engorged udders had finally exploded. Others had died of starvation. Now they stood imprisoned and rotting inside their pens. Insects crawled over their hides and into their flesh, and the droning buzz of flies almost drowned out the incessant mooing.

Martin coughed, and quickly covered his nose with the back of his hand. Grimacing, he backed out of the barn, and threw up in the tall weeds along the side.

Jim slowly walked down the aisle, methodically shooting each of the cows and stopping only to reload. When he was finished, he walked back outside. His ears were ringing and the gun smoke had irritated his eyes, making them bloodshot.

"Let's check the house. See if there's some keys for that truck or van."

"Maybe we should just siphon the gas and go." Martin wiped the bile from his lips, but Jim had already walked away.

They approached the front door, their boots clomping up the wooden steps. A wheelchair ramp had been built onto the side of the porch. Martin remembered the handicapped tags he'd noticed on the mini-van.

Jim tried the knob and found it unlocked. The door creaked open and they stepped inside. Jim flicked the light switch uselessly.

"Power's out here, too."

They found themselves in a neat and orderly living room. A layer of dust covered the furniture and knick-knacks, but the house seemed undisturbed. There was a hallway to the right that led to the kitchen, and an open doorway to their left that was concealed in a layer of white lace curtains. A stairway led up to the second floor, and the banister had a motorized lift attached to it. The lift sat halfway up the flight of stairs, and Martin assumed that it had gotten stuck there when the power went out.

"Yoo-hoo," Jim called, "anybody home?"

"Stop it," Martin hissed. "What's gotten into you?"

Jim ignored his whispered protests. "Come on out! We've got something for you!"

Silence was the only answer. Jim began scouring the shelves and tables for a set of keys.

"See if there's any keys for that mini-van in the kitchen and that side room. I'll look upstairs. Be careful."

Swallowing, Martin nodded and crept down the hall, his rifle thrust out in front of him, arthritic finger on the trigger.

The kitchen was also covered in dust. White cupboards displayed porcelain dishes and silverware. The sickly-sweet smell of rotting food drifted from the refrigerator, and Martin noticed thin strands of white, fuzz-like mold growing around the seam of the door. He had no desire to peek inside. A coat rack stood next to the back door, and a rain slicker and flannel jacket hung from the pegs. He checked the pockets of both, but they were empty.

Jim's footsteps pounded over his head, searching the rooms above, and Martin jumped. He walked back down the hall, crossed the living room, and parted the lace curtains with the barrel of his gun.

The bedroom was dark. The shades were drawn over the windows and Martin stopped to let his eyes adjust. After a moment, he began to make out the objects in the room; a bed, dresser, and a nightstand. A door in the rear stood slightly open, revealing a toilet. Parked next to it was the partial outline of a wheelchair.

"Nothing up here!" Jim shouted from upstairs.

Holding the rifle in the crook of his arm, Martin felt along the nightstand, knocking bottles and pocket change to the floor. Then his fingers closed upon a key-chain.

"Found them, I think!"

He sniffed the air. The stink from the kitchen was worse than he had first realized. He could smell it all the way in here.

He heard Jim's footsteps heading back to the stairs. Martin turned to leave, and from the bathroom came an electronic hum. The bathroom door swung open.

Martin turned, swinging the rifle up, just as the motorized wheelchair flew out of the bathroom and buzzed towards him. The occupant grinned toothlessly, revealing shriveled, blackened gums, and waved a disposable razor at him.

"Ain't got my teeth and you look pretty chewy," it slobbered. *"Nothing on you but gristle."*

Martin squeezed the trigger and the rifle cracked, punching a hole through the zombie's breast. The wheelchair continued to speed towards him. He fired again and ripped out the side of the creature's neck. As he was ejecting the empty shells, the zombie rammed him, knocking him backward. His teeth slammed together as he banged his head against the floor, and he tasted blood.

The force of the collision threw the zombie from the chair. It landed on top of him and cackled. Its fetid breath was in his face and Martin screamed.

He heard Jim hollering, and struggled to push the thing off of him. It coiled in his grasp like a snake, and licked his cheek with its scabrous tongue.

Balling his fist, he struck the creature in the face. The rank, toothless maw snapped at his knuckles, gumming them. Then the creature swiped at his face with the razor, sliding it across his cheek and savagely pressing down. He felt the dull blade bite into his skin, and Martin screamed again.

Wrapping a slimy hand around his throat, the creature drew the razor away and licked it.

"Mmmmm. Tasty. Not much on there, though. This might take awhile."

It sliced at him again, and suddenly, the crushing weight was gone from his chest and the fingers were ripped away from his throat.

Grabbing the zombie by its stringy hair, Jim flung it into the wall. Before it could move, he turned his gun around, holding it by the barrel, and smashed the stock against its face. The nose flattened, driving the bone into the brain, and Jim swung again. He brought the rifle down a third time and there was a wet, cracking sound as the zombie's head split open.

Flinging the rifle onto the bed, Jim grabbed the wheelchair, struggled to lift it off the ground, and then brought it down on the pulped remains as well. He hefted it a second time, then a third.

"Jim, it's dead!" Martin dabbed at his bleeding cheek with a corner of the bedspread.

Jim stood over the thing, breathing heavily.

"Thank you," Martin offered, then picked himself up off the floor with a groan.

"You okay?"

"Yes, I think so." He felt the knot on the back of his head, but his fingers came away bloodless. "Lucky I didn't break a hip."

"You found the keys to the van?"

"Yes, but I dropped them when that thing rushed me." He felt around on the floor. "Here they are."

"Let's go."

* * *

Shortly after dawn, they encountered a southbound caravan of survivors. The rag-tag group was traveling in a camper, several cars, and what appeared to be a modified dump truck. Both groups stopped, eyeing each other warily from across the wide, shrub-covered median strip.

Finally, a man exited the lead vehicle, an AR-15, the civilian version of the M-16, slung over his shoulder. He held his hands palm up in a cautious greeting. Jim and Martin got out of the van and did the same.

"He looks familiar," Martin whispered as they walked closer. "Is he somebody famous?"

Jim had been wondering the same thing. The stranger had an athletic build, recognizable even though it was hidden beneath layers of ragged clothing. His face was what Carrie would have called 'ruggedly handsome'— the same thing she had referred to Jim as being.

"Hi," the man greeted them. "You guys looking to trade, maybe?"

"Maybe," Jim agreed. "What have you got?"

"We've got fresh vegetables," the man said proudly. "We came across a greenhouse yesterday."

Their mouths watered at the thought. They hadn't eaten since leaving the Clendenan house.

"We can trade some guns and ammunition," Jim offered, "and maybe exchange some information."

The man laughed. "Well then gentlemen, allow me to invite you to lunch."

They walked around to the back of the dump truck, and Jim started when he caught sight of the two figures that had been lurking atop it: a boy and a woman, both pointing rifles at them. The two relaxed and lowered their weapons, and then Jim did the same.

The dump truck had been modified. A sheet metal roof was built over the open top, forming a camper of sorts. The man ushered them inside, and they found themselves staring at a group of people, comprising all ages and races.

"I'm Glen Klinger," the man offered.

"Jim Thurmond." They shook hands. "This is the Reverend George Martin."

"Pleased to meet you both." Klinger then introduced the other nine people in the back of the truck.

"Say," Martin mused, "aren't you that surfer fellow who was on Extreme Sports?"

Klinger grinned sheepishly. "That I am. I'm afraid you've got me."

Incredulous, Jim turned to Martin. "*You* watched Extreme Sports?"

"Used to love it," the preacher laughed. "This guy here was famous!"

They traded weapons and ammunition for vine-ripe tomatoes, as well as cucumbers and watermelons.

"Where you heading?" Jim asked him.

"Anywhere, I guess," the man shrugged uneasily. "We don't really have a plan. Someplace better than what we've seen so far. Somewhere alive. I was in Buffalo, doing some charity work when things started happening. I would have flown back to California, but by the time I made my decision to go, the NTSB had grounded all flights because of that pilot that had the heart attack while in the air."

"I didn't hear about that," Jim said. "News was spotty in West Virginia. What happened?"

"Well, he died in mid-flight, somewhere over Arizona. I guess they have a procedure for that, but they couldn't revive him. The co-pilot took over, then the dead Captain came back to life and attacked him. The plane crashed, taking out a swath of downtown Phoenix. They reconstructed the events from their calls to the controllers and from the black boxes. Of course, by the time they figured everything out, things were snowballing worldwide. How about you guys? Where are you heading?"

"New Jersey."

"Jersey?" Klinger scoffed. "That's suicide, friend. You'd be better off letting them get to you now. Anything close to New York City is pretty much wall-to-wall zombies."

"You've been there?"

"No, but we've heard. We drove down from Buffalo, picking up survivors along the way. It doesn't sound good. New York, Philly, Washington D.C., parts of Pittsburgh and Baltimore—really bad. Lot's of people lived in those cities, and they're staying there after they die. And it's not just the zombies either."

"What do you mean?" Martin quizzed him.

"There's a lot of crazy stuff going on. Gangs, skinheads, militias—all kinds of paramilitary survivalist nutcases on the loose. Hell, we even heard that the Army or somebody was trying to take over south-central Pennsylvania. There's no government anymore, man. No leaders. It's everyone for themselves. You guys would be better off heading back the way you came. Or come with us, if you'd like! We could use the extra help. At least in a group like this you've got a chance."

"Thanks for the offer," Jim said, "but there's somebody in New Jersey who only has one chance—us. We've got to be moving on now. Thanks for the food."

"It's your funeral."

"Is it?" Jim asked.

* * *

They drove in silence, hungrily sharing a watermelon on the seat between them and spitting the seeds out the window. At one point a bird darted downward, and Jim assumed it was going after a seed—until he noticed that it had no legs and was flying towards his open window. He sped up and they quickly passed it by.

"That's one bright point about all of this," Martin said.

"What's that?"

"Less roadkill. The carcasses along the side of the road get up and walk away now."

Jim laughed and the sound of it filled Martin with relief. Perhaps it was a signal that his friend was starting to come out of the fugue that Jason's suicide had induced.

But Martin noticed that the laughter, while genuine, never reached Jim's eyes.

* * *

An hour later, crossing the border into Maryland, Jim spotted a cluster of motorcycles ahead of them.

"Friendly?" Martin asked.

"We're about to find out," Jim answered, and floored it.

The van accelerated toward the six figures. The biker bringing up the rear turned as they approached. He wore no helmet, and was naked from the waist up. Most of the flesh on his chest and back were gone, exposing ribs and raw muscle. His eyes were hidden behind a pair of mirrored sunglasses hanging crookedly from his face.

"They look dead to me."

"Unfriendly then."

The motorcycles filled both northbound lanes, and Jim roared directly toward them, straddling the dotted line.

Hefting the shotgun, Martin leaned out the window. He fired, hitting the zombie's exposed chest.

"The head, Martin! Shoot for the head!"

"I'm aiming for the head! It's hard to do in a moving vehicle!"

A second zombie reached into his leather vest and pulled out a small caliber pistol—a Ruger. There was a sharp crack and the bullet pinged against the passenger side of the van.

"They're shooting at us!" Martin ducked back inside. Ejecting his spent shell, he leaned out of the speeding van and fired again. This time the zombie's sunglasses disappeared, along with its head. The bike collapsed, sliding into a second creature and sending them both careening towards the breakdown lane.

The zombie with the pistol squeezed off another shot, and a small hole appeared in the windshield.

"Jesus!" Jim exclaimed. "Hold on!"

He swerved into the right lane, bearing down on the shooter. The other three were slowing now, letting the van pull ahead of them. The zombie pointed the pistol over his shoulder, his outstretched arm aiming at the windshield again.

"Get ready!" Jim called and then zoomed the van into the breakdown lane. The zombie turned in confusion, swinging the pistol towards Jim.

"Now!"

Jim leaned back into his seat as far as he could go, and Martin leaned past him, pointing the shotgun out the driver's side window. The blast ripped the creature from the bike, and Jim swung around the wreckage and back onto the highway.

The rear window exploded, spraying glass all over the interior of the van.

"Get down!" Jim ordered, and Martin flung himself beneath the seat. Jim slouched down as far as he could and pressed the gas pedal to the floor.

"Fucking four-cylinder! Why couldn't we steal a good old V-8?"

Another volley of shots peppered the rear of the van. Martin cringed, waiting for it to stop, then popped up over the seat and returned fire. The zombies wheeled out of the way, and the van sped ahead of them.

"I'm empty," Martin informed him. "Can you buy me a minute?"

"Take the wheel."

"I don't think so."

"Then reload fast!"

Jim raced ahead with the zombies in pursuit and

then, at the last minute, bounced over the grass median strip and into the southbound lanes toward an exit ramp. The motorcycles shot past him, firing wildly. The van veered down the nearest exit ramp and then screeched away.

"Did we lose them?"

"I think so," Martin panted, watching for signs of pursuit. "There's no sign of them, anyway."

"We'll stay off Eighty-One for a while, just in case."

"Where are we?"

Jim searched his memory for the trips he'd used to take to see Danny.

"If I remember correctly, this runs over the Pennsylvania border and right into Gettysburg on Route Thirty. We can get back on Eighty-One there, by either doubling back to Chambersburg or going through York and taking Eighty-Three to Harrisburg. Either way, in Harrisburg we'll want to jump over to Seventy-Eight and that will run us into New Jersey."

"How long, do you think?"

"Six or seven hours," Jim answered. "A little more if we stop to piss or screw around with more of these things. If not, we'll be there by nightfall."

CHAPTER SIXTEEN

Baker cried out in horror when he saw the bodies.

They were suspended on X-shaped crosses, lining both sides of the road. Most of them were dead. Some of the dead were still moving, struggling uselessly against their bonds and the heavy railroad spikes that had been used to secure them.

The stench was overwhelming, and Baker pulled away from the small hole in the truck's side that he'd been peering through. He'd recognized the landscape and monuments as they drove by them as being Gettysburg, and he guessed correctly that the downtown district was their destination.

He briefly checked on Worm, and found the boy still curled up and sleeping soundly in the corner. What little light the holes in the truck allowed to filter through, made him look pale and drawn. Baker reached out with bound hands and gently brushed the boy's brow with his fingertips. Worm stirred in his sleep, and the worried creases in his forehead smoothed and vanished.

Holding his breath, Baker returned to the hole and peeked outside again. The truck was passing through some type of checkpoint, built from sandbags and barbed wire. Armed guards were posted every few feet, watching the direction they'd come from.

The truck rolled to a halt, and Baker heard muffled voices and laughter. Then they started forward again, into the group's stronghold.

Baker was reminded of footage he'd seen of the Warsaw ghetto during World War Two. Pitiful, filthy civilians slaved over their labors as the truck passed by; filling and piling sandbags, stretching thin but sturdy survival netting between the rooftops in an attempt to keep the birds and other airborne zombies out, hauling heavy furnishings from abandoned buildings, repairing the buildings that were still being used, pulling burned-out cars with harnesses strapped to their backs, cleaning the gutters along the streets—all done with a uniform look of hopelessness on their grimy faces. He noted the puzzling absence of women among the laborers; save for a few elderly crones here and there.

Bodies, not living dead but just plain old dead, dangled from the traffic lights, the poles having been turned into makeshift gallows. Baker wondered if they were there to serve as a warning to the workers, but then he noticed that a few of the hanging corpses wore military uniforms.

The truck halted again and Baker heard the motor cough, then cease. He moved away from the hole, kneeling on the floor next to Worm. The deaf-mute woke with a start and struggled in the darkness. Baker motioned for him to remain still.

Booted footsteps crunched along the side of the truck and then the back door rolled open, flooding the compartment with light. They blinked, momentarily blinded, and the soldiers pulled them out, forcing them to stand. Baker bent his knees, trying to work out the kinks in his legs.

An unkempt man in a soiled uniform strode toward them. His hair hung well past his collar and several days' growth of beard clung to his face. Baker noticed two silver vertical bars on his shoulder.

"Second Lieutenant Torres," Staff Sergeant Michaels saluted, "we completed our reconnaissance and have a full report. We lost Warner, I'm afraid, but we also captured two prisoners of remarkable interest."

Torres brusquely returned the salute and eyed Baker and Worm.

"They don't look that remarkable to me, Sergeant."

Michaels handed him Baker's credentials, and the officer studied them with interest.

"Hellertown, huh? Havenbrook—that was a weapons lab, wasn't it?" He clapped Michaels on the shoulder. "Well done, all of you. Colonel Schow will be very interested in talking to these gentlemen."

He turned to Baker.

"Welcome to Gettysburg, Professor Baker. I'm afraid your accommodations will be more rustic than you're used to, but perhaps if you cooperate, something better can be arranged."

"Cooperate how?" Baker asked.

"Well, we'll let the Colonel decide that."

He turned, addressing the rest of them. "Good job, men. Shame about Warner. Still, I think twenty-four hours leave is warranted for each of you. Staff Sergeant Miller's squad is on their way back as well, Michaels, and once they return we'll expect a full report from both of you. Their ETA is about another hour. You have time to grab a shower, if you'd like."

"Thank you, sir!" He snapped off another salute and Torres walked away.

"Oh hell yeah," Blumenthal cheered, "I'm heading for the bowling alley and then the Meat Wagon!"

"No you're not," Ford told him, "first you and Lawson are going to transfer the prisoners to the containment center. Make sure you tell Lapine to separate them from the rest of the scabs. I don't want anything happening to them until after the Colonel has interrogated them."

Lawson leered, grinding his pelvis against Worm's backside. "They'll make you squeal like a pig, boy!"

Worm hooted in indignation and Baker leapt forward.

"Leave him alone, god damn you!"

"Shit, you'll wish we'd kept him with us once the Colonel's done with you!"

Baker's fists clenched in anger, his nails digging into the skin of his palms. Blumenthal shoved him forward. He stared at Lawson as Blumenthal led him away, and he did not back down until the other man looked away, busying himself with Worm's bonds.

The containment center was an old movie theatre, one of the single-screen kind that had gone out of fashion with the arrival of the multiplex. Heavily armed guards patrolled the sidewalks surrounding the building, and stood watch from the roof. More loitered in the lobby, eyeing the new arrivals indifferently.

Blumenthal approached the ticket booth and addressed the guardsman inside.

"Two newbies for you, Lapine. Sergeant Ford wants you to keep them apart from the others."

"How the fuck am I supposed to do that?" the man complained. "We ain't got room for the townies we have now, and now you want me to find separate room for these two fucks?"

"I'm just doing what I'm told. You figure it out."

"There's a balcony we can put them in, I guess." He pointed at Baker. "What'd you do before the rising started, dickhead?"

"I'm a scientist," Baker told him, and bit his tongue to keep from saying *and I'm the one of the guy's who brought you this.*

"Scientist, huh," Lapine scoffed. "Well, I guess you can pick up trash or toss sandbags like everybody else."

"Not these two," Lawson informed him. "At least, not yet. Colonel wants to see 'em."

"Ooooo," Lapine mocked, "visiting dignitaries are they? Well then, let's get them stowed away safe and sound."

He stepped out from behind the glass window and motioned for two guards to relieve Blumenthal and Lawson. Then he marched them through the double doors and up a winding flight of stairs, stopping in front of a chained and padlocked door.

One of the burly guards pointed his M-16 at them while Lapine produced a key ring from his pocket and unlocked the chains. Then they escorted them inside.

"Most of the townies sleep below," he motioned, as if he were a tour guide, "but you two will be up here in the penthouse."

They stood in a balcony, overlooking the movie theater. The alcove had four reclining red velvet seats that were covered in mildew, and not much else. Below them, most of the chairs had been ripped out and thrown into corners. Moldy mattresses and heaps of straw littered the floor in their stead. The movie screen itself still stood, but was covered with scrawled graffiti and gouged in places.

Baker noticed a fifty-caliber machine gun protruding from the window of the projection booth. He also noted that steel plates had been welded over the two fire doors at the rear of the theatre, on each side of the screen.

The center aisle was filled with glittering shards of glass, visible even in the dim light. Baker looked upward and saw a brass chain dangling from the ceiling.

"Chandelier," Lapine said conversationally. "It was a beautiful thing—all crystal. The townies knocked it down and used the glass to try and cut up a bunch of our guys. Didn't make it far, but we lost some good men. Rounded up the ringleaders and crucified them out along the highway. You probably saw the crosses on the way in."

Reluctantly, Baker nodded.

"That's one way of dealing with them." His braying laughter echoed off the high-domed ceiling and dirty alabaster walls. "Of course, the funny part is when they die after they've been crucified. We really nail them down; restrict their muscles and everything.. They come back as the living dead and they're stuck! Ever see a zombie starve to death? Well, neither have I. So they just hang there, day in and day out. A couple of them eventually got to the point where their hands or feet rotted enough that they could tear free, so now we use 'em for target practice."

"Sounds very economical," Baker muttered sarcastically. "I'm sure Uncle Sam's accountants would be proud."

"Oh, that's not the only way Colonel Schow has for dealing with troublemakers," Lapine assured him. "Hangings are pretty effective. Firing squads. My favorite is the helicopter rides."

"And what are those, exactly?"

"Piss the Colonel off, and maybe you'll find out."

They left, shutting the doors behind them. Baker heard the chains rattle and the lock snap into place.

"Moovee," Worm said, pointing to the screen. "Moovee, Baykher."

"Yes indeed," he sighed to himself, collapsing into a damp seat. "Perhaps it's a double feature. *Night of the Living Dead* and *Apocalypse Now*. All we need is popcorn."

* * *

Because the interior of the HumVee was crowded with people, booty, and weaponry, they forced Frankie to sit in Skip's lap. The seating arrangements changed quickly when Miccelli discovered her working the ropes around her wrists against the Private's belt buckle, trying to saw through them. This earned them both a beating, and Frankie was thrown to the floor, where she was used as a footstool for Miccelli and Kramer.

Defiantly, she sank her teeth into Miccelli's calf, relishing his screams as his blood welled around her mouth.

That was when they raped her.

Frankie made no sound; did not move—even as they laughed, even when the pain started, even as they thrust in and out of her orifices, as she was battered inside and out, as they spilled their semen on her stomach and face. She lay completely still; drifted, going to her special place and reminding herself that it wasn't so bad, it was just like any other business transaction, and if she submitted, she would live.

Don't be ashamed, she reminded herself. *It's not your fault. You can't fight back now. If you do, they'll kill you. It's just your body. They can't touch your mind.*

She stayed in the secret place as Kramer relieved Miller at the wheel, and the Staff Sergeant took his turn with her.

In the secret place, she did not think about heroin or the baby.

This time, her fantasies were of revenge.

I'm a survivor. I've lived through worse, I can live through this.

Grunting in orgasm, Miller rolled off her prone form and wiped himself on her shirt.

"What do you think of that, bitch?"

"Is that the best you three can do?" Frankie replied. "I bet your wives all left you, didn't they?"

"She needs to be hosed off," Miccelli muttered. "Hold her down, will you Sarge?"

Perched atop her, Miller straddled her breasts, crushing her back to the floor. Miccelli unzipped his pants and urinated, the bitter yellow stream arcing over her face and running in rivulets down her neck. Frankie closed her eyes against the flow, gagging and coughing as the urine flowed over her eyes and nostrils and mouth.

"Don't you hit me with it!" Miller warned, then joined them in laughter.

"You bastards!" Skip groaned from his seat. "Leave her alone!"

Miller backhanded him, and Skip's already swollen lips burst open again.

"Don't worry about your girlfriend, Private. Better worry about yourself instead."

"Feel better after your shower?" Miccelli jeered.

"Shit," Frankie grinned. "My pimp was doing that when I was seventeen, you dickhead. And he did it better. At least he had a prick to pee with."

Miller and Kramer laughed at this, and Miccelli glared down at her.

"We'll see how you talk after the rest of the boys have had a turn with you."

He raised his foot, aiming a kick at her head, but Miller stopped him.

"Enough. Don't mess her face up. Let her rest for now. She'll be getting hers soon enough, that's for sure."

They went to work on Skip next.

* * *

Frankie was horrified by the same things Baker had seen as they drove into town, but she stared at them anyway so she wouldn't have to see Skip's face. Kramer, Miller and Miccelli had taken turns with him, just as they had her, and while he hadn't been raped, physically he was in worse shape than she was.

His broken nose had swollen to a bulbous, fleshy knob, and dried blood had crusted both nostrils. More blood caked his battered lips and when he breathed through his mouth, she could see the raw spaces where teeth were missing. There was a massive gash above his left eyebrow and another on his forehead. The skin of his right cheek had been flayed open and hung in a flap down the side of his face. One eye had swollen shut and the other was dark and bruised.

Despite all of this, he had remained conscious, and Frankie thought that perhaps that was the most horrible part of all. Skip apparently had no secret place in which to mentally retreat. He had been brave at first, but after numerous merciless and savage blows and cuts, he had begun to scream. It was a long time before he stopped.

The screams still rang in her ears, though now the injured man only wheezed.

The squad was met by Second Lieutenant Torres, just as Michaels' squad had been, and were given their orders. Torres nodded grimly when he was informed of Skip's dissent, and ordered him confined to the containment center.

"Put her with the rest of the whores and let her get cleaned up," Miller told Kramer after Torres had left. "And Miccelli, you take this traitorous fuck over to the movie theater like the Lieutenant said. I've gotta go to the debriefing."

Kramer grabbed Frankie's arm and dragged her away, while Miccelli forced Skip to walk ahead of him at gunpoint. Suddenly, Frankie whirled.

"Skip!"

He turned slowly, with great effort, and Miccelli shoved the gun into his back.

"Thank you," she said simply, and despite the pain that it caused him, Skip smiled at her. It was a horrible image to behold, and Frankie had to struggle not to turn away at the sight. Then Miccelli shoved him, leading him away from her.

"Blow your boyfriend a kiss goodbye," Kramer jeered. "You won't be seeing him again."

"You're name's Private Kramer, right?" Frankie asked.

"Private First Class Kramer," he corrected her, puffing out his chest proudly. "And don't you forget it."

"First class asshole is more like it," Frankie said calmly. "Before this is all over, Private First Class Kramer, I'm going to kill you. And don't you forget it."

He glared at her, his face turning red with fury. He swung the M-16 up, aiming it at her face and grunted something unintelligible.

"What was that?"

"I said move!" he screamed.

As she let him lead her away, Frankie couldn't help but smile.

* * *

Miller entered the debriefing room to find Michaels, Torres, Captains Gonzalez and McFarland, and Colonel Schow already seated and waiting for him. A service station map of the state of Pennsylvania hung from one wall and a topographical survey map hung from another. He snapped off a quick salute, poured himself a cup of instant coffee, and took a seat next to Michaels.

"Sorry if I kept you all waiting."

"That's quite alright," Colonel Schow smiled. "Sip your coffee and relax, Sergeant Miller." His voice was soft, and there were times when the other men had to strain to hear it; but it was also cold.

Very, very cold.

Schow was not a big man, but his presence filled the room regardless. His five-foot eight, one hundred and seventy-five-pound frame wasn't imposing, but the way he carried it was. He moved like a cat; swift, graceful and deadly. He never raised his voice above the brittle, clipped tone, but when he spoke, people listened. He displayed the uncanny ability to finish the thoughts and sentences of those under his command, almost as if he could read minds. But perhaps the most disconcerting thing about him, Miller thought, was that Colonel Schow never blinked.

Never. He'd bet Michaels a case of beer on it one time, back when they were still both new recruits, fresh out of boot camp, and he'd won.

Schow was like a snake; silent and watchful.

And venomous.

Captain Gonzalez cleared his throat.

"Staff Sergeant Michaels, why don't you begin." It was not a question.

"Yes sir. We did recon on Harrisburg. The city is uninhabitable. High undead concentration, and what survivors are left are mostly marauders—gang-bangers, bikers—groups like that. No heavy weaponry—nothing that would withstand an armored regiment at least. We could take it as an expansion base, but if we went in, we'd be doing a lot of urban combat, for which the tanks would be useless; we'd just destroy what we were trying to obtain. They have enough resistance to where I feel our casualties would be excessive. The city presents no desirable incentive for re-supply either, as scavengers have looted most of the non-perishable food stores and other goods."

"What about the two prisoners you captured, Sergeant?" Schow asked. "Tell us about them."

"Well sir, we ran into them, almost literally, on the return trip. The zombies launched an aerial and ground attack, primarily using undead birds. During the skirmish, we lost Private Warner."

"Otherwise you were unscathed?" Schow interrupted.

"Yes sir."

"That's acceptable then. Please continue."

"During the confrontation, we encountered the two men in question, and after obtaining their I.D., we were able to determine that one of them worked for the Havenbrook National Laboratories facility in Hellertown; a Professor William Baker. He was the director for the RHIC project. You might remember that from the news?"

"That thing that was gonna make a black hole, right?" Miller asked.

"The Relativistic Heavy Ion Collider." Schow steepled his fingers together. "There was a series of fascinating articles about it in several of the trade publications."

"Well, that's what this Baker was working on." Michaels pulled Baker's identification from his pocket and slid it across the table. "Pretty high level security clearance, I would think."

"The highest," Schow mused, then passed the laminated badge to Gonzalez and McFarland. "As Director, he would have had access to virtually everything in the facility."

"Permission to speak, Colonel?" Miller interrupted.

"Go ahead."

"Begging your pardon, but how does this help us?"

Schow paused, his thin smile parting to reveal a set of gleaming white teeth.

"Havenbrook was one of the U.S. Government's foremost research facilities, Sergeant. That's what the public was told. Forget what your amateur conspiracy theorists said about Area 51 and Groom Lake. Oh, those facilities exist as well, as most Americans know, but they are used for mostly experimental aircraft development."

"Havenbrook," Gonzalez told him, picking up where the colonel had finished, "was, among other things, a weapons lab. Biological, chemical, ballistics—you name it, they did it. They had more bugs than Fort Deitrich."

"So we're gonna help ourselves to the arsenal?" Miller guessed.

"You only see part of the picture, Sergeant," Schow told him. "Havenbrook is vast—huge. It would have to be, to contain all of those different projects. On the surface, it looks like any other facility. Heavy security around the perimeter, but once inside there's only a few office buildings, or perhaps a hangar or two. That's because the majority of the complex is underground. From what I've read, there are miles of tunnels. It's impregnable."

Miller whistled. "That would make one hell of a base of operations."

"Indeed," Schow grinned, "Think of the possibilities that presents. Every day, we are beset by more and more of these creatures. The Sons of the Constitution militia holds sway over much of Western Pennsylvania and it is only a matter of time before they turn this way. Renegade, makeshift armies squabble in the ruins and all the while these creatures multiply. We need to establish a permanent stronghold, something other than Gettysburg. Otherwise, we won't last the winter here. Indeed, we'll be lucky to last another month, because despite all of our weaponry and manpower, we are dealing with a primary enemy that has a distinct advantage over us. It needs only a dead body. These days, the number of dead bodies far outweigh the number of living. We are not fighting for conquest or land or ideals. We are fighting for survival—for our very right to stay alive! And only the strong can do that. This thing that has happened is nature's way of winnowing out the weak. But we are not weak, are we men? No! We are strong! That's what those civilians out there don't understand. They think us cruel and harsh because of our means. But the fact that they do not agree with our methods proves them weak, and therefore, unfit to survive. This is a war that we must win, and Havenbrook may prove a very suitable place to start doing just that."

He paused, took a sip of coffee, and then finished. "And now Miller, in the popular idiom of today's youth, you know what time it is."

"Is this Baker cooperative?" McFarland asked Michaels.

"Not so far," the Sergeant told him, "but I'm sure he can be persuaded to be."

"What about the other man that was taken with him?"

"No, just a deaf mute—a retard of some kind. Not sure how they came to be together, but the scientist definitely has a bond with him."

"Then he'll cooperate," Schow said. "Have them brought to me. I want to learn everything this man knows about Havenbrook before we go there. Layout and design, if there is still power functioning, what security systems are still working, manpower, and most importantly, how many of those things are holed up there, if any. He'll serve as a very useful tour guide, I believe."

Pursing his lips, he blew on his coffee to cool it, took a sip, and then turned to Miller.

"Now, Sergeant, I'd like you to advise us of your findings."

Miller reported all that had transpired on the mission. When he was finished, they sat in silence for a moment.

"That's a shame about Private Skip," Torres said finally. "I actually liked that kid."

"Perhaps we can use his punishment for insubordination as a learning tool for our new resident scientist. Lieutenant Torres, have the helicopter made ready. I want all three prisoners, our wayward Private, the Professor, and his unfortunate companion, brought to me. We're taking them for a little ride."

* * *

"If we put him in with the rest of the townies, they'll rip him apart when they come back from their work details tonight, just like the zombies would."

Baker recognized the voice outside the door as Lapine's, and he pulled his feet off the ledge where he'd propped them while he rested. The key clinked in the lock and the chains rattled as they were drawn away from the door. Worm noticed Baker's quick movements and followed his pensive stare.

The door to the balcony swung open, and a severely battered soldier stood flanked by four armed guardsmen, as well as Lapine. They shoved the injured man forward and the door slammed shut behind them.

The man sprawled over the back of the chair and then collapsed, huddled and twitching, onto the seat.

"Are you okay?" Baker took a tentative step towards him.

"Ahm fyn," the man mumbled through his ruined mouth. "Mah namez Schip."

Jesus, he sounds like Worm! Baker thought.

"I'm William Baker, and this is my companion Worm."

"Hu were on Shee Enn Enn—the blak hole mashine."

"Yes, I was on CNN," Baker admitted in surprise.

"You remember me?"

"Shoor, buht kin hu echzcuse mee fo' a shecond?" the man grinned, and pink drool ran down his mangled cheek. He bent over, coughed, and then spit three broken teeth and a wad of bloody phlegm onto the floor. Baker stared, horrified.

"Sorry about that." His voice, while still hoarse, was clearer now, but Baker could still see that it hurt him to talk.

"It's okay," Baker assured him. "Let's take a look at you, Mr. Skip. I'm afraid the light in here isn't so good, but I'll see what I can do."

"You a medical doctor too?" Skip winced as Baker gently but firmly felt his head.

"No, but I did take pre-med in college." He turned Skip's head to the left and right. "Does that hurt?"

"Yes," Skip grimaced "but that's okay."

"What happened to you?"

"This is what happens when you don't follow orders. What about you guys? They raid the Hellertown facility?"

"No," Baker answered, "but how do you know so much about us?"

"I told you—I saw it on CNN. You guys were the ones working on the black hole machine. Had some other guys working on sentient computers and cloning and all kinds of stuff."

"The Relativistic Heavy Ion Collider was what I worked on—what you called the black hole machine. It was just one of many projects, and they kept us pretty much in the dark about the others so I can't verify those."

"Well Professor, you better hope Schow doesn't know about the others. That's why you're here, right?"

"It would seem so, yes. They said he would want to question us. They seemed to think Hellertown was primarily some type of weapons lab."

"So how'd they get you, and who's he?" Skip cocked a thumb at Worm, who was staring down into the theatre.

"I guess you could call him my son, of sorts. I'm his

guardian at least. I found him during my travels and I've become quite attached to him. He's a remarkable young man. As to your first question, we were captured by some of your fellow National Guardsmen near Harrisburg. I take it you're from the same platoon or squadron?"

"Something like that," Skip agreed, not in the mood to give a lesson in military terminology. "But I ain't like the rest of them. They're animals. And Schow's the worst. Him and McFarland and Gonzalez. They're fucking crazy!"

He spat more blood over the side of the balcony. It made a distant splat below. Worm watched it, giggled, and then followed suit. Skip grinned at him and ruffled his hair.

"What will this Colonel Schow do to us?" Baker asked.

"Hard to say," Skip shrugged, dabbing at his face with his shirttail. "But if I were you, I'd tell him whatever he wants to know."

"But that's just it!" Baker exclaimed. "I don't know what he wants us for! I don't know anything. And even if I did know something, doesn't it stand to reason that he'd just kill us after I'd told him whatever it is he thinks I'm good for?"

"He probably would," Skip said, "but trust me, if you're in Schow's hands, you're better off as one of those things out there than as his prisoner. Speaking of which, I've got something to do."

He limped back over to the balcony, where Worm was still spitting over the side in delight, and looked down.

"Hmmm, only thirty feet. Not a far enough drop."

"What do you mean?" Baker asked.

"Like I said, you're better off dead than in their clutches. They've got me already. I planned to throw myself off this ledge but the drop isn't far enough. I could end up just breaking my legs and then I'd be even worse off."

Horrified, Baker wondered how sinister this Colonel Schow could be, to inspire this man to commit suicide rather than face him. Surely, he couldn't be that bad?

A moment later, when he heard voices outside the door again, Baker knew that he was about to find out.

"On your feet, assholes," Lapine sneered, "Colonel Schow has requested your presence. You're going for a little ride."

CHAPTER SEVENTEEN

Martin leaned forward in the seat, his wrinkled hands gripping the dash.

"Is that what I think it is, Jim?"

They'd just passed the sign for Gettysburg, and Jim slowed to a stop. Directly ahead of them, two HumVees and a tank blocked the road. Several men in military uniforms milled about the roadblock, their attention now focused on the car. The tank's turret swiveled toward them.

"I don't believe it! They're soldiers, Jim!" Martin exclaimed. "It's the Army!"

"National Guard, I think," Jim corrected him, "but what the hell are they doing here?"

"Maybe this is a buffer zone! Maybe we're leaving the affected area?"

"No, that doesn't make any sense. If that were true, then why would New Jersey be affected? This was worldwide. And remember what Klinger told us?"

"He said the army was taking over south-central Pennsylvania."

"Right. I don't like this, Martin."

"What can we do? Those guys have machine guns, Jim! We can't outfight a tank!"

Weapons pointed at the car, two of the men approached them and tapped on the window. They did not smile.

"Gentlemen, I'm going to ask you to exit your vehicle."

"Sure," Jim replied, trying to stay calm. "Can you just tell us what's going on?"

"We've got zombies in the perimeter, sir. It's for your own protection."

As if to verify this, one of the soldiers seated behind the HumVee's machine guns suddenly looked alert.

"Two o'clock!" he called, and swung the weapon towards the field.

A cluster of zombies were weaving their way through a row of civil war monuments, heading towards the road. Jim and Martin could smell them even from this distance.

The man atop the HumVee opened fire, mowing them down in their tracks. Limbs and torsos were scattered, and still the creatures advanced, until the barrage reached their heads. Then they lay still.

"If you would, sirs." The soldier indicated the door, and reluctantly they complied.

"Lucky you fellows came along," Martin said. The troops did not reply.

"Sirs, we're going to have to check you for weapons. I'm sure you understand."

"But just tell us what is—"

"Put your hands on the fucking car now!"

Two more ran forward and slammed Martin against the car. Blood spurted from his nose and he cried out in pain and terror.

"Hey," Jim shouted, "you son of a bitch, can't you see he's old? What the hell is going on?"

Enraged, his fists balled in anger, he started forward. The soldier behind him kicked at his legs, knocking him to the ground. Two more fell on him, wrestling with him until they could snap a pair of handcuffs on him. Two more trussed up Martin.

"What is the meaning of this?" Martin demanded.

"You gentlemen are now civilian volunteers," the soldier informed them. "Please come with us."

"Do we have a choice?" Martin quipped.

"You don't understand!" Jim struggled in their grip. "I've got to get to my son!"

"Not any more you don't," the man told him, "as of this moment, you've both been drafted."

"You bastards," Jim screamed. "You god-damn fucking bastards! Let us go! My son needs me!"

They dragged them toward the vehicles, and Jim watched the car, and New Jersey, get farther and farther away.

* * *

Frankie shivered, crossing her arms to her breasts as she walked down the corridor. The hospital was cold, and she could see her breath under the bright fluorescent lights.

The hallway was silent except for her footsteps. She grimaced as she breathed in the sterile, chemical smell that permeated all hospitals. Underneath it, Frankie detected another smell, faint but still unmistakable. The reek of spoiled meat and carrion flesh.

The perfume of the undead.

She stopped in front of a set of double doors and ran her fingers over a sign hanging on the wall.

MATERNITY WARD

She pushed and the doors swung silently open. She stepped through. The stench was stronger in this wing of the building.

She stood in front of the glass observation window, staring at the dozens of little white cribs that were lined up in neat, orderly rows. Each crib was occupied. Tiny fists and feet pumped the air, and here and there she spied a tuft of downy hair peeking over the rims.

I wonder which one is mine?

Her question was answered a moment later, as a pair

of mottled, grey arms gripped the side of the crib and her baby pulled itself upright. Standing on diminutive legs, the baby climbed down to the floor and scampered over to its nearest neighbor. It scurried into the crib and fell upon the other newborn.

The other babies began to cry as one.

Frankie could hear the chewing sounds, even over the cries of the other babies and through the thick glass partition.

Even over her screams.

"Stop it! Stop it!"

Somebody was poking her and she opened her eyes, lashing out.

"Stop it!" she hollered one last time, and then glanced around in bewilderment.

A young girl, no more than fourteen, flinched away from her. The girl was pretty, and Frankie thought to herself that she was going to be a heartbreaker. Probably of mixed descent, possibly Hispanic and Irish. But underneath her mournful, dark eyes were black circles. Both the eyes and the circles beneath spoke of harsh lessons learned before they should have been. Frankie had had the same look when she was the girl's age.

"Sorry," the girl apologized. "You were having a bad dream."

"Where am I?"

"In the Gettysburg Fitness Center," the girl said. "This is where we stay in between shifts on the Meat Wagon."

"The what?"

"The Meat Wagon," the girl repeated. "It's where they make us do the sex things. My name's Aimee."

"Hello Aimee. My name is Frankie. Now would you mind telling me how I can get out of here."

"You can't. They'll kill you if you try. It's not so bad, really. Some of them are even nice to you while they stick their thing in you."

"Aimee, come away from there now!"

The woman who spoke was obviously the girl's mother. Frankie noticed the same pale skin, high cheekbones, and flowing, raven-like hair. Like the daughter, the woman's eyes spoke of suffering and pain, humiliation and hopelessness.

Frankie knew the look well. She'd worn it herself, in what now seemed like a lifetime ago.

"I'm Gina," the woman introduced herself. "Are you thirsty? Would you like some water?"

"Don't suppose you have any painkillers I can wash down with it?" Frankie winced, touching her bruised face. Her shoulder and ribs were in agony, and her split lip throbbed in pain. She wished for some skag, then forced the thought away.

"Sorry," Gina said, "but they won't let us keep anything like that. I guess they're afraid some of the girls might swallow a handful of aspirin. Sometimes I think that might be a better alternative."

She handed Frankie a bottle of water and a cigarette. Frankie drank eagerly and then took a drag, letting the bitter, acrid smoke fill her lungs. She exhaled with a sigh.

"I never used to smoke," Gina said, "but I figure lung cancer is the least of my worries now. At least it's a quiet death."

"Yeah," Frankie mused "it sure as shit beats becoming a midnight snack for one of those things. Thanks."

She took another drag and looked around the room. True to the girl's word, she was in the gutted remains of a gym. The weight benches and exercise machines had been removed, and strewn in their place were mattresses and blankets. About two dozen other women lounged about, most of them eyeing Frankie with laconic interest, while a few others slept. The oldest woman appeared to be in her late fifties. Aimee was the youngest.

"So what's the deal?" Frankie asked.

"They work us in shifts," Gina told her. "They've got a massive tractor trailer that they've outfitted into a mobile whorehouse. Keeps up the spirits of the troops and all that. They call it 'The Meat Wagon'. It's got bunk beds and office cubicle partitions that form little rooms. It—it gets easier. As long as you don't resist, most of them treat you okay, or at least indifferently. A few of them are rough, but I've managed to distract them from Aimee so far."

She paused and took another drag from the cigarette. Then she exhaled and said, "Still, every night, I die a little."

"You've got to put yourself somewhere else while it happens," Frankie counseled her. "Detach from your body."

Gina stared at her, mouth open but unable to speak.

Frankie shrugged. "I used to do this for a living."

The door opened and twelve more women entered, looking tired and smelling of sex and sweat. Several of them were crying softly. Four armed men followed behind them and took positions at the door.

"Next shift," one of them barked. "You twelve! Get a move on!"

Moving with a resigned shuffle, twelve more women followed them out and the women who had just come from the truck took their places, collapsing onto the vacant mattresses.

"Aimee and I will have to go in a few hours," Gina said, "but I imagine they'll let you recuperate at least one night."

"Hey," called a nasally, shrill voice from across the room, "who's the skinny black bitch sleeping in my bed?"

"Oh shit," Gina muttered and moved away quickly, not meeting Frankie's eyes. "I'm sorry."

"Whatchu doing in my bed, ho?"

The woman shoved her way forward through the crowd, and Frankie lazily watched her approach. She was big; bloated to the point of obesity, but solid. Lifeless, dishwater blonde hair clung to her head in a bowl-cut, and her mounds of flesh strained against her faded jeans and black t-shirt.

"That's Paula," Aimee whispered, but Gina quickly clamped a hand over the girl's mouth.

"I didn't see your name on it," Frankie said, and deliberately took another puff. "But then again, we haven't been introduced, so I wouldn't have known what name to look for."

"Oh, ain't you a fucking smart mouth!" Paula exclaimed. "What's your name, sweetheart?"

"Frankie."

"Frankie? That's a guy's name." She brayed laughter, hands cocked on her ample hips. None of the other women moved, hypnotized by the scene unfolding before them.

"Well, *Frankie*," she emphasized her name, "I'm Paula."

"Paul?"

"Paula! What the fuck, you deaf? P-A-U-L-A...Paula!"

Frankie looked down at the mattress. "Nope, no Paula here. It does say 'Property of a Bull Dyke Bitch' though. Is that you?"

The women in the room gasped as one, and began to back away from the combatants. Paula gaped at Frankie in astonishment, clearly unaccustomed to this type of response.

"What did you say?"

Slowly, Frankie rose to her feet and faced the larger woman. She pressed forward till their breasts were almost touching. Then she removed the cigarette from her mouth and blew the smoke into Paula's eyes.

"I said to fuck off bitch, before I jack your fat ass up."

Paula moved fast, but Frankie was quicker. The big woman swung a fist at the side of her head and Frankie dodged it. With her other hand, Paula reached and grabbed a fistful of Frankie's hair, twisting it savagely. Grunting, Frankie thrust forward with the still glowing cigarette butt, and shoved it into her attacker's eye.

Screaming, Paula let go of Frankie's hair and reared

backward, her hands clawing at her face. Frankie aimed a kick at her mid-section and felt her foot sink into the doughy flesh. Paula sank to her knees, shrieking in agony.

"I'll kill you bitch!" she screamed.

The other women were shouting now, unanimously cheering the newcomer on. The door burst open and two guards dashed in, attracted by the commotion. Seeing a catfight in progress, they held back and watched in enjoyment, quickly placing bets.

Paula lashed outward blindly, grasping at Frankie's legs, but she darted back and circled around behind the crouching woman. As Paula turned in pursuit, Frankie slapped her face, then backhanded her a second time. It felt like hitting a side of beef, and Frankie's hand stung, immediately going numb. The wounds she'd received during the rape were reopening, and Frankie knew she had to end this quickly.

Suddenly, Paula rose to her feet and charged her, frothing with rage. Frankie tried again to sidestep her, but this time the larger woman was too quick. Her massive weight bore them both to the floor, and Frankie's breath was forced out of her lungs as Paula crushed down on top of her.

Paula head-butted her, and then began to pound her chest and face, clubbing her senseless. Frankie tried to shout, tried to scream, and found she could do neither.

The crowd was circling them now, some chanting for Paula but the majority openly encouraging Frankie.

Paula tilted her head backward and brought it crashing down again. Just before it struck her, Frankie opened her mouth and bit down on her attacker's nose. Blood and mucous ran across her tongue and she clamped down hard. Paula thrashed on top of her, shaking her head furiously, but Frankie ground her teeth together, locking her jaws.

With a mighty effort, Paula heaved herself backward, and suddenly, Frankie could breathe again—after she spit out the tip of the woman's nose.

Paula had forgotten all about her now. Delirious from shock and pain, she cupped her mangled face in her hands. Blood streamed from between her fingers, flowing from both her nose and her right eye.

Frankie moved in for the kill.

One of the guards fired a single shot into the air. Plaster rained down upon them, and the cheering women scattered.

"That's enough," one of them warned her. "Step away."

Training their weapons on Frankie, they moved toward them and pulled Paula's gore-stained hands away from her face.

"Take her out back and shoot her," one of them dismissed her casually. "This new one's a good enough replacement. She was too fucking fat anyway."

With some effort, they dragged the sobbing woman from the room, her blood leaving a trail behind them.

The room was completely still for a moment, and then all of the women began talking at once. Frankie's numb hands were pumped repeatedly, the bruises on her back slapped in joy and exultation.

"She was horrible," Gina said. "She beat several of the girls in here, even raped them herself, in between shifts."

"You're welcome," Frankie muttered, collapsing onto the bed. "Now give me another cigarette, would you?"

* * *

The space inside the helicopter was cramped and tight, and Baker felt a wave of claustrophobia that was even worse than the spell that had gripped him while climbing up the elevator shaft during his escape from Havenbrook.

Skip, Worm, and he sat back to back on the floor. Their hands and feet were tied behind them. Schow, McFarland, and Gonzalez were seated around them.

Torres sat up front, next to the pilot.

"We've spotted some just up ahead, Colonel!" Torres shouted above the roar of the rotors and Schow nodded in understanding. When he spoke, he didn't raise his voice, but Baker could understand him perfectly, despite the din.

"Enjoying the view, Professor Baker?"

"I'm afraid that I can't see much from where I'm sitting."

"That will change soon enough, Professor. I promise you a better vantage point. Now tell me, is there anybody left alive at Havenbrook."

"I've told you repeatedly, not that I know of. But Havenbrook is a large facility! You can't imagine the scope and size. As for the rest of it, I can't speak for some of the other secure areas, since I was never inside them."

"Indeed," Schow trimmed his fingernail calmly, "so you've insisted. Just you and this—Ob—I believe you referred to it as, yes?"

"Correct," Baker said. "Ob was what it called itself. You've got to understand, Colonel, these things are not the people we knew when they were alive. Once the body dies, these creatures inhabit it. They use it as a host; a vehicle of sorts."

"Fascinating. And why do you suppose this possession occurs only after the victim has died?"

"Because these demons, for lack of a better word, occupy the place where the soul was. The soul needs to have departed before they can move in."

"The soul, eh? Then tell me Professor, if this is true, why do the animals become zombies too? Do animals have souls?"

"I don't know," Baker exclaimed, "Nor do I want to have a philosophical argument with you Colonel. I'm a scientist. I'm only reporting what I've learned."

"You were a fairly celebrated scientist, were you not?"

Baker didn't reply.

"You were. My men tell me they saw you on CNN.

Never watched it myself. Too biased. But I read a great deal, and I'm familiar with your work. You were numero uno. The big man. The head cheese. I'm sure there's more than you're willing to tell me. I can respect that. Perhaps you don't want to betray your security clearance. But there's no government left to betray, Professor. I'm it—all that's left in this part of the country. Consider that for a moment, if you would."

"I've already told you, Colonel, that I will not go back to Havenbrook. It's madness to try! Whatever it is that you think you'll find, let me assure you that you won't. The only thing left at Havenbrook is a creature of great evil!"

Ignoring him, Schow turned his attention to Skip.

"What are *your* thoughts, Private?"

"I think you're insane," Skip responded. "You're going to kill me anyway, so fuck you, Colonel Schow. Fuck you very much, you crazy asshole."

"Kill you?" Schow put on a show of mock wounding, clasping his hand to his chest. "Kill you? No, Private, you misunderstand. You were found guilty of treason, and worse yet, cowardice. We're simply going to give you a chance to prove your bravery again."

He began to laugh and a second later, Gonzalez, McFarland and Torres joined him.

"We're over the target now sir," the pilot reported from the front.

"Good!" Schow became animated. "Let us begin. Gentlemen, if you would."

McFarland and Gonzalez left their seats and removed something long and black from the storage box. Baker couldn't tell what it was, but it appeared to be made of rubber. Even though he couldn't see Skip, he felt the man shaking against him.

They hooked one end of the item to a winch, and Baker realized that it was a bungee cord.

"Take us down a bit," Torres ordered the pilot, "then level it off."

"Oh no," Skip pleaded. "Come on, Colonel. Not this! Anything but this!"

"I'm afraid it's too late for that, Private. I lied. We are going to kill you after all. Of course, as you've already indicated, you were well aware of that fact when we got on the helicopter. Just take heart in the fact that you will get to prove your bravery before you die."

The two officers strapped a harness around his midsection. His hands and feet still tied behind him, Skip was unable to resist. Instead, he began to make choking noises in his throat. Baker realized the man was literally choking on tears.

"Please," he begged, "don't do this, man! For God's sake, don't do this! Not like this. Just shoot me—shoot me and be done with it!"

"There is no honor for you in that," Schow told him calmly. "And to be honest with you, Private, I would not want to waste the ammunition."

Skip moaned. They dragged him over to the door and slid it open. A blast of cold air rocked them all, and Baker cringed against it. Skip's mouth was moving silently, and his eyes looked ready to explode from his head.

"Please, shoot me! Cut my fucking throat! But don't do this!"

"Any last words?" McFarland asked him.

"Yeah," Skip said, his panic suddenly replaced with an icy resolve. "Fuck you crazy, sadistic mother-fuckers! I hope you all die! Don't tell them anything Baker! Don't lead them to Havenbrook cause they'll just kill you too when you're done!"

He leaned forward and spat in Schow's face.

Schow's expression remained calm, emotionless. He waved a disinterested hand at Skip and wiped the saliva away with a handkerchief.

"Bon voyage!" Gonzalez called, and pushed him out the door.

Skip's scream was one long, drawn out wail, and Baker closed his eyes and waited for it to fade.

"Show them," Schow ordered, and they dragged Baker and Worm to the door.

Skip plummeted headfirst toward the ground, the bungee cord trailing along behind him. Below the helicopter lay a barren field, and in the field, a crowd of zombies had gathered in anticipation.

Skip fell directly toward them. He closed his eyes as the wind whistled in his burning ears, feeling his stomach drop into his throat. His bowels and bladder weakened at the same time, and the foul warmth inside his trousers seeped out and ran down his back, his chest, then into his hair, before falling ahead of him.

As Baker watched in horror, the zombies craned their heads and arms toward the offering from the sky. Skip landed in their midst, but then the cord snapped tight and he shot upward again, the helicopter rocking slightly as he did.

Down he went again and this time, the zombies managed several bites before he was pulled back skyward.

Worm cried out and buried his chin against his chest, squeezing his eyes shut. Baker found he could not look away, even though he desperately wanted to.

Bleeding and screaming, gravity brought Skip down for a third descent, and this time the zombies latched on tight. They clustered around him, pushing and shoving at each other in their rush to get at him. The wave of human bodies crashed upon him, bearing him to the ground, and began to tear at him. Skin and muscle were torn away, and limbs were gnawed down to the bone.

The helicopter rocked again under the sudden additional weight.

"Steady," Torres cautioned. "Don't lose it."

McFarland and Gonzalez were laughing.

"I love this shit!" Gonzalez clapped the other man on the shoulder. "Look at them go! It's like a school of piranha. They're so hungry, they ain't even leaving enough to get up and walk around."

"Yes, they will," McFarland argued. "They always do. They'll leave the head at least."

Schow said nothing, watching impassively, as if he was bored.

"Heh," Gonzalez snorted. "Did you see his intestines fall out on that other one's head? Too funny. Gut shampoo!"

"Enough," Schow ordered. "Bring him up."

The winch began to hum as the rope and the bungee cord attached to it began to rise. Something red and wet and unrecognizable was attached to it. Grimacing, they unstrapped the remains and shoved the carcass back out, where it splashed into the midst of the clamoring zombies.

Schow pointed at Worm.

"Now the retard, if you would please."

Baker froze. "No, you can't! Leave him alone!"

"It's too late for your protestations, Professor. While you've certainly been taught a lesson today, I think it's time we made it more personal."

"For God's sake, Schow, the boy did nothing to you! He's harmless! He doesn't even understand what's happening!"

"He'll understand soon enough," McFarland grunted, lifting Worm from the floor. "Stop struggling you fucking dummy!"

Worm's teeth sank into the Captain's hand. Shrieking, he pulled it back and Worm rolled away.

"Bayhker! Dohnt leht thim hurht mee!"

"God damn you Schow, he's innocent! He's just a boy!"

Gonzalez sat on Worm, forcing him to lie still. McFarland strapped the bloodstained harness onto him. Tattered bits of Skip still hung from the straps. Worm began to scream Baker's name over and over again; a shrieking, siren-like keening that had no end.

"Bayyyyyyyyykherrrrrrrr!"

"Say goodbye to your friend, Professor."

They shoved Worm towards the doors.

"Okay!" Baker cried. "Okay, I'll do it! I'll lead you inside Havenbrook! Just please don't hurt him." He broke down, sobbing into the seat cushion.

"You see gentlemen," Schow said, "how well the power of persuasion works? Very good, Professor. I trust that you are a man of your word. But just in case, I think I'd better keep your young companion with me. Think of it as insurance."

"And you won't hurt him."

"I give you my word. He'll be fine. In fact, he'll have much better quarters than you will, I'm afraid. But remember your promise."

Baker glared at him. "I'll take you to Havenbrook, Colonel. But you're not going to like what you find there."

CHAPTER EIGHTEEN

"I'm getting out—now."

Martin blinked the sleep from his eyes. "You can't, Jim. They'll catch you and kill you before you even get out of town."

"I've got no choice, Martin! Danny's life depends on it. He's alive, and I don't know how I know, but he is! I can feel it."

"Jim, I know you want to get to your boy, but think about it. You can't just waltz out of here!"

"Would you two shut up? People are trying to sleep!"

The angry whisper came from their left. The movie theatre was pitch black and they couldn't see the speaker until he crawled forward. He wore wire-rim glasses and one of the lenses was cracked. His small goatee and mustache were unkempt and wiry, as was his hair. At one point he had probably been very collegiate looking, but weeks of forced labor and the hellish conditions of the movie theatre had undone that.

"Sorry," he apologized, "I didn't mean to be so harsh. But some of these guys in here will carve your heart out with a spoon just for an extra piece of bread. You don't want to disturb them."

"Thanks for the tip," Jim said, "but we don't intend on being here long enough for them to try."

"Yeah, I couldn't help but overhear that. That's another thing you want to be careful of. We've got snitches in here, and they'll sell your soul to Schow quicker than anything."

"How has he managed to get away with this?" Martin whispered.

"I don't know the whole story, because I'm not from here," the man said. "I'm originally from Brooklyn. They captured me a few weeks ago, on my way through Chambersburg. I'd planned on getting into the Appalachians and hiding out; finding some place safe. My friend said we should just go to the Hamptons, but I hated that fucking place even before all this shit started. The Appalachians sounded pretty good."

"The country's just as dangerous as the populated areas," Jim told him. "You'd be no better off there."

"I'm sorry, Mister?"

"Thurmond. Jim Thurmond. This is Reverend Thomas Martin."

"I'm Madison Haringa. I was a schoolteacher. Now, I don't know what I am. Lost, I suppose. Alive. Anyway, you seem pretty pessimistic about our chances for survival, yet if I overheard correctly, you're risking your life breaking out of here to rescue a friend of yours?"

"Danny. My son. He's still alive and I need to get to New Jersey and find him."

"Jersey?" Haringa coughed. "Mr. Thurmond, if he's anywhere near the Big Apple, then that's the most dangerous place of all. You said the country isn't safe, but I'm here to tell you, New York and New Jersey are *teeming* with those things. The only relatively safe parts of Jersey are places like the Pine Barrens and the farmlands."

"I can imagine New York City is pretty bad," Martin said, "but surely some people made it out?"

"Not that I know of," Haringa answered. "I haven't met a single survivor who was in New York City since I left. The undead seem to be massing there. And I've heard of them gathering in other locations as well. It's almost like they're building armies."

"Then I'll fight their army if I have to," Jim said. "But

in any case, I've got to go now."

Haringa sighed. "Mr. Thurmond, weren't you listening? If you're lucky, very lucky, you'll be shot trying to escape. If you insist on doing this, hope for that. Schow's alternatives are much worse."

"Who is he," Martin asked, "and why don't these people fight back?"

"From what I gather, the unit was assigned to protect Gettysburg. But as things fell apart, so did the sanity of the men in command, especially Schow's. It started simply at first. He imposed martial law and curfews and selected 'volunteers' for various work details. The townspeople complied. What choice did they have? It was either that, or the zombies. By the time things around here got really twisted, most of them had already been lulled into compliance."

"They're like sheep," Jim spat. "Afraid to fight back so they just blindly accept it all."

"How would they fight back, Mr. Thurmond? They don't have any weapons. Clubs and rocks won't stand up against heavy armor and machine guns. They may outnumber the soldiers, but the soldiers would even those odds pretty quickly. And what would happen if they did rise up? If they overthrew Schow's men? Would they be safe then? No. It would be worse. Despite all of the atrocities being committed here, these people are still alive. They know who's responsible for that. You'd be surprised what people will do to survive."

"No I wouldn't. Because I'd move heaven and earth to save my son, and Mr. Haringa, I intend to do just that."

Haringa ruefully shook his head.

Jim glared at him. "Do you have children, Mr. Haringa?"

"No. No I don't, but—"

"Then shut the hell up."

They fell into a brooding silence, then the schoolteacher leaned in closer, and motioned for them to huddle.

"You really think your son is alive?"

"I know he is."

"Then I'll help you. But wait till morning. You'll never make it tonight."

"How can you help?"

"I'm betting that they'll assign both of you to the sanitation crew. With that wound on your shoulder and his age, they won't want to stick you on heavy duty yet. Despite their callousness, they do try to keep the workers alive, if they can, and they're not going to waste the two of you right away."

"Go on."

"I'm on trash pickup too. When we get close to the edge of town, I'll start a distraction and you can make a break for it then."

"Will that work?"

"Probably not. But you'll get farther than you would now, and it beats a bullet in the dark."

A sudden noise from behind alerted them and Haringa disappeared into the darkness. Both Jim and Martin feigned sleep, but Jim kept a watchful eye open.

"It won't work."

The speaker crawled up between them.

"I know you're not asleep. I heard everything. Your plan won't work because they plan to move us all out tomorrow."

"Who are you?" Jim asked.

"Professor William Baker. No need to introduce yourselves. I was listening the whole time."

Martin sat up again and a moment later Haringa rejoined them.

"You're new too," Haringa observed. "I haven't seen you before."

"My companion and I were captured early this morning."

Jim cracked his knuckles. "Where is your friend now?"

"Schow is holding him hostage, using him as leverage

against me."

"What the hell are you talking about?"

"As I said, they plan on moving the entire operation tomorrow. I worked for the Havenbrook Laboratories in Hellertown. It's a secure research complex. Massive in scope and size. You could easily fit an army there. Schow intends to make that his permanent base of operations. He's using my friend as insurance to make sure that I guide them there and get them safely inside the complex."

"What," Haringa quipped, "does it have laser beam alarms that are still functioning or something?"

"The Center is equipped with security devices that you wouldn't believe," Baker responded, "but I've explained to the Colonel that most of them are now inactive."

"So then what does he need you for?" Martin asked.

"Schow believes we were designing and experimenting with new weapons for the military. He wants me to give him access to those."

Haringa sat up quickly. "Do you have access to stuff like that?"

"No."

"But you're playing along so that he doesn't kill your friend," Martin guessed. "What happens when we get there and he finds out, Professor Baker?"

"I don't intend to let him find out, and to be honest Reverend, we most likely won't make it that far. Not if Havenbrook is occupied by what I think it is."

Martin frowned. "What would that be?"

"Evil, gentlemen. Pure evil. It calls itself Ob and it would appear to be just another zombie. But it speaks with such authority and arrogance—almost as if it were smarter than the others. It whispered to me of things..." He trailed off, shaking his head, then continued. "I think he's a leader of some kind."

Jim had been silent while Baker spoke. Now he stirred and addressed the shaken man.

"You're from Hellertown. That's close to my son. Hell, that's less than an hour away from him! How sure are you that they plan on leaving tomorrow morning?"

"I'm quite positive that is what they intend to do. Schow gave orders to that effect before I was brought back here. They are to start assembling before dawn."

Jim turned to Haringa. "Hellertown is about two hours away by car. How many people are we talking about here in this camp?"

"Counting both troops and civilians?" He paused a moment, wiping his smudged glasses on his dirty shirt. "I'd say somewhere around eight hundred."

Jim whistled softly. "That's a lot of people. How would they transport them all?"

"I don't know," the schoolteacher admitted. "They've made us walk in front of the convoys before, on smaller trips. Used people for bait. Figured if there were any zombies in wait, they'd rush out and attack the easiest targets first."

"I can't see them doing that all the way to Hellertown," Jim said. "That would take days."

Baker removed his boots and began to massage his feet. "Schow seemed very eager. I can't see him rolling along at walking speed. He'll want to expedite things."

"They've got trucks," Haringa offered. "At least two dozen big rigs, all of them reinforced and adapted since the rising began, and lots of those big green National Guard trucks you see on the highways sometimes. Do you know what I mean? I'm not sure what they are called."

"The ones with the canvas tops that the troops sit in the back of?" Martin asked.

"Yeah, those are the ones. Jeeps too, and all of those have been outfitted as well."

"What else do they have?" Jim grilled him.

"HumVees and Bradleys and a few tanks. The HumVees move just like a car, but I'm guessing the tanks are a little slower. They've got a helicopter. And I don't know how many civilian cars and trucks. Even a couple of motorcycles, though I doubt they'd take those. Too risky. Leaves the driver exposed."

Jim frowned. "Eight hundred. That's still a lot of people to move. It makes for a pretty big target."

"But there's safety in numbers too," Haringa countered, "and I've got a feeling the convoy will be better armed than the living dead."

"Don't be so sure," Jim told him. "These things can think, use guns, drive cars."

"We've seen them plan ambushes," Martin chimed in. "They calculate—they're more cunning than you think."

Baker thought back to Allentown. "I concur. I saw them hunting a young couple, the way we would hunt a deer. And if Ob is doing what I suspect he's doing, you can be assured he will have arrayed his forces in anticipation of this very thing."

"What is it you think he's doing?"

"Gathering them together. Building an army. During the brief time I had to study him, he demanded that I release him. He said he needed to 'summon his brethren.' I didn't understand his true intentions then. I thought he wanted to simply scare me, perhaps acquire help in escaping. Now, I fear I know all too well what he really meant."

He paused to listen. The darkness around them was silent, save for a few snores and someone mumbling in his sleep.

Baker leaned in conspiratorially.

"I'm sure by now, that all of you realize the things walking around out there are not our loved ones. These creatures come from another place; a place outside our reality of being. Ob called it the Void. Perhaps its real name is Hell. I don't know. I beg your pardon, Reverend Martin, but I've never been a believer. I trusted science, not religion. But all that has changed now. I believe that demons do exist, and that this is what they are. Ob confirmed as much. He indicated that they wait in this other dimension, and as soon as the spark of life leaves the body, they take its place. They're like parasites, taking over a host and using the body for themselves. Our empty shells provide a vehicle of sorts for them."

"I would almost agree with you that they are demons, Professor," Martin said "for demons surely exist. But if these disembodied spirits inhabit our dead bodies, why is it that they eat human flesh? Why is it that the only way to kill them seems to be by destroying the brain?"

"I don't know why they eat," Baker admitted. "Perhaps they convert the flesh into some form of energy, just as we do when we eat. Or maybe they just do it to violate us further. They hate us very much, of this I am certain. As to the particular method of dispatching them, I've given that some thought. I think the brain is where they go. Think about it; all of our bodily and motor functions stem from the brain. Movement, speech, thoughts, instincts—voluntary and involuntary, it all starts up here." He tapped his head.

Martin rubbed at his chin. "So by destroying the brain, they become a spirit again, and have to find a new host body?"

"I don't know if it merely releases them or if it destroys them completely, but I hope it's the latter. If it merely inconveniences them for a period of time, then all life on this planet is doomed and our situation is hopeless."

"Why," Haringa asked, "are there *that* many of them?"

"Ob boasted that their number was 'more than the stars and more than infinity'."

Jim jumped as if he'd been shocked.

Martin placed a hand on his shoulder. "What is it?"

"I've been hearing it over and over the past week. More than infinity. Nothing. It's just a game Danny and I used to play together. I'd say I loved him more than pepperoni pizza and he'd say he loved me more than Spider-Man, and so on and son on, until we'd finish with we loved each other more than infinity."

The others said nothing and Jim's next words caught in his throat.

"It was how we used to say goodbye."

* * *

When the second shift of girls returned, the third shift didn't leave the gym. Instead, a meal of watery, brown soup and stale bread was served. Frankie picked at the stringy, unidentified bits of meat in her broth, and then wolfed it down in several quick gulps.

Now the meal was finished, and still no women had departed for the Meat Wagon. The gym was getting crowded and Frankie wondered if this was usual.

Gina, Aimee, and another woman, a blonde barfly type, walked over to where she sat.

"What's up?" Frankie asked.

"They've canceled all the other shifts tonight," Gina reported. "Apparently, they want the men to get a full night's rest. Those not on duty have been ordered to their barracks."

"Why? What's going on?"

"This is Julie," Gina introduced the woman, "and this is Frankie, the woman who beat Paula."

"Wow," Julie beamed. "It's so cool to meet you! Great job with that. We all hated her."

"It was my pleasure, believe me."

"Tell Frankie what you told me," Gina prompted.

"Well, there's this one Private who does it with me. He says that I'm his favorite and I think he's got kind of a crush on me. I don't mind. He's gentle and he only lasts a few minutes. Anyway, he says the rumor is that the entire town is bugging out tomorrow."

"Bugging out?"

"Yeah, moving. They're going to move us all further north to some underground army base or something."

Frankie set her soup bowl down. "How the hell are

they going to move all these people?"

"Most of us will probably ride in the backs of the rigs. That will suck cause we'll be packed in there like sardines, with no ventilation or anything. But my Private says he's gonna arrange it so I can ride in a HumVee with him and his friends."

Frankie grinned. "Sounds like a party. Think there's room for one more?"

"I can ask him tomorrow and find out," Julie said, "I don't think his friends would mind. You do understand what they'll expect from you though, right?"

Frankie stared soberly at her.

"Julie, I'm a professional."

The girl laughed, then shook her hand.

"You're all right, Frankie. I'm glad you took down Paula. I'll see you tomorrow. We'll have some fun!"

She walked away to join another group of women, adding her voice to the steady drone of gossip buzzing through the room.

"Why would you do that?" Gina asked, shocked. "My God, do you know what you're exposing yourself to?"

"Nothing more than what happens to us every night in the Meat Wagon."

"Then why volunteer for it?"

"Research."

"Research? What do you think you're going to be studying?"

"For starters," Frankie said, leaning back on her mattress, "I want to learn how to drive a HumVee."

* * *

Later in the night, with the room overcrowded, Gina and Aimee shared her bed. Aimee slept between the two women, and snuggled up against Frankie in her sleep.

Frankie lay there unmoving, staring at the ceiling.

It was a long time before she slept.

CHAPTER NINETEEN

At four the next morning, the battery-powered bullhorns squawked to life, blaring reveille throughout the empty streets. Within five minutes of the first note, the troops fell out accordingly: dressed, armed, and eager to go. The town buzzed with activity. Guardsmen darted back and forth, carrying out orders. The motor pool thrummed with the sound of revving engines, and the HumVees, trucks and transports began to file out of the buildings. Some carried food stores and other essentials; blankets, water, gasoline, oil, spare parts, generators (under interrogation Baker had made sure they understood that Havenbrook had no power left), weapons, ammunition, textiles, and everything else they would need. Other trucks were designated for human cargo.

The doors to the fitness center, movie theatre, and other detainment areas were thrown open, and the sleepy and frightened civilians were herded outside. They hugged one another at gunpoint, huddling for warmth against the chilly pre-dawn air. A column of trucks roared to a halt in front of them, and the soldiers began ordering them into the trailers.

A former banker and a grocery store clerk tried to slip away in the confusion. Gunshots exploded in the darkness as they were discovered and gunned down. After that, there were no further attempts at escape.

Jim, Martin, Baker and Haringa stayed clustered

together as their line shuffled toward a waiting trailer. Two guards stepped toward them and grabbed Baker by his arms.

"Sir, I'm Private Miccelli and this is Private Lawson. You need to come with us."

Jim stepped between them. "Why? Where are you taking him?"

Miccelli looked him in the eye and smiled. "How would you like to be gut shot and left behind? If not, then mind your own fucking business, friend."

Planting his feet, Jim's fists clenched at his side. Martin placed a quick hand on his shoulder, and whispered in his ear.

"Not now. Not like this. This isn't going to help Danny."

Gently, he pushed Jim forward toward the truck.

"Good luck, gentlemen!" Baker called after them. "I'm sure we'll meet again before this is through."

Martin waved. "And to you too, Professor. God is with us all."

As they marched the scientist away, Baker suddenly turned and cried out.

"Mr. Thurmond! Your son is alive. I can feel it too!"

"Let's go!" Miccelli shouted. He smacked Baker in the back of the head with a fist and unslung his M-16.

Jim, Martin and Haringa filed towards the truck with the rest of the men. The trailer was filled before they got to it and their line was halted. The soldiers swung the doors shut, sealed them with a thin, metal shipping band, then waved the truck on. It pulled away and another one rolled up to take its place.

One by one they were forced to climb up into the trailer. Jim paused at the top and held out his hand to Martin, pulling the old man up with him.

"Keep moving," one of the guards barked, "all the way to the back!"

They herded them in, and the trailer filled with pressing, unwashed bodies. The three of them were pushed all the way to the rear. They crouched down, Jim and Haringa shielding Martin from the other prisoners, making sure he wasn't crushed against the walls.

"I hope you guys aren't claustrophobic," Haringa remarked. "That would really suck."

Finally, the trailer filled to capacity with its human cargo. The doors slammed shut, plunging them into dense, stifling darkness. The motor sputtered to life and they began to move.

* * *

Julie waved to them through the crowd, and Frankie thought the woman almost looked giddy; as if this were nothing more than a weekend road trip with some guys they'd met at a party.

Giggling, she sidled up between Frankie and Gina. "You ready to have some fun?"

"Word! You know it," Frankie smiled. "I hope these guys are cute."

"Oh, they are," Julie assured her. "And like I said, they're gentler than most. You should try to hook up with one of them."

Gina grabbed Frankie's arm and pulled her aside.

"Are you sure you know what you're doing?"

Frankie nodded. "I'm sure. You just watch out for Aimee and yourself. I'm going to start making some friends. Learn what I can."

Two soldiers approached and one lifted Julie from the ground, swinging her through the air. She squealed in delight.

"Put me down," she playfully insisted, then turned to Frankie.

"This is Blumenthal." She ran a hand over his broad chest. "And this is Lawson. Lawson, this is my friend, Frankie. She's the one that beat that bull dyke's ass last night."

Lawson eyed her, lingering on her breasts and hips.

The Rising / 255

"Little thing like you? You don't look like you could have kicked her ass."

Frankie licked her lips suggestively. "I'm full of surprises."

"I bet you are." He turned to Blumenthal. "She can ride with us?"

The other Private laughed and pulled Julie to him. "Sure bro, I ain't got no problem with it. We just gotta make sure Sergeant Ford doesn't find out."

"I was hoping you'd offer to give us a ride," Frankie said. "What are we waiting for? Let's go."

Lawson let out a low whistle and patted her ass.

"Right this way, ladies."

Gina watched them disappear into the crowd, and then went in search of Aimee.

She found the girl clustered protectively among another group of women. PFC Kramer stood nearby, leering at the girl.

With revulsion, Gina noticed the erection bulging in his pants.

They were directed toward a trailer and shuffled toward it.

Kramer's eyes never left Aimee, marking her location in the convoy. Gina didn't think Aimee had noticed.

She shuddered as the trailer doors slammed shut.

The last thing she saw was Kramer's grin.

* * *

"Welcome aboard, Professor Baker. I'm pleased that you could join us."

Worm sat bound and gagged, his eyes bulging in a mixture of terror and relief as Baker climbed into the command vehicle. McFarland sat to his left, a pistol casually pushed against the young man's ribs. Gonzalez sat directly in front of them and the seat next to him was empty. Schow indicated with a wave of his hand that Baker should sit there.

He complied, mouthing assurances to Worm. "It's okay. We're just going for a ride. They won't hurt us."

The boy softened, his body going slack. He leaned back in the seat, his eyes remaining on Baker.

"He trusts you," Schow observed from the front passenger seat. "Almost like an adoptive son. That's good. You wouldn't want to betray that trust. You'll do well to remember that, Professor Baker."

"I'm a man of my word, Colonel. I hope that you are as well."

"Your insinuation wounds me, Professor." He turned to the driver. "Silva, what's our status?"

"The first group left on point ten minutes ago sir," the driver reported. "And I've just received confirmation from Lieutenant Torres that the chopper is in the air and performing aerial surveillance as well. We are go."

Schow nodded forward.

"Proceed."

The convoy began to roll.

* * *

"How fast do you think we're going?" Martin whispered.

Haringa grunted. "Hard to tell from inside here. Forty miles an hour maybe."

It was cold inside the truck, and the dank, musty air stank of stale urine and sweat. The wound in Jim's shoulder, though healing, still throbbed.

In the darkness, somebody farted. This was followed by nervous laughter and cries of faux dismay.

"Anybody bring a flashlight?" someone called, followed by more laughter.

"I've got a deck of cards," came the answer. "Not that they'll do us much good right now."

"Somebody know what's going on? Where the hell are we going, anyway?"

"They're gonna gas us," answered a voice near the

front, "just like the Nazis did to the Jews. Gas us and feed us to them zombies."

"Bullshit!"

"We're relocating to a scientific research center in Hellertown." Jim's voice rang out in the darkness and all other talk ceased. "Schow wants to set up base there. Much of it is underground, and the location is better protected than Gettysburg was."

"What are you, some kinda collaborator?" someone challenged him.

"No, and if I could get up there and get my hands on you, I'd choke the living shit out of you for saying that."

"I know that voice. You're that guy what thinks his son is still alive. I heard you last night."

"Yeah, what of it?"

"You're a stupid fucker, is all. Ain't no way that boy is still kicking. Better get used to the idea."

Jim tensed and Martin reached out in the darkness, steadying him.

During the night, Jim had begun to experiment with the idea that it was possible—perhaps even likely—that Danny was dead. But even if that were the case (and it was a reality that he wouldn't let himself accept—not yet), then he still needed to see, to *know*, or he would drive himself crazy.

He thought of Danny: bright and cheerful. He tried to imagine him as one of them now. His mind refused.

"My son is alive," he insisted quietly, "and if you say that again, you won't be."

"Fuck you," the disembodied heckler retorted. The tension inside the musty trailer was building, almost palpable. Suddenly, Haringa spoke out.

"Now is this anyway to act, guys? Here I throw this nice party for all of you, and all you do is bitch about the lights being out and that there's no room to move. And I didn't want to say anything, but which one of you forgot to put on his deodorant this morning?"

The trailer exploded with laughter and the tension

quickly dissipated.

"Anybody want to sing 'Ninety-Nine Bottles of Beer on the Wall'?"

The laughter turned to groans.

Jim was silent, the rage within him building, refusing to subside.

* * *

Frankie moaned with false passion as Lawson thrust into her. Wrapping her legs tightly around his back, she pulled him close. His breath, reeking of tobacco, blew against her neck.

"Oh God," he murmured into her hair. "Oh shit, yeah baby. I'm gonna come."

She ground her hips and urged him on, watching over his shoulder the entire time, studying how the vehicle was operated. It was pretty much like a car, she noted. She was confident that if and when the time came, she wouldn't have much trouble with it.

She felt him spurt inside her, and the frenzied thrashing increased, then subsided. She faked her own orgasm, then went limp. Behind them, Blumenthal and Julie were finishing up as well.

"That was fucking great," Lawson exclaimed, rolling off of her. He turned to the man up front. "Too bad you've got to drive, Williams."

"Well shit man, give me a turn."

Lawson shook his head and looked down at Frankie with a smile. "No way. She's all mine. Aren't you baby?"

Frankie winked at him, then reached out and wrapped her fingers around his softening penis.

"Think you can shoot this gun off again?"

"Yeah, if you help me."

"I think I can do that," she purred. "Maybe later you can teach me how to shoot that gun up there?"

"What, the fifty cal? Baby, you keep this up and I'll teach you anything you want!"

* * *

They rolled on as dawn turned to daylight, and the impassive sun climbed higher into the sky, shining its light on the horrors below. Their progress attracted the unwelcome attention of the living dead, and the trip became a constant rolling battle. The sharp crack of single-shot pistols and the heavy staccato of the machine guns marked their passage as they swept by exit ramps and small towns and fields and forests.

In Chambersburg, Baker experienced a surreal moment of astonishment when he spied a lone fawn, its soft brown coat still covered with white spots, poking its way through the broken window of a farmer's market and foraging on half-rotten fruits and vegetables. Even Schow and the other officers were silent and reflective as they passed it by. The fawn was not alarmed by their presence, and made no move to run.

"Baybee," Worm cooed in momentary happiness, and Baker was glad for it. He'd convinced them to remove the boy's gag, and Worm had relaxed some.

The deer was the only living creature they saw during the trek. Everything else was dead.

Near Shippensburg, four zombies in a pickup truck waited until the point vehicle had passed and then tried ramming the first truck in the procession. Torres' watchful eye from the hovering helicopter alerted them, and a well placed tank shell turned both the vehicle and its undead inhabitants into shrapnel before it ever reached the convoy.

Other creatures tried similar tactics and met with the same fate. Sharpshooters mowed down some, while others were simply run over to save bullets. All morning long, the civilians inside the trailers heard the intermittent but gruesome sounds of battle.

The troops were not without their own casualties, however. Near York, a well-aimed shot from a zombie sniper atop a billboard took out a gunner on one of the HumVees. The undead sniper was using a .223 round, and the soldier was killed instantly.

Half an hour past Harrisburg, a group of undead bats launched themselves at another HumVee, and the young recruit in the turret, panicking and frightened, rolled off his perch and into the road while trying to get away from them. He disappeared beneath the tires of his own HumVee before the driver could stop. He writhed in the road, legs crushed and bats gnawing at his exposed flesh, before a soldier in the next vehicle ended his misery for him by running over his top half.

They left the interstate and were only ten miles from Hellertown when they lost their first point team.

The Clegg Memorial Orphanage had, at the height of its operations, been revered as a perfect example of modern childcare. Overlooking a scenic and wooded portion of the highway near Havenbrook, the home provided mental and physical health care and support services to neglected, abused, homeless, and emotionally troubled children. The orphanage had a spotless record, and averaged more permanent adoptions than any of its kind nationwide.

When the dead began returning to life, it had housed over two hundred children.

Those two hundred children swarmed from the building as the HumVee and Jeep on point drove past it.

The soldiers stared in shock at the tide of undead children pouring forth from the doors and running towards them.

The shooting started a moment later.

Then the screams...

* * *

"Say again, Lieutenant, everything after 'trouble'."

Schow stared impatiently at the radio, waiting for a

response, but none was forthcoming.

"Silva, get them back on the air!" The driver busied himself with the radio, keeping the other hand on the wheel. The command vehicle began to swerve along the road.

"God damn it, Silva, watch where you're going!"

"Sorry sir!"

Torres' terrified voice flooded the radio again. The whir of the helicopter's blades could be heard in the background.

"I repeat, our point team is under attack! They are under attack! Two klicks away from your current position."

"Can you see Havenbrook?"

"Affirmative, sir. But—my God..."

Schow seethed with anger, and both Baker and Worm cringed back into their seats.

"What is your status?" he barked into the radio.

If Torres heard him, he gave no indication. Instead, it sounded as if he was talking to the pilot. "What the hell is that?"

Static, and something unintelligible; then "No it's not a fucking cloud! Lead them away from the rest of the convoy! That's an order!"

"What the hell is going on up there?" McFarland wondered aloud.

Nobody answered him.

*   *   *

In the helicopter, Second Lieutenant Torres cowered in horror as death approached them.

Birds. The sky was blotted out by a black storm cloud of undead birds. They soared toward the chopper as one, the sun vanishing in their wake.

"They're everywhere," the pilot screamed. "I can't shake them sir!"

"Keep going! The others can make it to Havenbrook

from here! We've got to lead these things away from the convoy!"

"Fuck that and fuck you, sir!"

Torres didn't reply. Closing his eyes, he reached beneath his shirt and pulled forth his dogtags. He'd seen men do the same with their Catholic medallions, but he himself had never been a believer.

He wondered if it was too late to change that.

He placed the metal tags between his teeth and clamped down on them, trying not to scream as the first of the wave crashed against the cockpit. It was followed by another, then five more. Then a dozen. Their heads and beaks splatted against the glass, sounding like gunshots above the noise.

The pilot was screaming, and Torres wished briefly that he would shut up. He bit down harder on the dogtags as the helicopter began to spin out of control. There was a sickening lurch, and Torres knew if he opened his eyes, he'd find himself upside down.

There was a cacophony of sound now; the screech of the birds, the whine of the helicopter, the pilot's screams. And above them all, a roaring sound, as the ground came rushing up to meet them.

It sounds like a freight train, he thought to himself, *roaring through a tunnel.*

For the first time in his life, Torres wondered if there would be a light at the end of his tunnel.

The glass windows shattered and dozens of rotting, feathery bodies swarmed them.

He was thankful when the helicopter hit the ground, welcoming the explosion that took away all pain and knowledge. It looked very much like a light.

* * *

"We've lost contact with them, sir."

"Do you really think so, Private? Eyes left!"

Schow pointed to the fireball blooming on the

horizon, beyond the treeline.

"Fuck," Gonzalez gasped, staring at the smoke and flames, "Let's just can this whole thing now, Colonel. Let's head back to Gettysburg!"

Schow whipped around in his seat. A vein throbbed in his reddening forehead.

"Captain, you will sit there and guard our prisoners or by God, I will shoot you myself. Is that understood?"

"Yes sir." Gonzalez thrust the barrel of his pistol into Baker's side.

Schow changed channels and addressed the convoy.

"Now hear this! Be advised, we've got incoming. I repeat, we have incoming. I want all fifty-cal gunners to man their posts. I want snipers atop the rigs, and I want them now. Secure the non-combatants and lock them down. I want every available man ready. Let's move, gentlemen!"

The line of vehicles halted abruptly, and the men began moving as one, carrying out their orders. Gunners swept the perimeter from atop their perches, searching for movement. Newly hardened veterans, whose only combat experience before the rising occurred had been drills and wargames, now sniffed the air knowingly, catching a telltale hint of the approaching force.

They did not have long to wait.

The children appeared as one atop the hill. They raised a horrible cry, and swarmed forward, running down the road toward them. The soldiers opened fire, unleashing a barrage that slammed into the horde, shredding their rotting flesh. Limbs were ripped from bodies and entrails were left lying on the road and still they advanced. The soldiers readjusted their fire, and heads began to disintegrate, but for each zombie that dropped, another one took its place.

The dead children's laughter echoed above the gunfire.

* * *

Blumenthal swiveled in the turret, shouting over the staccato roar of the fifty caliber.

"Get the girls to the Meat Wagon!"

Drawing his pistol, Lawson shoved Frankie and Julie forward.

"You heard him! Let's go!"

Julie planted her feet. "We want to stay with you!"

"You'll be safer inside the truck," Lawson insisted, "and besides, if the Colonel sees you out here, he'll shoot us all."

He led them forward through the chaos. Bursts of gunfire and the angry shrieks of the undead erupted all around them, and Frankie's nose wrinkled at the smell of cordite and zombies.

Then she saw one of them. A girl, no more than six years old. She carried a battered stuffed bear. Her flower-print dress was stained and torn, and her skinny arms and legs were swollen and ulcerated. She grinned, revealing blackened gums, and skipped towards them.

"Can I have a hug?"

Lawson stepped between the women and the zombie and squeezed off a shot. A crimson flower bloomed in the girl's forehead, and she dropped to the ground, still clutching the stuffed animal.

Shuddering, Frankie covered her ears, trying to drown out the noise. Above the din of battle she could suddenly hear her baby crying again. She found herself wishing for some heroin, and then forced the urge from her mind.

"Move!"

Lawson pushed them both forward again, running as more zombies made it into the perimeter. They were attacking from four sides now; the road, the hill, and the woods flanking the highway.

He dropped four more of the creatures before they reached the truck. Quickly, he threw the bolt and swung the door open.

"Get in!"

"Let me have a gun," Frankie pleaded.

"Trust me, baby, you'll be safer in here than you will outside. I'll come and get you when this is over."

Julie and Frankie clambered aboard and he slammed the door behind them. Frankie heard the bolt slide into place with a dull click.

The interior of the trailer was not what she'd expected. Plush red carpet cushioned the floor, and kerosene lamps gave off a soft, dim glow. Cubicle partitions looted from an office formed separate rooms, and each space had a cot. A few women slept fitfully, even with the pitched battle outside, but other than their snores, the Meat Wagon was quiet.

Then Frankie heard the cries from the rear, and the unmistakable sound of flesh striking flesh.

"Yeah, that's it. Take it you little bitch."

Frankie recognized the snarling voice immediately. Julie placed a cautious hand on her shoulder, but Frankie shoved it off and crept forward.

Another slap, and this time the girl's cry was louder, and followed by sobs of pain and shame.

Aimee.

Gritting her teeth, Frankie rushed into the last cubicle. Kramer thrashed on top of the girl; his pale, white ass gyrating in the air, his bulk crushing her to the cot. One hand was around Aimee's throat, and the other was curled into a fist. As Frankie burst forward, the fist came crashing down again. The sickening sound of the blow resonated in Frankie's stomach.

Aimee was gasping for air, her dilated pupils far away and unseeing. Her eyes rolled back into her head, showing only whites, and her back arched so much that Frankie thought her spine would snap.

"Hey, fat boy!"

Kramer turned, still on top of the girl, and grinned.

"Oh, I was hoping you'd be here, bitch. I got something for you."

He rolled off Aimee, and she lay still and unmoving. Frankie noticed the blood on her thighs, and the rage seethed within her.

"What do you have for me, that little thing?" She pointed at the Sargent's blood-slickened penis, bobbing in the air.

Kramer reached into the pile of clothes at the foot of the cot, and pulled out his pistol.

"Maybe I'll just fuck you with this instead."

"At least it's bigger."

Julie came up behind her. "Frankie, don't antagonize him."

"Keep out of this, Julie. Go back up front and watch the door. Make sure no zombies try to get in." She kept her eyes on Kramer. "We wouldn't want to be interrupted."

"That's right," he drooled, "while everybody else is having target practice, we can have some fun."

Julie backed away, her frightened eyes watching in disbelief. The sounds of battle surrounded them now, punctuated by screams of agony and terror.

"Your friends are dying out there, and all you can think about is getting your dick wet," Frankie observed coldly. "Some man you are."

"I'll show you how much of a man I am, bitch." He pointed the pistol at her. "On your knees, or I'll shoot you and then the girl."

* * *

"I wonder what's going on?" Martin whispered as the truck ground to a halt.

Bullets whizzed by the outside of the truck. There were unintelligible shouts and then more gunfire, followed by the sound of running. An explosion rocked them back and forth on their tires.

"We must be under attack." Jim shifted his weight, trying to coax the blood back into his legs, which had grown numb from inactivity.

Something slammed against the side of the trailer, and then a quarter-sized hole appeared, letting in a thin shaft of daylight. In the darkness, one of the men cried out.

"He's been shot!"

"Everybody down!" Jim shouted, dragging Martin to the floor with him. Another bullet punched through the trailer, near the roof.

Haringa adjusted his glasses. "What the hell is going on?"

He crawled above the other men toward the slim shaft of light. As he leaned closer to peek outside, something white and puffy poked its way through.

A finger. A dead finger.

Something tittered on the outside and the finger withdrew, decaying flesh flaking off against the twisted metal.

A fist pounded against the trailer, then another.

Jim noticed that the gunshots were distant now, scattering away from them.

Something knocked playfully on the trailer doors; rapping out 'Shave and a Hair Cut'.

Before they could stop him, one of the men knocked back.

Tap Tap. 'Two Bits'

The doors began to rattle.

* * *

"It's like they were waiting for us," McFarland mused, staring at the carnage on all sides. "Like they'd been told we were coming."

"Perhaps they were, Captain," Baker told him. "The birds. The bats. I've tried to make you understand that they are possessed by the same entities possessing the human dead."

"Bullshit," Gonzalez spat. "If that's true, then why

aren't the bugs infected, huh? How come there's not zombie mosquitoes buzzing around? Fucking zombie gnats?"

"I don't claim to have all the answers. Maybe insects don't have enough of a life force. Maybe their frames are too fragile. I don't know. All I know is that when our—or an animal's—energy or life force or soul or whatever you want to call it departs, these things take over."

Schow threw down his headphones and in one fluid motion, pulled his pistol and shoved it against Worm's temple. Worm whimpered and tried to draw away from the barrel, but Schow grabbed him by the hair and yanked his head forward. A single drop of blood ran down the frightened boy's face, forming a tear.

"Tell you what, Professor. Let's test your little theory right now. You knew this was going to happen, didn't you? You set us up!"

"No, Schow," Baker thrust his hands out, "I had no idea! I went a different way when I fled Havenbrook. Why would I lead us into a trap, and endanger Worm and myself in the process?"

"They're all around us," a voice screamed over the radio, "I repeat, they've broken through the perimeter!"

"Watch your flank, watch your—" There was a strangled scream, followed by a burst of static.

Schow leaned over and flung the door open, pushing Worm outside.

Baker lunged for him, but Gonzalez was quicker. He punched him once in the face, followed by a blow to his stomach, then shoved him back down in the seat

"Baykhar!"

Worm rolled across the road, and then scrambled to his feet, pawing at the door. Schow slammed it shut and re-locked it, then pointed the gun at Baker.

Four children circled Worm, their dead faces alight with malicious glee.

"Baykhar!"

Schow turned to the driver. "Silva, give the order to

retreat. I want every man on the ground back in his vehicle. We're moving forward, and we'll regroup at Havenbrook."

Worm clawed at the HumVee, pounding frantically on the door. Then the children fell on him.

Baker shut his eyes, but he couldn't block out the screams.

"Look at that," Gonzalez whistled, "they took his throat out with one bite."

"And his ear," McFarland snorted, "although, I guess he wasn't using those anyway."

"You bastards," Baker sobbed. "You god damn bastards, I will see you burn. I will see you fucking burn! Why would you do this?"

"Move out," Schow ordered, and the HumVee lurched forward with a jerk.

With his eyes twisted shut and his fists balled against his ears, Baker wept.

"Look at that," Gonzalez said, "the retard must have been a bug. I don't see him getting back up."

But after they crested the hill and passed from sight, Worm rose.

CHAPTER TWENTY

"**F**all back, you college-boy asshole!" Miller shoved the cringing Lieutenant forward, all thoughts of rank forgotten.

Along the roadside, an injured private screamed as a group of zombies clawed open his stomach, plunging their hands into his steaming innards. Miller swung his M-16 toward them and emptied the clip.

He grabbed a fleeing officer and pulled him close. The frightened man squirmed in his grip.

"Where is PFC Kramer?"

"I don't know," the man stammered, "last I saw he was heading for the Meat Wagon with some little girl and then the shit hit the fan and those things killed Navarro and Arensburg and they looked just like my daughter, one of them looked just like my daughter—"

Miller flung the raving man to the dirt, where he lay continuing to babble.

Fuck Kramer and fuck Schow and fuck everyone else, he thought to himself. *This whole operation is one gigantic cluster-fuck.*

He ejected his spent clip, popped in a fresh one, and shot the Lieutenant in the face. Then he flagged down a passing tanker truck and climbed up into the cab.

The driver looked grim. "I'm thinking we should have stayed in Gettysburg, Sergeant."

"Six of one, half dozen of the other," Miller shrugged. He rolled down the window, sighted a zombie, and squeezed the trigger.

* * *

"They're trying to get in!"

The men in the truck scrambled backward, crushing those behind them against the sides of the trailer. Martin wheezed, clutching his chest, and clawed for enough room to stand.

"Are you okay?" Jim asked.

The old man shook his head, fighting for breath.

The doors rattled again, as the zombies sheared through the metal band holding them shut. They swung open with a bang, flooding the trailer with blinding sunlight and the sounds of battle—the sounds of men dying.

They're children, Jim thought. *They're Danny's age!*

The men closest to the door clawed in terror at those behind them, but there was no room to move. They pressed against each other as decaying hands clutched at them, hauling them down into the hordes. Hungry mouths snapped in anticipation, and the zombies began to climb onto the truck in their place.

Haringa pushed his way forward and kicked one in the head, sending it sprawling back into the others. He aimed his boot at another, but it latched onto his leg and pulled him down. The creature's teeth sank into his pants leg, and blood welled through the denim as Haringa wailed.

More of the creatures climbed aboard.

* * *

"You heard me, bitch. Get on your fucking knees, now!"

Frankie complied, kneeling on the carpeted floor.

Her eyes never left Kramer's.

Leering, the big man moved forward, thrusting his still erect penis at her face. Taking a deep breath, Frankie let the rancid thing slide past her lips.

He's no different than any other john.

Kramer groaned, caressing her cheek with the pistol.

"Remember," he grunted, "don't get any ideas or I'll kill all of you."

Frankie made no indication that she'd heard him, but her pace quickened. She bobbed her head faster, working him like a professional. She felt him relax, leaning into her, and she continued.

She blocked out his stench, his sounds, thoughts of Aimee, and the noise of the fight raging outside. She was in her private place now, and the world didn't exist. Nobody else was there. Just her—

—and her baby.

She wanted a fix, and the craving filled her with revulsion and self-loathing.

She felt Kramer stiffen, his legs knotting together, knees locking. He groaned, and the gun dangled uselessly at his side as he erupted in her mouth.

Frankie slid all the way down to the base of his penis, letting his dank pubic hair tickle her nose.

Then she bit down. Hard.

Kramer shrieked.

She ground her teeth together, feeling them meet through the flesh and muscle. With a savage jerk, she twisted her head back and forth, and then pulled away from him.

The severed member dangled from her lips. She spat it onto the floor as Kramer screamed, staring in disbelief. Eyes glazing over, he raised the gun toward her; his other hand clutching at his mangled groin. Blood gushed from between his fingertips, spattering the carpet.

Frankie grinned with crimson teeth. "Maybe I could get used to being a zombie."

"You bitch..." He waved the gun, then fell over, still

clutching between his legs as the blood pumped out of him.

Frankie stepped over his limp body just as the truck began to move again. She plucked the pistol from his hand and pressed it against the back of Kramer's head. Then she squeezed the trigger.

Next, she went to Aimee. The girl lay still.

"Aimee?" She patted her cheeks gently, then raised her limp arm and felt for a pulse. There was none. Her skin was growing cold. Frankie sighed, then dropped the girls arm and turned away.

Aimee's eyes opened and she sat up, swinging her legs off the cot.

"Frankie, look out!" Julie screamed.

Frankie spun just as Aimee launched herself at her. She sidestepped and the zombie slid across the floor, colliding with Kramer's corpse. Frankie fired, and the shot tore the girl's throat open. The next one went in just above her eye, and Aimee lay still again.

Julie was sobbing, and the other women were awake now, crying out in confusion and horror. Frankie grabbed the corner of a sheet and wiped the blood from her arms and face, then walked towards them.

"What now?" Julie asked.

"These doors won't open from the inside," Frankie said, "so we wait. Help me look for more weapons."

* * *

Jim tried desperately to push through the crowd, but it was no use. He turned away as the zombie took another bite from Haringa's leg. The men inside the truck were screaming now, crushing each other in desperation.

Outside, the truck's engine suddenly coughed, then roared to life. The truck jerked forward, and both the zombies and the men nearest the door tumbled onto the road. Jim caught a brief glimpse of Haringa's outstretched hand and then he was gone as well. Only his eyeglasses remained behind.

The truck picked up speed, leaving those on the ground behind. Two of the creatures remained on board, and they struggled with the prisoners as the truck squealed away.

One of them, a teenage girl, sank her teeth into the back of her victim's neck and hung on while the man spun in circles, beating at her with his fists. Jim finally was able to push forward, and he shoved both the zombie and the man out the open door. The other zombie turned on him, then teetered, arms pinwheeling, before it dropped out the open space as well. Jim cheered as its head burst upon the road.

Still clutching his chest, Martin made his way forward.

"What now?" he wheezed.

"We get the hell off this truck."

The truck's speed increased, leaving the zombies and their victims behind as the yellow line in the middle of the road became a fast moving blur.

"Jump?"

"That's what I'm thinking," Jim nodded. "Wait for the truck to slow around a curve or something and then jump off."

"Jim, this isn't the movies. You'll be of no use to Danny if you break your leg escaping."

"He's right, Mister." Another man shuffled forward. One of the zombie children's fingernails had gouged two ragged furrows in his cheek, and he wiped at the blood absentmindedly. "You'd be road pizza if you jumped at the speed we're going."

"I've got to try. I can't just stand here and do nothing!"

"What about them?" Martin pointed out the door.

A fleeing Jeep sped along behind them. The driver was shouting into the radio, probably reporting that the doors were open on the truck.

"Even if you did land safely, I suspect they'd either

run you over or shoot you. What help would you be to Danny then?"

Jim punched the wall of the trailer.

The soldier in the Jeep fired at a zombie in the road.

"You wouldn't stand a chance on foot, either," Martin continued. "How many of those things do you think are out there? You said it yourself, Jim. The closer we get to the populated areas, the more of them there'll be."

Jim didn't reply. He stared at the Jeep, then turned back to Martin.

"I want to thank you for all that you have done, my friend." He clasped Martin's hand and squeezed. "I don't have the words to tell you how much it means."

Then, before Martin could blink, he let go, bent his knees and jumped off the back of the truck.

* * *

"What the hell?" Ford turned as the Jeep he was riding in swerved into the passing lane.

"What Sarge?"

"Somebody just jumped off that rig up ahead!"

He picked up the handset.

"Charlie-Two-Nine, this is Six."

"Go ahead, Six. Over."

"Sharpes, what the hell is going on over there?"

"We tried telling them their backdoor was open, but their radio's busted. Did you see that guy jump off?"

"Hell yes, I saw. Handle it."

There was a pause, and then "Sergeant, are you sure? Don't you think the zombies will take care of him for us?"

"Handle it before the rest of the men on that truck get the same idea. Six out."

* * *

Jim rolled into a ball as he fell; tucking his heels against his buttocks and wrapping his arms around his knees. He'd seen his father demonstrate the maneuver when he'd been younger, and the old man had told him stories of parachuting into the jungles of Viet Nam.

He landed in the grass along the side of the road, and his left side slammed against the ground. A thousand tiny needles of white-hot pain shot through him as he tumbled into the ditch, forcing the breath from his lungs. He continued rolling. When he tried to breathe again, it felt like something was stabbing him in the chest.

Then the motion stopped and he was lying there in the gutter, alive. In pain, but alive.

He took a tentative breath and though it still hurt to do so, it wasn't excruciating. He crawled onto his hands and knees. Nothing seemed to be broken, but his back and side were bleeding, and he'd reopened the gunshot wound in his shoulder.

The truck was speeding away and he saw the men in the trailer cheering him, their arms upraised in salute.

A sudden burst of machine gun fire peppered the ground around him, sending gravel and dirt and bits of rock flying in all directions.

Jim scrambled into the woods as the shooter readjusted his aim. Bullets tore through the ground where his feet had been seconds ago. They slammed into trees and whizzed through the weeds as he dived into the heavy brush. Thorns tore at his face and hands.

"Fuck," Sharpes cursed. "I missed him."

The driver shook his head in disgust.

"Sergeant Ford can't see right now. That tanker truck's in the way. Want to go after him?"

"Screw that. We'll tell him we nailed him. Besides, with all these zombies around, the fucker'll be dead in minutes anyway."

Schow's voice crackled over the radio.

"Be advised. We have reached the location. Standby."

* * *

The lead vehicles slowed as the convoy turned down the private lane leading to Havenbrook. The sign at the entrance had once read:

HAVENBROOK NATIONAL LABORATORIES
TOMORROW'S FUTURE TODAY
HELLERTOWN, PENNSYLVANIA
AUTHORIZED VEHICLES ONLY

Baker remembered passing by it when he'd escaped from Ob and fled south. Since then, somebody had vandalized the sign. Some of the words had been blacked out and the garish, spray painted letters now read:

HELL
TOMORROW'S DEAD
HELL, PENNSYLVANIA
AUTHORIZED VEHICLES ONLY
ENTER MEAT

They stopped at the entrance. The security fence stretched away on both sides, and the guard post was unmanned.

Schow's smile was tight-lipped. "Welcome to our new home, gentlemen."

"Looks deserted." Gonzalez observed.

"Not according to our friend here." Schow patted Baker on the head, and the scientist pulled away from him.

The rest of the convoy rolled up behind them. During the attack, they'd lost two HumVees and three civilian trucks. Schow had not yet been given exact figures on how many men hadn't survived, but he considered the probable estimates acceptable losses. The only thing that angered him was the irreplaceable loss of the helicopter.

At his order, the tanks crept forward, turrets leveled at the entrance.

Nothing moved.

*　*　*

"We've stopped," Frankie said. "Get ready. As soon as they open those doors, we make a break for it."

"They'll have guns—" Julie argued.

"We've got one too," Frankie interrupted her, "and besides. I'd rather swallow a bullet than another one of these pig's dicks." She turned to face the other two women.

"I heard that," a Puerto Rican woman named Maria nodded. "I've got your back."

"Me too," agreed the other. "I'm ready."

"What's your name again?"

"Meghan."

"Alright," Frankie turned back to Julie. "Maria and Meghan are with me on this. Are you? Because if not, Julie, then you're nothing more than the whore they want you to be."

Anger flashed across Julie's face, then slowly subsided.

"I'm no whore."

"Then be a warrior, god damn it. Survive. Live!"

Frankie aimed the pistol at the door, and they waited.

* * *

"So," McFarland asked, "do we just drive through the front door?"

Schow's laughter was short and clipped.

"What do you think, Professor?" He grabbed a fistful of Baker's hair and jerked his head upward. "Look at me when I address you! What do you suggest? Is there anything we should know about before we proceed?"

"I'm not telling you anything!" Baker snorted, then spit on him.

His eyebrows arched, Schow calmly wiped the spittle from the silver eagle on his shoulder.

"Then we have no further use for you."

He yanked the pistol from his holster.

"Colonel Schow, this is Charlie-Two-Seven."

Silva picked up the handset and looked at the officers questioningly.

McFarland grabbed it from him.

"Go ahead, Sergeant Michaels."

"Sir, we've got the remnants from that orphanage coming up on our rear flank. We thinned their numbers during the last skirmish, but I suspect that some of our men are now with them."

"How far back?"

"A couple miles. They're coming on foot. Sir, there's enough of them that we probably don't want to be caught out here in the open."

Still clutching both Baker's hair and the pistol, Schow nodded his head to McFarland.

"Have one of the tanks go through the gate first. Tell them not to knock down that fence. It sounds like we'll need it in a while. After the tank has gone through, send a unit along behind it. If the entrance and the grounds are secure, then the rest of us will follow."

"Yes sir." McFarland began relaying the orders over the radio.

Schow twisted Baker's hair savagely, and despite his efforts not to do so, the scientist groaned in pain.

"The United States Government thanks you for your assistance, Professor."

Baker grimaced. "Burn in hell, you twisted piece of garbage."

Schow raised the pistol to his head and then paused, thinking.

"Captain, delay that order. Have the tank crew stand down."

"Sir?"

"We're going to have the Professor Baker here go in before the tank."

"What?"

"You heard me. Point detail."

Laughing, McFarland gave the orders.

Pulling him by his hair, Schow opened the door and gestured for Baker to get out.

"It's easy, Professor. Just walk up and ring the doorbell."

* * *

The soldiers had shut the door again as soon as the convoy stopped. Martin and the others huddled in the darkness, peering through the bullet holes and listening to what was going on outside.

Martin ignored the shocked and frightened mutterings of his companions, and turned his thoughts to Jim. He knew that the Lord had protected his friend from harm, at least as far as the leap from the truck was concerned. Jim had been up and moving even as they'd passed from sight.

But what had his friend escaped into? How many zombies had been involved in the initial attack, and how many still lingered in the area? How many guardsmen had died at their hands, and now joined their ranks?

Jim was on foot, weaponless, and alone amidst the living dead. The only thing in his favor was that single-minded determination and love for his son.

Martin bowed his head and began to pray harder than he ever had in his life.

* * *

Baker considered his options. If he refused Schow, they would shoot him where he stood. On the other hand, if he re-entered Havenbrook, there was a chance he could run past the gate and hide in one of the buildings. If his theory regarding Ob was correct, however, the complex would offer an even worse fate—death at the hands of the undead.

With both Schow and Gonzalez pointing their weapons at him, he turned toward the gatehouse. His feet felt light, as if he were standing on a conveyer rather than walking toward it. His senses were hyper-aware. The sun was hot on the back of his neck. His scalp ached where Schow had pulled his hair. It was quiet, as if the land was holding its breath. No birds or insects—living or otherwise. From behind him, he heard the squawk of a radio set. Somebody sneezed and someone else jacked a fresh clip into their weapon.

Now he was in front of the guardhouse. He'd driven through this entrance twice a day for many years. When he'd fled from Havenbrook, only days before, he'd never expected to see it again. He'd known the guards by name; asked about their children and wives and gave them a bonus at Christmas. Where were they now? Perhaps inside the shack, lurking in the shadows and waiting for him to pass by?

No, that was ridiculous. If they'd returned to their posts after being reanimated, they would have been there when he escaped. Then again, who had vandalized the sign out front? That had been recent—extremely recent.

There was a burst of static as a nearby radio squawked again. He heard gears turning as the tank turret tracked his progress.

"Let's go, Professor!" Schow yelled. "We don't have all day. We've got incoming to our rear! Five seconds and I start shooting. Pretend you're selling Girl Scout cookies!"

Raucous laughter from the troops greeted this.

Baker took a deep breath, held it, and thought of Worm.

"I'm sorry." He whispered it over and over, like a mantra.

Then he walked through the open gate.

CHAPTER TWENTY-ONE

The wind was blowing in the opposite direction, and Jim heard them coming before he smelled them. Their slurred grunts and curses echoed through the forest. Leaves rustled beneath their shambling feet as they advanced toward his location, trailing after the convoy. A live bird took flight, startled from its hiding place in the branches overhead. Seconds later, it screeched as one of its undead brethren seized it in mid-air.

Pulse hammering, Jim glanced around, his senses hyper-aware. The road would be quickest, but it was too open. He'd be a sitting target out there. The woods offered protection, but the thick undergrowth that hid him would also slow him down.

Something rustled toward him, and he froze, holding his breath. He caught a rancid whiff as it passed by and his eyes began to water. The zombie was close enough that he could hear the flies buzzing beneath its skin.

It passed him by, slogging toward the road. Jim quietly exhaled, and waited for it to pass from earshot. When he thought it had passed, he broke cover and ran.

Immediately, a hoarse cry sprang up behind him. He'd been spotted.

"Here piggy piggy piggy!"

Running parallel to the road, Jim dashed through the foliage. Branches whipped at his face and jutting roots threatened to trip him with every step. The dead leaves crunched under his pounding feet, attracting further attention.

Something dead erupted from the bushes in front of him and he veered to the right, farther from the road. The zombie hobbled along in pursuit, dragging one useless leg behind it. Armed with a fiberglass compound bow, it launched an arrow at him. The missile whistled over his head, embedding itself in the trunk of an old oak tree.

Another zombie burst forward, and though Jim didn't know it, the corpse had once been Worm.

"Guhnnuh git ewww."

It shambled toward him, its tongue flopping around in its mouth like a dead fish.

Jim shouldered his way through a jumble of raspberry bushes and continued on. His shirt caught on the thorns and he shrugged his way free, leaving the garment dangling like a flag.

Scrambling up a brush-covered hill, he reached down and grabbed a fallen limb. It was about the length of his arm and it felt solid as he hefted it.

A groundhog, entrails protruding from a hole in its side, chittered angrily and snapped at his ankles. Jim swung, bringing the makeshift club down across its head. The creature backed away and he brought the limb down again with a mightier blow. The thing's head collapsed, one eye bulging out of its socket.

Worm was right behind him now. Gaining higher ground, Jim turned to face him.

More zombies were pouring from the woods toward his position. Six, then a dozen. Then two dozen. He could hear more of the creatures crashing through the undergrowth, and plodding down the highway to his left.

Worm clawed at him and he shoved him backward, sending the zombie tumbling down the hill. It crashed into three more, and they sprawled in a heap on the forest floor.

He swung the club again, connecting with another zombie's jaw. There was a sharp crack, and Jim cheered, until he realized that it was his weapon, and not the zombie, that had broken.

The jagged limb looked like a spear now, and using it like one, he thrust it forward, jabbing it into the creature's jaundiced eye. He pushed with all his weight and heard a pop as the broken stick penetrated the membrane and sunk into the soft tissue of the brain. Jim tugged on the stick but it wouldn't budge, embedded in the zombie's skull. Dropping it, he turned and ran again.

He headed back towards the road again, searching desperately for an abandoned vehicle, or at least a weapon, dropped during the battle. He'd gone about five hundred yards when he almost tripped over the injured soldier.

The man lay with his back against an oak tree. One arm dangled uselessly at his side, and both legs were broken and covered with bite marks. Remarkably, despite the damage, the man was alive.

After a moment, Jim recognized him.

"Hey man," the guardsman pleaded, "help me out. I need to get back to the unit. Need to find a medic."

"You're Private Miccelli, aren't you?"

The man's eyes narrowed in a mixture of suspicion and surprise.

"Yeah," he panted, "and you are?"

"Jim Thurmond. I remember you from this morning. Let me help you."

He knelt down, prodding at Miccelli's legs. A jagged splinter of bone had poked through his calf, and Jim touched it with his fingertip.

Miccelli shrieked, clawing at the dirt and leaves.

"Shhh," Jim warned him. "You'll let them know where we are. Those things are all around us."

"For fuck's sake, man, help me! What the fuck is wrong with you?"

With his foot, Jim casually pushed Miccelli's rifle out

of the soldier's reach.

"They'll be on us in a minute or so. I'll have to protect us both. How the hell do you work this thing?"

Between grunts of pain, Miccelli explained the weapon, and how to change the clip. Satisfied, Jim stood up and pointed it at him.

"What are you doing man?"

"This morning, when you took Professor Baker away before we were put on the truck, you asked me something. Do you remember what it was? Do you?"

Miccelli shook his head in frustration.

"You asked me if I would like to be gut shot and left behind. Remember that?"

His eyes widened in comprehension.

"Hey man, don't!" He held his palms out in surrender. "Please? Don't fucking do that man! If you're gonna shoot me, shoot me in my fucking head! Don't shoot me in the stomach! Why would you do that?"

"I wanted to get to my son, and you got in my way."

He gave the trigger a short, quick squeeze and Miccelli's screams were lost beneath the report.

Blood gushed from the hole in his abdomen, and he grappled with his intestines, fighting to keep them inside. The tendons in his neck and face stood out, taught with pain. He began to shake, his teeth clattering together.

"You asshole," he whined. "You fucking asshole."

"So tell me Miccelli, how does it feel to be gut shot and left behind?"

Jim took off quickly, as the zombies, attracted by the gunshot and Miccelli's cries, began to draw towards them.

He burst through the foliage and onto the road, then turned. He was well ahead of the zombies, but they were still within sight, plodding steadily toward Havenbrook.

This can't all be for me.

From the woods, Miccelli began to scream louder. His cries were punctuated with the horrible laughter of the zombies. But there were also the sounds of further pursuit. More were coming his way. Only a few of the creatures had stopped to take advantage of the dying man. The others were moving forward. Why? Where were they going? He thought about it and decided that they must be pursuing the convoy. Only a small handful of the creatures were armed, but apparently, they planned to continue the fight.

Almost as if they were following orders from someone...

The knowledge chilled him. Slinging the rifle, he ran on. Jim had always laughed at horror movies where the victim ran down the middle of the road, rather than hiding in the woods, but now he found himself doing the same.

Miccelli's screams followed him, then turned to squeals, and finally faded.

* * *

He found a hollow oak stump, a long-ago victim of a lightning strike, and he hid inside the dry-rotted, musty confines. He waited there, along the edge of the road, hidden in the tree, until the shambling, rotting forces had passed by him.

The zombies were representative of all walks of life. The majority were children and teenagers from the orphanage, but the residents of Hellertown, and even a few dozen soldiers from Schow's rag-tag group also marched toward their destination. Black, white, Hispanic, and Asian—death did not discriminate. Some carried weapons while others carried nothing but their hunger, hanging over them in an almost palpable cloud of menace. Some moved along at a quick pace while others lagged behind, slowed by mangled or missing limbs. One in particularly bad shape paraded by, and the flesh sloughed off its leg as it passed his hiding place, landing on the road like a discarded banana peel.

They were all around him now, and Jim slouched

down inside the tree as far as he could go. If they found him now it would all have been for nothing. The confines of his hiding place offered no escape.

Eventually, their reek and clamoring subsided. They were gone, drawing closer to what he was sure was their destination: Havenbrook.

He left the tree a short time later. He crossed through a marsh on the opposite side of the highway. If a major confrontation between Schow's troops and the zombies was about to erupt, he should be able to skirt around it unnoticed, and make his way north. If he could find a car, he could conceivably be at Danny's within an hour or a little more.

He slogged through the stagnant, ankle-high water, pushing through the reeds with his hands. He was glad Martin wasn't with him. The old man would have had a difficult time wading through the bog.

A flash of memory hit him; their conversation in the Clendenon's living room, while Delmas lay dying.

Maybe this is how it's supposed to be, Jim. I could stay here with them while you went on.

No, Martin, I can't leave you here. You came with me, offered your friendship and support. It wouldn't be right.

He thought of Baker, and what he'd said as Miccelli was dragging him away.

Your son is alive. I can feel it too!

He pushed forward and suddenly a white, pallid arm thrust up from the swamp and clutched at his legs. The zombie pulled itself up, brackish water dripping from its mouth and nose and ears. Not wanting to announce his location with a shot, Jim unslung the M-16 and in one fluid motion, brought it down on the creature's head. He did it again and again, blow after blow, hammering the thing back into the muddy marsh bottom.

They don't need air, don't need to breathe. So it just lay there at the bottom, waiting for somebody to come by. There's still so much we don't know about them.

Wonder if Baker figured that out yet?

He stood, panting heavily.

Danny was ahead of him. His friends were behind.

Thrashing at the weeds in frustration, he turned and ran back towards Havenbrook. He ploughed through the fronds and cattails, and prayed.

"God, I'm not even sure that I believe in you anymore, but I know that Martin does. I hope that you'll repay his faith by watching over him. Please let him and Baker and the others be safe. And please, please Lord, watch over my son. I'm so close. So very close now. Just keep him safe for a little longer."

CHAPTER TWENTY-TWO

B aker shuffled past the silent, brooding guardhouse. The only sound was that of his feet scuffing through the gravel, and the idling engines of the vehicles and tanks. He then crossed through the open gate and let out a breath that he hadn't realized he'd been holding.

Perhaps I was wrong. Maybe Ob is long gone— Powell's body rotted away and Ob had to go back to the Void and then back here again to find a new one.

He crept forward. The stillness of the place was ominous, and Baker was filled with a sudden sense of dread. Something felt wrong. He knew of no other way to describe it, but he was certain of it nevertheless. He could feel it in the air.

To his left, empty buildings and hangars. To his right, the employee parking lot, holding only a few abandoned cars. In front of him, the office buildings watched ominously with broken windows for eyes. He glanced back at the army, then started toward the buildings.

There was a sudden flash of movement behind the windows.

Baker froze. He sniffed the air, and smelled corruption.

The thing that had once been his colleague and that now called itself Ob stepped out from between the buildings. He saw more movement out of the corner of his eye. Zombies lurked inside the cars, behind trees, and even in the bottom of the fountain; its still waters disturbed and rippling now.

He knew Schow couldn't see them. The zombies were still hidden from their vantage point outside the fence. Even if they used infrared scanners or other technology, the corpses wouldn't register.

Ob grinned at him; a terrible grimace that split Powell's face in half.

Schow couldn't see them. Schow couldn't see the rocket launcher in Ob's hands.

"It looks clear, Colonel," he shouted. "I think they've abandoned the place!"

Behind him, the tanks began to rumble forward through the gate.

Ob nodded, waiting.

Baker crouched down and prayed for a quick death.

* * *

"All units go!"

They rumbled forth; HumVees and half-tracks and tanks, and in between them were men on foot, weapons at the ready. Schow steadied himself as his own vehicle passed through. Clouds of fumes and dust rose into the air.

They poured through the gate like invading ants, and Schow was surprised to find he had an erection—

—until the first tank exploded in a blast of orange flame and shrapnel.

"What the hell?"

"We are under attack! I repeat, we are under attack!"

"Colonel, they've got anti-tank weaponry!"

"No shit, McFarland! Do you really think so? Give the order to fall back!"

"Sir, Sergeant Ford reports we've got zombies in the rear. They're coming up the driveway now."

The sounds of battle exploded around them; tanks,

rifles and machine guns were all booming at the same time, and the noise was so tremendous that it seemed beyond the limits of human endurance. Zombies advanced into a storm of steel and fire, but as they were cut down, more took their place. Unlike the previous assault, Ob's forces were heavily armed. They fired indiscriminately, giving the fight back to the unit.

Men were running everywhere, falling back and then advancing, only to fall back again. Most were beyond the fence, on the grounds of Havenbrook. Others had turned to flee, only to be caught by the creatures at their rear, now forming an impenetrable wall.

"We're surrounded," Schow said, indignantly. His officers simply stared at him.

A volley of bullets slammed into the command vehicle and Gonzalez and McFarland both jumped.

Schow laughed. "It's about time! Finally, we've got a real fight on our hands!"

He flung the doors open and ran out to greet the firestorm.

* * *

An explosion rocked the trailer and then the doors swung open.

Frankie brought the pistol up and into the frightened face of Private Lawson.

"Hey," he gasped. "What is this?"

"Where's your HumVee?" she snapped.

"Blumenthal's bringing it around now. We were coming to get you and Julie. Everything is going to hell out there! You want to put that fucking gun away?"

Frankie shot him in the face, just between the eyes, and he looked surprised as he collapsed to the pavement.

"Let's go!"

She jumped off the back of the truck, scrambling for Lawson's rifle. Julie and the other women followed her.

A group of zombies lumbered towards them, pistols

and rifles raised menacingly. Before either group could fire, Blumenthal careened around the corner in the HumVee and crashed into the cluster of zombies. They crunched under his wheels, and he skidded to a stop, dragging several of them underneath the carriage.

He stared at the sight of the armed women, but before he could react, Frankie flung the door open and shot him. He screamed, fumbling for his pistol and she shot him again, pumping a third and fourth shot into his head. Then she climbed through the passenger seat and pushed his dead body out the driver's side door. Julie and Maria followed.

Meghan was halfway in when she screamed. One of the zombies beneath the HumVee had latched onto her leg, and was gnawing at her exposed ankle. Blood ran down the thing's cheeks as it bit down harder, shaking its head like a dog.

Meghan fell backward, beating at the creature with her hands. Frankie leaned over Julie, put the pistol to the creature's head, and squeezed the trigger.

"Get her onboard," she snapped. "Now, let's see if I remember how to do this."

They jerked forward, and then the ride smoothed as Frankie grew adjusted to it.

"Drive toward the field!" Julie shouted. "We can four wheel in this thing, right?"

"First, we've got to let the others out of these trucks," Frankie said, and wheeled up to a trailer. "We can't just let those people stay trapped inside."

She pulled along beside it, so that the HumVee's passenger door was even with the trailer's doors.

"Get out and open it!"

"I can't!" Julie shouted. "They've got some kind of metal band holding it shut!"

A bullet whined over their heads. Another slammed into the truck trailer. Inside it, Frankie could hear people screaming for help and pounding on the walls with their fists.

She fumbled through the debris on the floor, until she found a pair of wire cutters.

"Use these. They should snip right through it."

Julie flung the door open and ran the few steps to the trailer, while Frankie and Maria laid down cover fire. They were not choosy, aiming at both the soldiers and the undead.

"My ankle hurts! What if it's infected?"

"Swallow it up, Meghan," Frankie hollered over her shoulder, "because right now we're a little busy!"

Julie cut through the thin seal and yanked the doors open. She dashed back toward the HumVee as a human flood poured out of the trailer.

"Go!"

Frankie sped away toward the next truck and they repeated the process. This one held many of the women, and Frankie was relieved to see Gina spring forth. Julie escorted the frightened woman back to the HumVee and Frankie pulled away again.

She looked in the rearview mirror and what she saw chilled her. The freed captives were being mowed down by the dead, who in turn were being shot at by Schow's men. A zombie and a woman grappled, only to be mowed down by a soldier, who in turn was dragged to the ground by another group of captives. Then the zombies fell on them both. All three groups melded into a grisly, face-to-face confrontation.

Several of the captives were freeing others, using rocks and sticks and even their fingers to snap the metal bands and open the trailers. Several of the trucks exploded before those inside were freed, killing both captives and their would-be saviors, and the smell of burning flesh mixed with the acrid smoke of battle and the stench of the undead.

A soldier ran towards them, his clothes on fire, and the right side of his face charred black. He waved his arms at them, begging Frankie to stop.

She drove straight towards him, closing her eyes as he

crunched beneath their wheels.

Julie shivered. "Let's get the fuck out of here!"

"Wait, what about Aimee? Please Frankie, we've got to find her!"

Swallowing hard, Frankie braked. Gripping the wheel tightly, she turned to face the frantic mother.

"Gina," she began, then struggled for the words. "She's—"

"No. No no no, don't you say it! Why would you say that? Did you see her?"

"Kramer had her in the Meat Wagon. He—he did things."

Before Frankie could finish, Gina ripped the door open and ran across the battlefield, charging towards the Meat Wagon.

"Gina, get back here! Julie, stop her!"

Cursing, Julie ran after her. Frankie slammed the HumVee into gear and chased after both of them.

"Meghan, close Gina's door!"

The injured woman leaned forward, fingertips grasping for the handle. Then she slumped over.

Frankie turned in horror as a second bullet finished the woman off.

She stomped the accelerator and Meghan's dead body slipped to the floor. Frankie glance around, looking for Gina or Julie, but there was no sign of either of them amidst the carnage.

Unaware that she was crying, she drove into the storm.

* * *

The gunner's lower jaw and most of his throat were gone, and Sergeant Ford knew it was just a matter of minutes before the corpse started moving again. He clambered up onto the sling seat, unbuckled the dead man, and flung him unceremoniously to the ground. Then he squeezed his bulk behind the fifty caliber, pointed it to their rear, and opened fire.

The creatures were coming from everywhere. They shambled forth from all directions, and Ford's eyes widened when he saw that some of them were his own men, killed and forgotten during the orphanage attack.

"Come on you fuckers! Come and get it!"

He fired in a sweeping pattern. Heavy rounds slammed into the zombie's lines, destroying many and cutting others to pieces. The injured; those with missing limbs and severed spinal cords, flopped on the ground, dragging themselves back toward the battle.

The creatures returned fire, and bullets ricocheted off the heavy armor. Ford stayed low and kept firing, sweeping back and forth as the creatures advanced. The gun grew hot in his hands, and the smoke was beginning to burn his eyes.

Something screeched from above him. He threw his hands up to protect himself as the blackbird swooped down, clawing at his eyes. In panic, he stood up, swatting at the creature, and the zombies on the ground opened fire.

Ford jerked as the bullets slammed into him. He tried to scream, but only managed a small, stuttering wheeze. As he fumbled for the machine gun, the zombies responded with a second barrage.

Clawing at his wounds, he swayed, then fell to the ground, landing atop the dead gunner.

As his lifeblood drained from him, the dead gunner began to squirm beneath him.

Mercifully, Ford was dead before the feeding began.

* * *

"Let's go! If you're going to die, die like men!"

They swarmed from the trailer, and Martin heard many of them begin screaming just seconds later. He cowered against the back wall, terrified of what must be occurring outside.

One of the Psalms echoed through his head, and his voice trembling, he began to recite it aloud as the rest of the men from the trailer leapt into the fray.

"My heart is pained within me, and the terrors of death are fallen upon me."

A horrid shriek interrupted him, and something slammed violently against the trailer.

"Fearfulness and trembling are come upon me, and horror hath overwhelmed me. Oh that I had wings like a dove! For then I would fly away, and be at rest."

Something outside exploded, and the trailer shook. He braced himself with one hand against the wall, and opened his eyes. The truck was empty now, but all around him on the outside, men were dying.

"I would hasten my escape from the windy storm and tempest."

Gunshots rang out, followed by a scream. Then something wet hit the ground.

"As for me, I will call upon God, and the Lord shall save me."

"No he won't."

The thing bubbled laughter as it clambered up into the truck. It squelched toward him, and Martin was horrified to see a priest's collar embedded in the bulbous, sagging flesh of the zombie's neck.

"He won't save you. He didn't save me."

"Of course God didn't save you," Martin said, pressing himself against the wall. "But He saved the soul of the man whose body you've stolen. Your desecration means nothing. You may have taken the body of a man of God, but you couldn't touch his soul!"

The zombie hissed, then reached into its rancid clothing and pulled forth a very large kitchen knife. The blade gleamed in the light. It advanced toward him, slashing at the air. Outside, the sounds of battle continued.

"Yes. Your kind go to Heaven. Our kind didn't have that luxury. We were sent to the Void. You have no idea

how long we've suffered there, waiting for this, our release. We gnashed our teeth and cried aloud and waited for the day of the rising."

Martin repeated the verse. "As for me, I will call upon God, and the Lord shall save me."

The zombie-priest snarled at him, edging closer.

"It will be better if you do not fight. You are one of His, as was this body I inhabit. I will make it quick, so that one of my brothers can join me in you. Then we shall go forth and spread a new gospel."

Martin took a deep breath. "He hath delivered my soul in peace from the battle against me; for there were many with me."

It charged him, thrusting the knife toward his stomach. Martin twisted away, and grabbed the creature's wrists. Grappling with each other, they crashed backward, and the zombie landed on top of him. Martin squirmed beneath it, fighting with all his strength as the zombie pushed the knife towards his throat.

"I will feast on your liver," the thing spat, and Martin winced at the reek pouring from its mouth. *"I will wear your intestines as a necklace and give them to the one that will soon dwell in you."*

Weakened by old age and fear, Martin's arms quivered. The knife slid closer, inches away from his throat. The creature laughed again, and leaned its mouth toward his face. He let go of one of its wrists and shoved his palm under the zombie's chin, desperately pushing the head upward. Its hand freed, the zombie clawed at his throat.

Martin twisted his head toward the arm clutching the knife and bit down. His teeth sank into the zombie's forearm and he ripped away, taking a chunk of rancid flesh with him. Something wriggled inside his mouth, and Martin spit it out, gagging.

"See, you're getting the hang of it already—"

The gunshot was deafening in the confines of the trailer. Martin was sprayed with blood and tissue as the zombie's head exploded inches away from his own.

"I've got to tell you Preacher, I've seen some sick fucking stuff since this whole thing started, but I ain't never seen somebody take a bite out of a zombie. How'd it taste?"

Gasping, Martin wiped the gore from his eyes. He retched, picking the strands of dead flesh from between his teeth. Then sat up on his haunches.

"Thank you, Sergeant...?"

"Miller. Staff Sergeant Miller. Not that three chevrons with two loops at the bottom means fuck-all anymore. And don't thank me Preacher-man. I'm going to kill you in a little bit too."

"Why? You just saved me."

"Yep, saved you for cannon fodder. We're safe in here for a second, and I can hold off any zombies that try to crawl up inside with us, but we can't sit around here all day. Those fucks've got rocket launchers and grenades and all kinds of shit. Sooner or later, they'll take this trailer out, which means I've got to go back into that mess out there. Only I'm gonna send you out first, so you can draw their fire."

"That's—that's evil! You're no better than the zombies!"

"Yep. But don't sweat it. You've got a few minutes to live still. I need a smoke first."

Miller fumbled for his lighter and cigarettes. Finding both, he sat his M-16 out of Martin's reach and lit up. The flame cast shadows on his haggard face, and for a second, Martin thought it looked like a skull, gleaming and fleshless.

"Ahhhh," Miller inhaled, a look of bliss crossing his features. "I always thought these things would be what killed me. Don't know what the fuck I'm gonna do when we run out of smokes."

"You could let me go. There's no reason to kill me. I can help you fight them."

Miller snorted and took another drag.

"Help me? Some team we'd make huh? An old fart like you teamed up with a hardcore motherfucker like me? No, I think I'll just let them use you for target practice—make my getaway while they do."

Another muffled explosion shook the trailer, and Miller turned to catch his M-16 before it clattered to the floor.

In one fluid motion, Martin grasped the knife and thrust it upward. The blade slid into the man's skin, just beneath his chin. He opened his mouth to scream, and as his cigarette fell out, Martin caught a glimpse of the knife as it penetrated the roof of his mouth and sank into the cavity above it. The hilt was tight against the man's chin.

Miller toppled over, curling into the fetal position as he died.

Martin tugged at the knife's handle but it was lodged tight. He stood, wiping his bloody hands on his clothing.

"But thou, oh God, shalt bring them down into the pit of destruction. Bloody and deceitful men shall not live out half their days; but I will trust in thee."

He kicked Miller's body, then picked up the discarded weapon and examined it.

"Psalms fifty-five, verses four through twenty-three."

He experimented with the rifle, recalling his own experience in the military, and then readied himself. He glanced back at the two bodies, making sure neither was moving, and a shudder ran through him. His rescue at the hands of Miller reminded him of the wheelchair zombie. Jim had saved him then.

"Please Lord, watch over him. Help him find his son."

A strange peace settled upon him. Filled with renewed confidence and strength, Martin ignored the arthritis stabbing at his joints and the shortness of breath in his chest, and moved toward the yawning exit.

"Yea, though I walk through the valley of the shadow of death, I will fear no evil; for thou art with me."

He went out into the valley, and though the shadow of death covered all, he knew no fear.

* * *

Staff Sergeant Michaels kicked the door in, shattering the glass all over the sidewalk and carpet. He ran through the office building's lobby, and the sounds of his men dying trailed in his wake.

A zombie leapt up from behind the receptionist's desk where it had been hiding, and fired at him. Something burned across his shoulder, like a bee sting but sharper. Something else punched his leg. Hollering, Michaels gunned the creature down and gasped.

He paused in front of the elevator doors, panting heavily and trying to figure out what to do next. His shoulder and thigh both felt warm, and it was only then that he realized he'd been hit. He peeled away the cloth of his shirt and appraised the wound. It was bad. The hole in his thigh was even worse. Feeling light-headed and sick to his stomach, he pressed a palm to his shoulder and considered his options.

The complex was without power, so the elevators were out. He briefly considered prying one of the doors open and hiding inside the shaft, but decided against it. To his left, a stairwell led upward and a men's room sat off to his right.

He limped toward the stairwell and edged the door open a crack. Voices and running footsteps echoed down to him.

"The gunshots were from downstairs!"

The voices were not human.

Michaels let the door swing shut and staggered toward the restrooms. Several zombies stalked through the front entrance and more were storming down the stairs. He shouldered through the men's room door and glanced around in panic. There were three sinks, four stalls and a row of urinals. No windows, and the only exit was the door he had just come through.

The zombies shouted to each other in the lobby.

Whimpering, he hid inside the stall farthest from the door, and collapsed on the toilet. As he drew his feet up from the floor, he noticed that it hadn't been flushed since its last use. The water inside it was dark brown, and the remnants of months-old feces and urine had congealed into a toxic soup. Michaels gagged and tried to hold his breath.

They won't find me in here.

The bathroom door squeaked open and footsteps plodded towards him.

Michaels looked down at the floor and froze. Shining quarter-sized drops of blood had dripped from his wounds, leaving a trail brighter than any breadcrumbs.

"Come out, meat, and we'll make it quick!"

More of the creatures crowded into the restroom.

Sobbing, Michaels pointed his rifle at the stall door. The barrel shook, the pain in his arm intensifying. Fear, adrenaline, and blood loss merged with the stench of both the toilet and his pursuers, and nausea took over. Michaels retched, his rifle clattering to the floor as the cramps seized him. He couldn't move, couldn't think.

They forced the door open as the bile spewed forth, and he couldn't even scream as they dragged him out and forced him down onto the cold, hard tiles. He choked on his own vomit as they began to feed.

* * *

"Welcome back, wise man." Gangrenous fingers seized Baker by the hair, yanking him to his feet. *"I see that you've brought some friends. I appreciate the gesture."*

Baker couldn't speak. He coughed as the miasma of cordite and burning fuel and Ob's rotten flesh coated his lungs. The battlefield rang with the screams of the dead and the dying. Bullets whizzed by and explosions peppered the air like fireworks. Both sides were suffering heavy casualties, but most of those killed in the human army were quick to rise again and replenish the ranks of the dead.

"What was the purpose of this, Billy-boy"

"They—they wanted to use Havenbrook as a base of operations."

"Really?" Ob shook his head, stroking the rocket launcher almost lovingly. *"Your kind must learn that your time is over. You are food. Meat. Transport. Nothing more. Your time here is over."*

"I've been wondering about that," Baker ventured, holding a hand over his nose and mouth. "Surely you must realize that if the human race is hunted to extinction, then your kind will be endangered as well."

Ob stared at him with Powell's dead eyes.

"There are other worlds than these."

Something whined by Baker's head and a hole blossomed in Ob's shoulder. The zombie staggered backward, raising the rocket launcher.

Baker flung himself to the ground as a second bullet smashed into Ob's face, destroying his nose and upper lip. The rocket launcher slipped from his grasp as he roared in indignation. His words were unintelligible, but his intent was clear.

"You fucked up, Professor!" Schow stalked toward them both, oblivious to the bullets whizzing by them. He raised the pistol and fired again, this time obliterating the side of Ob's head. The brain glistened through splintered fragments of skull. It reminded Baker of bloody cauliflower.

Ob collapsed, twitching in the dirt.

Baker curled into the fetal position as Schow aimed a savage kick at his ribs. He screamed as the heavy boot connected, and something snapped inside him.

"You son of a bitch! Those are my men dying! My men! You led us into a trap!"

He lashed out again, catching Baker in the side of the head. Pain exploded throughout him and his vision grew blurry.

Kneeling, Schow pressed the pistol against his crotch. Baker groaned and tried to roll away, but Schow shoved him flat on his back.

"I'm going to put an end to you right here and now, Professor. But it's not going to be quick and it's not going to be painless. I'm going to shoot your dick off. How do you like that?"

He punctuated the threat by pressing the barrel hard into Baker's testicles. Baker screamed.

"Doesn't feel good, does it Professor? It's about to feel much worse. You'll bleed to death, but not before these scumfucks get a hold of you. Most likely, you'll still be alive when they start on you. Then you know what I'm going to do?"

Baker closed his eyes.

"I'm going to wait for the zombie version of you to rise up, and then I'm going to do it all over again. I'm going to shoot out your kneecaps and your spine and both your arms. Hell, I might just cut them all off. But not your brain. I want what's left of you to lay here in the dirt, alive."

"Go ahead, Schow," Baker grimaced. "You'll be the first one I eat when I come back."

Ob sat up behind them, tissue and fluid running down the side of his face. His brain, still intact, pulsed from inside his ruined head.

He grabbed Schow from behind, wrapping his fingers around the Colonel's throat, and yanked him backward. The few remaining teeth in his lower jaw slavered across the back of Schow's grizzled neck, and Ob squeezed.

Baker snatched at the pistol, but Schow clutched it tight. Squirming in Ob's clutches, he thrust it behind his back and squeezed the trigger, emptying the clip into the zombie's chest and abdomen. Ob squeezed tighter, and Schow began to kick and flail.

A burst of machine gun fire raked the ground around them, and Baker spun to see Schow's command vehicle bearing down on them. Gonzalez was behind the wheel, and McFarland sat perched in the gunner's seat, sweeping his machine gun towards them.

Something heavy punched him in the stomach, and Baker tried to breathe, only to find that he couldn't. His mid-section felt warm, and he was afraid to look down.

He fell to the side as the next volley slammed into both Schow and Ob. McFarland cackled madly as the barrage decimated both flesh and bone.

Something wet was running down Baker's legs, and he didn't want to look at it. He felt very weak, and still he could not breathe. Grappling with the rocket launcher, he sat up and pointed it towards the vehicle.

Schow had been pulped, and the rest of Ob's head had vanished, leaving only a chin and one staring eye.

Baker felt the strength ebbing from him and knew it was only a matter of seconds. He could smell himself now, and the crimson pool spreading around him left no doubt. He braved a glance at his wound and found that his stomach was missing; replaced by something that looked like raw hamburger.

"Oh God..."

He belched and blood sprayed from his mouth.

Still laughing, Gonzalez and McFarland bore down on him.

"I'm sorry for what I've done, and I'm ready to face the consequences."

They fired at the same time, and the last thing Baker saw before the beautiful orange flower bloomed was the look of disbelief on both Gonzalez's and McFarland's faces.

The pain in his stomach ceased, and Baker closed his eyes. The explosion felt warm on his skin, and he relished it.

Something was screaming at him from far away, and a second later, he found out what it was.

* * *

Carrion birds hovered over the site in a thick, dark cloud. Jim remained beneath the shelter of the trees, staring in disbelief. He'd found a pair of binoculars on one of the zombies he had killed, and though he wanted to look away, he found that he couldn't. Instead, he watched in dreadful fascination as the horrors were magnified before him.

Schow's forces were decimated. The burned out husks of tanks and vehicles still smoked, their inhabitants smoldering with them. Zombies littered the landscape, each one brought down by some form of head trauma. Dozens more thrashed in the mud; appendages severed, bodies cut in half, but still moving. Hordes of them swarmed about the lawn, feasting on the fallen.

Jim shuddered, noting that many of the creatures partaking in the massacre were once Schow's men. Even worse were the once captive civilians, now freed from bondage but their dead bodies a prisoner of something even worse.

Not all of the humans were being killed. Several dozen had been rounded up, stripped of their weapons, and were now being herded inside the complex. Jim could only imagine what the creatures would do with them. Would they be used for food? Livestock? Or perhaps, something even more sinister?

His shoulders slumped. Martin was nowhere in sight, and Jim could only hope that the old man had not suffered. There was nothing more he could do here.

He started to turn away, and then froze, staring through the binoculars.

Baker walked toward the captives, talking to the group of zombies that guarded them. His flesh was burned black in places, and his mid-section was an empty cavity.

Jim lowered the binoculars, gathered as much weapons and ammunition that he could carry, and turned away.

Martin was dead. Baker was a zombie.

Nothing else now stood between him and Danny.

* * *

Ob looked out at his kingdom through Baker's eyes, and he saw that it was good. He gave orders regarding the captives, and then traversed the battlefield, welcoming the newly risen and joining in the feast. He had no stomach but it didn't matter to him. He was enjoying this new body.

From somewhere far away, Baker screamed.

Ob's laughter drowned out the sound of it in his head, and soon, the screams faded away to nothingness.

Chapter Twenty-Three

J im hobbled along the side of the road, sticking close enough to the edge so that he could seek cover in the treeline if he needed to. As near as he could tell, most of the undead in this area, both two-legged and otherwise, were concentrated around Havenbrook. He hoped to travel as far as he could while they were occupied at the site.

He readjusted the M-16, shifting its weight in his hands. An identical weapon was slung across his back, and he wore a pistol holstered at his side. The straps on the second machine gun chafed his skin as he walked. He tried to ignore the protests from his aching muscles, but his blistered feet were balls of flame, and the reopened wound in his shoulder trickled blood and pus. His upper arm felt warm where the infection burned in him, and the flesh around the bullet hole was red and puffy.

He had never felt so exhausted. He shuffled northward and swirling clouds of dust, kicked up by his boots, marked his passage. All around him, the land was silent, as if nature were holding her breath. The cornfields did not hum with the buzzing of insects or the chorus of birds. The houses sat like stones, dour and mournful. The sounds of the battle's terrible aftermath faded with every step he took, until they vanished completely.

Jim wiped the sweat from his eyes and listened to the silence, losing himself in the strange beauty of the moment. He wished he was more articulate, wished he could define what he felt. He found himself wondering if Martin would have appreciated the serenity, and thought that he would have.

Thoughts of the old man brought a smile to his haggard face, and he began to replay the journey in his mind; Carrie and the baby, Martin, Delmas and Jason Clendenan and the other scattered survivors they'd encountered, Schow and his men, Haringa, Baker—it all flashed before him, leading him to now. This road. This final road. If he could find a car, he'd reach his destination within an hour. If not, he could still be there before nightfall, as long as he kept this pace.

He patted his pocket and felt the letter he had written to Danny after Jason had killed his father and then himself. Knowing that the letter was safe brought him a strange sense of reassurance. Things would turn out all right yet.

As he plodded along however, his body began to rebel against him. The pain began in his feet and rocketed up his legs; great stabbing spasms that threatened to drop him in his tracks. Refusing to stop, Jim halted only long enough to drain the last few mouthfuls of tepid water from his bottle. Then he cast it aside with the rest of the litter along the road and stumbled on.

He didn't hear the motor until it was almost upon him. The HumVee crept purring up behind him, and Jim whirled, twisting his ankle as he did so. He tumbled to the ground, and lay there sprawled out while the vehicle pulled alongside him.

"No! You're not going to stop me now!" He raised the M-16 and pointed it at the HumVee.

"Jim! Is that really you? Thank the Lord!"

Martin leaned out the passenger window, hands triumphantly upraised in thanks.

"Martin?" Jim exclaimed, and despite the exhaustion

in his bones and the pain in his ankle, he sprang to his feet and ran toward the old man. "Martin! I thought you were dead!"

They clasped hands, and both of them were crying.

"It would seem that the Lord still wants me to help you, Jim."

They laughed, and Martin stepped out of the vehicle and hugged him.

"Come on, let's go find your boy."

"Amen, my friend. Amen."

Jim ducked inside the HumVee and a beautiful but tired looking black woman smiled curtly at him from behind the wheel. Jim nodded at her, puzzled.

"This is Frankie," Martin introduced her. "She was kind enough to give me a ride."

"Give you a ride, hell. I saved your sorry ass and you know it."

Martin laughed. "Yes, you did, and I thank you for it. You should have seen it, Jim! A group of them had me surrounded, and Frankie here just crashed right into them, driving over them all."

"Thanks for watching out for him."

"No problem."

They rolled forward and Frankie turned her attention to the road. Jim studied her, wondering who she was and what her story had been before all of this. She'd definitely seen some hard times. The echoes of it showed in the lines of her face and the very air around her. Jim had never believed in auras, but Frankie definitely had one. Despite the rough edges, she was beautiful, and Jim had the feeling that her true beauty had only recently begun to shine.

"So where are we going? You guys have any ideas?"

"Bloomington, New Jersey," Jim told her. "About an hour away."

"Bloomington?" Frankie stared over her shoulder. "That's all suburbs, isn't it? It'll be knee-deep in undead. Forget about it."

"Then you'll have to let us out here," Jim said, "because that is where we're going."

Frankie turned to Martin in disbelief, but the preacher only nodded his head.

"We have reason to believe that Jim's son is alive in Bloomington. That's where we have to go."

Frankie whistled. "Jesus. How do you know he's alive?"

"Farther south," Jim began, "the power is still on in some places. My cell phone was working up until a few days ago, and my son, Danny, called me on it. His stepfather had been turned into one of them, and Danny and my ex-wife were hiding in the attic of their home."

Frankie shook her head. "The power was still on in some parts of Baltimore too, but still—I mean, think about it. How do you know he's still alive?"

"Faith," Martin answered for him. "We have faith. God has seen us this far."

Jim was quiet for a few minutes. Then he spoke up again.

"At this point, I can't be sure he's alive, Frankie. I hope and pray that he is, and somewhere deep down inside I feel it. But I've got to know either way. If I don't, I'll drive myself crazy."

"Fair enough, but can I ask you something? Have you thought about what you'll do if we get there and Danny's one of them?"

Jim looked out the window.

"I don't know."

Frankie didn't respond. She shifted gears and they drove on in silence.

Monuments of their former civilization sat just off each exit they passed; houses and apartment buildings, churches, synagogues, and mosques, shopping centers and strip malls. The golden arches of a fast food restaurant hung askew. A bowling alley had burned to the ground. A pet store had provided a captive smorgasbord for the zombies, while a supermarket sat gutted and empty. They spotted a motel sign promising vacancy and cable television, and a movie theatre offering thirty different blank screens.

Frankie stirred. "What's going to happen to all of this?"

Martin shook his head. "I don't know."

"It's over, isn't it? If they don't have the numbers by now, they will soon. They'll start hunting us down, finding the survivors. Or maybe just waiting for us to die."

"I'm not ready to die yet," Jim said from the back, "and something tells me you're not ready to die yet either."

They drove on.

Martin began to quietly hum "Rock of Ages" while Jim fiddled with his weapons. Frankie sat brooding, lost in thoughts of Aimee, and of her own baby.

My baby...

What kind of life would it have had, had she not been a junkie and a whore? Obviously, it probably wouldn't have lasted long in this new world, but maybe they could have had some time together, even if just for a day. Instead, it had been ripped away from her, dead before it even got a chance to experience life, even for a second.

Her fault. She'd failed as a mother, just as she had failed at everything else in her miserable life up until she kicked the junk and was reborn.

She made up her mind that she would not fail again.

About twenty minutes later, they passed a sign for the Garden State Parkway.

"You can let us off at the entrance ramp," Jim sighed. "We appreciate your help."

"Bullshit!" Frankie said. "I'm taking you the whole way."

"You don't have to do that," Jim told her, "Like you said, it's going to be dangerous."

"I want to help you," Frankie insisted, "I need to help you. For me, and for my own child."

She turned to him and her eyes were wet.

Her voice cracked. "I lost my own. I want to help you find yours."

Swallowing hard, Jim nodded.

"Take this ramp then."

He checked the pistol, then handed it up to Martin.

"We'll be there in a little bit."

They rolled onto the ramp, and Frankie accelerated, heading towards the line of tollbooths.

"Anybody have any change?" Martin quipped.

Frankie gunned the engine and pointed. "Look at that!"

Ahead of them, zombies were forming a blockade. Concrete construction barriers had been stretched out across most of the entrances beyond the tollgates. In the others, the creatures themselves formed a wall, standing shoulder to shoulder and several bodies thick.

"They must have seen us coming from the bridge."

Jim scrambled up into the turret while Frankie sped towards the cluster of zombies.

"Jim," she warned, "the fifty caliber doesn't have any ammo!"

His response was lost in the burst from his M-16. Zombies dropped in front of them, their heads exploding. Martin leaned out the window and carefully picked his targets with the pistol. He squeezed off two shots, then yelped and ducked back inside.

"They're shooting at us!"

"Hang on!" Frankie shouted and mashed the accelerator to the floor.

They crashed headlong into the knot of zombies, scattering the creatures and crushing them beneath the wheels. Jim ducked back down inside the vehicle just as the front grille clipped a zombie. The impact sent it careening over the hood and through the windshield. Its head and most of its shoulders poked through the shattered glass, halfway between Frankie and Martin.

"Shit!" Frankie brushed bits of broken glass from her

lap and leaned forward, trying to see through the cracks spider-webbing through the windshield.

The zombie struggled, gnashing its teeth together as it snapped at Martin.

"Say folks, I appreciate the ride, but don't you know it's not smart to pick up hitchhikers?"

"I've noticed something about your kind," Martin told it calmly. "You all have that same black humor. I think you do it because you are afraid. You're afraid of being sent back to wherever it is you come from, and you try to cover it up."

The creature jerked itself forward another inch, cracking more of the glass on both sides.

"Do something!" Frankie urged.

"I'm not afraid of you, Preacher," it snarled. *"Your time is over. We are the rulers now. The dead shall inherit the earth!"*

Martin shoved the pistol into its mouth in mid-snarl.

"Well the meek aren't done just yet, so you'll have to wait your turn."

He pulled the trigger and the windshield turned red.

With the shot still echoing, Jim turned and looked for pursuit. A bullet pinged off the roof, and then they roared onto the Parkway, leaving the tollbooths behind.

"Where are we?" Frankie panted, craning her head out the window so that they wouldn't crash.

"Near West Orange," Jim told her. "I think we lost them for now. Pull over and we'll get rid of that thing quickly."

Frankie pulled onto the median strip and stopped. All three of them jumped out, and Martin and Frankie stood guard while Jim grabbed the zombie by its feet and pulled. He grunted with the effort, but the body was lodged tightly into the windshield.

"Martin, give me a hand."

The old man didn't reply.

"Martin?"

Jim looked up to find both Martin and Frankie

staring off into the distance. Along both sides of the Parkway, a cemetery stretched as far as the eye could see, and the highway cut right through its center. Surrounded by tenements and overgrown vacant lots, thousands of tombstones thrust upward to the sky. The horizon was littered with them. A few tombs and crypts dotted the landscape, but the sheer number of gravestones almost blocked them out.

"Yeah," Jim said, "I remember this place. It used to freak me out every time I drove up here to pick up Danny or drop him off. Creepy, isn't it?"

"It's something," Frankie whispered in awe. "I've never seen so many tombstones in one place. It's huge!"

Martin whispered something beneath his breath.

"What'd you say, Martin?"

He stared across the sea of marble and granite.

"This is our world now. Surrounded on all sides by the dead."

Frankie nodded in agreement. "As far as the eye can see."

"How long after all these building crumble, will these tombstones remain standing? How long after we're gone will the dead remain?"

He shook his head sadly, then turned to help Jim. With effort, they managed to free the mangled body from the windshield. Then they continued on their way.

* * *

As the sun began to set, its last, faint rays shone upon the sign in front of them.

BLOOMINGTON—NEXT EXIT

Jim began to hyperventilate.

"Take that exit."

Martin turned around in concern.

"Are you okay? What is it?"

Jim clenched the seat, gasping for air. He felt nauseous. His pulse pounded rapidly in his chest, and his skin grew cold.

"I'm so scared," he whispered. "Martin, I'm just so scared. I don't know what's going to happen."

Frankie turned down the exit ramp, and flicked on the headlights. This time, the tollbooths stood empty.

"Which way?"

Jim didn't answer, and Martin was unsure if he'd even heard her. His eyes were squeezed shut, and he'd begun to tremble.

"Hey!" Frankie shouted from the front seat. "You want to see your kid again? Snap the fuck out of it! Now which way?"

Jim opened his eyes. "Sorry, you're right. Go to the bottom of the ramp and make a left at the red light. Go up three blocks and then you're going to make a right onto Chestnut. There's a big church and a video store on the corner."

He exhaled, long and deep, and began to move again. He sat the rifles aside and double-checked the pistol, shoving it back into the holster after he was satisfied. He pressed himself into the seat and waited, while his son's neighborhood flashed by outside.

"There's one," Martin mumbled, and rolled down the window enough to squeeze off a shot.

"No," Frankie stopped him, "don't shoot at them unless they directly threaten us or look like they're following."

"But that one will tell others," he protested. "The last thing we need to do is attract more!"

"Which is exactly why you don't need to be shooting at it! By the time it tells its rotten little friends that the lunch wagon is here, we can grab his boy and get the fuck out. You start shooting and every zombie in this town is gonna know we're here and where to come find us!"

"You're right," Martin nodded, and rolled the window back up. "Good thinking."

An obese zombie waddled by, dressed in a kimono and pulling a child's red wagon behind her. Another zombie sat perched in the wagon, its lower half missing and its few remaining entrails spilling out around it. Both creatures grew agitated as they sped by, and the fat zombie loped along behind them, fists raised in anger.

Frankie slammed on the brake, slipped the HumVee into reverse, and backed up, crushing both the zombies and the wagon under the wheels.

"See," she grinned at Martin, "now wasn't that much quieter than a gunshot?"

Martin shuddered, but Jim barely noticed. His pulse continued to race, but the nausea was gone.

How many times had he driven down this same suburban street, either to pick Danny up or to take him home? Dozens, but never suspecting that he'd do so in this fashion one day. He remembered the first time, right after his first complete summer with Danny. Danny had started crying when Jim turned onto Chestnut, not wanting his father to leave. The big tears had continued to roll down his little face when they'd pulled into Tammy and Rick's driveway, and they were still flowing when Jim had finally, reluctantly driven away. He'd watched Danny through the rear-view mirror, and had waited until he was out of sight before he pulled over and broke down himself.

He thought of when Danny had been born and the doctor placed him in his arms for the first time. He'd been so small and tiny, his pink skin still wet and his head still slightly misshapen from the birth. His infant son crying then too, and when Jim cooed to him, Danny had opened his eyes and smiled. The doctors and Tammy insisted it wasn't a smile, that babies couldn't smile; but deep down inside, Jim had known better.

He thought of Danny and Carrie and himself playing *Uno* and of both of them catching him cheating, hiding 'Draw Four' cards under the table in his lap. They'd wrestled him to the floor, tickling him till he'd admitted the deception. Later, they'd sat on the couch together, eating popcorn and watching Godzilla trash Tokyo and

Mecha-Godzilla.

He remembered telling Danny on the phone that he was going to be a big brother, right after Carrie's pregnancy had been confirmed.

He shuddered, recalling his escape from the shelter and the house, and what that joyous pregnancy had become. He thought of Carrie and the baby. He'd shot them both.

Danny's phone call echoed through his mind as Frankie turned down Chestnut.

"Daddy, I'm scared. I'm in the attic. I..." That burst of static and then *"I 'membered your phone number but I couldn't make Rick's cell phone work right. Mommy was asleep for a long time but then she woke up and made it work for me. Now she's asleep again. She's been sleeping since... since they got Rick."*

"I'm on Chestnut," Frankie reported from the front, "now what?"

"I'm scared Daddy. I know we shouldn't leave the attic, but Mommy's sick and I don't know how to make her better. I hear things outside the house. Sometimes they just go by and other times I think they're trying to get in. I think Rick is with them."

"Jim? JIM!"

Jim's voice was quiet and far away. "Past O'Rourke and Fischer, then make a left onto Platt Street. It's the last house on the left."

In his head, Danny was crying.

"Daddy, you promised to call me! I'm scared and I don't know what to do...."

"Platt Street," Frankie announced and made the turn. She drove past the houses, each lined up in neat rows, each one identical to the next, save for the color of their shutters or the curtains hanging in the vacant windows. "We're here."

She put the HumVee in park, but did not shut off the engine.

"...and I love you more than Spider-Man and more

than Pikachu and more than Michael Jordan and more than 'finity, Daddy. I love you more than infinity."

Jim opened his eyes.

"More than infinity, Danny. Daddy loves you more than infinity."

He opened the door and Martin followed. Jim placed a hand on his shoulder.

"No," he said firmly, shaking his head, "you stay here with Frankie, my friend. I need you to watch our backs out here. Make sure we've got a clear shot at escape."

He paused, and still squeezing Martin's shoulder, he raised his head and sniffed the breeze.

"This town is alive with the dead, Martin. Can't you feel it?"

"I can," Martin admitted, "but you'll need help. What if—"

"I appreciate everything you've done for me and Danny, but this is something I have to do alone."

"I'm afraid for what you might find."

"So am I. That's why I need to do this by myself. Okay?"

Martin nodded reluctantly. "Okay Jim. We'll wait here for both of you."

Frankie leaned over the seat and pulled one of the M-16s to the front. She placed it between her legs and checked the rear view mirror.

"Coast is clear," she said. "Better get going."

Jim nodded.

Martin sighed heavily. "Good luck, Jim. We'll be right here."

"Thank you. Thank you both."

He took a deep breath, turned away, and crossed the street. His feet felt leaden, just like they had in his dream.

"More than infinity, Danny..."

He broke into a run, his boots pounding the sidewalk as he sprinted for the house. He turned into the yard, dashed onto the porch, and drew the pistol from its holster. Hand trembling, he reached out and tried the doorknob. It was unlocked.

Slowly, Jim turned it and, calling his son's name, he went inside the house.

* * *

They waited in the darkness.

Martin hadn't realized he was holding his breath until Jim vanished through the front door.

Frankie checked the street for movement again. "What now?"

"We wait," he told her. "We watch and we wait for them to come out."

The night air had turned chilly, and it whistled through the hole in the ruined windshield. Frankie shivered.

"Tell me Reverend, do you *really* think his son is alive in there?"

Martin watched the house. "I hope that he is, Frankie. I hope."

"Me too. I think that..." Her voice trailed off and she checked the street and surrounding yards again. Carefully, she hefted the rifle.

"What is it?"

"Can't you smell them? They're coming."

Martin cracked his window and inhaled, his nose wrinkling a second later.

"They know we're here, somewhere. They're hunting for us."

"What should we do?"

"We wait. Not much else we can do."

They grew quiet again, and watched the silent houses around them. Martin turned back to Danny's house. His jittery legs bounced up and down, and he cracked his leathery knuckles in the dark.

"Stop fidgeting."

"Sorry."

Random Bible verses ran through his head, and Martin focused on that, so that he would not have to wonder what was going on inside the house. *Blessed are the peacemakers...Jesus saves...For God so loved the world that He gave his only begotten son, that whosoever believes in Him, shall not perish, but have eternal life...And on the third day, he arose from the dead...*

Martin glanced back to the house again, fighting the urge to run towards it.

He gave his only begotten son, that whosoever believes in Him, shall not perish, but have eternal life...And on the third day, he arose from the dead...

...His only begotten son... he arose from the dead...

A gunshot suddenly rang out, shattering the stillness. It was followed by a scream. Silence returned and then a second gunshot followed.

Both had come from inside the house.

"Oh God! Frankie, that was Jim screaming!"

"It didn't sound human to me."

"It was him! I'm sure of it."

"So what do we do now?"

"I don't know. I don't know!"

"Fuck this! Come on, Reverend!"

They jumped out of the HumVee, weapons at the ready, as the first cries of the undead drifted to them on the wind. The zombies appeared at the end of the street, and the doors to the houses began to open.

Martin's voice cracked. "Look at all of them."

Frankie aimed and fired, and the zombies charged.

"Come on!"

They ran towards the house, to see what had become of their friend.

Above them, the newly risen moon shined down upon the world, staring at a mirror image of its cold, dead self.

PEACEABLE
KINGDOM
JACK KETCHUM

When it comes to chilling the blood, fraying the nerves, or quickening the pulse, no writer comes close to Jack Ketchum. He's able to grab readers from the first sentence, pulling them inescapably into his story, compelling them to turn the pages as fast as they can, refusing to release them until they have reached the shattering conclusion.

This landmark collection gathers more than thirty of Jack Ketchum's most thrilling stories. "Gone" and "The Box" were honored with the prestigious Bram Stoker Award. Whether you are already familiar with Ketchum's unique brand of suspense or are experiencing it for the first time, here is a book no afficionado of fear can do without.

RED

JACK KE+CHUM

Fans and critics alike hailed Jack Ketchum's previous novel, *The Lost*, for its power, its thrills and its gripping style, and recognized Ketchum as a master of suspense. Now Jack Ketchum is back to frighten us again with . . . *Red*!

It all starts with a simple act of brutality. Three boys shoot and kill an old man's dog. No reason, just plain meanness. But the dog was the best thing in the old man's world, and he isn't about to let the incident pass. He wants justice, and he'll make sure the kids pay for what they did. They picked the wrong old man to mess with. And as the fury and violence escalate, they're about to learn that . . . the hard way.

Dorchester Publishing Co., Inc.
P.O. Box 6640   _5040-4
Wayne, PA 19087-8640 $5.99 US/$7.99 CAN

Please add $2.50 for shipping and handling for the first book and $.75 for each additional book. NY and PA residents, add appropriate sales tax. No cash, stamps, or CODs. Canadian orders require $5.00 for shipping and handling and must be paid in U.S. dollars. Prices and availability subject to change. **Payment must accompany all orders.**

Name: _____

Address: _____

City: _____ State: _____ Zip: _____

E-mail: _____

I have enclosed $_____ in payment for the checked book(s).

For more information on these books, check out our website at www.dorchesterpub.com.
____ Please send me a free catalog.

The
LOST
Jack Ketchum

It was the summer of 1965. Ray, Tim and Jennifer were just three teenage friends hanging out in the campgrounds, drinking a little. But Tim and Jennifer didn't know what their friend Ray had in mind. And if they'd known they wouldn't have thought he was serious. Then they saw what he did to the two girls at the neighboring campsite—and knew he was dead serious.

Four years later, the Sixties are drawing to a close. No one ever charged Ray with the murders in the campgrounds, but there is one cop determined to make him pay. Ray figures he is in the clear. Tim and Jennifer think the worst is behind them, that the horrors are all in the past. They are wrong. The worst is yet to come.

___4876-0 $5.99 US/$6.99 CAN

DOUGLAS CLEGG

THE HOUR BEFORE DARK

When Nemo Raglan's father is murdered in one of the most vicious killings of recent years, Nemo must return to the New England island he thought he had escaped for good, Burnley Island. But this murder was no crime of human ferocity. What butchered Nemo's father may in fact be something far more terrifying—something Nemo and his younger brother and sister have known since they were children.

As Nemo unravels the mysteries of his past and a terrible night of his childhood, he witnesses something unimaginable . . . and sees the true face of evil . . . while Burnley Island comes to know the unspeakable horror that grows in the darkness.

THE INFINITE
DOUGLAS CLEGG

Harrow is haunted, they say. The mansion is a place of tragedy and nightmares, evil and insanity. First it was a madman's fortress; then it became a school. Now it lies empty. An obsessed woman named Ivy Martin wants to bring the house back to life. And Jack Fleetwood, a ghost hunter, wants to find out what lurks within Harrow. Together they assemble the people who they believe can pierce the mansion's shadows.

A group of strangers, with varying motives and abilities, gather at the house called Harrow in the Hudson Valley to reach another world that exists within the house. . . . A world of wonders . . . A world of desires . . . A world of nightmares.

EDWARD LEE
CITY INFERNAL

Hell is a city. Forget the old-fashioned sulphurous pit you may have read about. Over the millennia, Hell has evolved into a bustling metropolis with looming skyscrapers, crowded streets, systemized evil, and atrocity as the status quo.

Cassie thought she knew all about Hell. But when her twin sister, Lissa, committed suicide, Cassie found that she was able to travel to the real thing—the city itself. Now, even though she's still alive, Cassie is heading straight to Hell to find Lissa. And the sights she sees as she walks among the damned will never be in any tourist guidebook.

___4988-0 $5.99 US/$7.99 CAN

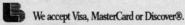